ST. MARTIN'S

MINOTAUR

MYSTERIES

GET A CLUE!

Be the first to hear the latest mystery book news...

With the St. Martin's Minotaur monthly newsletter,
you'll learn about the hottest new Minotaur books,
receive advance excerpts from newly published works,
read exclusive original material from featured mystery
writers, and be able to enter to win free books!

Sign up on the Minotaur Web site at:
www.minotaurbooks.com

"More funny adventures of John Marlin, amiable, estimable game warden of Blanco County, Texas . . . [A] winning sequel to *Buck Fever* . . . characters to chuckle at, yes, but Rehder never forgets he's got clues to furnish and a story to tell."

—*Kirkus Reviews*

"A humdinger. Funny, sardonic, and filled with clever metaphors and similes, *Bone Dry* is as cool and satisfying as a Lone Star beer on a hot Texas afternoon."

—*Sports Afield*

"Lots of twists and turns and authentic police procedures . . . [A] fast-paced romp."

—*San Antonio Express-News*

"Weird, wild, and wacky. One of the funniest mysteries of the year. [This] fast-paced novel has a variety of peculiar plot-lines that all converge in a wild and memorable ending. Rehder's first book was a finalist for the Edgar Award and the Lefty Award (for the funniest crime novel of the year). His latest effort is in the same category—it's a nifty, hilarious romp that's tough to put down."

—*Lansing State Journal*

"Funny . . . much like Carl Hiaasen's gore-spattered howlers."

—*Field & Stream*

"The pace of [*Bone Dry*] is steady and swift, the tone wry and playful."

—*Drood Review*

"Take a novel about hunting, throw in some unforgettable characters, and add a dash of ribald humor."

—*Abilene Reporter-News*

BUCK FEVER

"This fast-paced comic thriller comes with shooting distance of Hiaasen and Leonard territory...A promising debut."
—*Booklist*

"This debut novel is a complete success. There's sure to be a long career for this wacky, happy series."
—*Publishers Weekly* (starred review)

"A hilarious debut. *Buck Fever* does for Texas what Hiaasen does for Florida."
—*Clues Unlimited*

"A deserving, character-rich atmospheric crime novel that is deserving of the Edgar nomination."
—*Deadly Pleasures*

"Imagine Carl Hiaasen with a Texas accent. *Buck Fever* is a laugh-filled riot."
—*Denver Post*

"Briskly paced, amusing, spiced with deftly drawn good-old-boy portraits; an altogether promising debut."
—*Kirkus Reviews*

"A wild and crazy first novel."
—*Library Journal* (starred review)

ALSO BY BEN REHDER

Buck Fever

Bone Dry

AVAILABLE FROM
ST. MARTIN'S/MINOTAUR PAPERBACKS

FLAT CRAZY

A BLANCO COUNTY MYSTERY

BEN REHDER

St. Martin's Paperbacks

FLAT CRAZY

Copyright © 2004 by Ben Rehder.
Excerpt from *Guilt Trip* © 2005 by Ben Rehder.

ISBN: 0-312-99326-9
EAN: 80312-99326-9

Printed in the United States of America

St. Martin's Press hardcover edition / September 2004
St. Martin's Paperbacks edition / September 2005

St. Martin's Paperbacks are published by St. Martin's Press, 175 Fifth Avenue, New York, NY 10010.

10 9 8 7 6 5 4 3 2 1

For Martin and JoAnn Grantham
&
In memory of
Ann "Oma" McCroskey

ACKNOWLEDGMENTS

A LOT OF GREAT people provide information that shapes my books, and I want to make sure they realize how helpful they are.

Special thanks to Game Wardens Jim Lindeman and Bobby Fenton (retired), Director of Wildlife Enforcement David Sinclair, Tommy Blackwell (formerly of the Travis County Sheriff's Office), and Natural Resources Specialist Trey Carpenter.

Thanks also to Martin Grantham (for firearms information), Devon Millard and Jill Rodriguez (health care), Rob Cordes (helicopters), and Angela Lancaster (broadcasting).

A special nod to Phil Hughes for his insight on the Monrovian ground squirrel, Cisco Hobbes for his award-winning pudding recipe, and Tony Turpin for the scoop on computerized dating services.

As always, thanks to Helen Fanick, Mary Summerall, and Becky

Rehder for reading early drafts and providing excellent input, and to Stacia Hernstrom for providing an eagle eye in the later stages.

Once again, thanks to Ben Sevier for his deft touches and to Nancy Love for steering me through the maze.

FLAT CRAZY

1

DUKE WALDRIP WAS a damn resourceful hunting guide. In fact, he was so clever, his clients occasionally ended up with trophy deer mounts that weren't exactly authentic. Of course, the clients were unaware of this fact, but it was always at the back of Duke's mind that one of them might figure it out.

That's why he was a little uneasy about the man who was currently sitting in front of him—and there weren't too many things that made Duke Waldrip uneasy. As Duke liked to say, once you've done time in Huntsville, being outside is a walk in the fucking park. Most of the time anyway. Till shit like this came up.

The visitor—Oliver Searcy—had been a customer a few weeks ago, and he had called Duke early this morning, kind of rude, saying, "We have a problem." Duke had been in the middle of some important business—mounting a new scope on one of his deer rifles—but he put the screwdriver down on his desk and said, "What kind of problem?"

"I'll tell ya when I get there." Then, nothing but a dial tone.

Well, shit. Duke didn't like problems, especially the kind that would make a man drive nearly five hours from Houston. Matter of fact, Duke wasn't particularly fond of Searcy, either. The dickwad had first called Duke from Houston about a month ago, in the middle of deer season. He said he'd heard Duke was a hell of a guide, and he was in the market for a big buck.

"How big we talkin'?" Duke asked.

"At least one seventy," Searcy replied. "If you think you can handle it." He was referring to the standard scoring system for trophy whitetails. One seventy was the minimum to make the Boone & Crockett record books.

"Oh, I can handle it all right," Duke replied, thinking, *Okay, how am I gonna handle this?* Truth was, there weren't many deer that big in Blanco County. Sure, there were a handful of free-ranging bucks that scored 140, maybe 150 if you were lucky. But if you wanted one of their big brothers, well, you had to plunk down a lot of cash. Trophy deer like that were usually kept on large game ranches, behind high fences, unmolested by hunters. Those deer were protected like valuable livestock, which was exactly what they were. Many of the ranches were willing to make a commission deal with the guide—but Duke didn't like to go that route. Why part with most of the money when, with a little creativity, he could keep it all to himself? And that's what he had done with Searcy. Duke *did* make good on his boast—sort of. The important thing was, Oliver Searcy had gotten his deer and gone away happy. Something had changed, though. Now Searcy was sitting in front of Duke, looking none too happy at all. They were in Duke's two-room office, right next to the feed store, which was closed today, it being Sunday. Duke was behind the desk, sitting in his big leather chair, and Searcy was in one of the twin chairs in front of him.

So far, Searcy hadn't said a word, other than giving a gruff "No" to an offer of coffee. Duke smiled and placed his hands flat on the desk in front of him. "Okay, so what's up?"

Searcy didn't waste any time. "Last month, you said you could set me up with a trophy deer."

Duke nodded.

Searcy said, "You acted like it wasn't a big deal, like you did it all the time."

"That's 'cause I do."

Searcy shook his head. "The thing is, I've been hunting all my life, and I know big deer are hard to come by. I asked for the deer of a lifetime, and you acted like you could find it for me" — Searcy snapped his fingers — "just like that. Then you take me to a ranch and — bam! — first time out, I get a buck. It all seemed too easy. Now I know why."

Duke was sizing the man up, just in case there was trouble. Searcy wasn't a large man, only about five eight, maybe 160. Nothing compared to Duke's well-muscled six two. Plus, Duke's shaved head gave him a particularly menacing appearance. And his voice, full of gravel from twenty years of smoking, was a pretty good tool for intimidation, too. If things got rough, Searcy wouldn't be a problem.

Duke tried to act confused. "What exactly are you getting at, Mr. Searcy?"

"I'm a radiologist."

Duke didn't know what to make of that. "Yeah, so?"

"The deer mount you brought me last week — the 'outstanding trophy,' as you put it — it's a fake. I x-rayed it. Those antlers don't even go with that skull. They're bolted on."

Well now, aren't you a clever boy? Duke did his best to appear surprised. He contorted his face into an expression of Academy Award–winning amazement. He stood, walked around the desk, and sat with one butt cheek on the corner, now just a few feet from Searcy. "You gotta be shittin' me. For real?"

Searcy seemed nervous now, with Duke in such close proximity. He nodded. "Looks pretty realistic. You do good work."

Duke pointed one hand at his own chest, going for incredulous. "Me? You think I did it? Well, goddamn, I'm shocked, to be honest with you. I — it was probably the taxidermist I took it to." Not likely. Duke did all the taxidermy himself.

"The taxidermist," Duke continued, "that's who we oughta be lookin' at. They're experts at that sort of thing. Not me, that's for sure." Duke added a little extra head shaking, sort of an I-can't-believe-you-said-that gesture.

Searcy didn't buy it. That much was obvious. Especially when he reached under his coat and came out with a revolver. "I don't care who's responsible," he said, "as long as I get my five thousand dollars back."

Suddenly, Duke's raspy voice didn't seem like much of a weapon at all.

If Red O'Brien had known that the wetback he'd hired for the day was going to get hit by a truck, he probably would have insisted on a fatter one, one with a little more burrito on his bones. It might have cushioned the blow a little and the day wouldn't have turned into such a giant clusterfuck. Hell, a beefier guy might have walked away from it all.

But no, Red's friend Billy Don Craddock, who spoke the language some, had settled on this skinny little guy named Jorge, who was supposed to be damn good at rock work, and that was the important thing.

To be honest, Red wasn't all that crazy about using wetback labor, taking work away from genuine Americans. But in this case, as usual, Red couldn't afford to pay a regular white boy to do the job. It was one of those situations—what do you call it?—a catch-33. He'd wanted to hire a local worker, but they were all too pricey. He *didn't* want to hire the wetback, but the wetback was affordable. If Red didn't hire *anybody*, that meant he and Billy Don would have to take care of it all. And that settled that. What the hell. Mexicans were more cut out for that kind of work anyway.

Red and Billy Don had found Jorge early that morning, hanging around with the other illegals in their usual place—behind the Git It & Go convenience store. They'd buy orange juice and sweet rolls, then sit patiently with their backs against the brick wall, waiting for trucks to swing around the store. All those brown faces, none of them speaking hardly a lick of English. For the most part, Red had to admit, they were damn hard workers. They'd pick up manual labor at the rate of sixty bucks per day.

Clearing cedar, hauling rocks, digging ditches—hell, they didn't seem to care what the work was as long as they could earn a few dollars and send it home to Mexico.

The problem was, Red was pretty sure Jorge was hungover as hell, and it worried him. The schedule was tight, and the last thing Red needed was a Mexican who couldn't pull his weight.

In the truck, heading toward the job site, Red was driving, Billy Don's three-hundred-pound bulk was on the passenger's side, and the scrawny wetback was squeezed in the middle. As soon as the doors had closed, Billy Don had begun jabbering away at Jorge in Spanish. To Red, each sentence sounded like one long word. If there were any subjects or verbs hiding out in that mish-mash of sounds, Red sure couldn't find them. Plus, it made him feel left out, like when he'd get picked last for dodgeball back in grade school. So Red was trying to tune Billy Don and Jorge out, concentrating on the day's schedule, finding it hard to focus with the two of them rattling on.

Worse yet, every time Jorge opened his mouth, Red could smell last night's stale beer, stronger than bean dip. Then he smelled something even worse.

"Goddamn, which one a y'all cut the cheese?" Red groaned, rolling down the window.

"Jesus," Billy Don said, "it wasn't me," and opened his window, too. "Jorge told me he had *cabrito* last night. Plus a case of Budweiser."

Jorge just grinned, and Red gave him a frown.

"*No comprendo*," the Mexican said.

"Well, tell him he better be ready for a long day. We got a schedule to keep," Red said.

Billy Don translated, and Jorge fired a string of words right back, looking Red's way and smiling.

Billy Don laughed.

"What'd he say?" Red asked.

"I think he said you are a serious man."

Red snorted. "Damn right I am. Serious as a heart attack." And then he ignored them both. He had more important things to think about as he eased his old Ford truck and a trailer onto the shoulder of Flat Creek Road. Mr. Owen Pierce—yes, *that* Owen Pierce, owner of the most popular chain of barbecue joints in Texas—wanted the stone entrance to his ranch rebuilt, and he wanted it done *now*. He had some sort of party coming up this weekend, lots of bigwigs coming out, and Mrs. Pierce had decided just last night that the entrance wasn't quite up to par, thank you. "Kind of a last-minute thing," Mr. Pierce had said on the phone. "Think you can help me out?" Hell yes, Red could help out, for what the guy was willing to pay.

Red cut the engine, stepped out of the truck, and surveyed the elaborate limestone rock work on either side of the road leading into the ranch. Red didn't think it looked too bad. Sure, the concrete between the stones was crumbling in a few places, and there was a buildup of green mildew here and there. Nothing a little mortar mix and a few squirts of Clorox wouldn't fix. But Mr. Pierce wanted the whole thing torn down and reconstructed. In three days. "And let's make it granite this time," Pierce had said. "Mrs. Pierce likes the look of granite."

"Well, we're burning daylight," Red said. He gestured at Jorge. "Amigo, grab the jackhammer out of the truck and let's get busy."

Jorge stared back with bloodshot eyes.

"You know . . . ratatatat," Red said, making a jackhammering gesture with his hands.

The Mexican didn't budge.

Billy Don said a few words in Spanish, and that did the trick. Jorge grabbed the hundred-pound jackhammer, which weighed nearly as much as he did, and hefted it out of the truck like it was a toy.

Maybe he'll work out okay after all, Red thought.

But then the Mexican laid the jackhammer on the ground and leaned against the truck, moaning. Now he was bent over, grimacing, rambling on in Spanish.

Red removed his Dallas Cowboys cap with one hand and scratched his scalp with the other. "All right, what the hell's wrong with him?"

"Our boy says his stomach don't feel so good," Billy Don said. "Must be the *cabrito*."

"Yeah, that or the damn case of beer," Red said. "You picked a real winner for us this time, Billy Don. You ever try to run a jack-hammer after drinking all night?"

Billy Don shrugged.

Red and Billy Don watched as Jorge suddenly turned and scurried onto the ranch, tugging at his belt buckle, disappearing into some cedar trees.

"Well, hell's bells," Red said. "You found us a wetback with the runs."

Billy Don chuckled, then quit when Red glared at him. "Aw, give him a minute. He'll be fine. Just don't shake hands with him."

Red wasn't in the mood for jokes. "Well, let's quit wasting time. Gimme a hand with the generator."

The men pulled the generator out of the truck and carried it over to the stone ranch entrance. As soon as they had the generator running, they'd have juice for the jackhammer and they could tear this whole thing down in a matter of hours. The best thing was, Red could save the limestone and use it again on another job. Not only that, Mr. Pierce was *paying* Red to haul the rock away. Red was making money coming and going. Sweet deal. Now, if only the wetback would finish his business and get to work.

Red figured he'd have Jorge operate the jackhammer, the really hard work, while he and Billy Don used wheelbarrows to move the rock to the trailer. When they were ready to rebuild with the granite, he and Billy Don would have to provide the muscle, because Jorge had the masonry skills. Supposedly, anyway. That remained to be seen.

Red opened the choke on the generator and was just about to pull the starter cord when Billy Don said, "Here comes our granite."

Several hundred yards down the road, a loaded flatbed was slowly rumbling in their direction. *At least they're here on time*, Red thought. He yanked the starter cord and—in the instant right before the generator roared to life—there was a scream from the woods.

Red raised his head, puzzled, and locked eyes with Billy Don, who was mouthing something to him. The noise from the generator was too loud, but Red didn't need to read lips to know that Billy Don had said, "Did you hear that?"

They looked toward the woods, and here came Jorge, naked from the waist down, running—as Billy Don would later describe it—like the entire Border Patrol was on his tail.

Red had no idea what had Jorge so worked up—maybe a rattlesnake or a wild hog. But he figured whatever it was, Jorge would stop running once he came back through the ranch entrance. Then, as Jorge zipped through the open gate and loped across the shoulder of the road, Red was pretty sure he was running for the safety of the truck. It was only in the tragic half second after Jorge passed the front of the truck that Red realized the Mexican had no intention of stopping until he reached Laredo. By then, it was way too late. There was no way to warn Jorge about the oncoming flatbed, the sounds of which were covered by the generator.

The truck driver would later tell Red he had been planning on *bypassing* the ranch entrance, so he could back up and dump the load. That's why he hadn't slowed down much yet.

But right now, all Red heard was the awful sound of the truck's worn-out brakes grinding, metal on metal, followed by a sickening thump.

Red and Billy Don rushed over to Jorge, who was now writhing on the pavement, his leg obviously shattered, bone exposed.

"Oh man," Billy Don said, instantly going pale.

"Didn't see him in time," said the driver, who had climbed out of the cab of the truck. "Just never saw him."

"It wasn't your fault," Red said. "Meskin ran right in front of you."

Billy Don knelt down beside Jorge, grabbed his hand, and said something in Spanish.

"Oo, mi Dios! Chupacabra!" Jorge replied between clenched teeth, followed by a bunch of other words Red didn't understand.

"Que?" Billy Don asked.

"What's he babbling about?" Red asked.

Jorge's eyes got wide, and he said it again, much louder. *"Chu-*

pacabra!" Then he made the mistake of looking down at his ruined leg and promptly passed out.

Billy Don looked up at Red. "What do we do now?"

"Well hell, Billy Don, we gotta get the boy an ambulance," he hissed.

.But what he was thinking was, *There goes my damn schedule.*

2

SEARCY WASN'T EXACTLY pointing the pistol at Duke, just sort of holding it in front of him.

This was the kind of situation Duke had always worried about. For years, Duke had made a comfortable living by finding ways to gain access to beautiful animals so that wealthy hunters like Searcy could shoot them. Duke thought of himself as a broker, a man who paired hunters with the animals of their wettest dreams. He had set people up with all kinds of trophies, but white-tailed deer were the biggest market by far. And yeah, sometimes Duke had to skirt a few laws to get what the hunter wanted. Other times, if he really wanted to make good money in this business, he had to think outside the box. Which is what he'd done two years ago, when he'd first pulled off one of the most brilliant and profitable swindles ever concocted.

It was so slick, nobody had ever figured it out. Until now. Frankly, Duke couldn't blame Searcy for being a tad peeved.

"Take it easy," Duke said, his palms toward Searcy. "No reason to get all crazy on me."

"I just want my money."

Duke spoke softly. "I can understand that. You got ripped off, and now you wanna set things straight. Who can blame you? Just don't take it out on the wrong guy."

Duke was thinking there still might be a peaceful way out of this. Just return the guy's money, smooth-talk him a little, maybe even offer to take him on a free hunt—just to show there were no hard feelings. Duke could afford to give up the cash. What he couldn't afford was a guy like Searcy bad-mouthing him around the county.

But Searcy pushed him even further into a corner.

"I'm walking out of here with my money," Searcy said. "I paid cash, I want cash back. Then I'm gonna talk to the game warden and let him know what kind of operation you're running."

Duke could feel his heart pounding. If Searcy made good on his threat, Duke would be facing a lynch mob. Once word got out, every hunter Duke had ever guided would double-check their mounts for authenticity, and several of them would find reason to be seriously pissed off. Once the authorities got involved, Duke'd be looking at a return to the joint.

Duke held one hand up in the Boy Scout's gesture. "Mr. Searcy, one last time, I swear to you, I had nothing to do with this mess." With his other hand, Duke was reaching back behind him, feeling for the screwdriver on the desk.

Searcy waved his gun in Duke's direction. "Go on, now. Get my money. I'm sure you've got it stashed around here somewhere."

Duke found something with his hand—but it turned out to be the stapler. "See, now, I don't have any problem paying you back. No sir. You deserve it." He was buying time, still fumbling with his hand. Where was that damn screwdriver! "But see, I don't exactly have it on me," Duke said.

"Bullshit," Searcy said, coming around with the revolver now. "You're lying to—"

That's when Duke's hand found what it was looking for.

* * *

It was the final day of deer season, and Blanco County game warden John Marlin was thrilled. Yes, the season was the most exciting part of the year, but it was also the most tiring. It was an around-the-clock job, checking hunting camps during the day, chasing spotlighters at night. The weekends were especially hectic, and he was lucky to get a couple hours' sleep each night.

Then there were idiots who shouldn't be let loose in the woods with firearms, like the two Marlin had just pulled over on the side of Highway 281, north of Johnson City. He had spotted blood on the rear door, saw that the driver was wearing camo, and decided to do a license check.

"Looks like y'all had some luck this morning," Marlin said as the driver lowered the window.

"Yes, sir," the middle-aged driver said, nodding, clearly excited. "Shot my first buck. I got him tagged and everything, no problem."

Marlin peered through the side window, seeing a medium-size six-point lying on a tarp in the rear of the SUV. "If you'll cut your engine for me, sir, I'd like to take a quick look."

The man complied, and Marlin opened the rear of the vehicle. It was eleven o'clock on a Sunday morning in early January. But this was Texas, where winter didn't have much bite, and today the temperature was hovering around seventy. The interior of the vehicle, with the sun shining in, was probably at least eighty.

"You planning on icing him down?" Marlin asked.

This time, the passenger replied. He could have been the driver's twin: middle-aged, wearing freshly creased camos and some sort of safari hat he had probably ordered off the Internet. "Think we need to?"

"That depends. Where you headed?"

"Back up to Dallas."

Marlin shook his head. Most hunters were knowledgeable, law-abiding, salt-of-the-earth types. In fact, Marlin would stack hunters, as a group, up against the general population any day. But occasionally he ran into a pair like this. Utterly clueless. It was a four-hour drive to Dallas, which meant the venison would have plenty of time to spoil.

"When you shoot a deer," Marlin said, "you wanna get the carcass cooled down as soon as possible. This thing would be better quartered and in an ice chest. You realize it's a violation if you fail to keep the meat in edible condition?"

"Yes, sir, I understand that," the passenger replied. "I've hunted before."

Marlin examined the tag that was attached with twine to the animal's ear. There were small abbreviations for each month, plus the numbers 1 through 31, running along the border of the tag. "Then you should know you're supposed to *cut* the month and date out, rather than marking it with a pen," Marlin said.

"Well, uh, we were a little unclear on that," the man said.

Marlin glanced down at the Winchester he had noticed lying parallel to the deer. It wasn't in a rifle case, but was left to slide around in the rear compartment as the vehicle moved. That was dangerous in itself, but the hunters had made an even bigger mistake. "Whose rifle?"

"Mine," said the passenger.

"You mind?" Marlin asked, gesturing toward the rifle.

"No, go ahead."

Marlin lifted the rifle and worked the bolt. It was unloaded, but that wasn't what concerned him. Around the butt of the stock was an elastic band that was designed to hold bullets. This one was filled to the max.

"Guess you didn't do any shooting this weekend," Marlin said.

"I was waiting for a nice buck. Could have taken a couple of does."

"Good thing you didn't. This rifle is a thirty-aught-six and you're hunting with ammo for a three-oh-eight."

There was a brief pause as the hunters considered that fact.

"I, uh—is that a problem? I kinda figured since they were nearly the same caliber . . ."

"Thing probably would have blown up in your face," Marlin said. He heard the driver mutter, "Glen, you dumbass" under his breath. Glen, grimacing with embarrassment, opted to remain quiet for the moment.

Marlin was about to chastise the men further when he heard his unit number being called over his truck's radio. "What I want you to do is get some ice on this deer, notch those numbers, and secure this rifle. Put it in a case or something."

Both men mumbled that they would, and Marlin told them to have a safe trip.

Back in his state-issued Dodge Ram, Marlin keyed the radio mike and spoke his unit number. The reply was from Deputy Ernie Turpin: "Hey, John, can you swing over here to Flat Creek Road and take a look at something?"

"What you got?"

"Aw, we had a Mexican guy get hit by a truck earlier this morning. Garza was talking to him over at the hospital, and this guy was really freaking out. Said he saw some kind of weird animal chewing on a goat. Anyway, I found the goat, and I was wondering if you could take a look at it. I don't know what the big deal is, but Garza was getting kind of worked up about it. I called Trey Sweeney, too, and he's en route."

"No problem," Marlin replied, somewhat puzzled. "Did Garza say what kind of animal this guy saw?" Bobby Garza was the Blanco County sheriff, the most fluent Spanish speaker in the department. Trey Sweeney was the state wildlife biologist assigned to Blanco County.

"Yeah, some kind of weird thing I've never heard of," Turpin replied. "A Spanish word. *Coopa* something? *Coopacobra?*"

Marlin grinned. Surely Turpin was joking. "*Chupacabra?*"

"Yeah, that's it!" Turpin said. "Chupacabra. What the hell is that, anyway?"

Duke would have preferred to talk it out, to strike some kind of deal they could both live with.

But Searcy had to be an asshole about it all. He had to act like a big man and put the pressure on. Goddamn it, he hadn't given Duke time to figure a better way out. And what was Searcy thinking, coming in here with a gun? All that did was force Duke's hand.

Yeah, it was more or less Searcy's fault. That's what Duke was thinking as his arm came whipping around, the screwdriver clenched in his sweaty fist.

The thing was, Duke didn't really want to hurt the guy too bad. Just take the gun away from him, scare him away for good.

Duke was aiming for the meaty part of the guy's upper arm. Just the arm, that's all. To make him drop the revolver.

But Searcy saw what was coming. He raised his hand and tried to deflect the blow, but he was too late. All he did was bump Duke's forearm and change the path of the screwdriver.

And it plunged into the flesh on the side of the man's neck, just below the ear. It sank in all the way up to the handle.

Then there was silence. Duke was wondering if he should pull the screwdriver out or leave it in, and he was starting to freak because of the fucked-up look on Searcy's face.

Just then, the phone rang, and Duke twitched.

Searcy made a hacking sound, like a cat choking on a hairball. His revolver bounced on the linoleum floor.

The phone rang again.

Duke grabbed Searcy by both shoulders, easing him gently out of the chair and onto the floor.

The phone rang again.

Searcy's eyes became still, and just that quick, he was gone. Duke had always wondered what it was like to kill a guy. *It's a fucked-up mess, that's what it is*, he thought.

Duke turned and grabbed the phone, just to shut it up. "What?"

"We got a problem." *Damn, that's just what Searcy had said.* But this time, it was Kyle Dawson, Duke's best friend.

"Shit, what now?"

Kyle told him.

Duke sighed heavily and plopped down into his leather chair. "You're right, Kyle. I'd say that's a definite problem."

3

MARLIN SPOTTED DEPUTY Ernie Turpin's cruiser and Trey Sweeney's old Jeep on a remote stretch of Flat Creek Road, but neither man was in sight. Marlin tapped his horn as he stepped from his truck, and he heard Ernie give a directional shout from within the thickly wooded ranch.

He found them about fifty yards into the brush. Ernie was standing with his hands on his hips, staring down at a small dead goat, while Trey was circling the carcass, snapping photographs with an expensive Nikon.

Marlin always had to suppress a grin when he saw Trey. Most people around Blanco County referred to him as "eccentric" or "colorful." The less tactful ones called him "downright peculiar." Marlin knew from experience that Trey, a man with an off-the-charts IQ and a wild imagination, didn't pay much attention to what was said. The biologist had an unruly beard, round-lensed glasses, and a thick mop of auburn hair, which hid the fact that he was missing an ear. It had been removed by a black bear several years before, when Trey, doing research, had trespassed into the bear's den while it was hibernating. As Trey had once said over several rounds of beers, "The bear decided to relieve me of that particular appendage, and I was in no position to argue."

When Trey saw Marlin approaching, he immediately began speaking at a rapid clip. "John, you gotta see this. We've got this dead goat here, no wounds at all except fang punctures in its neck like a dog's been after it, and sure, that's the first thing I thought, until I took a look around and found some tracks over there under that oak tree, and damn if I can tell what they came from, and you and I both know I can identify the track of every damn critter that wanders these woods." Trey was making a come-with-me gesture now, as hopped-up as a kid at a carnival, wanting to show Marlin the tracks.

Marlin glanced at Ernie, who shrugged and said, "Looks like a damn coyote to me, but y'all are the experts."

The area around the slaughtered goat was too grassy to hold tracks, but ten yards away, Trey pointed out half a dozen fresh prints in firm mud. Like the tracks from a coyote or a dog, each of these prints had four toe pads, with claw marks evident in front of each toe.

Trey knelt down beside one of the tracks. "Look here. See how the pads are grouped together a lot tighter than a coyote's or a dog's? Besides, the two middle toes on either of those animals are the same length. This animal has one middle toe that is clearly longer than the other. More of a dominant toe. And—"

Marlin waved a hand. "Hold on a second, Trey. Let's just start at the beginning, okay? I haven't even heard what the Mexican man said. The guy who got hit by the truck."

Trey looked over at Ernie. The deputy said, "It was a wetback out here working with those two rednecks, Red O'Brien and his running buddy, the big guy."

"Billy Don Craddock," Marlin said. He knew the men well. He had caught them poaching so often, he could probably recite their driver's license numbers from memory. Just last year, Marlin had gotten a call about suspicious activity on a county road west of Blanco. He'd responded quickly and found a truck driving in circles in a large pasture. It turned out to be Red O'Brien driving, and Billy Don Craddock was in the bed of the truck. With a rope. Trying to lasso a terrified deer. Marlin had been tempted to use the lasso on both of *them*.

"Yeah, Craddock." Ernie nodded. "Anyway, I responded to the call, we got an ambulance out here, and the Mexican was about halfway loco, going on about—" He looked at Marlin. "What was that animal we talked about?"

"Chupacabra."

"Exactly. He kept saying that word, but I couldn't understand anything else. One of the paramedics spoke pretty good Spanish, so he told me the guy said he saw a chupacabra. Hell, I never even heard of one, so I just wrote it up in my report. When I got back to the station and told Garza, he wanted to talk to this Mexican guy himself at the hospital. About thirty minutes later, he radioed and told me to come back here, locate this goat, and call both of you. That's all I know. Garza said he'd be in touch."

Marlin took a moment to let that information soak in. Bobby Garza was about as intelligent and levelheaded as they come, and Marlin couldn't imagine that the sheriff would place any credence in an alleged chupacabra sighting. Of course, smarter men than Garza professed to believe that Martians are among us and the Earth is flat.

"So what do you think?" Trey asked, still kneeling by the tracks. "Weird, huh?"

Marlin squatted for a closer look. "I don't know, Trey. Yeah, they look a little unusual, but come on. How many different breeds of dogs are there? It's not like all of their tracks look exactly the same."

Trey shook his head. "I don't think this is a dog. Or a coyote or fox."

"Cougar?" Ernie offered.

"No, not with the claws showing," Marlin said. A cougar, also known as a mountain lion or a panther, has retractable claws, which don't show in its prints.

"And these aren't round enough for a cougar," Trey added.

"Well, damn, would someone just tell me what a chupacabra is?" Ernie asked, getting fidgety.

Marlin replied first: "What it is, is a myth. A fantasy creature, kind of like Bigfoot. I think it started—where was it, Trey?—in Mexico?"

"It's been reported all over Latin America, but most of the sightings have been in Puerto Rico."

"Alleged sightings," Marlin added.

"Whatever," Trey muttered.

"Okay," Ernie said, looking from Marlin to Trey, "but what is it *supposed* to be?"

Marlin said, "You don't believe in all that crap, do you, Trey?"

Trey let out something like an indignant huff. "I'm not saying *this* is a chupacabra, because I don't know *what* it is. I'm just saying it's something different, not a dog or coyote. And remember, just because you don't believe in the chupacabra doesn't mean it doesn't exist. For all we know, there could be dozens—hell, thousands—of unidentified species out there. We discover something new every year. You have to keep an open mind; you know that."

Marlin felt like he was back in college, receiving a talking-to from a disappointed professor. He grinned but said nothing. He'd learned long ago that there wasn't much use in arguing with Trey. And besides, it was too damn tough to keep up with the biologist in a serious debate. The three men stood in silence for a moment, surrounded by the gentle sounds of the woods.

"Goatsucker," Trey said softly.

"What?" Ernie asked.

"That's what *chupacabra* means in Spanish," Trey said. "Goatsucker."

Gus Waldrip had his good days and his bad days. Today, so far, was a good day. He hadn't had a single episode yet. Not that the episodes were scary or dangerous or even particularly upsetting. They were just weird. Of course, that didn't concern Gus too much, either. True, when you were weird, sometimes people would stare or point. Other times, they'd whisper behind your back. Gus would just smile and go on. He smiled a lot. Most of those people were strangers anyway. So why should he care? But Gus's brother, Duke, on the other hand—he was the person who had the biggest problem with Gus's condition. He was always teasing Gus about it. So was Kyle, Duke's snotty friend. They'd laugh at him. Or sometimes Duke would get pissed off about something and yell at Gus, telling him to straighten up and get control of himself. Like Gus had any say in the matter. And despite his deep, burning anger, Gus would grin. Sometimes, he'd even giggle, right when Duke was hollering at him. That *really* made Duke mad. But Gus could never understand why. What was the big deal? So he was a little different than he used to be. Life was good. Why get all upset about it?

Gus enjoyed getting away from Duke on occasion—not just because of the way Duke treated him, but because Duke was so damn high-strung. It was nice to get a break from that every now and then. Like today. While Duke was back at the office, Gus was driving the caliche roads of the Macho Bueno Ranch, Kyle Dawson's place. Snotty Kyle. Riding beside Gus in his Ford Expedition was Norman Raines. The old man had hair as white as snow. At first, Gus assumed he was about 160 years old. Raines had a Winchester .270 cradled between his knobby legs, the barrel pointing down at the vehicle's floorboard.

"How's your eyesight today, Mr. Raines?" Gus asked, grinning. He popped an Altoid into his mouth.

"How's that?" Raines replied, shifting his body in Gus's direction. Gus noticed that Mr. Raines always moved his entire torso, rather than just his head, as if he had a permanently stiff neck.

"Your eyesight," Gus said more loudly. "Think you'll be able to shoot okay today?"

"Hot damn, we'll shoot the shit out of 'em!" Raines replied, cackling; then he snapped the laugh off short as his dentures began to pop out of his mouth.

In reality, Norman Raines was eighty-three years old, a World War II veteran, and former president of the Texas Board of Independent Insurance Agents. He'd retired ten years ago, at the age of seventy-three, just weeks after his wife had died. Gus knew all this because Mr. Raines had told him, several times, in detail. Gus didn't mind listening, although it made him feel kind of sorry for the old man.

On the day they had first met, Mr. Raines had given Gus a brief history of his adult life.

"The first time I went to Africa," Raines had told Gus, "I was twenty-two years old. Shot a goddamn charging rhino—can you believe that? Nothing between me and him but a four-twenty-five Westley Richards Magnum. I'd never experienced anything like it, even in the war. So I went back every chance I could. Hunted lions, tigers, you name it. I wanted to bag every wild beast those negras had down there."

But, according to Mr. Raines, real life got in the way. He got married, had three children, and was always busy building his insurance agency. His dreams of African predators got side-tracked. Decades zipped by. And then his wife died.

"When Ginny passed over, I kinda moped around for a year or two, thinking my time would come soon, too. I sat around and waited for it, son—can you believe that? Is that gruesome or what? Well, as you can probably gather, I didn't die. Wasn't my time, I guess. My kids kept nagging me to get out more, so I did. Twice a week, I'd go down to the rec center—this crummy old place for geezers like me—and play a little shuffleboard or dominoes. Just marking time, really. I finally thought, What the hell am I doing wasting my time like this? I still got my health. Why not do some of the things I always wanted to do? That's what Ginny would have wanted."

So Norman Raines had made a choice. He decided to live out his final years "in a blaze of glory," chasing African predators and all the other crazy dreams of his youth. Nine years ago, when his health was still strong, he traveled to Maine and hiked the Appalachian Trail from Monson to Mount Katahdin. After that, Raines learned to fly a plane, caught a five-hundred-pound blue marlin, wrote a novel, crossed the country in an RV, surfed the

Gold Coast in Australia, attended the Republican National Convention in New York City, and took up pottery.

Now he was slowly completing the last item on his list. Three things really. The three animals Raines needed to complete his menagerie of dead African animals.

But the old man was facing a new hurdle. "Got me some health problems now," he'd told Gus. "Time's limited. I gotta hunt while I still can."

Gus didn't really understand hunting anymore, not like he used to. Now he didn't know why a man would pay thousands of dollars to shoot some beautiful, elegant creature and watch it drop to the ground. On the other hand, Gus really didn't have anything against it. Especially since Duke always came up with such clever ways for them to make money off hunters like Mr. Raines. Gus sometimes wondered about some of Duke's methods. But Duke always said, "Hunters like to outsmart their prey, bro. We're just doing the same thing."

Gus rolled the truck slowly along the caliche road, approaching a pasture he had visited a few hours ago, when he was preparing for the hunt.

"I saw the cheetah right around here yesterday," Gus said, pointing toward a grove of oak trees. "Duke figures it won't jump the fence as long as there's plenty of food for it to eat. So he shot a big hog yesterday and left it laying."

Mr. Raines slid the bolt on his rifle and chambered a round, which made Gus nervous. He liked the old man, but Mr. Raines had a palsy and there was no telling where that bullet might go if he got excited. "Well, let's get after it," Raines said.

"I figured we'd just drive around and see if we can spot—"

"A real man doesn't hunt from a truck," Raines declared.

That's what Mr. Raines had said last weekend, when he shot the jackal. Mr. Raines insisted on "stalking" it, though the old man could barely open his own truck door. Also, what Mr. Raines didn't know was that Duke had given the jackal some kind of drug, and it was snoozing quietly beneath some oak trees. Gus had had to throw some rocks at it when Raines wasn't looking to get it up and moving.

"That's fine with me," Gus said.

And then he felt it—the first twinge of the day. There was always a warning sign, an electric tickle down the back of his neck. He applied the brakes and brought the truck to a stop.

"Young fella, you okay?" Raines asked.

"Rutabagas," Gus said flatly. "Persimmons."

And then, just like that, the episode was over. It was even shorter than most.

Gus turned to Mr. Raines, who was eyeing him, puzzled. The old man said, "Rutabagas?"

"Uh, just thinking about lunch," Gus said. "You ready to go?"

"Let's do it!" Raines said enthusiastically, as if he were about to bound from the Expedition and begin a cross-country trek.

Gus stepped from the truck, opened the rear hatch, and removed Raines's walker from the storage compartment in the back.

4

DUKE WRAPPED THE body in a plastic drop cloth and dumped it in the back of Searcy's truck. Now the trick was getting rid of it. In the old days, Duke would have asked Gus to help, but not nowadays. He was just too damn strange—ever since the accident. Duke didn't even like to think about the accident.

Before, Gus used to be just another good old boy like Duke. He'd hunt and fish and drink beer and chase women, just like a man ought to. He'd poach deer without a qualm in the world.

But now he was a different man. Kind of goofy, like he'd been sniffing glue. He did all kinds of weird stuff, like laughing hysterically for no reason at all, or watching the History Channel. Plus, there was that bizarre thing with the words.

It happened two years ago, when Gus was still an electrician. Gus had been rewiring a dryer, and a customer, trying to be helpful, flipped a breaker too early. Gus got lit up with 220 volts of juice, and it was his brain that got the rewiring job.

In the few weeks that followed, Duke blamed Gus's mental haze on the fact that his brother had been damn near electrocuted. Surely the fog would lift and Gus would return to normal. But the days ticked by and the old Gus didn't show. He started popping mints all the time, complaining that the electricity had left a coppery taste in his mouth. But that wasn't the strange part.

A few days after the accident, Duke and Gus were sitting in a deer blind when Gus said, "Amebic dysentery."

At that point, neither of them had spoken for an hour.

Duke turned to his brother. "What?"

"Amebic dysentery," Gus said again. He was staring straight ahead, eyes focused on some faraway horizon.

"What about it?"

Gus turned to Duke then, blinking rapidly. "What about what?"

"Amebic dysentery."

"Yeah?"

"You just said it. You were just sitting there, and then you said, 'Amebic dysentery.'"

Gus smiled, but he looked embarrassed. "Did not."

"You sure as hell did. Just out of the blue. 'Amebic dysentery.'"

"Funny."

It didn't take Duke long to discover, in the days ahead, that Gus was prone to interject all sorts of random words and phrases into a conversation.

"Marsupial," Gus would say when they were watching motocross.

"Esophagus," he'd blurt out over dinner.

"Tort reform," he'd state on the telephone.

Over time, Duke more or less got used to it. In fact, it would be kind of funny if it wasn't so damn creepy. Kind of an *Exorcist* thing. And the thing that worried him: What if they got pulled over by the game warden someday and Gus said, "Poached a deer." Or "Spotlighting tonight." That could really screw things up.

Now Duke had a whole new reason to worry about Gus. His brother was the only one who knew Duke and Oliver Searcy had hunted together—and he wanted to keep it that way. Eventually, the cops would find records of the calls from Searcy to Duke, but that wasn't much for them to go on. Searcy himself had said he was calling several guides in the area. So Duke knew that in order to keep the cops from focusing on him, he'd have to say they never hunted together. The bitch of it was, he'd need Gus to play along.

As Marlin maneuvered the curves of Flat Creek Road, heading back toward Johnson City, he tried to remember everything he could about the mythical chupacabra. Sightings had been reported everywhere from Puerto Rico and Nicaragua to Chile and Mexico. A few years ago, there had even been a sighting reported just five hours south, in the border town of Brownsville.

The chupacabra was known as a stalker of livestock, leaving scores of dead goats, sheep, and calves in its wake. Allegedly, the animals' throats were punctured, the chupacabra feasting on every last drop of blood.

Descriptions of the beast varied, anywhere from a large scaly reptile with bulbous red eyes and fangs to a flying monkeylike creature with razor-sharp claws.

Despite hundreds of alleged sightings, the chupacabra had never been captured. In fact, it had never even been photographed or filmed. Not once.

In other words, it was total bullshit.

Marlin was surprised that Trey Sweeney appeared to believe it might actually exist. But then, the biologist, while brilliant, tended to exhibit a complete lack of good sense on occasion.

Why else would he hole up with a hibernating black bear?

Why else would he dress up in a deer costume and approach a massive lovesick buck?

Why else would he attempt to hand-feed a Komodo dragon?

Trey had done all these things and more, reminding Marlin that while he could trust Trey's scientific expertise implicitly, the biologist's judgment was another story.

Back at the scene, Sweeney had made a cast of one of the animal tracks, and he'd insisted on taking the goat carcass with him.

Marlin smiled as he envisioned Sweeney asking Lem Tucker, the medical examiner, to conduct an autopsy. *Subject is an adult, uh, goat with multiple visible puncture wounds to the carotid artery.*

Marlin was inclined to forget the whole thing, but he decided he'd better have a talk with Bobby Garza. After all, Marlin still hadn't heard the facts directly from the sheriff. Maybe there was more to the witness's account than Marlin knew so far. There had to be some reason why Garza would ask Marlin and Trey to check out a dead goat, which was an everyday occurrence in Blanco County. But then, of course, there was Garza's Hispanic heritage to take into account—and Marlin felt a twinge of that damned political incorrectness even considering it. The truth was, the chupacabra was a bit of folklore that thrived almost exclusively among Hispanic populations. Yeah, Bobby Garza was a first-generation central Texan. But his parents were natives of Mexico, and they might have regaled Bobby with tales of the chupacabra as he was growing up. Something like that could be hard to shake. Much like the otherwise-sane people who believed in Bigfoot or the Loch Ness Monster.

Marlin turned east on Highway 290, drove into Johnson City, and pulled into the parking lot at the Blanco County Sheriff's Department. Marlin had a small office there, though he didn't spend much time at it. It was more or less a place to grab coffee, store some equipment, and return calls (since he still hadn't given in and bought a cell phone).

Marlin walked into the building, said hello to a few of the deputies, and made his way to Garza's office in the back. He stuck his head through the doorway and saw Garza concentrating on some paperwork. "What's this wild goose chase you sent me on?" Marlin said.

Garza glanced up, saw who it was, and smiled. "So did you catch it? The notorious chupacabra?" Garza motioned at a chair and Marlin took a seat.

"Yeah, I got him in a cage in the back of my truck. I'm charging a nickel for people to see it."

Garza laughed. "Don't you wish. You'd be a rich man if you did. You know how many people believe in that thing?"

"Just please tell me *you* don't." He and Bobby Garza were old friends, and Marlin knew he didn't need to mince words with the sheriff. "I had enough trouble keeping Trey's imagination from running wild on this one."

Garza rolled his eyes. "Give me a little credit, will you? No, I just wanted to get it checked out because, in case you haven't noticed"—the sheriff lowered his voice and glanced furtively out his office door—"we got a lotta Meskins around this county."

Marlin smiled, though he felt a twinge of guilt for thinking as he had earlier. "You don't say."

"No joke, though," Garza said. "All kinds of people, not just Hispanics, believe in this stuff. We've gotten about two dozen calls already, mostly from people who know Jorge."

"The guy who got hit?"

"Right. Word's spreading fast. I was thinking at first they were concerned about him—and they are. But that isn't why they're all calling. It's this chupacabra business. I was talking to one of his cousins, down in Nuevo Laredo, and when he told his grandmother what happened, she crossed herself and then fainted on the spot."

Marlin couldn't completely smother a smile.

"Yeah," Garza said, "I know it sounds kinda silly, but not if you were brought up to believe in it. Anyway, I just wanted to get the jump on this thing before it got out of hand. That way, we can say no, it was just a dog or coyote, or rogue elephant, or whatever you wise old woodsmen determined that it was. So what's the story?"

Marlin shrugged. "Looked like just another dead goat to me, probably killed by dogs or coyotes. None of the meat was eaten, and that usually means dogs got it. But this guy Jorge might have spooked a coyote just as it was sitting down to breakfast. We found some tracks that looked like a dog to me, but Trey wasn't so sure."

"What'd he think it was?"

"You'll have to ask him. All he'd say is that he thought it was"—Marlin made quotation marks with his hands—"'something different.'"

"How so? Based on what?"

"Just on the tracks. And I guess on the eyewitness. I think Trey figured any idiot would recognize a dog or a coyote right off the bat. Speaking of which, what exactly *did* Jorge say?"

Garza took a breath and leaned back in his chair. "Man, I don't know. He was pretty rattled. Said he saw a creature with big fangs and a real long neck. And a huge head, too, like a lion. Oh, I almost forgot: It had the face of the devil. That's what he said. That should narrow it down some."

Marlin was glad Garza was showing a sense of humor about this thing. "So any animal wandering around looking like Satan, we can be pretty sure that's him?"

Garza winked. "Do me a favor. Let me handle the press, okay?"

"You really think there'll be any interest?"

Garza gave a slight nod toward his office door. Out in the main room, Susannah Branson, a reporter with the *Blanco County Record*, was making her way toward Garza's office.

When Red and Billy Don got back to Red's trailer that evening, all four of their traps had squirrels in them. That was the only good news of the day. The rest of the day had been a total loss. Red was still plenty pissed at the wetback—and at Billy Don, for that matter, for choosing that crazy Meskin.

Mr. Pierce, the barbecue king, had canceled the job after he found out what had happened. Said his wife was just too distraught by the whole thing to worry about the rock work right now. He gave Red two hundred bucks in cash and thanked him for his time.

Red's first inclination was to take the money and head straight to the electric cooperative and pay off his growing bill. But he and Billy Don kind of got sidetracked and ended up at the Friendly Bar, playing dominoes and consuming large quantities of beer and pork rinds.

Red grabbed a water hose and began to fill the kiddie pool he'd stolen from the Save Mart that summer. (He couldn't believe they'd just leave the pools out on the sidewalk like that. It was almost like they were *daring* him to throw one in the bed of his truck and drive off.) As soon as the water was high enough, he'd submerge the traps, drown the squirrels, and clean them for dinner. Red felt like a humanitarian for drowning the squirrels rather than shooting them, since it was painless. Plus, it saved ammo.

Billy Don was sitting in a nearby lawn chair, drinking a tallboy. Red, still intoxicated, couldn't resist taking another stab at the huge redneck. "Just had to pick that particular Meskin, didn't ya?" he muttered for about the tenth time.

Billy Don glared at him. "Don't get crossways with me, Red. Let it lie."

"I'll tell you one thing," Red said, wanting to get the last word in, "we're gonna need to come up with some cash pretty soon. The bills are piling up. Plus, you still owe me rent." Billy Don had moved into Red's trailer the previous fall.

"Yeah, but you said you'd just take the rent out of the money I'd earn from your great new masonry company. Remember?"

Red was quiet for a moment. In fact, he *did* remember saying that. He just didn't think Billy Don would remember it. "Well, like I said, if you hadn't gotten us a suicidal wetback with the runs—"

Billy Don growled and crumpled the beer can against the side of his skull.

Red decided to let the topic drop.

5

BARRY GRUBBMAN, AN assistant producer for *Hard News Tonight,* came into work early on Monday morning because he had a lot hanging over his head. He needed a good scoop, and he needed it bad. Something big and wild and juicy enough to get him back into his boss's good graces.

Last Friday, Chad Reeves, the show's arrogant executive producer, had made it clear that Barry's job was on the line. No, Chad hadn't come right out and said it, but Barry wasn't an idiot. He didn't need it spelled out for him.

Barry had pitched some segment ideas, but Chad had not been receptive whatsoever.

"I got a stringer with footage of Madonna sunbathing topless, rubbing oil on her . . . uh . . . herself," Barry had offered.

"Bor-ring," Chad replied in that annoying singsong voice of his. It was something he did when he wanted to be condescending.

Barry clumsily thumbed through some notes.

"A woman who claims to be the Pope's illegitimate daughter?"

Chad sighed heavily.

"How about a hiker in Michigan who got lost and ate his own dog?"

"Move along."

"Rap star Heavy Dogg Joe arrested during a drug bust?"

Chad shook his head.

"But . . . the guy was dressed in drag."

"I'll pass."

Barry was starting to get discouraged. "A blind lesbian in Georgia who became the surrogate mother for her brother's quadriplegic wife?"

Chad drummed his fingers on his desk.

Dejected, Barry said, "That's all I've got right now."

Chad leaned forward and made eye contact with Barry. It was somehow unsettling, the sense of intimacy too great. Barry struggled to maintain eye contact but failed. Chad spoke softly: "Let me ask you something, Barry. Let's say you just got home from a long day at work. You've been selling shoes or teaching first graders, or whatever the fuck you've been doing. Now you're tired, you've got a glass of booze in your hand, and you're looking for a little entertainment. Do any of those stories sound even mildly entertaining to you?"

The truth was, Barry thought they did. Madonna's hooters? Let me at 'em! A man who barbecued his own yellow Lab? Hell yeah!

"No, I guess they don't," Barry said quietly.

Chad rose from his chair and began to pace, a signal to Barry that a lecture was coming. "You know how I got my big break in this business, Barry?"

Oh God. Not this one again.

"I was on a flight from L.A. to New York—riding first-class, naturally—and as luck would have it, Jessica Hyatt was sitting right next to me."

Jessica Hyatt had achieved worldwide fame in the early nineties as a hip-swiveling, midriff-baring pop superstar before she drove her Ferrari into a tree at eighty miles per hour. She had been affectionately known to her fans as J Hi. Her death had made her an instant legend.

"Now, riding next to J Hi wasn't news in itself, of course," Chad said. "But as we reached cruising altitude and she began moaning and clutching her chest, I knew something was wrong. When it became apparent that her new breast implants had exploded, I knew I was onto a huge story. As soon as we landed, I got on my cell phone, made a few calls, and the rest is history."

There was a long pause, and Barry knew from experience that if he tried to say something, Chad would immediately interrupt him.

Barry said, "So you—"

"My point is," Chad said, "you have to have a nose for this business. You have to be able to spot the big story and react instantly. Not everyone has that gift. No, I'm afraid that sort of intuition is reserved for just a precious few."

Long pause.

Barry said, "And what—"

"I want you to do something for me, Barry. This weekend, I want you to take a long hard look at yourself . . . and decide whether this is the career for you. Figure out whether you have that special gift or not. Will you do that for me?"

Another pause. Barry wasn't sure if he was really supposed to answer.

He said, "Well, if you think—"

"That's my boy!" Chad placed a hand on Barry's shoulder, steering him toward the door.

That meeting had taken place last week. Now it was Monday, and Barry had to come up with some killer ideas fast.

He turned to the Internet, expecting to slog from one useless site to another. But as it turned out, he found something that caught his eye in about five minutes.

"Got a call this morning—maybe something you can help out with," Bobby Garza said.

John Marlin was sitting across from him at Ronnie's Ice House

& Barbecue in Johnson City. Marlin was waiting on a sliced beef sandwich, Garza for a rib plate. The rich aromas in the large one-room restaurant always made Marlin's mouth water before his meal even arrived.

"What's up?"

"Well, about a half hour ago, we got a call from a woman in Houston. Said her husband had come out this way yesterday to talk to a hunting guide. He was supposed to be home last night, but he never showed."

"Which guide?" Marlin knew most of them.

"That's the problem. The woman was practically useless. Didn't know the guide's name, the name of the ranch, or even what part of the county her husband was hunting in. The one thing she did know was that he had hunted with the guide a few weeks ago. I asked her to check with her bank, see if there were any checks made out to names she didn't recognize. In the mean-time, I told her we'd keep an eye out, and she could file a missing person report tomorrow if she wanted."

"Probably nothing," Marlin said. During deer season, it wasn't uncommon to receive a call like that, a frantic wife wondering where her husband had disappeared to. Usually, the hunter had decided to stay an extra day and either forgot to call or couldn't get good cell phone service where he was hunting.

"Anyway," Garza said, "the guy's name is Oliver Searcy. Drives a blue Ford truck, couple years old. Keep an eye out, will ya?"

"Sure, no problem. I'll be checking some camps this after-noon. I'll ask around."

Garza noticed Ronnie placing their orders on the counter, so he hopped up to get them while Marlin refilled their iced tea glasses.

Marlin tore into his sandwich, which was loaded with plenty of barbecue sauce. Pure heaven. On Wednesdays, Ronnie served a legendary hamburger made from three-quarters of a pound of meat—way more than Marlin could comfortably handle.

As Garza was gnawing on a rib, he said, "Also got a call from Trey Sweeney this morning."

"Oh yeah?" Marlin hadn't talked to Trey since yesterday on Flat Creek Road. "What's Trey up to?"

"He's decided he's going to pen a few goats and set up one of those automatic cameras."

In the past five years, motion-triggered cameras had become all the rage among hunters. You simply aimed the camera at your feeder or a trail, and anything that passed by was photographed. Great for scouting.

Marlin shook his head and grinned. "Man, once he gets his mind set on something . . ."

"Tell me about it. Like a dog with a bone."

Marlin had seen the *Blanco County Record* that morning. Right there on the front page was the article:

CHUPACABRA REPORTED IN BLANCO COUNTY
Undocumented Immigrant Struck By Truck in Bizarre Mishap

Fortunately, Susannah Branson hadn't taken the chupacabra angle too seriously. Marlin figured the buzz would die off quickly and that would be the end of it.

The lone coyote was white at the muzzle, old and lean, and not as fast as he used to be. He had had little success hunting for three straight days, and hunger was ravaging his insides. It ruled his existence and propelled him endlessly forward. He had found the remnants of a deer earlier in the day, but the carcass had offered little, the entrails long gone, the bones picked clean by scavengers that had been there in the preceding days.

Later, he was navigating a familiar hunting trail, the moon providing light by which to stalk, when he encountered the scent of the man. At first, his instincts—finely honed by untold generations of his forebears—told him to retreat. The coyote's brain equated *man* with *death*, and rightly so.

But he lingered. This scent was different, somehow enticing. This man was no longer a threat.

He crept through the cedar trees, moving upwind, his senses on full alert, prepared to flee at the slightest provocation. Moments later, his eyes, still sharp, spotted the source of the scent, a shapeless bulk sprawled on the ground.

The coyote lowered his belly to the dirt, the tall grass providing cover. For a full two hours, he lay in waiting, scanning the surrounding woods for signs of danger. There was no movement, and no other animals happened by.

Finally, when he could stand it no longer, the coyote moved forward, wary and watchful. The smell was overpowering, though, and he began to salivate.

In the middle of the night, a twelve-year-old boy named Charlie Riggs woke when his dogs began whimpering in the kennel outside his window. The dogs whined, but they knew better than to bark—because when they barked, Charlie's stepdad would go outside and kick them. Especially if he was drunk. Charlie hated when that happened. It scared him, and he knew it made his mother sad.

After a few minutes, the dogs were quiet again, and Charlie hoped they'd go back to sleep. It was probably nothing but a raccoon or possum that had wandered too close. But just as Charlie was drifting off again, the dogs began to whimper more loudly than before.

Charlie looked at the clock radio on his nightstand and saw that it was nearly 4:00 A.M. His stepdad would likely be in bed by now and wouldn't be able to hear the dogs. *As long as they don't bark*, Charlie thought. *Please don't bark*.

But Scout gave in. First, Charlie could hear her growling; then she let loose with a high-pitched yap.

Charlie pulled the covers back and stepped into his slippers. He made his way down the darkened hallway and was relieved to see that the door to his parents' bedroom was closed, no light showing through the space at the floor. He went through the kitchen to the back door, grabbing the flashlight off the counter as he walked outside.

He turned the corner of the house and approached the kennel. The dogs were quiet now, wagging their tails with excitement.

He opened the gate and stepped into the kennel, the dogs immediately nuzzling his hands and rubbing against his legs. Scout was the dominant one of the pair, a six-year-old female spaniel. Ace, a three-year-old pointer, was male, but submissive. Charlie knelt and petted each dog, calming them. They were warm and soft, and Charlie never felt more loved than when he was with his dogs.

He sat and leaned with his back against the chain link of the kennel. Ace stretched out on one side of Charlie, resting his muzzle on the boy's thigh. But Scout stood with her nose to the fencing, staring into the darkness, whimpering softly.

"What is it, girl?" Charlie asked. "Possum?"

The dog whined for a while, but finally she settled down and lay on Charlie's other side.

Charlie stayed in the kennel, dozing on occasion, until he began to see the glow of the sun in the east.

6

TUESDAY MORNING, JOHN Marlin woke before sunrise to a warm tongue scraping like sandpaper across his cheek. He turned his head and tried to ignore it, but that didn't stop the young dog from climbing across his head to get to the other side, planting a paw squarely on Marlin's ear as it went.

The licking continued.

Marlin covered his face with a pillow, but in a matter of seconds, the determined pup burrowed underneath and continued the assault.

"Okay, you win," Marlin muttered, raising up on his elbows. The gangly pup knelt on her front paws, butt in the air, and yapped. This was her I-want-to-go-outside bark, and Marlin had become intimately familiar with it. In fact, his alarm clock was quickly becoming obsolete.

Marlin pulled the covers back and the dog leapt to the floor, excited now, dashing back and forth, barely able to contain herself.

Her name was Geist and she was a seven-month-old found-ling. The previous July, Marlin had discovered her whimpering in the darkness, dehydrated, hopelessly lost in the middle of a large ranch. Marlin had saved the pup's life—that's what the vet had told him later.

But looking back on it now, considering everything that had been happening in his life the past summer, Marlin liked to think it was Geist who had come along at just the right time.

Two hours later, Marlin was driving down A. Robinson Road when he passed the gate to the Shorthorn Ranch. Maggie Mason, the owner, lived in Dallas and made it to the ranch about twice a year at most. She was a widow and had inherited the ranch from her deceased husband's side of the family. Maggie was not particularly fond of hunting, and she usually called Marlin at the beginning of each deer season, asking him to keep an eye on the place. They both knew poachers would be tempted to trespass in Maggie's absence. That's why there shouldn't have been tire tracks going into the ranch. And yet there they were, fresh in the mud from Saturday's light rain.

Marlin reversed, then swung up to the gate. Even before he climbed out of his truck, he could see that the chain was hanging loose and the lock was gone.

Duke Waldrip needed to talk to Kyle about the animal situation, so he drove over to the Macho Bueno Ranch, sorting things out in his head along the way.

This was the second animal they'd lost—but the first one, Duke had to admit, had been his own fault. Hadn't used enough tranquilizer on a jackal. When Gus hauled old man Raines over to shoot it, the damn thing was nowhere to be found. Hadn't seen it since. Coyotes probably got it. Duke had fixed the problem the next time around, dosing the second jackal with enough drugs to keep it from wandering. Duke had been lucky to find another one so quickly. But this new escapee would be much harder to replace, Duke knew.

Oddly, Duke felt remarkably calm about the Oliver Searcy fuckup. There hadn't even been anything on the news yet. And once there was, as long as he and Gus kept quiet, nobody would ever know Duke had guided Searcy on a hunt. Chances were good that Kyle didn't even know Searcy had set foot on the ranch. Duke couldn't remember specifically mentioning Searcy's name to Kyle, but if he had, it was doubtful Kyle would remember, being half blitzed most of the time. Kyle didn't seem to care who Duke brought out to the ranch, as long as Duke kept feeding him some of the profits. Like he really needed the money.

Kyle's daddy had been a big-time oilman, a millionaire before he turned thirty. When the old man died three years ago, Kyle was the sole heir to the fortune. Had to be something like twenty million bucks, according to the newspapers. Since then, Kyle had lived a life of fast women, fast cars, and expensive drugs. In other words, nothing had changed at all. Kyle had always driven in the fast lane, and there were times when Duke went along for the ride.

Like nine years ago. They were riding in Kyle's Lotus outside Houston, and Kyle had decided they should rob a liquor store. Just for kicks. "Hell, let's try something new," Kyle had said, high as a kite. If Duke hadn't been so drunk, he never would have done it. Or if Kyle hadn't bet him ten grand he didn't have the balls. So Duke went in alone, ended up shooting the slant-eyed clerk in the leg, and the whole scene was captured on video. It didn't take long for the cops to come calling, and for Duke to end up in Huntsville for four years. Shit, it could have been longer, if it wasn't for the overcrowded Texas prison system. Sure, Kyle had paid for Duke's lawyer, and he had even given Duke twenty grand in cash to keep his name out of it. But now Duke was an ex-con with a violent crime on his record.

That's what made the Searcy situation so dicey. Even if he managed to skate on the killing, the game violations and the fraud were enough to send him back to the joint.

Besides, who would believe that Duke had killed Searcy in

self-defense? The grand jury would string him up like a piñata and hand the district attorney a cane. And even if Duke *had* claimed self-defense and called the cops, they would have dug into his business and eventually nailed him for the hunting scams.

Okay then, Duke felt like he had done the right thing. He knew he'd probably have to answer some tough questions at some point, but he was prepared for that. With a little coaching, Gus would be, too.

One other loose end nagged at Duke's insides. What about Searcy's trophy mount? It had Duke's fingerprints all over it, inside and out. Should he try to find out where Searcy lived and go get it back? Duke figured that was probably overkill, at least for the moment. Hell, the heat wasn't even on yet. No sense in putting himself at risk if he didn't have to.

The best thing to do was to go back to life as usual. That meant trying to round up the escaped animal—or get ahold of another one—so Raines could shoot the damn thing and Duke could collect his money.

Marlin followed the tire tracks until the mud ended and turned to hard-packed caliche. He continued along the rough road, hoping to find soft ground that would reveal additional tracks.

Four hundred yards farther, he came to a Y in the road and kept to the right. He followed it for a few minutes, until he reached a muddy spot where a seasonal stream crossed the road. No tracks. He returned to the Y and went left this time. The road made a slow, sweeping curve, then crested a small hill. Coming over the rise, Marlin immediately spotted a blue vehicle a hundred yards away. As he neared, he identified it as a Ford truck. Fairly new, judging from the looks of it. The cab appeared to be empty, and the driver's door was open.

Marlin grabbed his radio mike. "Seventy-five-oh-eight to Blanco County."

"Blanco County, go ahead seventy-five-oh-eight." It was Darrell Bridges, one of the dispatchers for the sheriff's department.

"Darrell, Bobby told me yesterday about a missing hunter. . . ."

"Yeah, his wife called again this morning."

"Can you give me his plate number?"

"Uh, yeah, hang on a sec."

Marlin shifted his gaze to the license plate on the truck in front of him.

Darrell came back and recited the number.

It matched, just as Marlin figured it would.

Duke felt the usual pangs of envy as he pulled through the entrance to the sprawling Macho Bueno Ranch. It always made him do a slow burn, this place. Here he was, working his ass off year in and year out, and he'd never own a place like this. All Duke and Gus had was the old Waldrip homestead, a stone house on twenty acres. But Kyle, hell, he'd had it handed to him on a platter. Didn't seem right. Even though Duke and Kyle had been best friends since childhood, their properties sharing a common fence line, it always nagged at Duke that Kyle had it so easy. When Duke and his Gus were young, before they could drive, they'd hop the fence behind their house and follow a worn trail to Kyle's place, marveling the whole time at how big the ranch was.

Duke parked in front of the massive ranch house, which, like a lot of homes in Texas, was built from large slabs of limestone, durable cedar-plank siding, and seamless metal roofing. The place was huge and rugged and a little bit overstated, just like the whole damn state.

Walking to the front door, Duke heard a shriek—part giggle and part scream—coming from behind the house. *Cheri*, Kyle's current girlfriend. Oops, check that. Cheri was Kyle's wife now, at least on paper. The two of them had flown to Vegas two weeks ago. Kyle had gotten wasted and married, in that order. He was planning on having it annulled.

Duke couldn't blame him. Cheri wasn't the type you married. She was the type who'd look right at home with a wad of dollar bills sticking out of her G-string. Lots of brittle bleached hair. Long painted nails. A fake tan, even in the winter.

Duke followed a bordered path around the side of the house and found Kyle and Cheri wrestling in the hot tub in back, next to the swimming pool. The recreational area at the rear of the house—pool, tennis courts, barbecue pit, picnic tables—had an astounding fifty-mile view of the Hill Country. But Duke was distracted by another breathtaking view: Cheri, topless, her pendulous fake breasts swinging to and fro while she and Kyle played grab-ass. Damn. He might not like the girl much, but she had a tight little body on her. Wasn't bashful about showing it off, either.

"Couldn't afford the whole suit?" Duke said as he pulled up a chair on the patio.

Kyle and Cheri managed to shake their lust long enough to realize they had a visitor.

"There he is, Mr. Sunshine," Kyle bellowed, liquor in his voice. "Done snuck up on us. What's up, big man?"

Cheri giggled. She was always doing that. Giggling like a simpleton every time Kyle said something. Maybe Duke should set her up with Gus. The two pea brains would probably have a lot to talk about.

"I've always wanted to ask you something, Cheri," Duke said. "If you were on a plane that went down in the ocean, would those two things act as flotation devices?"

Cheri looked down at her gently bobbing orbs, then looked back at Duke, confused. "No, I don't think so. God, what a weird question."

"Aw, give her a break," Kyle said. "Grab yourself a drink." He pointed toward a wet bar beneath the latticed arbor.

Duke walked over, filled a glass with ice, and grabbed the lone bottle of vodka on the bar. Empty. He turned back to Kyle and shook the bottle back and forth.

"Hey, baby?" Kyle said.

"Whattie?" Cheri replied.

"Would you run in the house and get another bottle of vodka?"

"What am I, your slave? Go get it yourself."

Duke smiled. He liked to see Cheri giving it to Kyle that way.

"Don't be a bitch, Cheri," Kyle said. "Can't you see I'm talking to Duke here?"

Cheri glared at him. "Baby, it wouldn't hurt to say *please* now and then."

"Pleeease." Lots of sarcasm.

Cheri rolled her eyes and climbed out of the hot tub.

"That's my girl," Kyle said.

As she strutted toward the house, Kyle called out, "Have I told you lately that you love me?"

Cheri responded by flipping him the bird over her shoulder.

Kyle laughed. "God, I love to watch that girl walk, don't you?"

Duke gave a grunt.

"Damn, you're in a pissy mood," Kyle said. "Need to get laid or what? Maybe Cheri'd be willing to help you out."

Kyle, trying to be funny. What Kyle didn't know was that Duke had already been there and done that. Several times.

"Naw, man, it's this damn Raines thing. It's a package deal, and he ain't payin' until he gets his last animal. Tell me again what happened."

"Simple. I went to check on his last animal and it was gone."

Duke pulled a pack of smokes out of his pocket and lit one up. "Just like that? Gone?"

"As in not present. No longer there. Adios, muchachos. Sayonara and—"

"Awright, enough already. I get it." Duke was in no mood for Kyle's smart-ass bullshit. "How'd it get out?"

"Wish I knew. Checked on it two days ago and it was fine. Mean as a damn grizzly, but fine. Yesterday, the cage was wide open and it was gone."

Duke grimaced.

"Man, what's the big deal?" Kyle said. "Just call one of your buddies and get another one."

"My problem is, it never should have gotten loose in the first place. Know what I mean?"

Kyle set his drink down on the concrete beside the hot tub. "Hey, now, don't blame it on me. You want to use my ranch, fine. But keepin' 'em locked up—I don't remember applying for that particular job. I ain't no goddamn zookeeper."

"But damn, Kyle, how hard is it to make sure the cages are locked?"

"Man, that's your deal, not mine."

Duke knew Kyle was right. But still, there was something about Kyle that was damn irritating. Always had an answer for everything. Duke rattled the ice in his glass and looked toward the house, wishing Cheri would hurry the hell up with the vodka.

"Like I said," Kyle continued, "just get on the phone and round up another one."

"Snap my fingers and make it happen?"

"Isn't that how things work?"

"Maybe in your world."

Finally, Cheri emerged from the house, carrying a bottle of Stoli. About damn time.

"Besides," Kyle said. "How hard can it be for them to find another hyena? Worthless damn animals, if you ask me."

"Eww, hyenas. Gross," Cheri said, handing the bottle to Duke. She stepped into the tub and said, "Hey, baby, look what I found." She made a *voilà* gesture with one hand and revealed a small amber vial filled with white powder.

"A woman after my own heart," Kyle said.

While Duke poured some vodka, Kyle unscrewed the vial, poured a generous amount into the small lid, and passed it to Cheri. She sucked it into her left nostril, like a vacuum cleaner sucking up lint. Kyle took some for himself, then said, "You want a bump, Duke? Nothing like a little white stuff to chase your blues away."

Normally, Duke wasn't much of a cokehead. But at the moment, he couldn't think of a good reason to turn it down.

Ernie Turpin had brought a dog with him, a skinny, hyperactive coonhound named Jessie that pulled eagerly on its leash, anxious to hit the trail. Marlin watched from beside his truck, along with two other deputies, as Turpin was dragged into the brush.

He was back in five minutes, grim-faced.

The deputy pointed to the south. "He's right over there, under some oaks. Varmints have already been after him."

Bill Tatum, the chief deputy, said, "Look like Searcy?"

"Yeah, it's him. Looks just like the photos his wife faxed."

There was a moment of silence, and Marlin knew the deputies were thinking about the wife, and the call one of them would have to make.

Turpin spoke up again, almost in a whisper. "He was pretty torn up and everything, mostly through the torso, where the varmints got at him. But I think I could see what killed him. He had a puncture wound right here on his neck." Turpin pointed to a spot below his right ear.

"Gunshot?" Tatum asked.

"Hard to tell."

For a few seconds, Marlin couldn't remember where he had heard about that type of fatal injury: a single puncture wound to the neck. Then it came to him.

"You gotta admit, it's pretty strange," Bobby Garza said. "One day, we got a guy screaming about a chupacabra; two days later, we got a corpse with a hole in his neck." The sheriff had arrived shortly after the body was discovered. Now, two hours later, he and Marlin were sitting in Garza's cruiser, having a private conversation before Marlin left the scene. Marlin had already given the deputies a full report, telling them how he had happened upon Searcy's truck.

"Oh man, don't get started on that," Marlin said. "You're as bad as Trey Sweeney."

"It's weird, that's all I'm saying."

"Pure coincidence."

Bill Tatum, the chief deputy, approached the sheriff's window. Tatum was short and stout, with biceps that bulged like grape-fruits. He had gone straight to police work after a tour in the Marine Corps when he was younger. On the job, he was as tena-cious and focused as they come—which was why he had earned the respect of every man and woman in the department. Off the job, he had a dry sense of humor and a fishing addiction that kept him on the lake most weekends.

"We pulled some prints from the interior of the truck," Tatum said. "But nothing at all on the steering wheel or the door handle. Not even partials. Looks like they've been wiped clean. No footprints anywhere. The caliche's too damn hard. No other tire tracks in the vicinity, either. Henry's going over the body right now."

Henry Jameson was the young forensics technician Garza had hired seven months ago. The Blanco County budget alone couldn't afford Jameson's salary, so Garza had worked a deal to pool resources with several neighboring counties, giving them all access to Jameson's services.

"How's Lem doing?" Garza asked, referring to Lem Tucker, the medical examiner for Blanco County.

"He'll be ready to move the body as soon as Henry's done. Neither of them have said much so far."

"How about you? Any thoughts?"

"Pretty obvious we're looking at a dump job. No blood at the scene. My guess, someone drove Searcy's truck with the body in the back, then wiped it down later. We'll talk to the neighbors, and I'd say somebody needs to have a talk with the vic's wife."

Garza nodded, and Tatum retreated from the car.

Garza turned to Marlin. "Well, we're really in trouble now."

"Why's that?"

"Damn chupacabra knows how to drive."

7

TWO CHINESE DWARVES were having sex in front of Marty Hoffenhauser, and he definitely didn't like what he was seeing. Marty himself was not particularly aroused by the sight of two small Asians going at it, but there were certain people who not only craved but *burned* for this type of adult action. Fetishists. Marty had developed a keen eye for what these fetishists liked, and what they didn't. And this was definitely not working.

As far as Marty could tell, the dwarves' hearts just weren't in it today. They were merely going through the motions—and if they weren't fooling Marty, they sure wouldn't fool the audience when the video was released.

"Cut!" he shouted, making no attempt to mask the frustration in his voice. "Let's break for lunch, people. Back in sixty."

As the crew dispersed, Marty pulled the naked male dwarf to the side. The man's name—his screen name anyway—was Mike Hung, and Hung was, by far, the leading performer in Asian dwarf pornography. Marty had discovered Hung working as a busboy in a Chinese restaurant in Austin. As Hung had cleared the dishes from a nearby booth, Marty couldn't help but notice the bulge in Hung's slacks. Marty called him over and discreetly asked the young man whether he would be interested in an audition. That was two years ago, and since then, Hung's popularity had skyrocketed (and Marty's fortune along with it). In crude terms, Hung was the most important horse in Marty's stable, and the director did whatever he could to keep the little stallion happy. At times, that was quite a chore.

"Mike, you doing okay?" Marty asked, draping a robe around the actor. "You seem kind of . . . I don't know . . . distracted."

Hung began to answer, then shot a sideways look at the sound guy, who was still within earshot.

"Tony, give us a little privacy here, will ya?" Marty said.

Tony nodded and left for lunch.

"So what's up, little guy? Everything all right?" Marty asked, doing his best to appear empathetic.

Hung plopped into a nearby child-size chair. Marty had ordered half a dozen to accommodate the unique needs of his cast.

"T'ings velly bad with Wanda."

Hung was referring to Wanda Ho, a superstar adult actress in her own right, and Hung's costar in this film as well as the previous one, *Big Trouble in Very Little China*. It was common knowledge that Hung and Ho had been dating for several months. Marty would have preferred that his actors not socialize off the set, but there was really no way to prevent it. Especially among a population that was rather limited.

"Bad? Bad how, Mike? Everybody knows Wanda adores you." Marty had taken a seat in one of the small chairs himself, and his knees were up to his shoulders.

"Aw, that just acting," Hung replied. "She velly good actless. But she lose intelest in me."

"Oh, now, Mike, I don't think that's true. Why do you say that?"

"Last week, she have dinner with Willie Wang." Wang was the other male performer in Marty's current production, *Fortune*

Nookie. "She say it innocent, but I see way she look at him. I aflaid I not satisfy her." Hung's head dropped dejectedly and he stared between his legs. "Beside, he bigger than me. She like that."

"Bigger? Come on, Mike. Nobody in the industry is bigger than you. You're a regular Godzilla." Too late, Marty remembered that the *Godzilla* films had been made in Japan, not China. But Mike didn't seem to notice the faux pas.

"No, not that!" Hung replied. "Taller. He taller than me."

"Oh." Marty wasn't sure what to say to that. Wang *was* a couple of inches taller than Hung. But Hung had those extra two inches where it really counted.

"I aflaid of losing her." Hung's eyes were starting to glisten.

Marty patted Hung on the shoulder, trying to offer some measure of comfort. But truthfully, he wished he was someplace else, doing anything but counseling the diminutive porn star on his love life. How was Marty supposed to know what to say? He wasn't a counselor, just a director of adult films. Yeah, a pretty good one, but his expertise ended when the camera quit rolling.

On Wednesday afternoon, Sheriff Garza stuck his head into John Marlin's office and was happy to find the game warden behind his desk. He hadn't seen him since the day before on Maggie Mason's ranch.

"I think I got a leak," Garza said quietly.

"Bathroom's down the hall," Marlin replied.

"No, smart-ass," Garza said, closing the door behind him. "I mean a leak in the department. Like someone flapping his gums too much to the press. Susannah Branson just called. Told me she heard Searcy had a puncture wound to the neck. Wanted me to verify it."

"Wouldn't that have been in Lem's report anyway? And she would have found out that way?"

"Yeah, unless we sealed it."

Marlin gestured toward a chair and Garza sat down. Garza had a lot of respect for Marlin, and he wanted the game warden to join his department as a deputy. Garza had run the idea past Marlin a number of times, but to no avail. Being a game warden was in Marlin's blood, through and through. So Marlin remained an employee with the Texas Parks and Wildlife Department—and Garza remained content that Marlin was assigned to Blanco County, where Garza could include him in investigations when the need arose. Marlin had a natural instinct—that much was clear to Garza. Some people would say it was luck, Marlin stumbling upon Searcy's truck that way. But Garza knew better. Some people just have a knack.

"What'd you tell Susannah?" Marlin asked.

"'No comment.' Not that that will stop her from running with it anyway. The whole county's buzzing about the chupacabra. This'll only feed the fire."

"So where does the investigation stand?"

"Slim pickings. Neighbors didn't hear or see anything. Tatum and Cowan drove over to Houston last night to talk to the wife, but that went nowhere. They went through Searcy's office, looking for notes or something that would tell us who he hunted with, but came up empty. They talked to his friends, neighbors, family—everybody. Got nothing. They're still in Houston. Meanwhile, Ernie's getting the phone records and maybe that'll lead somewhere."

"Any word from Lem yet?" Marlin asked.

Garza checked his watch. "I was just fixing to go see him. Want to join me?"

John Marlin enjoyed the latitude his position gave him. His primary role was to enforce hunting and fishing laws—and he loved every minute of it. But as a peace officer with the state, he was free to assist the sheriff anytime Garza asked. These investigations added a little extra excitement to the job.

At the county morgue, Garza parked his cruiser next to Lem Tucker's ancient Chevy Suburban. The morgue was housed in an old Dairy Queen building, with the windows painted black and the signage removed. But the exterior of the building still featured a perky red-and-white color scheme. The only indication that the building had any official capacity was a small sign on the door that read BLANCO COUNTY CORONER'S OFFICE.

Both men stepped inside and Garza called out Lem's name.

"Back here."

The interior of the building hadn't changed much since its restaurant days, except that the booths had been replaced by desks and filing cabinets. Garza and Marlin found Lem behind the walk-in freezer, in a corner that housed an autopsy table, a hanging scale, and several other stainless-steel tools of Lem's trade. Lem stood next to the autopsy table, where Oliver Searcy's body still rested.

"I'm just about finished," Lem said. He was a lean man in his late thirties, with sandy hair quickly going gray. All three men had known one another since childhood, though Marlin was a handful of years older than the other two. Nobody shook hands, chiefly because Tucker was still wearing bloody latex gloves.

"What's the story?" Garza asked. On the occasions when Marlin had reason to visit the morgue, he noticed there was rarely any small talk.

"Just to set your curious minds at ease, it definitely wasn't a chupacabra," Tucker deadpanned. "I know you gentlemen were hoping for a little *X-Files* kind of excitement in your lives, but this ain't it."

Marlin and Garza chuckled to be polite.

Tucker pointed toward the wound on the neck, which was no longer recognizable. It had been deeply splayed open, like a flower in bloom, and Marlin found himself staring at what he assumed were Searcy's vertebrae. The torso was even worse, the rib cage cracked open, the chest cavity empty. The abdomen was a grotesque mess, the skin ragged, rather than cleanly incised.

"It was the neck injury that killed him," Tucker said. "Near as I can tell, the wound was made from a long pointed instrument, more than likely made of steel. Round shaft, about ten millimeters thick. It slammed directly into the spinal column, and he died in seconds, if not instantly. Not a great deal of blood loss, since it missed the carotid. Difficult to determine if he had any other injuries through the torso, because of the damage from scavengers. Most of the organs were gone or pretty mangled. What the hell got after him, anyway? Wild pigs?"

Garza looked to Marlin.

"Hard to say. Not pigs, though, because you wouldn't have this much left to work with."

"Lucky me," Tucker said flatly.

"Back to the steel instrument," Garza said. "Any guesses as to what it was?"

"This'd be speculation, now . . ."

"Sure."

"I'd say maybe a screwdriver. Driven in all the way to the handle."

8

HARD NEWS TONIGHT was anything but, in Rudi Villar-real's opinion. Heck, in anyone's opinion, the show was nothing but fluff. A lot of gossip and speculation and innuendo, plus a healthy dose of titillation. Who's sleeping with whom? Which Hollywood hunk is allegedly gay but afraid to come out of the closet? Whose boob popped out on the red carpet at the Oscars? Pure pabulum really.

And Rudi Villarreal was the show's rising star.

No, she wasn't the anchor yet (and it was really a stretch to use the word *anchor* anyway); she was still a field reporter. But she knew Chad, her boss, had big plans for her—beyond his ongoing plans to get her into bed, that is.

That wasn't much consolation.

Looking back, Rudi sometimes wondered how her career had gotten so pitifully sidetracked. Thirty-six years old, and she was nowhere near the network news position she had always envisioned for herself. And if not one of the major networks, then maybe CNN, MSNBC, or even—God help her—Fox News.

But *Hard News Tonight*?

It was more than depressing; it was enough to make her cry into her pillow at night.

Amazingly, Rudi's coworkers appeared to enjoy their jobs, seemed to thrive on dishing out garbage on a nightly basis.

Well, there was one guy who seemed to share the same lofty ambitions as Rudi. A producer named Barry Grubbman. Kind of a quiet guy. Young. Semicute. Kind of passive, though, and Rudi could never picture him producing a network newscast. Regardless, they had become friends, kindred spirits in a sea of empty souls, as far as Rudi was concerned. They grabbed lunch together about once a week, the occasional drink after work.

Late Wednesday afternoon, Rudi stopped in Barry's office doorway on her way to the coffee machine. He was staring intently at his computer screen, so preoccupied he didn't even notice her standing there.

"Haven't I warned you about those porn sites?" Rudi said, causing Barry to jump.

"Oh man, you startled me. What's up, Rudi?"

"Getting some coffee. You want some?"

"Hey, let me run an idea past you," Barry said, ignoring her question. "You got a minute?"

Rudi took a seat in the chair in front of his desk. His office was tiny, not much larger than a closet, and there was hardly room for the chair between the desk and the wall. "Let's hear it." Maybe Barry had discovered a way for them both to get hired by *60 Minutes*. Yeah, sure.

"Well, you know how Chad is always talking about fresh concepts? He glanced at his computer screen again. "I've been following a story in Texas. Small newspaper site, not much content, but there's something kind of interesting. At least *I* think it is."

Rudi stood, about to make her way around his desk.

Barry put up his hands. "First, though, you gotta promise not to laugh."

Rudi promised, and they switched positions, Rudi leaning for a closer look at the screen. She held one hand to her blouse. Yeah, Barry was her friend, but she still caught him trying to sneak a peek now and then.

She read the first few paragraphs. "A chupacabra?" she said. "Is this for real?"

Barry nodded.

"And it supposedly killed a man?"

Barry started to turn red. "It's just an idea. Maybe it's stupid. Just be honest, okay?"

Rudi scrolled down and read the entire story. Then she read it again as Barry fidgeted.

Finally, she looked up. "I think it's got potential."

She had never seen Barry grin quite so hard. "You do? You really do?"

"Yep, and Chad will, too."

"Think so?"

"Uh-huh. Just leave it to me."

Holed up in his office, Duke longed for the good old days. It used to be, you could kill just about any kind of exotic animal you wanted to in Texas. Impala and gemsbok. Zebra and kudu. Hell, you could even shoot a giraffe, if that's what got your rocks off. And, of course, the all-time favorites—the big cats. They were all fair game, and it wasn't anybody's damn business who was shooting what.

But there was always someone who wanted to come along and drop a turd in the punch bowl, and in this case, it was liberal groups like the Humane Society, PETA, and a bunch of other Commies with sticks up their butts. They were always whining that these so-called canned hunts were unsporting and most of the animals were too tame even to know they should run. *Well, so what?*—that's what Duke thought. Beef cattle didn't know to run, either, and those were slaughtered by the thousands every day. Where did those morons think Big Macs came from—wild, free-ranging Black Angus?

Besides, if some rich guy wanted to shoot a lion, that was

between the hunter and the lion, just like Mother Nature intended. You didn't see the lion complaining about it. Exotic hunts were big business, too, pumping millions of dollars into the economy every year. Some guys, that's the only way they made a living, finding animals and guiding hunts. Just like the pinkos to try to take away a man's right to earn a decent living.

Well, they hadn't completely ruined everything yet. You could still hunt a wide variety of imported animals, and you could hunt them in just about any manner you chose. But the liberals had had one big victory, and it gave Duke a migraine every time he thought about it. The bunny-huggers kept putting pressure on the state, and the Parks and Wildlife Department finally caved in with a new hunting law. It was now illegal to hold various "dangerous" wild animals in captivity and then release them for hunting—including lions, leopards, and cheetahs, wolves and bears, rhinos, and, yes, even hyenas.

Fortunately, there was still a healthy black market. You could get your hands on any type of animal you wanted if you knew the right people. Luckily, Duke knew several of them. Most of them were licensed animal dealers or legitimate breeders, but they ran some of their business under the table for guys like Duke. They got the majority of their stock from zoos that needed to get rid of surplus animals—out with the old gray lion, for instance, in with the cute new lion cub born last week. Those displaced animals had to go somewhere, and to Duke's good fortune, they often went to dealers who were willing to pay a fair price.

Duke picked up the phone and called one of his most reliable contacts. "Hey, Ryan, it's Duke."

"What's up, man?"

"Nothing, except I was wondering: How hard would it be for you to get me another hyena?"

"You serious? You find someone who likes shooting the damn things?"

"Long fucking story. Need another one, though."

"Well, yeah, I can help you out, but it'll take a couple weeks. Maybe a month."

Shit. That geezer Raines might die by then, Duke thought. Duke pushed, but Ryan couldn't deliver any faster.

He hung up and made a few more calls. One guy said he was lying low for the moment, trying to renew his license, and he didn't want to screw anything up. Another said, "Hey, how about a couple of wildebeests and a Thomson's gazelle instead? I'll make you a hell of a deal."

Duke told him no, it had to be a hyena.

"Sorry."

Duke continued down his list, and struck out on every call. The problem was the time frame. Duke wanted the hyena *now*, not in a month or two. Who knew how long Raines would be willing to wait. For that matter, who knew how long the fucker would even be able to write a check, much less shoulder a rifle.

And Duke really needed that twenty grand. Oliver Searcy had been found, the county was buzzing with the news, and Duke needed to be ready if he had to haul ass. Maybe get out of town until this whole mess blew over. Lord knows, Duke's girlfriend, Sally Ann, wouldn't give a shit if he was gone. Probably throw a goddamn party. All because she'd heard that Duke was slipping it to a barmaid down in Blanco. Duke denied it, but Sally Ann didn't want to listen. Of course, it *was* true, but she didn't know that for a fact. Just like a woman to believe loose gossip instead of her old man.

Anyway, Duke figured he and Gus could head up to Alaska and guide caribou hunters for a season or two. A man would be damn hard to find in a state that size—if anybody even came looking. But they damn sure couldn't make the trip without some cash.

Duke shuddered when he thought about his feeble-brained brother. He was the weak link in all this, the one who could blow it all and land them both in prison. And since the telephone account at the office was in Gus's name, the cops would probably go to him first. Just this morning, Duke had sat Gus down and warned him the cops might be nosing around. "They're gonna try and pin it on me, even though I had nothing to do with it," Duke said. "So as far as you're concerned, you never met Oliver Searcy. And for Christ's sake, don't tell 'em I took Searcy hunting."

Gus had responded with a prolonged giggle—not exactly a confidence builder. So Duke had given him strict instructions: "Just lay low for a while, okay? Hang out at the house—and whatever you do, don't answer the goddamn phone or doorbell."

Rudi stuck her head back into Barry's office. "Pack your bags, cowboy. We're going to Texas."

Barry's eyes snapped up from his computer screen. "What? Really? When?"

"Right now. Tonight. We've got a flight in three hours."

Barry was standing now, excited. "You're kidding! Chad liked it?"

Rudi whispered, "At first, I pitched it like it was my idea—and he loved it! I showed him the Web site, and once he bought in, I said, 'Oh, by the way, Barry found this.' It worked like a charm."

Barry giggled. "Did he know you played him?"

"Not a clue. There is one tiny bit of bad news, though. He wants to go with us."

Barry groaned. "To Texas? You're shitting me."

"I wish I was. But we'll have fun anyway. Now go home and get packed." She tried a drawl: "We gotta skedaddle."

Something else Dr. King, the vet, had told Marlin the day after he had found Geist: "You got yourself a pit bull here, you know that?"

The pup was back on her haunches atop a stainless-steel exam table, staring at Marlin with those large brown eyes. She gave him a somber look that seemed to say, *Okay, now you know. Are we still friends?*

Up to then, Marlin had thought of her as a generic puppy. Gangly legs, wet nose, and a tail that wouldn't stop wagging. He hadn't put much thought into what breed she was. But a pit bull? No, Marlin hadn't realized that. "You sure?"

"No doubt. See the size of her head and how wide her jaw is?

And through here, the broad chest. I would say she's not even a mix. One hundred percent pit is my guess, but there's no way to know for sure with a stray."

Marlin considered that. He'd never had a problem with a pit bull before, but then again, he hadn't dealt with very many. He wondered if the media hype matched up with reality. Were pit bulls sweet and loyal right up to the minute they chewed your arm off?

"Don't look so concerned." Dr. King laughed.

"Well, no, I'm not, really."

"It's all in how you raise 'em, John." The vet tussled Geist's head, and she immediately wanted to play tug-of-war with his fingers. Suddenly, Marlin became painfully aware of how much play biting the dog seemed to do. He wondered if that much aggression was normal.

"She's a sweet one," Dr. King said.

"Yeah, yeah, she is, but how big is she going to get?" Marlin asked.

"Oh, maybe forty, fifty pounds. That's about average. But some get up to seventy or eighty, sometimes even larger."

An eighty-pound pit bull? Marlin began to wonder what he was getting himself into. He'd been thinking about keeping the dog, but now he was having second thoughts. Did he really need these responsibilities right now? He was having a tough time just remembering to feed himself lately.

There had been a warm and beautiful light named Becky in Marlin's life until a month ago, but she was gone now, and Marlin was doing his best to cope with it. People are drawn together and pulled apart by all types of forces, and in this case, it was Becky's career. She was a nurse, and even the promise of a new high-tech county hospital hadn't been enough to make Blanco County her permanent home.

"It's a commitment," Dr. King said, almost as if he were privy to Marlin's thoughts. "Any dog is, though. If you decide she's not for you, no big deal. Just let me know and I'm sure I can find a home for her."

Marlin had taken Geist home that day, thinking he'd give it a week or so and then make up his mind. Looking back on it now, watching the dog romp in the backyard, a bittersweet smile crossed Marlin's face. Geist had made up his mind for him.

He opened the door and Geist bounded inside. Marlin stepped into the kitchen and poured a bowl of kibble. He was preparing his own dinner when Bobby Garza called.

"You ever hear of Gus Waldrip?" the sheriff asked.

"Yeah, I've checked his license once or twice. He lives on Flat Creek Road. I think he guides over at Kyle Dawson's place now and then."

"That's good to know. Oliver Searcy called a couple of different guides here in the county. Three, actually. We've talked to the other two and they check out okay. Searcy called Gus Waldrip on Sunday, but we haven't been able to track him down."

Marlin said, "He has a brother who lives with him, I think. Goes by Dirk, or something like that."

"Yeah, the records show his name as Richard, nickname Duke. Do you know if he guides, too?"

Marlin checked so many hunting camps each season, it was difficult to remember. "You know, I don't think so. I believe I've seen him and Gus hanging around with customers, but I don't remember him guiding. I could be wrong. I've only seen them for the last couple seasons. I think they were born around here but moved away for a while. Then they came back when their mother died."

"You know where they were living before?"

"Let's see. Up in Burnet County? I think it was just south of Lampasas."

"Tell you what: I'm gonna check with the sheriff up there, but would you mind giving the warden a call? See what he has to say about them?"

"Will do. I'll give you a ring back."

"Okay, pardner, I appreciate it."

At nine o'clock, the cops showed up for a third time—and Gus thought it was hilarious. He was peeking through the window, grinning, and could see the sheriff and one of his deputies getting out of a squad car. Gus quickly closed the curtain. It was kind of fun, actually—like a game of hide-and-seek.

Then Gus thought, *Clambake*.

Crap. Now was not the time for one of his episodes.

The cops were at the door, knocking again, but Gus could feel himself fading out. He sat on the couch.

Ocelot.

Chimichanga.

Deputy Ernie Turpin knocked again. There was no answer, no sound from within the home, even though the porch light was on and a Ford Expedition sat in the driveway.

"What do you think?" Turpin asked. "Leave another card?"

Garza tried to peek between two curtains, but all he could see was a sliver of carpet. "Yeah, and then let's try their office again."

Back in the cruiser, Turpin said, "I thought you wanted to talk to Kyle Dawson next."

"I've been thinking. I want to send Marlin out there, go at this from a different angle."

"The Waldrip brothers? Hell, yeah, I remember them." The man on the other end of the line was Howell Rogers, Burnet County's game warden since the early seventies. He was one of the old-timers and could tell some good stories about Marlin's dad. "You need to keep an eye on Duke," Rogers said.

"You ever write him up?" Marlin asked.

"Dadgummit, no, but I sure as hell tried. Man's smart, I give him credit for that."

"And his brother?"

"What, is he smart?"

"No, was he trouble, like Duke?"

"Well, he was always hanging around, but Duke was the ring-leader, that's for sure."

"But you never nailed them for anything?"

"The closest I came ... one time some lowlife broke into a shed behind my house. Stole a bunch of my supplies, a few power tools, even an old carbine I kept out there. I heard it was Waldrip who done it, so I started asking around. One of the locals told me they'd seen him with a rifle just like mine. So I got a warrant and checked his place out. No luck." Marlin could hear the regret in the older man's voice.

"You ever see him get violent? Get into a fight maybe, stuff like that?"

"Not me, no. You should check with the sheriff."

Rogers's cell phone crackled. Even old Howell had joined the mobile crowd. Marlin was aware that he himself was in danger of becoming the last game warden in Texas without one of those gadgets.

"Now he's back in your part of the country?" Rogers asked.

"'Fraid so."

"Do me a favor. Send that son of a bitch to jail, will ya?"

9

DRIVING THROUGH JOHNSON City early Thursday morning, John Marlin noticed a sign in the window of Big Joe's Restaurant: ASK FOR THE CHUPACABRA SPECIAL! ONLY $3.99!

Great. Sure, some people would get a laugh out of it, but others would take this chupacabra business seriously and the calls would start to come in. "I just saw the chupacabra running through my backyard!" Or "I think the chupacabra is hiding in the crawl space under my house!"

Marlin remembered when a mountain lion was allegedly on the loose in the area four years ago. The whole county was nervous, keeping their children and pets in sight at all times. Late one night, Marlin was awakened by a call from an elderly man living up near Round Mountain. "I got the cougar trapped in my henhouse!" he said. Of course, when Marlin arrived on the scene, he had to be cautious—even though he was sure it would be another false alarm. He swung the door of the henhouse open slowly, a spotlight in one hand and a shotgun in the other.

That's when the house cat—granted, a damn big house cat— streaked right between Marlin's legs.

The cougar was never seen. But it showed how easily things can be blown out of proportion.

Marlin put those thoughts aside and concentrated on what Bobby Garza had told him last night. The sheriff had done some digging, and it turned out Gus Waldrip's brother, Richard—aka Duke—had done some time for armed robbery. Gus's record was clean. Now Garza wanted Marlin to drop by Kyle Dawson's place, like it was just a casual hunting check, and see what he could find out about the Waldrip brothers, especially Gus. Marlin had only run into Gus on a couple of occasions and didn't know him well. His general impression, though, was that the guy was sort of odd. Kind of spacey.

Dawson's place, the Macho Bueno Ranch, didn't have a gate at the entrance—just two ornate stone columns on either side of a cattle guard, a holdover from the days when Dawson's father, Floyd, raised a large herd of Angus on the place. Marlin remembered the elder Dawson: a quiet, hardworking man who had managed to assemble a sizable fortune in the oil and gas industries. His son, on the other hand, didn't seem to have any sort of occupation at all, other than squandering the assets his daddy had left behind. Nothing more than white trash with money.

Marlin's tires thrummed over the cattle guard, and then he was on the quarter-mile driveway up to the large house, pavement all the way, a luxury in these parts. He parked in the circular drive, walked to the door, and rang the doorbell.

In the living room, Cheri was snorting a fat line off a small mirror. Her first bump of the day, just a little pick-me-up to get her blood flowing. Not that she needed it or anything. She could take it or leave it, no big deal. If it ever got to be a problem, she'd just quit cold turkey. No sense in turning into some kind of coke slut. *The slut part is okay, though*, Cheri thought, giggling, feeling the warm buzz of the drugs.

Kyle was still crashed in the bedroom, and she could hear him snoring hard. Maybe she'd sneak back in there in a minute and see if his dick was awake yet. She didn't need the rest of him.

She had just finished a second line when the doorbell rang.

Damn it. Probably Duke again. She licked the remaining coke residue off the mirror and stuck it in a drawer behind the bar. Dropped the coke vial in there, too. No sense in sharing it with the whole world.

Marlin rang the bell again.

He would have called first, but that would have been unusual. Landowners on ranches where people hunted were used to the game warden dropping by unannounced, no big deal. After a full minute, he was turning to leave when he heard the door being unlocked.

The door swung open, revealing a young woman in a short red robe, kind of a kimono thing, loosely tied around her waist. She had that semicheap look, with long bleached hair, lots of makeup that was a little rough around the edges, maybe slept in. The robe was open to her navel, plenty of cleavage on display. Marlin wouldn't have been surprised if Hef had suddenly appeared in his pajamas. Just another morning after at the Playboy mansion.

The woman appeared startled, her eyes wide. "Oh!"

"Morning," Marlin said. "I, uh, I'm sorry if I woke you."

"No, I was just . . . No, I wasn't sleeping. You looking for Kyle?"

"Yes, ma'am, if he's here."

"Yeah, hold on." There was a moment of hesitation, as if she wasn't sure whether to invite him in or leave him standing on the front porch. "Here, come on in," she finally said. Marlin stepped into a foyer that was as large as the living room in his own house.

The woman closed the door and said, "Can I tell him, like, who you are?"

"Yes, ma'am. John Marlin. I'm the game warden of Blanco County. He'll recognize the name."

"Oh, a game warden." She smiled. "I thought you were a deputy."

Marlin shrugged. "Well, the uniform and everything . . ."

"Wait right here," she said, and disappeared down a hallway.

Half a minute later, Marlin could hear voices murmuring deep within the house. Finally, the woman reappeared. "He'll be right out." She offered a hand. "I'm Cheri, by the way."

Marlin shook her hand. "Nice to meet you, Cheri."

"Why don't we go in here," she said, leading him into a large living room with a huge stone fireplace. "Have a seat. You want some coffee?"

"I don't want to trouble you."

"No, I've already got it perking in there. How do you like it? Have a seat."

"Black's fine," Marlin said, settling down into a leather couch.

"Coming right up."

She sashayed through a swinging door, the robe barely covering her butt as she walked out, then came back thirty seconds later with a coffee cup on a small saucer. "It's just Folgers," she said, leaning over to set the coffee on the table in front of him. The front of her robe was hanging free now, both breasts clearly exposed, her nipples large and brown.

"Thank you," Marlin said.

"Nice rack, huh?" It was Kyle Dawson, coming into the room, still buttoning his shirt.

"Excuse me?"

"That six-by-six," Kyle said, pointing to an elk mount hanging above the fireplace mantel. "Got it last year up in Colorado. Big sumbitch. Took me all day to cut it up and pack it out." Kyle extended a hand now. "How you doin', John?"

"Real good, Kyle. I didn't mean to barge in this morning, but I was out this way and thought I'd stop in and see how it's going this year."

"Oh, hey, no problem. I was wondering when I'd see you."

Dawson dropped into a large stuffed chair. He looked over at Cheri but remained silent.

She stood there for a moment, then said, "Okay, I'll leave you two alone. Nice meeting you."

"You, too," Marlin said, staring down at his coffee cup rather than at Cheri's ass as she left.

Kyle hiked one leg up over an arm of the chair, getting comfy. "Well, we're doing some hunting out here this season, but not as much as last. It gets to be a hassle, you know—all the lease forms, the insurance, having to worry about rednecks wandering all over your property, tearing shit up. Can be a real pain in the ass. And the lease fees don't really amount to much. Thousand a gun."

"So you're not leasing it out this year?

"Nah. Kinda limiting it to friends only for now. A guided hunt every now and then."

"Yeah? Getting any good deer?"

"So-so. Nothing too impressive."

Marlin said, "Hey, what about that friend of yours? Gus Waldrip? He still guiding?"

"Gus? Well, kinda. It's really his brother, Duke, that does the guiding, and Gus is sorta his helper." An exaggerated expression of concern crossed Dawson's face. "You know, because Gus is a little—I don't mean to be an asshole—but Gus is kinda goofy. Got shocked a few years back, and he ain't been all there since."

"That right?"

Dawson nodded and began to sit up. "Listen, I'm gonna grab me some coffee. You need some more?"

"No, I'm all set."

In the kitchen, Kyle paced for half a minute. *Damn, am I telling this guy too much?* he wondered. The game warden was being awfully nosy, and Kyle wondered if word had gotten out about some of the animals Duke had been bringing out lately. Kyle wished he hadn't snorted a line in the bedroom before coming out to speak to the game warden. Cocaine always made him talk too damn much. And he could never keep his thoughts straight.

He poured a cup, then went back into the living room, ready to wrap this up, get the warden out the door. He didn't sit back down, but stood instead, drinking his joe, hoping the guy could take a hint.

"So Duke does the guiding, then?" Marlin said, right back at it. "You usually go with him?"

Kyle shrugged. "Not usually. You know, we're such good friends, I more or less give him the run of the place."

"You ever meet any of his customers?"

"Not this year I haven't." Kyle wondered what the hell this guy was getting at. He figured the warden would be more interested in the *types* of animals they were hunting, rather than *who* was doing the hunting.

"You recall a man named Oliver Searcy?"

The name sounded vaguely familiar to Kyle, but he honestly couldn't recall where he'd heard it. "I don't think so. . . ."

The warden's tone had changed and he was starting to look serious now—and it made Kyle nervous. Somehow, this had become more than a casual discussion.

Marlin sat forward on the couch, drilling Kyle with his eyes now. "You might have heard his name on the news. We found his body two days ago. He was murdered."

Kyle hadn't seen the news in several days, and he damn sure didn't know what to make of *that* information. "What's that got to do with me? Or Duke?"

"Searcy made some calls to Gus, or maybe Duke, and we want to talk to them both."

Jesus, Marlin wasn't here about hunting; he was here for a murder investigation. Kyle knew Duke was a bit of a hothead, and he wasn't one to back down from a fight. But killing a guy? Could Duke have done that?

Marlin added, "We haven't had much luck getting hold of them. I thought maybe you'd know where they are."

Now Kyle was really getting antsy, and he wanted the man out of his house as soon as possible. "I got Duke's cell phone number," he offered, thinking that would send the game warden on his way.

"Great," Marlin said. "Let's give it a try."

10

DUKE'S CALLER ID read DAWSON, KYLE, so he picked up after the second ring. The problem was, it wasn't Kyle.

"Hey, Duke, this is John Marlin. Remember me? The game warden?"

"Yeah, hey, how's it going? You surprised me there. I thought it was Kyle."

"Well, I'm calling from his place."

Yeah, I know that, you tricky son of a bitch. "Kyle ain't been poaching again, has he?" Duke said, forcing a laugh. "Damn outlaw is what he is."

"Nothing like that. I was just talking to him about a few things. And I need to chat with you for a couple minutes, too. Where are you right now?"

"My office, next to the feed store." Damn! Why had he said that? Since he was on his cell phone, he could've lied, said he was out of town or something. He could have bought some time and found out from Kyle what the game warden wanted. He was worried it had something to do with the exotic animals. Maybe one of his hunters had gotten nailed and pointed the finger at him.

"Good. Hang tight, will you? I'll be there in a few minutes."

"If you don't mind me asking, what's this about?"

No reply. The game warden had already hung up.

Duke gave it five minutes, then called Kyle back.

It rang ten times before Duke finally slammed his cell phone down on his desk.

In his cruiser, Marlin radioed the sheriff's office for Bobby Garza. He knew the sheriff kept a handheld unit in his office.

After a few seconds, Marlin heard Garza's voice: "Blanco County to seventy-five-oh-eight. Go ahead."

"Bobby, I got a line on Duke Waldrip. You want to talk to him?"

Threesomes were always tricky. Not just the lighting and the sound and the camera angles, but, in this case, the personalities. This was the most important scene in *Fortune Nookie*—the climax, so to speak—and Marty didn't know what to expect. Would Mike Hung, Wanda Ho, and Willie Wang recapture some of the magic from their earlier films? Or would their offscreen tensions put a damper on it all?

Yesterday, Mike Hung had managed to complete his scene with Wanda Ho, but the results were hardly scintillating. Everyone on the crew noticed an obvious sense of uneasiness between the two actors, and it made for some fairly blasé adult entertainment. Certainly not up to the usual Marty Hoffenhauser standards.

On the other hand, being realistic, not every scene could be an award winner. If Marty could just get the three performers to finish off with a flourish, this could still be another moneymaking picture. Marty had given Mike a little pep talk an hour ago, and now he was desperately hoping it would pay off.

"You ready, Mike?" Marty called from behind the camera.

Hung appeared lost in thought and didn't respond. He was seated at a table on the set, which was supposed to resemble a Chinese restaurant. Wanda Ho was playing a slutty waitress, one who gave her favorite customers a special treat when the restaurant closed for the evening. Meanwhile, she was also a secret agent for the U.S. Treasury, trying to nail the restaurant owner for money laundering. Marty had written it himself.

The script called for Mike to hoist Wanda up onto the table, climb onto a chair, and go at it for seven or eight minutes, changing positions a couple of times. Eventually, Willie Wang would emerge from the kitchen, just a curious cook wanting to get in on the action.

Marty called again: "How 'bout it, Mike? You good to go?"

Hung glanced up and nodded. His expression didn't give Marty a great deal of confidence.

"All right, then, people. Everybody ready?"

Tony, the sound guy, gave a thumbs-up. Blake, the lighting technician, had the set softly lit.

Marty said, "Let's roll it!"

The scene began with Mike studying a menu. Wanda entered the frame, holding a pen and pad, ready to take his order.

"Good evening," she said. "Welcome to Fung Yu." Big smile. Nice. Looked genuine. "What you have?"

Mike pointed to the menu. "I like pork special," he said, giving emphasis to the word *pork*, just like he was supposed to.

"Ah, velly good choice," Wanda replied. "You like peanut sauce on side, or . . . on top?" She raised an eyebrow suggestively. Nice touch.

Mike looked up now, making good eye contact. "Supplise me."

"Coming right up," Wanda said.

"I'll say it is," Mike replied.

Wanda winked and exited the frame.

Perfect. This was all going well so far.

Mike busied himself with unfolding his napkin and preparing his chopsticks, while Wanda, just off camera, stripped to a bra and panties and grabbed a plate of food. Marty would add a dissolve later to indicate a passage of time.

Wanda walked back onto the set, now in her underwear, and placed the food on the table.

Mike did a good job of appearing surprised by Wanda's change of wardrobe. Excellent.

Wanda also carried a small metal canister, supposedly filled with soy sauce or something. "You like it hot?" she asked.

"The hotter the better," Mike said, and swept everything, including the plate, off the table.

Kissing ensued, followed by clothes flying off and the fondling of various body parts. Plenty of passion coming across. Outstanding.

Off came Wanda's panties—and now they were getting down to it. Oh yes, this was good stuff. Just like the earlier films.

Marty kept the camera rolling even when the actors repositioned themselves. This was great material, and he didn't want to miss a minute.

A short while later, it was time for Willie Wang to join the fun. He entered the frame wearing a white apron, a chef's hat, and a big smile. He stood beside Wanda and Mike and said, "Wow, this what I call full-sevvice lestaulant."

Wanda was supposed to keep Willie entertained with her hands, and she reached out to unzip his fly.

That's when the action went all wrong.

As soon as Wanda grasped Willie's belt, Marty heard a guttural moan from Mike. At first, he thought Mike was giving the performance of a lifetime. Then he realized it wasn't passion, but anger. Mike was staring at Willie, not Wanda, with an expression of pure contempt on his face.

In a flash, the dwarf extricated himself from Wanda and vaulted from the chair onto Willie, getting the startled actor into a headlock.

Wanda shrieked.

A boom mike tumbled to the floor.

Marty rushed onto the set, hoping to separate his miniature stars before one of them was seriously injured.

* * *

The feed store's parking lot was fairly empty now that deer season was over. Marlin had noticed the office space at one end of the building before, but he hadn't paid much attention to it. There was no sign on the door, no indication whose office it was. He had always assumed it was used by the employees of the feed store.

Marlin and Garza stepped from Marlin's cruiser and approached the door. Before they could knock, the tall, muscular man Marlin remembered as Duke Waldrip opened the door. The guy was bald, too. Marlin had forgotten that part.

"John, good to see you again. You been doing all right?" Waldrip said, offering a hand.

"Just fine, Duke," Marlin said.

Duke turned to Garza. "Sheriff Garza, right?"

"That's right."

The men shook hands.

"Y'all come on in," Waldrip said, retreating into the building.

They followed him through a small reception area and then into a sparsely furnished office in the rear.

"I'd offer y'all some coffee, 'cept the damn coffeemaker quit on me a couple weeks ago."

"That's fine," Garza said.

Waldrip took a seat behind the one desk in the room, and Marlin and Garza sat in two worn chairs facing him.

"Mr. Waldrip, we've been trying to contact you," Garza said.

"Oh, yeah, I know. Sorry 'bout that. I've been real busy. I found your notes on my door." He glanced at Marlin. "You said you wanted to talk about something?"

"Yeah, Duke, I was wondering whether you and Gus—that's your brother's name, right?"

Waldrip nodded. "Good memory."

"Are y'all still doing some guiding around here? Out at Kyle Dawson's place?"

Duke grabbed a pack of Marlboros off the desk and shook a cigarette free. "Well, there, and in a few other places, some up in Burnet County. Mostly there, though. Why?"

Marlin ignored the question. "You get many out-of-towners?"

"Hell yeah. Almost nothing but. All the boys from around here already have places to hunt, and they damn sure don't need me." Duke laughed. He paused to light up. "Most of my customers come from Austin, San Antone, sometimes Dallas."

Garza said, "I'm curious about something. Does Gus mostly run the operation, or do you?"

Waldrip opened his mouth to speak, then closed it again. After a pause, he said, "Listen, if this is about, you know, my record . . . and whether I can possess a firearm, I was told it was okay after five years."

Garza waved him off. "No, that's not why we're asking."

"What, then?"

Marlin remained silent, letting Garza decide how to handle it. The sheriff decided to dive right in. "You know a man named Oliver Searcy?"

Duke answered immediately. "Yeah, sure. Guy found dead the other day, right? See, that really floored me, 'cause he called me up a coupla times about wanting to hunt somewhere in the county. He even came to scout the area and dropped by to see me once or twice."

Garza said, "Which was it—one time or two?"

Waldrip took a deep drag on his cigarette and expelled a large cloud of smoke. "Hell, I cain't remember for sure. I think twice. Been so busy, it's hard to keep track. And we only talked for a few minutes."

"Where did you meet with him?"

"Right here at the office."

"Was Gus here, too?"

"Gus? Uh-uh. Don't know where he was, but I remember it was just me and Searcy."

Marlin said, "Did you ever do any hunting with Searcy?"

"Naw, we couldn't agree on a price. He was wanting a nice trophy, but he wasn't quite ready to spring for it." Waldrip shrugged. "I get guys like that all the time. Tire-kickers. I'm used to it."

"When was the last time you talked to him?"

Waldrip stared at the ceiling, thinking. "Let's see . . . the first time was maybe two or three weeks back. That's when he came to do some scouting and he dropped by to see me. Then he called again this past Saturday. No, wait, it was Sunday."

"What did he want?"

Waldrip grinned and tapped some ashes onto the floor. "I think he figured I'd be running some kind of end-of-the-season special. He was trying to Jew me down."

It had been a long time since Marlin had heard that disgusting little phrase.

Garza said, "Did he ever mention talking to anyone else in the area? Any other guides?"

"Well, they all do. Shop around, I mean. Wondering if maybe one of us guides is a little hungrier than the others. Wouldn't surprise me at all if that's what Searcy did."

"So you never saw the man for more than a few minutes?" Garza asked.

"Nope. Just the phone calls and the meeting. That's it."

"He ever come to your house?"

"Nope."

"And Gus never met him?"

"Like I said—no."

"Where can we reach him?" Garza smiled. "He's as hard to track down as you are. I'm just thinking maybe he *was* at that meeting and it slipped your mind."

Waldrip fidgeted for a second. "You know, there's—I think I need to be real up front with y'all about my brother." He placed his palms flat on his desk. "He's kind of flaky. Got electrocuted a couple years ago, and he ain't been what you'd call normal ever since. Damn shame, really." He held his hands up in a what-can-you-do? gesture.

"All the same, we'd like to talk to him," Garza said.

"Try him at home, then," Waldrip said. "That's where you'll catch him."

Garza pulled out a small notepad and verified the phone number.

"Yeah, that's it," Waldrip said. "If he ain't there, just leave a message. He'll get back to you."

"Y'all have an answering machine?"

"Uh, no, that's right, we don't. It broke. Guess you could leave a note for him."

"We've already left several notes."

"Don't know what else to tell you. I haven't talked to him myself for a few days."

"But y'all live together, right?"

"What? Yeah. Different schedules, that's all."

"Tell you what. Why don't you let me use your cell phone real quick."

"Pardon?"

"I'd like to call him on your phone."

"Yours ain't working?" Duke asked.

"Been having trouble with my battery."

Smart move, Bobby, Marlin thought.

"Well, yeah, sure." Duke slid the phone across the desktop to Garza.

Even if the Waldrip brothers knew nothing about the Searcy homicide, they might be avoiding the police on general principles. Duke was an ex-convict, and many ex-cons didn't like talking to the cops. Maybe Duke and his brother had stopped answering their phone because of Duke's contact with Searcy, knowing the cops would show up eventually.

But Duke *had* answered a call when he thought it was coming from Kyle. If Gus really was at home, maybe he'd answer a call from Duke's cell phone, assuming he had caller ID.

The sheriff dialed the phone number and waited. Marlin could hear the shrill ring coming through the phone's small earpiece. Five rings. Then ten. No answer.

"Guess he's not home," Duke said.

Garza disconnected and slid the phone back over to Duke. After a pause, he said, "If you think of anything that might be important, you'll let us know?"

"Yeah, sure. No problem."

"Thank you for your time."

11

DUKE'S ARMPITS WERE damp and his heart felt like it was going to bust through his rib cage. It was bad enough when he thought it was just the game warden coming to see him. But when he saw the sheriff tagging along—Jesus!—he'd almost had a stroke. This wasn't about some candy-ass game violation after all. Good thing he'd mentally prepared himself for it.

And thank God Gus hadn't answered the phone. Duke thought he'd done a fairly good job with the interview just now, but what would Gus say if they came after him with the same questions? It wasn't all that easy to stay cool and keep your story straight. Thinking about it now, Duke realized it was crazy to have ever thought Gus could pull it off. He'd probably get rattled and start babbling, telling the cops everything they wanted to know.

Duke noticed that Garza hadn't said a word about Sally Ann, and he didn't appear to know they'd been shacked up for the past six months. They thought he and Gus were still living together in the old family homestead. Actually, Duke *had* been back staying with Gus again for the last week or so, because of Sally Ann getting pissed about the barmaid. But the cops didn't seem to know any of this, and that was fine with Duke. Best to keep Sally Ann out of it.

And what the hell was up with Kyle? The only thing Duke could figure was that Kyle must have heard him mention Searcy's name at some point. Did he know Searcy had been out to the ranch? And the more important thing: What did he tell the sheriff and the game warden? Hell, he didn't *know* anything—not about what had happened to Searcy anyway. But Kyle *had* known what the cops wanted to talk to Duke about—and he hadn't had the guts to answer the goddamn phone and warn him. There were no two ways about it: Just like nine years ago, the son of a bitch was covering his own ass again, and hanging Duke out to dry.

Duke decided he had to take care of a few things real fast.

First, go see Gus and make sure he wasn't freaking out, maybe getting cabin fever or something like that. Take him some food and remind him to stay put.

Second, go talk to Kyle—maybe even kick his ass a little—and find out what he'd told the cops. Maybe Duke was blowing this thing out of proportion. Maybe he wasn't even a suspect at this point. Hell, he couldn't blame them for wanting to question him, seeing as how Searcy had called him several times.

And lastly, he knew now he'd have to do something about Searcy's trophy mount. Duke had claimed he and Searcy had never hunted together, but the mount proved otherwise. He needed to get the damn thing back.

When Rudi's phone rang, she was in the buff, putting on mascara, swiveling her hips to the Rolling Stones song coming from the cheap clock radio on the nightstand.

Rudi, Barry, and Chad had spent the night at a small motel in Johnson City. Not a bad place. Nothing fancy—her room was small and appeared to have been decorated by somebody's senile grandmother—but at least it was clean.

Johnson City itself seemed to be an okay little town. A handful of restaurants, a few dozen small businesses, a large stone courthouse, and one traffic signal. That's all she had seen last night anyway. They had come in late, and most of the town appeared to be sleeping.

Rudi set the mascara down and picked up the telephone.

"Rudi, sweetheart." It was Chad, using that horrible syrupy voice he reserved for single women. "What are you doing in there?" Rudi suddenly felt a chill and placed one arm across her breasts. Just talking to this vermin gave her goose bumps. She couldn't remember the last time Chad had pursued a story in the field. The jerk just wanted to come along to see if he could get lucky.

"Almost ready," she said. "We said ten o'clock, right?" She glanced at the clock. It was five till.

"That's right, darling. Barry and I are waiting for you outside."

"Give me ten. I'll be right out."

Rudi hung up and quickly finished her makeup. She followed that with a tailored pencil skirt that hit just above the knee, and a French-cuffed, polished-cotton blouse. She checked herself in the mirror. *Not quite what I was ten years ago, but not too bad*, she thought. *Kind of a babe, actually*.

The plan today was to begin interviewing locals, maybe see if they could speak with some of the county deputies. When they had decent footage, they'd drive to Austin and send it back home via the network affiliate station. The anchors at *Hard News Tonight* would provide a lead-in and wrap-up to the segment. This was supposed to be the first of several reports from the land of the chupacabra. How long the reports would continue depended on whether there was any more strange activity.

"He didn't ask many questions, you know what I mean?" Bobby Garza said.

Marlin was driving slowly back to the sheriff's office. "That struck me, too. On the other hand, he's been through the system, which might've taken all the curiosity right out of him. Or he might be too dense to even realize we were checking him out. But I'll say one thing: He didn't seem to want us to talk to Gus."

"Yeah, I noticed that."

"And just because his brother's kind of nutty?"

"Man, in this line of work, who do we talk to that ain't?"

Marlin pulled into the parking lot at the sheriff's office. "So what next, then? Try to track down Gus?"

"Yeah, and I guess I'll get one of the deputies to talk to the other guides again. They checked out okay the first time around, but I think we better have another look."

"You want me to talk to them?" Marlin didn't mind getting more involved now that deer season had ended.

Garza glanced at his watch. "Actually, I had something else in mind. It's ten-fifteen now. What're you doing after lunch?"

"Nothing too urgent."

"I'm gonna drive over to Houston and reinterview the widow. Something just isn't clicking, and I want to dig a little deeper. You want to ride along? Maybe you can help me get something out of her."

"Yeah, I can do that. Tatum and Cowan already talked to her, right?"

Rachel Cowan was a deputy who had been with the Blanco County Sheriff's Department for just over a year. Young and very sharp.

Garza nodded. "Yep, twice. But I want to go in with some fresh eyes."

Red O'Brien was rumbling down Pecan Street after a trip to Dairy Queen when Billy Don yelled, "Holy whorebag!" It startled Red so bad, he dropped his Dilly Bar into the crotch of his pants.

Red tried to steer while wiping at a smear of chocolate along the inseam of his Wranglers. "Damn, Billy Don, take it easy, will ya."

"Check it out! Right over there! That's Rudi Vee!"

Red turned to see where Billy Don was pointing. Standing in

front of the courthouse was a woman facing a camera, with large cluster of people her milling around. The woman, who looked kind of familiar to Red, was holding a microphone in front of Ernie Turpin, one of the county deputies. Red couldn't quite place her, though he could tell, even from thirty yards, that she was definitely headboard-banging material. He figured it was another newscast about that Houston hunter who'd been found dead. Red had seen something about that a few days ago.

"What is she, a reporter from Austin? Big friggin' deal. What's everyone gettin' so excited about?" But Red pulled over to the curb to watch.

"Naw, man, Rudi Vee. Rudi Villarreal."

"You already said that, Skeezix. But who the hell is Rudi Villarreal?"

Billy Don looked as if Red had just said NASCAR was for pussies. "Jesus, Red. You know, from *Hard News Tonight*? That hot reporter who's always interviewing big stars and interpreting the economy and stuff."

Oh, *now* Red remembered. It was a news program, but not your typical tight-ass broadcast with guys like Peter Jennings. Red always wondered if Peter was Waylon's cousin or something. Anyway, *Hard News Tonight* was, to Red, every bit as informative and a whole lot more entertaining than, say, *Nightlight*. Okay, so maybe their stories weren't quite as in-depth as those other shows, but damn, look at those hooters! Red could see that ol' Rudi was packing some major mangoes.

"Damn, I've always had a thing for her," Billy Don said. "Why you think she's in town?"

Red didn't know, but—like the knot of bystanders—he was extremely curious. "Who gives a shit?" he said.

Billy Don didn't seem to hear. He was gazing through the windshield, mooning over the reporter.

"Well, damn," Red said, "if it means that much to you, we might as well go see what's going on. No sense in sittin' in the truck."

Billy Don heard *that,* and they both climbed out of the Ford.

As they approached the crowd, Red could hear Rudi Villarreal saying that funny word again: *chupacabra.* After the incident with the wetback on Sunday, Red had finally learned what that word meant. According to the papers, a chupacabra was some kind of devil-dog or mutant lizard or something—nobody seemed to know for sure. And you could find them down in Mexico, especially around the capital city of Puerto Rico. Red was listening, and now the deputy was saying no, there hadn't been any more reports of the chupacabra.

Rudi Villarreal asked about Oliver Searcy—apparently, that was the dead hunter. Rudi was wondering whether Searcy might have been a victim of the chupacabra. After all, she said, wasn't Searcy killed by a single puncture wound to the neck, the chupacabra's trademark?

Ernie Turpin shook his head and said he couldn't comment on that. Hell, this all sounded pretty interesting to Red. Kind of sci-fi and weird. You wouldn't see Dan Rather offering *this* kind of coverage.

Rudi thanked the deputy for his time, and Red could tell the interview was coming to an end. He figured he owed it to the world to tell what he knew. "Hey, Rudi!" he called out. "We was with that Meski—uh, that Mexican that was hit by the truck on Sunday. The one what saw the chupacabra."

Rudi looked his way, and so did the rest of the crowd. "You mind sharing your story with us?"

"Heck no!" Red elbowed his way through to the reporter, dragging Billy Don along. "Red O'Brien, ma'am. This here's Billy Don Craddock."

"Nice to meet you both."

"Awwbllghf," Billy Don said, apparently choking on his own tongue.

Red couldn't blame him. Up close, this Rudi Villarreal was one hot broad, and Billy Don wasn't as comfortable talking to a classy piece of tail as Red was.

Red said, "See, what happened was—"

Rudi cut him off. "Give us just a minute, please, Mr. O'Brien." She said a few things to the cameraman, using terms Red didn't understand. "Here, stand a little closer to me, please."

"I'll stand as close as you want, darlin'." Red leered, giving her his best smile.

She asked Billy Don to move to her other side, and then the interview began. "Tell us about your experience with the chupacabra," Rudi said, holding the microphone in front of Red.

"Well," Red said. "What happened was, we was working on some masonry with this wetback and—"

Rudi lowered the microphone and covered it with her hand.

"What?" Red asked.

"Mr. O'Brien," she whispered, "I would thank you if you wouldn't use that term."

"Masonry?"

"No. *Wetback*. It's very derogatory, you know."

Red couldn't remember what *derogatory* meant, but he figured it wasn't good. "What should I say instead?"

"How about 'day laborer'?"

Red nodded. "That'll work."

"Okay, let's start over," Rudi said, back to her normal tone of voice. "Tell us about your experience with the infamous chupacabra."

"Well," Red said, "We was working on this masonry job with a, uh, day laborer when he ran into the woods to take a dump and—"

Rudi lowered the microphone again. She whispered, "Mr. O'Brien, you have to remember that we'll be broadcasting this during the family hour. Could you please be careful how you phrase things?"

By now, the crowd was giggling. Red couldn't imagine why anyone would have a problem with the word *dump*. It sure beat the alternatives. "I'll do my best," he said.

Now the camera guy was saying something to Rudi. She glanced down at Red's Wranglers. "Did you know you have a large stain on your pants?"

"Yes, ma'am, it's chocolate. Wanna taste?"

12

DUKE PULLED THROUGH the entrance of the Macho Bueno at 10:30.

He'd stopped by to see Gus, and everything was fine. Duke had made Gus promise again that he wouldn't leave the house. Then, just for peace of mind, Duke had gone out to the box on the utility pole and unplugged Gus's phone line. *That* would keep the retard from making any calls.

Kyle's driveway forked just before it reached the house, and the right path led to the garage on the north side. Duke stayed left, which led to a circular parking area in front. He parked and followed the pathway around the south side of the house. Kyle was usually in the hot tub by now—if he wasn't taking a nap. It turned out he was doing both. Duke found Kyle snoozing soundly while the water bubbled around him.

Duke sat in a patio chair and pulled out the revolver he'd brought with him—Oliver Searcy's gun, which he still needed to ditch. He figured he'd just fire a round right into the tub. That would make Kyle wake up and come to Jesus, yessir. But then he thought of something even better.

He stood and walked into the house.

"Cheri! You here?"

No answer.

"Cheri! Get your skanky ass out here!"

Seconds passed. All quiet. Good. He didn't need that slut hanging around, whining.

He went through the kitchen and out into the four-car garage, where he found a hundred-foot extension cord. Walking back through the house, he grabbed the toaster off the kitchen counter.

He found an outlet on the side of the house—but instead of plugging the cord in, he laid it on the ground. Then he trailed the remainder of the cord over to the hot tub.

Kyle was still sleeping like a baby.

Duke plugged the toaster in and slid the knob down to the TOAST position. He stood at the edge of the hot tub and dangled the toaster over the water, holding it in such a way that Kyle wouldn't be able to see that the elements weren't glowing red.

Then he fired the gun into the tub.

Kyle woke with such a start, Duke had to stifle a laugh.

"Damn!" Kyle sputtered. "Duke, Jesus! Are you fucking crazy?"

"Don't get out of the water, Kyle. Don't even move."

Kyle's eyes went to the toaster. "Whatever you say, man. But what the hell's going on?"

Duke gave the toaster a little swing. "You know how Gus turned out when he got a little too much voltage."

"What are you doing, man? Be careful. Please."

Duke smiled. "We're going to have a little talk, Kyle. You tell me the truth and maybe this thing won't go in the water."

"Yeah, man. Yeah." Kyle was as white as a deer's belly.

Duke took his time, enjoying the power. "Okay, first question: What did you tell the cops?"

Kyle didn't answer right away, and Duke didn't like that. "What, you mean the game warden?"

"Him and the sheriff."

"Man, it was just the game warden that came out. Not the sheriff."

That was news to Duke, but he saw no reason why Kyle would lie about that.

"Okay, so what did you tell him?"

"What do you mean, *what did I tell him?* There wasn't anything to tell."

"Come on, Kyle. About Oliver Searcy."

Kyle was nodding now. "Yeah, the dead guy. He asked if I'd ever heard of him. That's all."

"What'd you say?"

"I told him no. Because I *hadn't* ever heard of the guy. Least not till he asked me. Did you know him?"

Duke ignored the question. "Did he ask about me?"

"Yeah, at first. He wanted to know if you were still guiding out here."

"And?"

"Well, I told him yeah, sometimes. Nothing official."

Duke reached over with one foot and pressed a button beside the hot tub, turning the jets off. The water slowly settled and it was much quieter now.

"He ask you if I guided Searcy?"

"No, not specifically," Kyle said. "I think that's what he was wondering, though. He said Searcy had made some calls to you, that's all. And he wanted to get hold of you."

"So you wanted to be a good citizen and gave him my cell number."

Kyle looked at the toaster again. "Well, yeah. I mean, I didn't have any reason not to. He didn't ask what kind of animals you were hunting out here, and I figured that was the only thing that might get you in trouble."

Duke believed him. It sounded like the cops had just wanted to ask Duke about the phone calls. Maybe he'd already been through the worst of their questioning.

"You didn't know Searcy, right?" Kyle asked.

Duke lowered the toaster, and now one shiny metal corner touched the surface of the water. "Did you tell him I did?"

Kyle was as far back against the rim of the tub as he could be. "No, man, I swear. I didn't say nothin'." He was starting to blubber now. "I didn't even know nothin' to tell. I swear."

Okay, then. It wasn't as bad as Duke thought.

"Dude, please," Kyle said, "lift that thing up a little."

The water was almost up to the bread slots.

"What, this?" Duke said. "It's not even plugged in."

He smirked and dropped the toaster into the tub.

And everything went all wrong.

Sparks shot from the toaster, and Duke jumped.

Kyle bucked and jerked, letting out a low wail. He went stiff, head back and feet straight out. Blood poured from his nose.

"Son of a bitch!" Duke grabbed the cord off the ground and yanked the toaster out of the water.

Kyle's body went limp and slowly settled into the water.

Duke was in a panic now, and he knelt to pull Kyle out of the tub. But then he heard something. A car engine, from the driveway in front of the side-entry garage.

Duke ran in that direction, even changed his course and went around the other side, the way he had come in. The driveway went south from the house, and this path would give him a better chance of catching the car as it left.

He raced around the corner, gasping for breath, but he was too late.

All he could see was the rear of Cheri's car as it sped away.

He yelled, "Cheri!"

She flipped him the bird.

Oh Christ. Duke couldn't believe what had just happened. *That little bitch. That crazy little bitch.*

Duke waited for doom to come, and while he waited, he had a chance to think.

Cheri's car had been parked in the driveway in front of the

garage. That's why he hadn't seen it. She *had* been inside the house when he had called her name. She must have been watching through a window while he was taunting Kyle with the toaster.

Then she went out the front door, snuck around the side, and plugged the extension cord in. That had to be the way it had happened. She was setting him up. Duke had nearly forgotten, but she was Kyle's *wife* now, even if Kyle had viewed the Vegas wedding as a joke. She stood to inherit everything Kyle owned, and the conniving little bitch was setting Duke up. He had to admit, it was a pretty good move.

He was certain the cops would show up any minute now. She must have called them, right? He could just imagine her on the phone: *Hurry! Duke Waldrip just killed my husband!*

That made two now. Two people Duke had killed—both by accident.

If he ran, he'd never make it out of the county. He had no choice but to wait for the cops, and then tell them the total and absolute truth. Even all of his hunting scams. It was the only option he had left, and it was a damn shitty one. Prison time for sure. Maybe the needle, if nobody believed him.

So he waited. And he waited some more.

The odd thing was, the cops never showed.

The phone was ringing in Marty Hoffenhauser's house when he walked through the front door. He'd just gotten home from the emergency room, and he didn't feel like talking to anybody right now. He didn't need any more headaches after the morning he'd had, so he let the machine take it.

He heard a familiar voice. "Hey, Marty! It's Drew. You around? Pick up, pal."

Just great. Drew Tillman, Marty's silent partner, calling from Los Angeles.

Marty picked up and tried to sound nonchalant. "Drew! What's up, buddy?"

"I figured you were there. Mr. Hotshot Director, screening your calls."

Marty chuckled politely.

He and Drew were partners—on paper anyway. But they both knew that Drew held the upper hand in the relationship. After all, Drew had saved Marty's career. And what a career it had been.

In the late seventies, Marty had written, produced, and hosted one of the hottest game shows on daytime television—*Show Me You're Nuts!* On the show, contestants performed some of the most harrowing, grotesque, and obscene acts imaginable. Feats involving the mouth were always popular. One guy swallowed a live rat, then regurgitated it, still alive. Another man French-kissed his own grandfather. In one of Marty's favorites, two young ladies from Newark performed mock fellatio on Popsicles made from Hudson River sludge.

One would think—in an environment as bizarre as *Show Me You're Nuts!*—that just about any type of behavior would be tolerated. Marty found out the hard way that this wasn't the case. Scandal erupted when he was caught banging two cheerleaders backstage. As it turned out, they weren't really in college, as they had said. They were high schoolers. Juniors, not even seniors. Marty was charged with statutory rape. He lost his job, was ostracized by the public, and was lucky to avoid prison. His days as an on-camera personality were over.

His problems, however, didn't prevent him from working *behind* the camera. In fact, from what Marty discovered, plenty of disgraced celebrities who disappeared from the public eye wound up working as producers. And that's what Marty did for two decades. The problem was, he wasn't very good at it. Over the years, he slowly slid in the ranks, going from executive producer to producer to production assistant. He knew it was only a matter of time before he'd be lucky to find work as a grip. He decided it was time to quit the business. It was the late nineties by then, and the dot-com frenzy was reaching its peak. Marty was only fifty years old, but he had ridden the Internet wave perfectly, bailing out before everything crashed. He had plenty of money saved up. So he had moved back to his home state of Texas. He had been born and raised in Austin, then moved to the West Coast when he was nineteen. Austin was bigger and busier now, though, like a miniature L.A., so he decided to relocate just an hour west of town in Blanco County.

He had been enjoying his retirement for exactly one week when Drew Tillman—one of Marty's oldest industry friends, a man who had stood behind Marty during the cheerleader scandal—tracked him down. And he had a very interesting proposition.

"How do you feel about adult videos?" Tillman asked.

"I, uh . . . What do you mean?" Marty replied, wondering what the question was leading to.

"You watch 'em? You think they're okay?"

"Sure, I guess. Why not?"

"How do you feel about Asians?"

"Well, the whole Pearl Harbor thing was kind of uncalled for," Marty replied, joking.

"But you're not, like, a bigot or anything?"

"Of course not."

"How do you feel about little people?"

"Little people?"

"You know, dwarves."

"Well, gee, Drew, I never really thought about it."

"But you have no problem with them, either?"

"No, I . . . What are you getting at, Drew?"

"Let me throw three words at you, chief. Chinese dwarf pornography. How's that hit ya?"

"Chinese dwarf pornography."

"It's huge, Marty. The hottest thing in the industry right now."

"You're kidding me."

"I kid you not, my friend. See, in the porn industry, there's something for everybody. The straight stuff, sure, but if you happen to have a thing for women with facial hair, say, or transvestites in wheelchairs, believe me, it's out there. And right now, the big thing is Chinese dwarves."

Marty thought about it. How large could that particular market segment possibly be?

Drew read his thoughts. "What's going on is, somehow these flicks have become all the rage at fraternity parties. It's like this big joke, having this funny little skin flick running in the background. And man, it's spreading all across the country. Sales are booming, buddy, and I'm getting in on it."

Drew described the situation. He and some of his "associates" wanted in on the new craze. They had decided to open their own production company, and they needed a director. Marty had never directed before, but, as Drew had said, how hard could it be? "It's not like you're shooting *Gone With The Wind* or anything. It's just your standard porn. Well, on a smaller scale. Besides, you've always had a knack for showmanship, Mart. Just like on *Nuts*. I think you're the man for the job."

Marty didn't know what to say. So he said yes.

Since then, Marty had directed some of the highest-grossing adult films ever made. He was quickly becoming a seriously wealthy man. Everything, on every film, had gone as smoothly as possible—until this morning's fiasco with Mike. Now, though, the entire operation was in jeopardy. And Marty would have to tell Drew all about it.

"How are things in Texas?" Drew asked.

These calls always followed a pattern. Drew would make small talk, pretend he was listening to Marty's answers, and then get down to what he really wanted to know: how the production was going. Everything revolved around the production. *Are we on schedule? Are we on budget? Are you getting some good footage? How are the dwarves? Tell 'em I said hi.*

After two minutes of forced banter, Drew finally asked about *Fortune Nookie*.

"Well, I'm afraid we've hit a bit of a snag," Marty said, fiddling nervously with his ponytail.

Silence. Then: "Snags are no good, Mart. What sort of snag?"

Marty's inclination was to lie, to conjure up some fake problem, like Wanda Ho having a cold or Mike Hung eating some bad sushi. But Marty owed a lot to Drew Tillman, so he told the truth. He described the fight between Mike and Willie Wang that morning, and the resulting trip to the hospital.

Again, he was met with silence.

Finally: "So now Willie has a broken arm," Drew said. "What are we going to do about that?"

"I guess we'll film around it."

"You *guess*?"

"No, I mean we *will*. We *will* film around it. I'll even write it into the script. I'll write a fight scene or a car crash."

"Car crashes are expensive, Marty."

"It doesn't have to happen on-camera. We'll show Willie speeding toward an overpass or something, maybe getting a hummer. He'll get distracted, lose control of the car, and then we'll cut to him in a hospital bed. No big deal."

Silence for the third time.

Marty spoke again. "Trust me, Drew. I'll make it work. This won't be a problem."

"I seriously hope not."

"It won't."

"What were they fighting about anyway?"

Marty sighed. "Mike thinks something's going on between Willie and Wanda. He's jealous."

"Jesus, what does the guy have to be jealous about? He's got a Damn python between his legs."

"That's what I told him."

"Didn't help?"

"No, in fact . . ."

"What?"

Marty hesitated. He hadn't told Drew the full story yet. The last part was a bombshell. "Well, at the hospital, Mike told me he's kind of lost his confidence."

"And?"

"And he didn't think he could shoot the threesome scene without losing his erection." Of course, Mike had pronounced it *election*.

"Oh my God," Drew gasped.

Now the cat was out of the bag. It wasn't a mere delay in production. They were in danger of losing their marquee performer on a permanent basis. Everybody knew that performance anxiety could wreck a man's career.

Drew said, "What the hell are we gonna do, Marty? This is some serious shit."

"Don't worry, I've got a plan. I'll shoot the rest of the scenes first—all the ones with just Mike and Wanda or one of the other actresses. I'll get his confidence back. I'll tell all the ladies to flirt with him on the set, tell him what a stud he is. You know—build him up, get his ego strong again."

"That's not much of a plan."

"Well then . . . you think I should ditch Willie?"

"Hell no! He's almost as big a draw as Mike and Wanda. We can't cut him."

Marty asked for other suggestions. Drew didn't have any.

"Let me mull it over," Drew said. "I'll call you back if I think of anything brilliant."

Ten minutes later, the phone rang again.

"I've thought of something brilliant," Drew said. "Actually, I talked to Lorraine, this sex therapist I know. Sex therapy is huge out here now."

"Yeah?"

"Anyway, Lorraine had a great idea."

"Let's hear it."

"Aphrodisiacs. Asians love them. Some pretty freaky shit, too."

"Like what?" Marty could hear Drew flipping pages in a note-pad, going through his notes.

"Ever hear of pickled tiger penis?"

"Uh, fortunately, no."

"Powdered rhinoceros horn?"

"Nope."

"Shark-fin soup?"

"Yummy."

"I'm telling you, Marty, the Asians are serious about this. Get your hands on some of this stuff and our problems will be over.

That's what Lorraine says. Says it's all a mind-over-matter thing, but who cares as long as it works, right?"

"Okay, great. But where am I supposed to get it? I don't suppose they carry any of that stuff at Seven-Eleven."

Drew paused. "Good point," he said. Marty could hear paper rustling. Then Drew said, "Let me ask you this: They got deer in Texas?"

"God yes," Marty replied. "All over the place. Why?"

13

"TATUM'S GONNA TALK to the other guides again, and we'll see if anything shakes loose from that," Garza said. "Meanwhile, I'm really hoping we can get something useful today."

They were in Garza's county car, heading east on Highway 290, about an hour past Austin. Marlin was getting drowsy from the warm winter sun, which was low in the sky, angling in through the window on the passenger's side.

"What do we know about Searcy?" Marlin asked.

"Married, no kids. Born and raised in Houston. Never lived anywhere else. Even went to medical school there."

"What kind of doctor was he?"

"A pretty good one, I guess."

Marlin shook his head at the lame joke.

"Radiologist," Garza said.

Marlin pondered that. "Have you talked to anyone at his office yet?"

"Yeah, Tatum did. I know what you're thinking: He's a doctor; maybe he misdiagnosed somebody, or beat somebody in a lawsuit. Nothing we could find. Plus, it would be kind of strange, wouldn't it? Someone following him from Houston so they could kill him in Blanco County?"

"Unless he had a patient from Blanco County."

"We checked, but he didn't."

A few miles passed in silence.

"Then there's the *way* Searcy was killed," Garza said. "Let's say Lem was right and it was a screwdriver. Doesn't seem like the weapon of choice if you were planning ahead, does it?"

"Something spontaneous, then?"

"Makes the most sense. Otherwise, why not a gun?"

"Maybe the perp wanted to keep it quiet."

"Then how about just a regular damn knife? Why a screwdriver? Who chooses a screwdriver when they have time to plan?"

Marlin agreed the theory made sense. A heat-of-the-moment homicide, no planning. Most of them were. One reason why so many perps got caught. Plus, with the enormous advancements in forensics over the past few decades, it was virtually impossible for a criminal—whether he was a killer or a poacher—to escape a crime scene without leaving physical evidence. The Texas Parks and Wildlife Department even had its own forensics laboratory attached to a state fish hatchery in San Marcos. The lab's capabilities were far greater than the average poacher assumed, including DNA testing, protein identification, and fatty-acid analysis. That meant, for example, that if a hunter claimed the blood or hair in the back of his pickup was from a feral hog rather than from a deer, the lab could quickly determine if he was telling the truth. Just the knowledge that samples were being sent to the lab was frequently enough to convince a poacher to confess.

The drive to Houston crept by, small town after small town, Duke keeping it well below the speed limit. He damn sure didn't need to get a speeding ticket. He didn't want any kind of record of his trip. He'd even topped off the tank of Kyle's Lotus before he left, so he wouldn't have to use a credit card along the way. Duke felt stupid being so cautious about these little things—it was like using a teaspoon to bail out a sinking boat—but there was no sense in losing his head now.

He'd sat by the damn hot tub with Kyle's body for half an hour, expecting to hear sirens at any second. He never did. With each moment that passed, he became more hopeful. After twenty minutes, Duke's spirits had begun to rise. It was only a ten-minute drive from the sheriff's office. Could it be that they weren't coming? Maybe—who the hell knows why—Cheri hadn't called it in. Duke could go insane trying to figure that woman out.

Ten minutes later, Duke couldn't stand it anymore. He carried Kyle to his truck and drove to a particular spot in the northeast pasture. There, when Duke and Kyle were kids, they had discovered a cave. Well, not so much a cave as a small underground hole, maybe the size of a Volkswagen. The entrance wasn't much wider than a basketball hoop. They used to slide down in there with flashlights and pretend they were Confederate soldiers hiding from the Yanks. Now Kyle was playing soldier again, the entrance sealed with the largest limestone rock Duke could find. Maybe it wasn't the best solution, but he hadn't known what else to do under the circumstances. He knew it looked bad: Kyle points the cops toward Duke, and then Kyle ends up dead just hours later. In the cops' eyes, Duke would be the only suspect.

Duke had something else brewing in his brain, though. A way to throw them off his tracks. After he'd hidden Kyle—and the cops *still* hadn't shown up—Duke had thought of a way to explain Kyle's absence. That's why he'd taken Kyle's car. Duke needed to go to Houston anyway, so why not kill two birds, so to speak, with one stone?

Duke reached the sprawling city limits at about four o'clock. He drove for twenty more minutes before 290 hit Loop 610. He went south for a few miles, wanting to get into the heart of town before he stopped and made the call. Finally, he exited the freeway and pulled into a gas station. He found a working pay phone—he wasn't stupid enough to use his cell phone—and dialed Information. He asked for the address of Oliver Searcy.

The operator said, "No Oliver Searcy, sir, but I do have an O. Searcy, M.D."

That had to be it. She gave the phone number, which Duke already had, and an address in the eight hundred block of North Third Street in Bellaire.

"No, lady, the guy lives in *Houston*," Duke said.

"Bellaire *is* in Houston, sir."

Duke hung up. He slid two more quarters into the slot and dialed Searcy's number. Four rings, then an answering machine.

Duke stepped into the store and bought a roll of duct tape— $4.99, plus tax.

Walking back toward the Lotus, Duke noticed a young guy filling his low-riding Honda, rap music thumping from the stereo. Smoking a cigarette, too, right there at the pumps. Even Duke wasn't *that* dumb.

"Any idea where Bellaire is?" Duke asked.

The punk had a smirk on his face. "Dude, you're standing in it."

Bellaire was actually a small city that had been swallowed by Houston many years ago. It was a decent little place, straddling both sides of Loop 610 on the west side of town. It appeared to Duke that the town used to consist chiefly of small frame homes, but most of them had been torn down, replaced by much larger brick homes. Small mansions, really, on prime real estate. Lots of money floating around the area. New construction on every block—including the house right next door to Oliver Searcy's place. *How damn lucky can a guy get?* Duke grinned. Plenty of construction workers coming and going. Now he didn't have to worry so much about being noticed. Except for the Lotus—and it was okay if somebody remembered that later.

Duke took two right-hand turns and parked at the curb one street over. He climbed out of the car, grabbing the roll of duct tape and Searcy's handgun, which he tucked into his waistband. He pulled his baseball cap down low and adjusted his sunglasses. Then he started walking around to the Searcy house.

He had absolutely no plan for what he was about to do, beyond knocking on the front door. If someone answered, he'd probably just say, "Oops, wrong address. Sorry about that."

If there was no answer, he'd scout the place out, check for an alarm system, then find a way in. That's what the tape was for. There was a clever little burglar's trick he had always wanted to try.

Duke peeked through the windows in the garage door. Three-car garage, two slots empty. A Lexus sitting in the middle bay. Searcy's SUV would still be with the cops. The question was, did the Searcys own three cars or two? If they owned three, that meant the wife was probably gone.

There was only one way to find out.

Duke walked right up to the front door—the construction workers next door were too busy sawing and hammering to even give him a second look.

He held his breath and knocked.

No answer.

He knocked again, more firmly this time. Nothing.

He casually strolled around the side of the house and found an iron gate leading into the backyard. No lock, just a latch. He popped it, stepped through, and closed it behind him. Thank God, he didn't see any sign of a dog.

The backyard was surrounded by an eight-foot rock wall, providing plenty of privacy. Huge oak trees towered overhead, completely shading the lawn. It was like a goddamn jungle back here, all kinds of big bushes and one huge shrub in the center of the yard. Some kind of fish pond, too, with a fountain bubbling away. There was a large gazebo in one corner. He couldn't even see the house that shared the rear property line.

He stepped onto a large redwood deck and walked to the French doors that led into the house. Locked. Hell no, it wouldn't be *that* easy.

He studied the door, then the windows along the back of the house. No sign of an alarm.

No time to fuck around. He pulled some gloves from his pocket and slipped them on. Then he picked the window closest to the construction site next door and covered it completely with duct tape. First he laid strips horizontally, then vertically.

He walked to the fish pond, pulled a large ornamental stone out of the water, and went back to the window.

Then he waited.

The sun was getting pretty low. Hopefully, the wetbacks next door weren't done for the day.

Then he heard it: the ear-piercing screech of the table saw. The neighbors had to be good and sick of all the racket by now.

He launched the rock through the window.

Susan Searcy thought she heard something odd, but it was hard to hear *anything* above the sound of the headboard slamming against the wall.

"What was that?"

"Uh! Uh! Uh!"

"Damn, Peter, would you ease up for a minute?" She whacked him on the head. Jesus, the man was like a rabbit. You'd think he just discovered sex yesterday.

"What's wrong, baby?"

"I heard something."

"Like what?"

He had stopped for the moment, and all was quiet.

"I don't know . . . it kind of sounded like breaking glass."

"Probably next door."

They heard hammering, then a power saw.

"See?" Peter said.

"This sounded closer—like in the house."

"You're imagining things." He started going at it again, slow strokes now, while Susan continued to listen for more sounds.

Okay, maybe it could have been the construction workers. From all the noise those guys made every day, you'd think they were tearing the house *down* rather than building it. The workers usually knocked off around 5:30, and now it was only—she glanced at her wristwatch—ten till five.

Ten till five!

"Jesus, Peter, get offa me! The cops are supposed to be here in ten minutes."

She squirmed out from under him and started collecting her clothes off the floor. She had no idea it had gotten this late.

"Get dressed!" she said. "You've gotta get out of here!"

Peter was moving slowly. "You drove me over here, remember?"

But she was already headed down the hallway.

It had worked perfectly. The window had shattered and fallen inward in one large sheet, only a handful of loose shards sprinkled on the windowsill.

Even better, when Duke had parted the curtain, he realized he had hit the jackpot. The room he had chosen was Oliver Searcy's office, with trophy deer heads mounted on all the walls.

Duke climbed through the window and quickly spotted the mount he had passed off as Searcy's deer. *Yeah, the guy knew it was a fake, but that didn't keep him from hanging it on the wall. Probably showed it off to friends, too, bragging about what a great shot he'd made. What a prick.*

Duke reached up, lifted the mount off the wall and—shit! He heard voices in the house! Not in the next room or anything, but close enough that he could make out what they were saying.

A woman: "Wait in the backyard until they leave. They'll be here any minute."

A man: "You're getting too freaked out about it. I'm an old friend of Oliver's, remember?"

Then the guy laughed, like it was some kind of inside joke.

Sounded like somebody was coming to see Searcy's widow, and for some reason, she was nervous about it. Duke made his way to the window. Time for a quick exit.

The woman: "That makes it even worse. You were his best friend, Peter, and you've been fucking me."

Duke stopped in his tracks. *That* was interesting.

The man: "So?"

"God, you're so dense sometimes. That makes you a *suspect*. Both of us."

Were the cops coming?

The man: "But we didn't do it. At least *I* didn't. I don't know about *you*." Another laugh.

"Very funny, asshole."

"Besides, they've already questioned both of us."

"Damn it, just wait in the backyard, okay?"

"All right, all right. Take it easy."

Damn! Duke hustled to the window, parted the curtains, and began to climb outside. But he heard a noise—the French doors opening—so he ducked back inside.

Shit, now he was trapped!

The doorbell rang.

"Mrs. Searcy?"

Marlin and Bobby Garza were standing on the front porch of an expensive home in Bellaire. Marlin noticed that Oliver Searcy's wife was a pretty woman, maybe in her early thirties, dressed casually in jeans and a pullover top.

"Please call me Susan. You must be Sheriff Garza."

"Yes, ma'am, and this is John Marlin, the game warden in Blanco County."

They shook hands all around, and Susan Searcy led them through the house and into a large, expensively furnished living room. They sat in overstuffed armchairs surrounding a mahogany coffee table. Marlin noticed there weren't any trophy animals mounted in the room. Odd, for an avid hunter like Oliver Searcy.

"Can I get you anything? Coffee?"

Both men declined.

"Well, then . . ."

"Mrs. Searcy," Garza said, "first, I'd like to offer my condolences. . . ."

"Thank you. This whole thing, really, it came as a shock."

"I'm sure it did. And I appreciate your willingness to see us. I'd just like to ask you a couple more questions. . . ."

"I'm not sure what more I can tell you. I've already spent so much time with your deputies."

"Yes, ma'am, and that's been very helpful. But sometimes we find that additional interviews . . . they can bring out facts you might've forgotten the first time around."

As Garza spoke, Marlin studied Susan's face. Her hair was disheveled, her makeup smeared. A widow grieving.

"I'll do what I can," she said.

Duke peered through the curtains and saw a man in a sport coat sitting in the gazebo, smoking a cigarette. Susan Searcy's lover, hiding out. Duke figured the shrub in the middle of the yard shielded the man from the view of anyone looking through the French doors. With the sun setting and the yard getting darker, the man probably wouldn't notice that the window into Searcy's office was missing. *As long as the douche bag stays put.*

Duke slowly stepped across the room and listened. Three voices now. He placed his ear against the door. The conversation wasn't as loud as the one earlier, and Duke had a hard time making out the words, but it sounded like they were somewhere in the center of the house.

Duke desperately wanted to hear what they were saying, to see where the cops were going with the case. He decided to take a chance. He gently placed his hand on the doorknob . . . and turned it slowly. He eased the door open two inches. Peeking through the crack, he could see a long tiled hallway leading toward the center of the house. Now he could hear much better.

With a chill, he recognized the voices of the Blanco County sheriff and game warden.

And one of the first things he heard was his name.

"No, I honestly can't tell you if he ever mentioned that name," Susan Searcy said. "Sorry."

"How about Gus Waldrip?" Garza asked.

Marlin watched her ponder that for a moment. He could tell that the questioning was difficult for her: She seemed anxious, glancing out the French doors occasionally as she gathered her thoughts.

"No, I really don't think so."

It was an awkward thirty minutes, Garza leading the conversation as he probed for new information. "Was anyone planning to go with Mr. Searcy when he came to Blanco County? . . . Did he have more than one cell phone? . . . Did he ever use yours? . . . Any enemies? . . . Any recent troubles at work?"

Susan Searcy had nothing to offer. "As you can tell, Oliver didn't tell me much about his hunting trips. See, to be honest, I'm not real fond of hunting. I find it cruel and unnecessary. But Oliver's hunted ever since I met him. I realize it's a tradition here in Texas, so we agreed to disagree. He never told me much about it."

Marlin gestured around the room and said, "Now I understand why there aren't any trophies hanging on the walls."

"No, he keeps those all in his study. Would you like to see them?"

Garza spoke up: "Actually, we'd like to see all of the things in his study, if you don't mind."

"The deputies have been through everything already."

"Yes, ma'am, but—"

She cut him off by standing. "That's fine. Follow me."

Sweet Jesus!

Duke eased the door shut. He knew he didn't have time to make it out the window.

He heard footsteps coming down the hallway. He gripped the handgun, aiming it at the door, feeling clumsy with his gloved hands.

The steps came closer, now just yards away.

He glanced down at the doorknob and realized it had a lock.

He quickly reached down and twisted it, and simultaneously felt a hand grab the other side.

"Oh, I must have locked it last time," Susan said. "Let me go grab the key."

Marlin and Garza waited in the hallway.

"We're really hitting a dead end," Garza said.

Duke tried to move as quietly as possible. He lifted the deer mount and stepped to the window. He parted the curtains, put one leg out the window . . . and heard the key in the door.

"You never know where danger is going to come from." After all these years, Marlin could still remember an instructor at the game warden academy telling that to his class.

But Marlin never expected it to come from a locked room in a quiet suburban home.

He and Garza were both unprepared for what happened next.

Susan Searcy returned with the key, unlocked the door, and swung it open.

Garza stepped through the doorway first.

Marlin was right behind him, still in the hallway, when Garza halted in midstride, his body tensed.

Later, Marlin would remember that Garza had just begun to utter something when the gunshot rang out.

Susan Searcy screamed and fled down the hallway.

Marlin flinched, and his hand instinctively went to his holstered .357.

Bobby Garza came tumbling backward, falling to the floor in the hallway.

Exposing himself momentarily to gunfire, Marlin reached out, looped a hand under Garza's armpit, and dragged the sheriff out of the doorway.

Garza was clutching his left thigh, his pants already soaked with blood. "Out the window!" he said.

"Call nine one one!" Marlin shouted. He could hear Susan Searcy sobbing somewhere in the house.

Marlin drew his weapon, flicked the safety off, and—in one quick move—dashed to the other side of the doorway, scanning the room. It was empty. A curtain was still gently moving.

He knelt over Garza and prepared to tear the left leg of the sheriff's pants open. He had to stop the bleeding.

But Garza clamped the leg himself. He was breathing rapidly. "Go! Out the window!"

"Bobby, I've got to—"

"Now, John! I'm okay!"

Reluctantly, Marlin moved through Oliver Searcy's study, stepped over a broken window on the floor, and parted the curtains. He looked left and right but saw nothing. He vaulted through the window . . . and that's when he saw a figure in the middle of the yard.

A man in a sport coat.

Marlin dropped to one knee and aimed his handgun. "On the ground! Now."

The man said, "But I saw a guy—"

"On the ground!"

14

DUKE'S HANDS WERE trembling on the steering wheel, sweat running down his forehead. Now he'd fucking done it. Now he was in this thing up to his balls. The question was, how good a look did the cop get? Shit, Duke had barely even got a look at the cop. He was pretty sure it was Sheriff Garza who had come through the door first, rather than the game warden. But had Garza recognized him? *No way.* He had been too quick—*bang* and out the window.

Duke was on Loop 610 now, heading north, wondering why things never seemed to go right.

It was a larger crowd than usual that evening at the Friendly Bar, standing room only, the place buzzing with excitement as the customers waited to see *Hard News Tonight.* Red didn't want to admit it, but he was excited, too—especially since his interview had gone so well. The television over the bar was tuned to an Austin station, and *Hard News Tonight* was supposed to start in ten minutes.

Red and Billy Don had prime seats at the bar, and Red wasn't about to leave his for a minute, not even for a trip to the john, where pictures of lingerie models were plastered to the walls. Red always wondered what was hanging in the women's bathroom, but he had never worked up the nerve to sneak a peek.

After Red had finished his interview with Rudi Villarreal, he'd invited her to be his guest at the bar. He could tell she was intrigued by the idea. Maybe she'd show up. Wasn't often a woman like her got a shot at a man like him—a real country boy, not one of those city sissies she was probably used to. It might break Billy Don's heart if Red got to her first, but Billy Don was a big boy. He'd get over it.

And if Rudi didn't show up tonight, Red had a good scheme brewing—something that would impress the pants right off of her. But he'd probably need Billy Don's help.

Red leaned over to Billy Don and said, "Hey, you wanna hear a wild idea?"

Billy Don answered immediately. "Not particularly."

"Damn, Billy Don, why you always gotta be so negative?"

Billy Don exhaled beer breath into Red's face. " 'Cause every bright idea of yours ends up with one of us either in jail or the hospital. That's why."

"Not this time," Red said. "This one's a beaut."

He waited for Billy Don to ask what the idea was, but the huge redneck showed no signs of curiosity.

"I'm telling you, Billy Don, this is the best, most wonderfulest idea I ever had."

No reply. In fact, Billy Don turned and faced in the other direction, watching two guys playing pool.

Red leaned in close, making sure nobody else could hear what he was about to say. His mouth was two inches from Billy Don's ear. "You and me, bud, we're gonna catch that chupacabra."

Billy Don slowly turned to Red. Red thought he saw the signs of actual mental activity on Billy Don's face, but it was hard to tell. Those occasions were few and far between.

Billy Don started to smile. Then he spoke. He didn't even say whether he liked the idea or not. He skipped right past that step and went straight to the heart of the matter. "Damn, Red, I can't believe nobody's thought of that. We could probably sell the damn thing to a zoo for a million bucks."

Red's eyes widened. That hadn't occurred to him. My God, Billy Don was right! The commercial possibilities were endless! They could set up a sideshow . . . or rent the animal out to carnivals . . . or sell it to the highest bidder. There'd be movies and books and calendars, and Red and Billy Don would make a stinking fortune. Until now, Red had figured capturing the chupacabra would be a great way to get laid. But now it was so obvious: The chupacabra was a gold mine waiting to be found.

"Exactly," Red said. "That's exactly what I was thinking."

"Have you fed the dogs yet?" Charlie's mother asked.

"No, ma'am," Charlie said. He had just finished rinsing the dishes and loading them into the dishwasher.

"Well, you'd better get to it before your dad gets home."

He's not my dad, Charlie wanted to say. He's my stepdad. There's a difference. But all he said was, "Yes, ma'am."

Charlie dumped all the table scraps into a pan. He went into the small utility room and filled the pan to the top with dry dog food, then carried the mixture outside to the kennel.

Ace, the pointer, began to gobble the food as soon as Charlie poured it into his bowl. But Scout, the spaniel, showed no interest. She stood with her nose to the chain link, staring into the darkness.

All week long, Scout had been behaving oddly. She had never been much of a growler, but now, like on other recent nights, a low rumbling came from her chest.

"Scout . . . hey, girl . . . come and get it."

Scout looked in Charlie's direction and wagged her tail, but then she turned back to face the dark night.

Charlie walked over and stroked her neck.

Scout's growl turned into a low bark.

Then Charlie saw it. An animal in the distance.

It was standing at the edge of the tree line, fifty yards away. The sun had set, and Charlie couldn't see the animal well, but it appeared to be a coyote . . . or maybe another dog.

Now Ace had quit eating and both dogs were growling, the hair on their backs standing up, looking more vicious than Charlie had ever seen them.

Charlie stepped from the kennel and took a few steps toward the animal, whistling. If it was a lost dog, maybe he could help it find its way home.

But the animal turned and vanished into the woods.

After Duke Waldrip parked the Lotus, he was in a taxi within ten minutes. Now he had to make a choice. Somehow, he had to get back to Johnson City, and his options were limited.

He could plant himself outside a convenience store, wait for someone to leave their engine running, and steal a car. But that was risky, and there was the question of what he'd do with the car once he got back home.

He could hitchhike, but that could take forever. Who'd want to pull over on a major highway just to pick up a stranger? Plus, cops all over the area would be on the lookout for the shooter, though he couldn't imagine they had a decent description.

He could grab a bus. That would work, except some of those bus lines routed you all over creation before they finally made it to your destination—especially a small town like Johnson City or Blanco. He could be on the road for a solid day. And didn't you have to show an ID to buy a bus ticket nowadays? Probably.

That left one alternative. "Take me to that truck stop west of town," he told the taxi driver.

"Which one?"

"Aw, hell, I cain't remember the name. Right there on Two Ninety."

"The Tasty Skillet?"

"Yeah, that's it," Duke said. Any truck stop would do, he figured.

The driver jumped onto Loop 610, drove for several miles, then swung west onto 290, heading out of town. He glanced in the rearview on occasion, but he stayed quiet. Duke discouraged small talk by staring out the window. Thirty minutes later, they were in the huge parking lot of a run-down café, the place packed with eighteen-wheelers. Duke paid the fare and stepped from the taxi, carrying the deer mount with him.

Duke proceeded away from the restaurant, weaving his way through the maze of big rigs. He spotted a group of four truckers standing next to the cab of a big blue Peterbilt. A couple of them were smoking, all of them drinking beer, smiling, listening to a large man in overalls telling a joke.

"... and so the guy says, 'Mister, I ain't really a nun. I'm on my way to a costume party and my name's Bob!'"

Laughter all around, but now all the truckers were studying Duke as he stood ten feet away. He imagined he looked kind of odd, carrying a trophy mount around.

When the chuckles died down, Duke said, "Any of y'all heading through Blanco County?"

None of the men answered.

Duke pulled out his wallet. "I got a hundred bucks for a ride."

The big son of a bitch in overalls said, "As a matter of fact, I'm driving right through there myself."

"Damn, Red, I said I's sorry."

"That don't even *begin* to cover it, Billy Don," Red muttered, driving his truck slowly along the quiet streets of Johnson City. He was adhering to his six-pack rule, which meant that if he'd drunk more than a six-pack, he avoided the highways and kept to the back roads. "How come every damn time I got a brilliant idea, you got to go and screw it up?"

Billy Don pouted. "Wasn't like nobody else was gonna think of it."

Back at the bar, the moment Red had finally given in and gone to take a leak, Billy Don had told Bart Norris about Red's plan to capture the chupacabra. After that, the plan had spread through the crowd like wildfire. Now every damn yokel in the county was going to give it a try.

"Nobody *had* thought of it, you doofus. Not until you opened your big mouth."

Billy Don turned the radio on. "Yeah, well, they woulda."

Red knew there was no point in arguing about it. "Would not," he said.

"Would too," Billy Don said.

Red let it slide. Even though Billy Don had ruined the plan, Red was even more disappointed that he hadn't been featured on *Hard News Tonight*. Yeah, there was one shot of the crowd where Red could see himself waving at the camera, but not one second of his interview had made it on the air. And to add insult to perjury, the news babe, Rudi Villarreal, hadn't ever showed up at the bar. Uppity bitch.

"Would not," Red said.

"And so the farmer says, 'Son, that ain't my daughter. That's my wife!'"

Duke gave a halfhearted chuckle, but he'd had just about enough. The trucker—Jimmy Earl Smithers—had told stupid stories and corny jokes for five hours straight. Duke could feel the weight of Oliver Searcy's revolver in his pocket, and he fantasized about popping ol' Jimmy Earl right between the fucking eyes. Now *that* would be funny. But no, Duke needed to play along, not make any waves. The less memorable he was, the better. And besides, they were now less than five miles from Johnson City.

As they rumbled into the city limits, not another vehicle in sight this late at night, Duke said, "You can just drop me at the traffic light."

Jimmy Earl nodded and downshifted, bringing the big truck to a stop. "Damn quiet tonight."

It's two o'clock in the morning, asshole. What do you expect? "Yeah, it's not bad," Duke said, opening the door.

"You know, I never did catch your name."

Duke leaned over and extended a hand. "Kyle Dawson."

"Nice to meet you, Kyle."

"Thanks for the ride." Duke jumped from the rig and closed the door.

Jimmy Earl gave a wave, turned left, and chugged down the highway.

Duke stepped to the shoulder and began the long walk to Kyle's ranch to retrieve his Ford Expedition. Then he froze in place and stared down at his empty hands.

Son of a bitch!

He'd forgotten the deer mount in Jimmy Earl's truck.

15

EARLY FRIDAY MORNING, operating on three hours of sleep, John Marlin found a parking spot at the hospital in Houston. In the lobby, he stopped at a pay phone and called his best friend, Phil Colby, again.

"How's Garza doing?" Phil asked.

Marlin had stayed at the hospital until three in the morning. The surgery lasted until midnight, and when the doctor finally came out, looking serious but not grim, he told Marlin the bullet had shattered Garza's femur. "It's not quite as bad as it sounds, though. We used titanium screws to reassemble it as much as possible. The rest, the body will fill in naturally. It'll take him a while to heal up, but there shouldn't be any lasting damage. Maybe a minor limp. The bullet missed all the major arteries, or he might've bled out right there on the scene."

Marlin had been agonizing over his decision to go after the

shooter rather than staying with Garza. He had been worried about blood loss, wondering if Garza might lose the leg.

After speaking to the doctor, Marlin had remained at Garza's bedside for several hours, partly out of concern, and partly because he was hoping Garza could provide a description of the shooter. Garza eventually emerged from the anesthesia, but the nurses convinced Marlin that Garza wouldn't be coherent until morning. Exhausted, Marlin left the hospital and found a room in a nearby hotel.

Now, Marlin told Colby, "I'm just heading up to his room, but when I left late last night, he was doing okay. Pretty groggy, though . . . not making much sense . . . so I told him I'd be back this morning. How's the mutt?"

Marlin had called Colby last night and asked him to feed Geist.

"She's fine, John. I'll swing by your place right now and check on her again," Colby said. "Keep me posted, will you?"

"Will do."

Marlin hung up and made his way to the elevator. He hated hospitals, but then, who didn't? The horrible smells. The cold institutional decor. And yeah, the fact that when you were in a hospital, you were probably there because a friend or loved one was in bad shape. A car wreck, maybe. Cancer. Heart attack. Marlin—knock wood—hadn't been a patient himself for years.

He exited on the proper floor, walked to Garza's room, and found the door slightly ajar. Inside were Bill Tatum and Rachel Cowan, who had already driven in from Blanco County. Garza was awake, two pillows behind his head, giving the deputies the details from the night before.

"Here he is," Garza said. "John can probably give you the full story." He looked at Marlin and grinned. "My memory is kind of foggy. Plus, they've got me on morphine. . . ."

Marlin moved to the side of the sheriff's bed and squeezed his shoulder. "You doing all right?"

Garza's face looked pale and drawn. His voice was raspy but strong. "Not so bad," he said. "You were up here late last night?"

"Yeah, but you were pretty out of it."

"Man, I don't remember much, to be honest with you . . . but I do remember you saving my ass." He looked toward the deputies. "I was a sitting duck, waiting to get popped again, and this guy dragged me out of the doorway."

The deputies murmured approval.

"It wasn't a big deal," Marlin said. "I think the perp was already out the window by then."

"Maybe, maybe not," Garza said. "Anyway . . . I appreciate it."

Marlin nodded. He didn't know what to say, so he said nothing.

Garza spoke again: "Why don't you shut the door, John."

Marlin swung it closed.

In lower tones, Garza said, "I've been trying to tell these guys what happened, but I haven't had much luck."

So Marlin told them everything—the facts as he knew them, plus everything Susan Searcy and Peter Wilson had told the Bellaire cops. Immediately after the shooting, Marlin had had to remain at the Searcy house for several hours to give his statement. He had also been present when Susan Searcy and Wilson were interviewed. Marlin described climbing out of the window and finding Wilson in the backyard.

"We talked to him on Wednesday," Cowan said. "Mrs. Searcy had mentioned him as a family friend. He said he had been in Atlanta for a week, up until Tuesday night."

"What was Wilson's story last night?" Tatum asked.

"He said he dropped by to have coffee with Susan and see if she needed anything."

Cowan frowned. "And they didn't hear the window break?"

"She said they heard a noise but thought it was the construction next door."

"What the hell was Wilson doing in the backyard?" Tatum asked.

"Supposedly grabbing a smoke. Said he didn't want to intrude on Susan's conversation with Garza and me. Anyway, according to him, he heard the shot, then saw a man come out of the window, carrying something. Too dark by then to see what it was. The man ran around the side of the house, and that was the last Wilson saw of him."

Marlin turned to Garza. "Did you get a look at the guy who fired the shot?"

Garza took a deep breath. "Man, I don't know. The Bellaire cops stopped by bright and early and asked me a million questions . . . but it all happened so fast." He shook his head. "I feel kind of stupid, because victims say that all the time. But now I know how true it is. I mean, she opened the door . . . I started to step through . . . I saw movement, a shadow or something, in the window . . . and then—*bam*—I was down."

Marlin frowned. "That pretty much sums it up."

"I *do* remember seeing this guy Wilson last night, though. Or at least I assume it was him. Guy in a sport coat?"

Marlin nodded. He had brought Wilson, cuffed, into the house. While the sheriff was slipping off, going into shock, Wilson had been standing just a few feet away.

Garza leaned his head back on the pillow for a moment. Marlin could see that his eyelids were heavy. Garza slowly said, "I saw the guy—the shooter—for just an instant . . . and I don't know, but for some reason, the sport coat sounds wrong. The curtains were in the way . . . and the room was dark. . . ."

"Maybe you'll remember more in a few days," Cowan said.

Garza nodded. "That's what the doctor said. Don't know if it will do us any good, though. Besides, it's Bellaire's case. How weird is that? I get shot, and my own deputies aren't in charge of the investigation."

"I don't think it's a stretch," Tatum said, "to figure the guy who shot you killed Searcy."

"No doubt," Garza said. "But let's explore all angles. I want Wilson checked out good." He turned to Marlin. "Bellaire said they didn't have anything on him."

"No, we searched the backyard, the neighbors' yards, the rooftops, everything. One guy even waded through the fish pond. No gun. If Wilson managed to get rid of it that quick, he's a hell of a magician."

"So it sounds like his story holds?"

"Even the part about the guy carrying something."

Garza looked confused. "Maybe I haven't heard the full story."

"Bellaire didn't tell you about the missing mount?"

"Apparently not."

Marlin figured the Bellaire cops were being tight-lipped, or maybe Garza didn't remember everything they'd told him. The sheriff was still pretty doped up. "Searcy had trophies hanging all over his office," Marlin said. "All of 'em big whitetails. Except there was one nail in the wall with nothing on it. A big empty space."

"Two things bother me about Peter Wilson," Marlin said. He was in the hospital cafeteria with Bill Tatum and Rachel Cowan, grabbing a cup of coffee before he drove back to Blanco County in Garza's cruiser. "First—and I realized this late last night—there wasn't a car parked along the curb out front. Or in the driveway."

"Yeah?" Tatum said, interested.

"I guess he could have parked in the garage," Marlin said, "since he's a friend of the family. But doesn't that seem a little too friendly?"

"Maybe he parked further down the street," Cowan said.

"With an empty driveway?" Marlin asked.

"Man, I wish I could have been there for those interviews," Tatum said. "You think there's something between Wilson and the widow?"

Marlin had been pondering that, wondering if he should mention his hunch. "Once Bellaire cleared Wilson on the shooting—when they were interviewing him as a witness, not a suspect—there just seemed to be, like . . . I don't know . . . eye contact between the two of them. Like they were getting their stories straight. But hell, I could have been imagining things. I was still pretty jumpy."

"Okay, but let's play this out," Tatum said. "Let's say Susan Searcy was sleeping with Wilson. Take it one step further—Wilson's

in love with Susan and he wants her all to himself. So he offs
Oliver Searcy. Why would Wilson *break into* Oliver Searcy's office
to steal a deer mount? He could have just walked out with it. And
why would Susan Searcy cover for him?"

Marlin smiled. "Hey, I didn't say it made sense."

All three sat in silence for a moment.

Then Marlin said, "You know why it's so hard to solve a murder in a small Texas town?"

Tatum didn't answer.

"I'll bite," Cowan said. "Why?"

"All the DNA is the same," Marlin deadpanned.

Cowan laughed, and Tatum allowed himself a slight grin. "You
about done?" he asked.

Marlin finished the joke: "And there're no dental records."

Even Tatum chuckled that time.

"Here's a wild thought," Rachel Cowan said, getting back to it.
"Assuming there *was* an affair, what if Mrs. Searcy and Wilson
both had something to do with Oliver Searcy's death . . . and what
if they staged the break-in to throw us off the track?"

Tatum took a sip of coffee. "Interesting."

"I've heard wilder theories," Marlin said.

Cowan said, "Bill and I interviewed Susan two different times.
And each time, we asked her about Oliver's hunting plans in
Blanco County. Who he was hunting with, that kind of thing.
Even though we never said it, it was *obvious* we were looking at
hunting guides as suspects."

"So she and Wilson are trying to push us even further in that
direction?" Tatum said.

Cowan shrugged.

"But why steal a deer mount?" Tatum asked. "To me, that
doesn't make a lot of sense. There are plenty of other things she
could have done to throw us off—like saying she recognized
Duke Waldrip's name, or any of the other guides, for that matter."

"And why do it in broad daylight, right when Garza and I were
coming, rather than later?" Marlin asked. "After all, we called and
told her what time we'd be there."

"I'll admit, it sounds pretty crazy," Cowan said. She drained the last of her coffee. "I'd say we need to have yet another interview with Mrs. Searcy. Wilson, too."

Tatum nodded.

"Anything I can do?" Marlin asked.

"We still haven't been able to contact Gus Waldrip," Tatum said. "If you happen to stumble across him, will you let us know?"

"Definitely."

"We've had Turpin sit on his place a couple of different times, but Gus hasn't showed. Either he's out of town or he doesn't want to talk to us. If we can find him, that'd be a big help."

Marlin nodded.

"I'm sure you're gonna be plenty busy when you get back, anyway," Cowan said.

"How's that?" Marlin asked.

"You didn't see that show? *Hard News Tonight?*"

Cowan and Tatum both grinned.

"No. What's up?"

"They did a special report on the chupacabra last night," Cowan said. "I imagine that's gonna bring all sorts of nuts out of the woodwork."

Marlin groaned and shook his head. "Just great." That was the last thing he wanted to hear.

"What was the other thing?" Cowan asked Marlin.

"Huh?"

"You said there were two things that bothered you about Wilson."

"Oh, yeah. Wilson said he dropped by to have coffee. But I checked the garbage for coffee grounds, and there weren't any. Then I looked in the sink and the dishwasher. No cups."

16

IN THE WORLD of high-end theft, few were as successful as Terry Hobbs. Or as lucky.

Five years ago, when he'd been facing hard time for the burglary of a mansion in River Oaks, the only witness—the eighty-year-old widow who owned the home—died before the trial. Weeks earlier, the prosecutor had been concerned enough about the woman's failing health that he had videotaped her deposition. The only problem was, the sound on the camera had malfunctioned and there was no audio. By the time the error was caught, the widow had been considerate enough to pass away. Subsequently, the prosecutor argued that a lip-reader could view the tape and tell the jury exactly what the old woman had said. Once again, there was a snafu. The woman was a Hungarian immigrant, and her accent had been so thick, the lip-reader reported that Terry had stolen the woman's "mayonnaise." While a charcoal study by Manet was on the list of stolen goods, Hellmann's cer-

tainly was not. The judge, worrying about other possible transla-
tion errors, ruled the entire tape inadmissible.

Then there was the incident two years ago, when Terry had
attended a lavish wedding reception, uninvited, at the finest
country club in Harris County. The bride and groom were both
from wealthy, pedigreed families. Normally, a wedding wouldn't
have been of much interest to Terry, but in this case, the bride's
father had made his fortune in the jewelry business. Terry could
just imagine the kind of stones she'd be wearing that night. So
he'd donned a tuxedo and a superior attitude and weaseled his
way into the party. As it turned out, the bride was dripping in
exquisite diamonds—a million-dollar necklace, earrings, her new
wedding band, even a tiara (which Terry found somewhat tacky).
He waited until the time was right—when all the guests were
good and liquored up—and then followed the bride into her private bathroom. His plan was to tape her mouth shut, handcuff
her to a pipe, and make his exit before anyone discovered what
had happened. But when he approached her from behind, the
bride, who by then had drunk a small river of champagne, mis-
took Terry for her amorous new husband and reached back to
unzip his fly. Terry was never one to let an opportunity pass him
by. He guided her into a stall, bent her over the toilet, and proceeded to give her the best wedding gift he could muster under
the circumstances. Midway through—and Terry didn't take this
as a comment on his performance—the bride passed out. The
stolen gems never even made the news. Terry speculated that the
bride, after speaking to her husband, had deduced what had really
happened and was too embarrassed to report the theft.

So when Terry was admiring the green Lotus—and noticed the
keys hanging in the ignition—he assumed the gods of good fortune were smiling down on him once again.

The first thing that concerned Marlin as he drove back into Johnson City was a Louisiana license plate on a Jeep parked at Ronnie's Barbecue. Right next to it sat a rusty Dodge truck from
Arkansas. Farther up, at the Exxon, a car from Oklahoma was

gassing up. Virtually every restaurant in town had a full parking lot, with plenty of out-of-state plates sprinkled throughout.

I imagine that's gonna bring all sorts of nuts out of the woodwork.

And today was only Friday. What would happen when the weekend officially began?

Some of these people must have hit the road as soon as they saw the show last night. Scary thought, that anyone would be that motivated.

Marlin had been planning to stop at his office, then go straight home to grab a short nap and a fresh uniform, but he changed his mind and drove west on 290, then hung a left on Flat Creek Road. Time for a quick stop at the Waldrip place. Maybe he'd get lucky and catch Gus at home. Marlin certainly couldn't stake the place out around the clock, but he could drop by on occasion and see if there was any activity.

Along one stretch of Flat Creek Road, there was a row of perhaps a dozen homesteads that had, at some point, been subdivided out of the Macho Bueno Ranch. Each tract was ten or twenty acres, and they all shared a rear fence line with the much larger property to the north. Those homes had been there for as long as Marlin could remember, meaning the tracts had been cut from the ranch at least thirty-five years ago, possibly much longer, before Floyd Dawson, Kyle's father, had bought the place.

Marlin spotted a mailbox with the name Waldrip crudely painted on the side, and he pulled into the gravel driveway. Behind a wall of brush at the edge of the road stood an old rock home. In front sat a late-model Ford Expedition. Tatum had said that Gus Waldrip's vehicle hadn't moved since the first time the deputies had dropped by. They'd checked the odometer each time.

Marlin parked and climbed the questionable wooden steps to the front porch. Before he knocked, he noticed that he could hear music from inside the house. Sounded like Willie Nelson.

He saw several business cards deputies had slipped between the door and the frame. If Gus had been coming and going, he was using the back door. There wouldn't be any way to get the cards back in position if he used the front door.

Marlin rapped on the door, waited a minute, then rapped again. He slipped one of his own cards into the door frame, then climbed into his truck and drove home.

Inside the house, Duke took a deep breath.

At first, he didn't know what to make of the game warden's visit. He had figured that if the cops were going to show, they'd show in force, guns drawn, ready to rip Duke a new asshole. But just one guy? And the game warden at that? No matter how he looked at it, Duke decided that was good news. They wouldn't send a game warden, solo, to arrest a suspect in the shooting of a sheriff. No damn way.

And the news reports hadn't mentioned Duke's name once.

Duke was careful not to get his hopes up, but he started to wonder if he just might get out of this mess unscathed.

And he still had another big card to play. He'd call Marlin later, and then Duke would know for sure where things stood. He'd be free and clear—or he'd have to get his ass out of Blanco County pronto.

He looked over at Gus, who was watching a Willie Nelson video. Well, Gus's eyes were on the TV, but Duke could tell he wasn't really watching it. He was zoning again. Freaked out by all this shit.

"Hey, Gus," Duke said. "You in there?"

"Trampoline," Gus replied.

As Marlin's truck bounced up his driveway, Geist tumbled from her doghouse and sprinted to meet him. Months earlier, Marlin had spent several hours a week training Geist not to leave the boundaries of his seven acres, and the time had paid off. Marlin scratched the dog's ears for a few minutes, then entered the house, where he found a note from Phil Colby:

Fed her this morning. Give me a call. P.C.

Marlin checked his answering machine, surprised to see no blinking light. If the out-of-state visitors were here for the chupacabra, they hadn't done much trespassing yet. But just as Marlin turned toward the bathroom to take a shower, the phone rang.

It was a cattle rancher named Clay Summy. He was excited as hell.

He said he'd just shot the chupacabra.

Sixty seconds later, Marlin was back in his truck.

"Slow down, Mr. Summy. Just tell me what you saw." Marlin was standing with Clay Summy on the rancher's front porch.

Summy was in his seventies, and Marlin knew the man's vision wasn't quite as good as it once was. And Summy was obviously still on edge from the incident.

"I was driving the east pasture"—he gestured to his right—"and I saw an animal out by my calves. First, I thought it was a coyote, but I grabbed my binoculars and, hell no, its ears was too tall. Had a long snout, too, like a fox, but not as pointed."

"But it wasn't a fox?"

Summy gave Marlin a glare. "I seen my share of foxes, son."

"Yes, sir, I know you have. It's just that . . . well, what color was it?"

"Kinda silver and brown."

"Silver, not gray?"

"Yeah, silver up top, brown on its belly."

The gray fox was common in Blanco County, and Marlin knew it would be easy to mistake gray for silver. Summy appeared to realize what Marlin was thinking.

"This wasn't no fox. But if it *was* this chupacabra everybody's talking about . . . well, hell, I don't see what all the commotion is about. Didn't look that dangerous to me."

"You said it ran off when you shot?"

"Yep, but I winged her. Found a lot of blood."

"Well then, why don't we take a look?"

Summy smiled patiently. "That's what I been tryin' to do, son."

The rancher led the way in his Ford truck and Marlin followed in his Dodge. Summy navigated along a bumpy caliche road, then pulled off between some cedars. After he'd gone about fifty yards, he parked beside a barbed-wire fence. Marlin noticed a red feed-store cap resting on a fence pole. Summy had marked the location.

"Right over here's where she crossed under the fence," Summy said.

Marlin saw small drops of fresh blood on the ground, and he could see that the trail continued on the other side of the fence.

"You didn't trail her over there?"

Summy frowned. "Getting too old to climb fences. Arthritis."

Marlin dropped to the ground and shimmied under the lowest strand of barbed wire. Then he followed the blood trail onto the neighboring ranch. It wasn't much of a trail, though, and after he followed it warily for a hundred yards, it petered out.

Marlin returned to the fence and slid back to Summy's side. He knew that two different ranches shared Summy's eastern fence line, but he wasn't positive where the cutoff was. "Who's your neighbor over there?" Marlin asked.

"Floyd Dawson's boy. Kyle."

That's what Marlin had suspected. *What the hell is up with Kyle Dawson?* he wondered. *Why does his name keep popping up?*

Marlin and Summy drove back to Summy's house, where Marlin asked to use the phone. First, he dialed Kyle Dawson's number. Marlin would be crossing deep onto Dawson's property, and he wanted to let him know—but there was no answer. Marlin left a message, and then he called the sheriff's office and asked for Deputy Ernie Turpin.

"What's up, John?" Turpin asked.

"You busy right now?"

"Little bit. Why?"

"How'd you like to bring your hound out for a little hide-and-seek?"

*   *   *

By the time Red and Billy Don composed a list of supplies and drove to the hardware store in Johnson City, it was early afternoon.

"Doncha think we're overdoing it a bit?" Billy Don asked.

In the back of Red's truck was Billy Don's favorite heavy-duty hog trap—a large steel cage with a spring-operated door. Red's plan was to reinforce the trap with an extra layer of heavy-duty cattle panel on the outside. He figured you couldn't be too careful with a wild animal like a chupacabra. Damn thing might just rip the cage apart with its bare paws . . . or claws . . . or hooves . . . or whatever the hell it had.

"We're gonna have to check the trap once a day or so," Red said. "When it's your turn to check it, maybe in the middle of the night, believe me, you'll want the trap as strong as possible."

Billy Don didn't look convinced. "But it's a waste of money, Red. Hell, that trap can hold a five-hundred-pound boar."

"Maybe," Red said, "but this ain't no boar. Shit, we don't even know *what* it is for sure. What if it's ten times stronger than the biggest hog you ever seen?"

Now Billy Don was starting to look a little more agreeable.

Red continued: "You don't want him busting out of there and planting his fangs right in your neck, do ya?"

"No," Billy Don said meekly.

"Awright, then. If we're gonna do this, let's do it right. Now let's get in there and get loaded up."

They walked up the concrete steps to the small hardware store and stepped inside. Red took one look around the place and immediately had a sinking feeling in his stomach. Most of the shelves had been stripped clean.

"Damn," Billy Don said. "Looks like they need to restock."

Red elbowed Billy Don in his ample gut. "Don't you know what this means? Everybody's already loaded up on supplies because they're doing the same damn thing we're doing."

Billy Don scratched his head. "Oh."

"Yeah," Red said. " 'Oh.' "

17

JESSIE WASN'T MUCH of a barker, and Marlin was grateful for that. He didn't want to spook the wounded animal—a fox or coyote, Marlin was sure of it—and cause it to run even farther.

Turpin had Jessie on a long leash, and both men slipped under the fence onto Kyle Dawson's property. Marlin was carrying the 30/30 he kept in his truck, Turpin was carrying a tranquilizer gun. Both men wished they had brought a video camera—just in case.

Marlin was about to offer to point out the last drop of blood he had spotted on the trail, but he saw there was no need for that. Jessie tugged on the leash and was raring to go, following the same path Marlin had walked earlier.

Without a dog, trailing a wounded animal can be a tedious and ultimately futile exercise, as most hunters know. Frequently, as was the case here, the blood trail thinned to a few meager drops, many yards apart. The pursuer could spend ten or fifteen minutes just looking for the next trace of blood, which might be lost in high grasses or underneath shifting leaves.

But with Jessie's powerful nose leading the way, the pursuit went so quickly that Marlin and Turpin could barely keep up. In less than five minutes, the trio had covered more than a quarter of a mile over the rugged, rolling terrain.

They crested a hill, and Marlin could see a rooftop on the horizon. Kyle Dawson's house, still half a mile to the east. Jessie continued downhill, where they came to a shallow creek, maybe ten feet across. The dog plunged right in, and the men waded after her. Back on dry land, Jessie picked up the trail again and continued her relentless tracking, meandering through juniper thickets, across caliche flats, and under fences that split the ranch into smaller pastures. Occasionally, Marlin spotted a small drop of blood, and at one point, a covey of quail burst from a clump of brush, startling both men. Jessie, however, paid the birds no mind at all, remaining focused completely on the job at hand.

"Pretty damn impressive," Marlin said, breathless, as they topped the far side of a ravine.

Turpin grinned. "And I hardly had to train her. It's just her nature."

For just a moment, the dog stopped and looked back at the men, wagging her tail, as if she were enjoying the compliment. Then it was back to business, nose to the ground, keeping the leash taut.

They reached a dense grove of towering western red cedars, the lower branches so thick, the men could barely make their way through. Jessie, however, simply scooted along underneath the lowest boughs, just as the wounded animal had done. The ground was covered with a thick mulch, and it was easy to see the animal's path. Marlin spotted several tracks in the mud, and he asked Turpin to hold up for a moment. He studied the prints and was more convinced than ever that it was a coyote.

Jessie barked, and Marlin had a hunch they were getting close. He worked the lever on his 30/30, chambering a round, then lowered the hammer to the safety position and nodded at Turpin to continue.

Jessie led them out of the cedars, and Marlin found himself staring directly at the front door of Kyle Dawson's house, roughly a hundred yards away.

"Damn, that's weird," Marlin said. He knew most wild animals completely avoided areas inhabited by man, especially during daylight hours.

"Maybe it's getting weak, not thinking straight," Turpin said, grinning, catching his breath. "I know I'm not."

Marlin took a breather, too. The brisk trek had made him realize how out of shape he was. He was feeling light-headed.

After a few minutes, Jessie couldn't stand the wait anymore and barked impatiently.

"Well, let's get after it," Turpin said.

The coonhound proceeded directly toward the house, then gradually veered to the north and began to go around it. Marlin noticed there weren't any vehicles parked in the circular drive out front, or in the driveway by the garage on the north side.

"Hold up a sec," he said. While Turpin and Jessie waited, Marlin walked to the front door and knocked. Then he went to the garage and peered through the windows in the retractable doors. He saw Kyle Dawson's truck, but Marlin knew Dawson also owned some type of sports car. It was gone.

He rejoined Turpin, and Jessie led them in a wide berth around the house. At the back, on the eastern side, was a swimming pool, hot tub, and tennis courts. Beyond that was a dilapidated riding stable inside a large corral made from split-rail fencing. No horses to be seen, though. Marlin remembered that Floyd Dawson used to ride horses on occasion.

Here, closer to the house, the landscape was maintained, the native grasses cut short. Kyle—or, more likely, a paid worker—probably drove a small tractor over the acreage on occasion to mow the grasses to a manageable level.

Jessie was getting excited now, barking more frequently, raring up on her back paws as she pulled on the leash.

"Looks like she's headed for the stable," Turpin said, trotting to keep up.

Marlin followed, and sure enough, Jessie squeezed under the fence and began to drag Turpin toward the wooden stable door.

The deputy brought the dog to a halt about ten feet from the door, which stood open about a foot. "Whatever it is," Turpin whispered, "I'd say it's in there."

Marlin nodded and walked to the front, taking the lead for the first time. With the rifle in front of him, he slowly approached the door. An animal could come busting out of there at any moment, and Marlin assumed it wouldn't be a house cat this time.

He reached the door and gently pulled it to until there was only about a four-inch space. Then he pulled a flashlight from his belt and shined the light inside the dark stable.

What he saw first, against the far wall, was a large steel-mesh crate, the kind used by dog owners who keep their dogs inside the house. As far as Marlin could remember, Dawson didn't own any dogs. The crate was about the size of a refrigerator laid on its side. Hay had been tossed inside the crate as bedding, and there were two metal bowls for food and water. But the crate was empty.

Right next to it was another crate, also empty.

Marlin swung the flashlight wider and found a third crate.

He saw a pair of eyes, red from the light, staring back at him.

He heard a low growl.

Then the animal stood up, blood matting its chest, and Marlin had a clear view.

He was so surprised by what he saw, he almost dropped the flashlight.

"So you really don't want the car?" Terry Hobbs asked. "Even for ten g's?" He couldn't believe what he was hearing. The man he was talking to was the only potential buyer Terry could think of, and this was a guy who bought just about anything of extreme value.

"Shit no, but thanks," the voice on the line said. "Got outta those high-dollar imports a couple years back. Too risky."

"Too risky? What about that Matisse last year?"

"Now, see, a Matisse I can stick into a suitcase and carry onto a plane. I got buyers overseas who won't ask questions. Try the same thing with a Lotus."

Terry saw his point. "You know anybody?"

"Top of my head, no. But I'll ask around. Where'd you pick it up, anyway? Never known you to boost cars."

Terry told him where he'd found it.

There was a sharp intake of breath on the other end.

"Problem?" Terry asked.

"You gotta be careful out there. Security and shit nowadays. Cameras all over the place."

Uh-oh. Terry hadn't thought of that. He hadn't thought at all. Just got in the car and took off.

"Didn't have to break in, though," Terry said. "Guy left the key in it."

"Seriously? Rich dude with shit for brains."

"How could I resist?"

"Next time, find a way. You'll have a tough time unloading it. If you don't get collared."

Now Terry was depressed. He thanked the man and hung up, promising to stay in touch.

Shit. He had seen an easy score, and he'd taken it. But this thing was turning into a headache. Not worth the hassle.

Just the fact that it was sitting out in his garage made him nervous. It was the first time he'd dealt with a piece of stolen property he couldn't fit into a crawl space or a safety-deposit box.

Marty Hoffenhauser had never been inside the feed store before, but it seemed like a good place to start. The store had a fenced yard outside, and Marty recognized many of the products inside the fence as hunting-related equipment.

The deer blinds were easy to identify: small squat boxes made from corrugated black plastic, with windows all around and a small door on one side. Some of the boxes were elevated, perched on thin legs made from steel tubing, with a ladder leading to the door.

Then there were fifty-gallon drums, also mounted on steel legs, with some sort of device attached to the bottom of the drum. Marty was fairly certain those were deer feeders.

Marty figured a place like the feed store would have deer antlers, and if they didn't have any, they could probably tell him where to get some. So he stepped through the door.

The store had many more hunting products inside—hundreds, actually—all arranged neatly in cabinets and on shelves. Marty had no idea it took this much equipment to go deer hunting. He figured you just grabbed a rifle and headed into the woods, but it was apparently more complicated than that. It was kind of interesting, actually. In one aisle alone, Marty found small bottles of deer, fox, and raccoon urine, hand warmers, earplugs, knife sharpeners, gun oil, battery-powered spotlights, compasses, rifle slings, reloading kits, varmint guards (whatever those were), solar panels to charge feeder batteries, and about a dozen other items.

Against a wall, there was a long rack of camouflage clothing—shirts, pants, shorts, coats, vests, socks, ski masks, caps, even long underwear—in a variety of patterns, weaves, textures, and colors. Marty noticed that most of the camouflage designs were actually trademarked, with names like RealTree and Mossy Oak.

But he didn't see any deer antlers.

A salesman approached, a young guy in Wrangler jeans, boots, and a pressed Western-style shirt. "Help you, sir?"

"Yeah," Marty said. "Do you carry deer antlers?"

"For rattling?"

Rattling? Marty didn't know what that meant, so he just said yes. He figured antlers were antlers, regardless of what they were to be used for.

The salesman moved to the next aisle over. On the bottom shelf was a pair of antlers connected by a leather strap. "Our last pair," he said. "Kinda late in the season for rattling. I guess you might still bring some does in, though."

Marty tried hard not to appear confused. The salesman handed the antlers to Marty, who studied the tag. "Oops. It says here that they're made from synthetic materials."

The young man shrugged. "Yeah, but they sound just like the real thing." He took the antlers from Marty's hands and began striking the antlers against each other, making a cacophony of sounds.

Marty smiled. "Very nice. But I'm really looking for genuine antlers."

The salesman placed the synthetic antlers back on the shelf. "Don't carry 'em. You might check with Junior Barstow."

"Okay, great. Where do I find him?"

"South on Two eighty-one. At the snake farm."

Marty couldn't hide his puzzled expression this time.

"He also runs a taxidermy shop," the salesman said. "He might have some sheds."

Sheds? What the hell did that mean? Marty didn't want to come across as a total idiot, so he thanked the man and walked back outside to his car. He drove south on the highway and spotted a hand-painted sign he had briefly noted in the past:

LIVE SNAKES! INDAIN ARROWHEADS!
DIRECTLY AHEAD!
THRILL THE KIDS! IT'S A SCIENTIFIC AND HISTORIC WONDERLAND!
(VISA EXCEPTED)

Marty pulled into the parking lot, stepped from his Jaguar, and surveyed the surroundings. He saw a collapsing fireworks stand, a sagging double-wide mobile home, and a rusty Blue Bell ice-cream truck with no wheels.

Marty remembered reading a newspaper article about this place once. The owner was a snake handler, taxidermist, butcher, and collector of Indian artifacts. Rare arrowheads, spear points, pottery, things of that sort.

"You need something?" An elderly man had exited the mobile home and was calling to Marty. Something long and black was draped over his shoulders. On closer examination, Marty realized it was a snake.

"Uh, you Junior?"

"That's what they call me." Barstow's accent was as thick as gin fresh from the freezer. It was times like this Marty wished he could enhance his mild Austin accent and blend in a little more with the Hill Country locals. It might prevent them from eyeing him suspiciously, as Barstow was now doing. Marty was sure the Jaguar didn't help matters much. One of the few foreign cars in Blanco County.

"Guy at the feed store said you might have some antlers for sale," Marty said, trying to bump his drawl up a little.

The old man didn't reply. His expression was stony.

"Sheds?" Marty said hopefully.

"Ain't got no sheds," Junior said, turning and disappearing behind the fireworks stand. A moment later, Marty heard him call out, "Well, you want antlers or not?"

"Um, yessir!" Marty said, trotting to catch up.

Hidden by the fireworks stand was a large blue Dumpster. Barstow was sliding open a door on the side.

As Marty got closer, he heard a loud buzz. In seconds, big blue flies were swarming around his head. He peeked into the Dumpster.

And he almost vomited.

He saw a shining, bloody pile of bones and hides, dismembered deer legs with hooves poking skyward, an occasional deer head, the eyes dull and flat, and twisted gray entrails. The stench was nearly unbearable.

Marty covered his mouth and stared at Barstow. The snake over the old man's shoulders stared back.

"Dig through there," Barstow said. "You can find all the antlers you want."

18

"YOU'VE LOST YOUR mind," Ernie Turpin said, studying Marlin's face for any sign that he was joking.

"If it's not a jackal," Marlin said, "then I don't know what the hell it is. Nothing native, that's for sure."

Jessie was whining, straining toward the stable door.

"I'll hold her," Marlin said, taking the leash with one hand, holding his 30/30 with the other. "Go take a look."

Turpin continued to eye Marlin while taking the flashlight off his belt. "Now if it's some damn coyote in there and it comes running after me . . ."

Marlin shook his head. "I'm not bullshitting you, Ernie. Promise."

The deputy stepped quietly to the stable door and eased it open. He played his flashlight around the interior. After a moment, he sucked his breath in. "Whoa!"

"Still in the crate?" Marlin asked.

"Yep. Staring right at me. Growling." Seconds later, he said, "I got a clear shot." Turpin swung the tranquilizer gun off his shoulder. He glanced back at Marlin.

"Take it."

They used Turpin's cell phone to call Trey Sweeney, and he was on the scene in thirty minutes. The wildlife biologist was as excited as Marlin had ever seen him, eyes wide behind his thick glasses, speaking loudly, rubbing his hands together.

They had already transferred the jackal—and indeed it was a jackal: a silver-backed specimen, to be precise—to a cage in the back of Sweeney's truck. Jessie had finally calmed down and now was sleeping in the cab of Sweeney's truck.

The three men were inside Kyle Dawson's stable, inspecting the three crates. With the overhead lights on, it was much easier to see the interior of the stable.

"When was the last time we saw illegal imports in Blanco County?" Sweeney asked.

"Other than some whitetails from Mexico," Marlin replied, "I can't even remember. Years."

Sweeney bent low and studied the jackal's crate, picking through the hay bedding. "He felt safer here. Came back when he got shot."

The bullet had grazed the front of the jackal's chest, leaving a bloody, though nonfatal, gash.

"What was he doing running loose?" Turpin asked.

Marlin said, "He probably got away before they could shoot him."

The deputy was confused. "They hunt them? Who in the hell would want to shoot that ugly thing?"

Sweeney muttered, "Doesn't matter what kind of animal it is. If it's alive, some idiot somewhere wants to kill it. Mount it on his wall."

"But why three of them?" Turpin asked, gesturing at the other crates.

Neither Marlin nor Sweeney answered. Marlin knelt in front of the middle crate. He shined his flashlight through the hay and spotted some hair. It wasn't the same color as the jackal's fur. "One jackal is all we know for sure," Marlin said. "We don't know what the other two animals were."

"Might even be more than three animals," Sweeney said, "if they kept more than one in a cage. Could be something smaller. But who knows?"

"Think they're loose, too?"

"Good chance," Sweeney said.

"No real way of knowing, though," Marlin replied, "until we talk to Dawson." *And probably Duke Waldrip, too*, he thought. Then he rebuffed himself for jumping to conclusions. It could be that Waldrip wasn't involved at all. Dawson might be allowing other guides to use his ranch, or he might have been importing the illegal animals himself. Best to wait and see.

Sweeney walked outside to his truck and returned with a camera and several small plastic bags. He began taking photos while Marlin used a pair of tweezers to place hair samples and fecal specimens in the bags.

"We'll send these to the lab in San Marcos," Marlin said to Turpin. "They'll tell us exactly what we're dealing with."

"Anything I can do?"

"You mind checking the house again?" Marlin said as he moved to the second crate.

The deputy nodded and exited the stable.

The two men worked in silence for a couple of minutes, the air stuffy inside the stable even though it was cool outside.

"This is fucked up, John," Sweeney said. Marlin knew the biologist was seriously pissed off. Rarely did Trey use a harsh word beyond *damn* or *hell*.

"Tell me about it."

"I mean, what's the point of this? They haul them out here in a cage, probably dope 'em up, and then shoot 'em with high-powered rifles? It's ridiculous."

"No argument here."

Sweeney fumed some more as he shot photos. "Who's the guy that owns this place?"

"Kyle Dawson."

"What's his story?"

Marlin moved to the last crate. "Well, they do some hunting out here, but it was all whitetail, as far as I knew. Never had any reason to think otherwise."

"How would you? It's pretty secluded out here."

Marlin stood and closed the plastic bags. Then he placed the empty food and water bowls inside large paper bags. The wire gauge of the crates was too thin to hold fingerprints, but the metal bowls might.

Sweeney said, "This might explain the chupacabra, huh?"

Marlin smiled. Sweeney sounded positively crestfallen. The biologist had probably been holding out hope of some breathtaking new species of animal. "Yeah, I guess so," Marlin said as they walked out the stable door. "You were right, by the way."

"How's that?"

"The tracks we saw last weekend. They weren't a coyote or a dog. Must've been this guy." He gestured toward the cage in the back of Trey's truck.

Trey said, "Or something from one of the other crates."

Turpin returned, shaking his head. "Nobody home."

Terry Hobbs was wearing nondescript clothes and had his collar turned up to mask his profile as much as possible. Sunglasses and a baseball cap completed the outfit. He even had a wig on the seat beside him, ready to go—just in case there really were video cameras.

He'd done some thinking, and had decided he'd take the Lotus back to where he'd boosted it. If he was lucky, he'd get the same parking spot, or at least close. Maybe the owner wouldn't even know it had been gone for a handful of hours. That way, nobody would have any reason to check the video from the cameras.

If he just left the car on an isolated street or in another crammed parking lot—which was his first inclination—the car would be reported stolen and they'd go straight to the video.

Terry had already removed the LoJack tracking device, but there wouldn't be any beating the video.

Damn, why had he gotten into this mess! Acting like a freaking amateur. *You don't ever pull a job unless it's carefully orchestrated*, he told himself. *Remember that!*

He swung onto the highway and headed north, enjoying the smooth ride of the Lotus. Hell, he had enough money to buy one of these babies with cash, so taking this chance was downright unforgivable.

Up ahead, traffic was moving slowly—which, in Houston, meant everyone was merely sticking to the speed limit rather than going ten or twenty miles above it.

Terry moved into the fast lane, behind a few other impatient drivers, and began to ease past the knot of cars. Then he saw why everyone was being so cautious.

There was a patrol car in the middle of the pack, gliding in the middle lane. Terry could see the cop glancing in his rearview mirror, looking back at Terry.

Terry began to sweat and focused on the lane ahead of him. He glanced at the speedometer. Still legal. Best to just ease on past the cop and go on his merry way. Terry inched past the patrol car. He even glanced over and nodded at the cop. He didn't nod back.

Now Terry was a car length ahead, one lane over. Then three car lengths.

Then the cop fell in behind him.

Son of a bitch!

Terry let off the gas and slowed to five miles under the limit. No sense in taking chances.

The cop was right on his tail.

Terry signaled and moved to the middle lane.

The cop moved over, too.

Terry moved to the right-hand lane and signaled for the next exit, a quarter of a mile ahead.

The cop stuck right behind him.

Lord, please say it isn't so! Terry eased off the accelerator and coasted off the highway onto the access road.

That's when the cherries on the roof of the patrol car lit up.

* * *

Terry had very little experience speaking to cops. Almost none. When he'd nearly gotten nailed on the River Oaks burglary, he'd immediately lawyered up during questioning, figuring it was the wise thing to do.

That was the only time he'd been arrested.

Hell, he'd never even gotten a traffic ticket.

That's why he was so nervous, the sweat beginning to trickle from his scalp. Well that, and the fact that the car he was driving was hotter than a ten-dollar Rolex.

The cop stepped to the window. Tall guy, built like a brick wall. Mirrored sunglasses. "License and proof of insurance, please."

Terry slipped his wallet from his back pocket and removed his driver's license.

The cop studied it and said, "The reason I stopped you . . . your registration sticker is expired." He glanced up. "Proof of insurance, too, please."

Terry didn't know where to look, so he popped the glove compartment.

Oh fuck! There was a handgun inside.

Terry snapped the compartment shut, but it was too late.

The cop had backed away a step or two, and now he had his hand on his pistol. "Step out of the car, Mr. Hobbs. Right now."

Trey Sweeney had several large enclosed pens at his house, so the men agreed that the biologist would store the jackal there for the time being.

"I'll drop Jessie off at your place, Ernie," Sweeney offered. The coonhound was still snoozing in the front seat of Sweeney's truck, tired out from the excitement of the chase.

After Sweeney left, Marlin and Turpin decided to have one more look around Kyle Dawson's place. Marlin wanted to hear what Dawson had to say about the other two crates. Were there other imported animals, possibly dangerous, running loose in Blanco County? If so, Marlin needed to know.

Turpin went around to the front of the house, and Marlin approached from the rear. He walked past the tennis courts, then skirted the edge of the pool. As he was making his way to the back door, he heard a phone ringing—but it was outside the house, not inside.

Marlin quickly backtracked and found a cordless phone on a chaise lounge next to the hot tub. He answered on the third ring.

"Who's this?" asked a gruff voice on the other end.

"You called me," Marlin said. "You go first." If this was one of Dawson's friends—maybe even the person who supplied Dawson with exotic animals—Marlin didn't want to spook him. So he waited.

Silence. Then the man said, "I'm looking for Kyle Dawson. Is this him?"

"I can get him a message."

"Yeah, well, you do that." The man obviously didn't like Marlin's coy attitude. "Tell him Sergeant McAlister from the Houston Police Department called. About his car."

Marlin chuckled. "Sergeant, this is John Marlin, the game warden in Blanco County. Dawson's a popular man today. We're looking for him, too."

McAlister warmed up now that introductions had been made, and he told Marlin the reason for the call. Kyle Dawson's car—apparently stolen—had been recovered by a patrolman during a routine traffic stop. Marlin, in turn, told McAlister what had brought him out to Dawson's house. Then Marlin asked, "What's the name of your suspect?"

"Guy who boosted the car? Terry Hobbs. Name mean anything to you?"

"Unfortunately, no."

"Blanco County . . . wasn't your sheriff shot over here yesterday?"

Marlin told McAlister that story, too, including some general details on the Searcy homicide. He mentioned that Dawson had been questioned regarding the Searcy case.

"Is he a suspect?" McAlister asked.

"At this point, we don't know."

"Sounds like we both have some things we need to share with our squads."

Marlin agreed. Then he asked, "Where was Dawson's car when Hobbs stole it?"

"Intercontinental Airport. Of course, Hobbs might be lying about where he got it. Then again, maybe your man Dawson skipped town."

19

"THIS IS TURNING into a tangled mess," Bill Tatum said. The deputy was still in Houston, and Marlin had called his cell phone to tell him about the jackal and the call from the Houston police. Neither Tatum nor Marlin was a big believer in coincidences. What were the odds that Kyle Dawson's name would come up in two separate investigations? They felt there had to be some kind of connection.

"I sure don't like Dawson's car being found in Houston the day after Bobby was shot," Tatum said.

"Me neither."

"There was never any indication that Dawson met with Searcy, right?" Tatum asked.

"According to Dawson, no." Marlin remembered the conversation in Dawson's living room. "No phone calls from Searcy to Dawson, either."

Tatum sighed. "When you talked to Dawson, he didn't say anything about leaving town?"

"Not a word, but Ernie's looking around. We'll see if we can find anything." Marlin and the deputy were inside Dawson's house now, having found the back door unlocked. Tatum had assured them that they could legally enter the home to check on Dawson's welfare. Anything that might be lying in open view was fair game, even without a warrant.

"What's the penalty for that kind of thing?" Tatum asked, referring to the illegal imported animals.

"Class-A misdemeanor," Marlin said. "First-time offense, he'd be looking at probation probably."

"I can't imagine him running because of something like that."

"Doubtful. Plus, he didn't know we were coming over here. We just stumbled into it, really."

Marlin waited as Tatum relayed some of the information to Rachel Cowan. "Tell you what," he said to Marlin, "have Ernie give me a call in a couple of hours. We're still working on Peter Wilson."

"How's that going?"

"He hasn't copped to the affair yet. We've got credit-card receipts from a local hotel, and the manager there thinks he recognizes Susan Searcy's car. Then there're calls on an almost daily basis from Wilson's cell phone to the Searcy house—but he's saying he was calling Oliver Searcy, not Susan. I think he's on the fence, about to give it up."

"What about Wilson's alibi?"

"Well, that's solid," Tatum admitted. "He was out of town when Searcy was killed, but that wouldn't have stopped him from hiring it out."

Marlin nodded as Ernie Turpin walked into the kitchen, carrying something in a latex-gloved hand.

"Hold on a sec, Bill." Marlin faced Turpin. "Is that what I think it is?"

The deputy nodded and came closer. In his hand was a combination lock that had clearly been snipped with bolt cutters. "Found it in the garage."

"What's going on?" Tatum asked.

"Ernie just found a lock that's been cut."

For a moment, Tatum didn't make the connection. Then he snapped to it. "Oh, jeez, like the one on Maggie Mason's gate."

"There's only one way to find out," Marlin said. "I know the combination."

"Try it," Tatum said.

Marlin recited it from memory. "Eleven- zero- seven."

Turpin called them out as he twisted the dial: "Eleven . . . zero . . . seven."

He tugged on the remaining stump of the lock shackle—and it popped loose.

"Bingo," Marlin said.

Red was starting to get blisters, and he wished he'd brought gloves along. The hog trap was a hell of a lot heavier than he'd thought it would be, but damn, was it solid. Like a jail cell, but for freaky-ass animals. And the smell of the road-killed possum they'd placed inside the trap as bait wasn't helping matters much.

"How much further we going with this thing?" Billy Don grunted, stumbling slowly through the cedar break. Even *he* was having trouble carrying his end, which showed what a chore it was to tote the trap onto Owen Pierce's ranch. Red had called the barbecue king and gotten permission, but only by enticing him with the idea of free publicity should they happen to catch the chupacabra. "Just keep the trap way off the main driveway," Pierce had said. "Don't need my wife getting all worked up about it." That was fine with Red, but it meant they had to haul the trap into the woods by hand; the brush was too thick to drive through.

"I'd say this"—Red let his end of the trap crash to the ground—"is just about far enough."

Red knelt with his hands on his knees, winded, then went ahead and sat down on the ground. Billy Don propped one massive butt cheek on a corner of the trap.

Red finally caught his breath and leaned on one elbow, surveying the moonlit area. "We're about two hundred yards off the road. I 'magine the chupacabra can find it easy enough."

"Yeah, if it ain't already made tracks for the next county," Billy Don said.

Billy Don was like that: downright gloomy, always trying to shoot holes in Red's plans.

"Well, shit, you got a better idea?" Red asked. "Now that we've lugged this sumbitch out here?"

Billy Don remained silent. Yeah, that always shut Billy Don up. Just ask him for ideas of his own.

"I figger they're just like deer," Red said. "You know how a big buck only wanders within a certain area? Kind of a home base? I bet the chupacabra's the same damn way. Makes sense, when you think about it."

Red knew Billy Don *didn't* think about it, which was why he never had anything worthwhile to contribute. But that suited Red just fine. There was room for only one set of brains in this operation.

After a long pause, Billy Don said, "Hey Red, what would ya do with half a mil?"

What *would* he do with money like that? An interesting question.

"Probably strip nekkid and roll around in it at first," Red said, enjoying the very idea.

In the moonlight, Red could see Billy Don grinning. The big man said, "I think I'd like to own a NASCAR team. Maybe get behind ol' Jeff Gordon. Can't you see my pitcher plastered all over his car, zooming down the Texas Motor Speedway?"

Probably scare everyone out of the bleachers, Red thought.

"Now, see," Red said, "that kind of dough won't go as far as you think it would. No, to be seriously rich, you need a couple million bucks. That's why I'd probably invest it." Red didn't know anything about financial stuff, but if he suddenly got rich, he could damn sure learn.

"Invest it?" Billy Don asked. "Even in today's volatile marketplace?"

Red shot him a suspicious glance.

Billy Don shrugged. "Something I heard on cable."

"Don't touch anything else," Bill Tatum said, excited. "Not until we get a warrant. In fact, just go ahead and get out of there."

Marlin agreed. They definitely didn't want to step over any legal boundaries and void their discovery. Losing the lock on a technicality would be heartbreaking.

"Great work, John," the chief deputy continued. "Tell Ernie, too. We're leaving right now. Be there in about four hours."

Obviously, finding the lock had virtually eliminated Peter Wilson as a suspect. Wilson might have been sleeping with Susan Searcy, but that wasn't a crime. Now the focus was on Kyle Dawson. Tracking him down, Marlin figured, would be the hard part. Marlin and Turpin stepped outside, closing the back door behind them.

"Our vehicles are still over at Clay's," Marlin pointed out.

Turpin nodded. "We can catch a ride when the others get here." Obtaining a warrant would likely take only a few hours, and the search of the house would begin as soon as Tatum and Cowan arrived.

One of the men needed to remain at the house anyway, just in case Dawson showed his face. Marlin assumed that wasn't likely.

"You mind if I take off?" Marlin asked. His part of the investigation was over, for now at least. Unless the deputies asked for his help, the homicide case fell squarely on their shoulders. Marlin would still try to determine what type of animals had been housed in the other crates, but that was something he could start in the morning, after he got some sleep. He'd only slept three hours the night before, and he was exhausted. Despite the excitement, he could barely keep his eyes open.

"Hell, man, you had a big part in this," Turpin said. "Stay and enjoy the glory."

"Thanks, Ernie, but I'm beat. I'm gonna head out."

They shook hands, and Marlin began the walk out to the

county road to make his way around to Summy's house. Thirty yards down the driveway, he stopped. "Make sure they talk to Duke Waldrip," he called back to Turpin. "He might have an idea where Dawson went."

Beulah Summerall's greatest love in life—next to her husband, Cal—was her poodle, Max. He was a spirited young male (a former champion on the show circuit), almost as spunky as Beulah herself. Yes, Beulah was well into her seventies now, but she always said that you were only as old as you felt. And she felt wonderful. She loved her long walks along the quiet county roads near her home, and she'd be darned if she'd let the mild arthritis that had been creeping up lately slow her down. A couple of aspirin and off she'd go.

Cal's emphysema, unfortunately, prevented him from accompanying Beulah on her strolls, but Max was always a willing volunteer, trotting ahead of her with a wagging tail, his toenails clicking on the asphalt.

This particular evening, Beulah decided to walk east on Flat Creek Road, admiring the lovely Texas sky as she went. There were always so many stars to see out here in the country, unlike back home in Chicago. There, the city lights blotted out the sky and you were lucky to get a decent glimpse of the moon. Here, the sky was literally shot full of millions of divine lights. She could even make out several of the planets on occasion.

Beulah and Cal had made the decision to retire to Blanco County three years ago, and they hadn't regretted it for a single minute. Their only child, a son named Michael, lived in San Antonio, and now it was a mere hour's drive to see the grandkids. And then there was the weather. How glorious, compared to Chicago's weather. Granted, the summers could be brutal, but that was what air-conditioning was for. And the winters more than made up for it. In Chicago right now, Beulah's old friends were digging out from under two feet of snow. Beulah, on the other hand, was enjoying a comfortable evening, the temperature in the mid-fifties.

Max was leading the way, tethered to a ten-foot leash, Beulah following with a flashlight. There really wasn't much need for the leash; traffic was generally light and slow on these smaller roads. But Beulah would never forgive herself if Max were to get hit. What a disaster that would be. Better safe than sorry. That's why Beulah always wore a shirt made from reflective material, and little Max's collar glowed in the dark. She preferred this eastward-stretching bit of road, in fact, because it was free of curves. She could see the cars coming from a great distance, and they could see her.

This evening, so far, only one vehicle had passed by—an old red Ford truck, going much too fast, in Beulah's opinion. Other than that, it was peaceful and serene and perfect.

Then Max started barking. Glaring into the dark, Max yapped at something unseen. Beulah shined the flashlight into the brush but saw nothing. It was probably just a small animal, maybe a raccoon. Some critter. She loved that word. *Critter.* Sounded so Texan.

"Come on, Max," Beulah said, tugging on the leash. He was behind her now, planting his little paws in the dirt on the side of the road. Putting up a perfectly brave show. He let out a few more courageous barks.

Then Beulah heard something moving in the brush.

She refined her theory. It was probably an armadillo. They were, after all, nocturnal creatures, and they made a tremendous amount of noise rooting through the native grasses.

Max growled and Beulah smiled. What would Max do if he actually caught one of those armored animals? Probably tuck his tail and run, if he was smart. It was silly to even think about it.

Then something strange happened. Max's growl turned into a whimper and he retreated behind Beulah's legs.

Well.

Beulah had never heard Max whimper quite like that. He seemed genuinely frightened. Poor little thing. Maybe it would be best to turn back now.

Max's whimper turned into more of a persistent yelp.

She shined her light again. Yes, it was definitely time to go home.

Then the brush exploded and the most hideous animal Beulah had ever seen lunged right at her.

Marlin had been asleep for less than an hour when there was a knock on the door. He pulled on jeans and a sweatshirt, wondering who'd be coming by his house without phoning. Maybe Phil Colby, since Marlin had never called him back. Marlin swung the door open and found a nice-looking dark-haired woman on his front porch. He couldn't place her, but she was definitely familiar.

"Mr. Marlin?"

"Yes?" he said, using one leg to keep Geist from escaping out the door.

The woman stuck out a hand. "I'm Rudi Villarreal, with *Hard News Tonight.*"

Now he recognized her. The reporter from that tabloid TV program that was in town. Marlin reluctantly shook her hand. Glancing behind her, he saw a minivan parked behind his truck, a couple of men staring out the front windshield. "How can I help you?" He figured he knew the answer already: They wanted to talk to him about the chupacabra.

"Well, I'm sorry to bother you at home," Rudi said, smiling, "but as you know, there have been a lot of strange events out here in your county." She said it more as a question, inviting him to respond. Marlin remained quiet.

She was undeterred. "We've talked to a couple of deputies and many of the local residents—but with you being the game warden, we thought you might like to give us your thoughts." Another question in the form of a statement.

"You're asking for an interview?"

Rudi nodded. "Just a quick one. Especially with the latest developments." Third nonquestion in a row. She raised an eyebrow, as if they shared a secret.

"What exactly are you referring to?"

"The animal you found this evening." The smile again, almost with a cat-and-mouse feel to it. "We spoke to Clay Summy."

There it is. That's what this is all about. When Marlin had returned to Summy's place to get his truck, he had felt obligated to tell the old rancher what he had found. He'd asked Summy to keep it under his hat, but news like that was hard to keep to one-self, apparently.

Marlin mulled it over. His gut told him to decline the interview, but then he realized it might be a good idea. If newcomers to town were after the chupacabra—and they thought it had already been caught—they'd pack their bags and go home. "I'm afraid I can't tell you much," he said. "It's an ongoing investigation."

Rudi nodded. "That's fine. We don't expect any more details than you'd put in your reports."

Marlin was warming to the idea. "When would it air?"

"Tomorrow night. It's our Saturday-evening show—our biggest audience." Rudi eyed him expectantly. "We can just talk to you out here on your porch. Won't take but a few minutes. Will you do it?"

Finally, a direct question.

"Yeah, sure," Marlin said. "Just let me put on a uniform."

Rudi turned and gave a thumbs-up to the men in the van.

20

WHOA, RUDI THOUGHT, waiting on the porch. *How come they don't grow 'em like this guy back in L.A.?* John Marlin was completely different than the Armani-clad power brokers out in Hollywood. Kind of rugged, without being some sort of hayseed.

Barry and Chad climbed the stairs, lugging the equipment with them. Barry would be running the camera, Chad on sound. Apparently, Chad had made his way up the ranks many years ago working audio. Fortunately, he seemed to be handling the components—new technology to him—without a problem.

"So he's going to do it?" Barry whispered.

"Well, of course he is," Chad said. "Wouldn't you if you found a gorgeous young lady like Rudi standing on your front steps?" He smiled at Rudi, but it came across as a leer.

Gross. Late last night, Chad had knocked on Rudi's motel door, saying they needed to talk strategy. "Who we're gonna interview next, things like that," he had said, slurring, ogling Rudi in her nightshirt. She'd smelled the scotch on his breath.

"Go to bed!" she'd hissed, closing the door with a bang.

This morning, he'd acted like it had never happened. *Lecherous bastard.*

She felt bad for Barry, too, because he was the producer and should be running the show. But since Chad was their boss, he was calling all the shots. He'd made all the decisions, from the approach they'd take to the story ("Deadly serious, not that light-hearted crap"), down to the motel they would stay at. And he'd been treating Barry like a gofer the whole time. In short, Chad was being his typical self: a grade-A asshole. He'd made his way to the top of the industry by being a world-class schmoozer, and he was quick to use his talents when the game warden returned wearing a khaki uniform with a badge pinned to the shirt.

"Good evening, sir," Chad said, shaking John Marlin's hand, "I'm Chad Reeves, executive producer of *Hard News Tonight.*"

Rudi noticed that John Marlin, to his credit, appeared unimpressed. "John Marlin," he said simply.

"You've already had the pleasure of meeting Rudi," Chad said. The game warden nodded.

Rudi waited for Chad to introduce Barry, but it became apparent that he wasn't going to. So she said, "And this is Barry Grubbman, the *producer* for this segment." Rudi hoped Chad noticed the emphasis she put on the word *producer.*

Barry waved from behind the camera. "Hi."

"Nice to meet you, Barry."

Rudi steered the game warden closer to the front of his porch. She decided she'd stand one step lower as she interviewed him, making the game warden appear even taller and more authoritative.

"How's this?" she asked Barry.

He had set up some klieg lights and was peering through the camera.

"Looks great," Chad said before Barry could reply.

Rudi shot him a glare. He winked at her.

She turned to Marlin, holding a microphone. "I'm going to ask you some basic questions. Just answer naturally. Don't worry if you get tongue-tied or anything." She gave him her best smile. "Lots of people get a little nervous when they're interviewed, but it's no big deal. We can edit it later and make it work."

"Sounds good," he replied. To Rudi, he looked anything but nervous. God, he was nice-looking, too, but not in a Tom Cruise pretty-boy kind of way. The camera—and the show's vast female audience—would love him.

Chad, listening on a headset, said the audio was ready to go. Barry gave her a thumbs-up, the camera rolled, and the interview began.

Rudi lobbed a few easy questions at John Marlin at first, just to warm him up. How long had he been the game warden in Blanco County? Did he work closely with the sheriff's department? What were his primary responsibilities? But in the middle of one of Marlin's answers, Chad gave her a let's-move-along gesture. So she said, "What can you tell us about the animal you captured late this afternoon?"

"Uh, I can say it wasn't a native species for the area. But nothing too unusual. Certainly nothing to be concerned about. There's been somewhat of a frenzy around here, and there's really no reason for it."

Rudi was pleased. The man was a natural—cool and confident in front of the camera. He had a comforting, easygoing demeanor. "So you're saying this was an animal you had never experienced before?"

"Well, I personally had never seen anything like it in Blanco County before, and we've had some odd animals get loose over the years. Ranchers and breeders can legally import all sorts of animals, and sometimes they manage to escape and cause an uproar."

"So this was a legally imported animal?"

"I'm afraid I can't comment on that."

"Okay, but you think this animal—whatever it is—was responsible for the so-called chupacabra sightings? Is this the animal that people have been seeing?"

"I imagine so. In fact, we discovered the animal after a man called in reporting it as the chupacabra."

Rudi smiled, wanting to draw the interview to a close with a playful question. "What exactly is the chupacabra supposed to look like, from what you know?"

The game warden grinned and played along. "Let's see . . . sort of a cross between a flying monkey and a large reptile. Huge red eyes . . . long fangs. Something ridiculous like that."

Perfect. "I take it you don't believe in it?"

"No, ma'am, I'm afraid I don't. And I hate to disappoint all the people who are here looking for it, but they're gonna come up empty. Better just to go on home."

"That's the end of the animal troubles, then?"

"That's right. No more animal troubles."

The horrible beast lunged straight for Max, and Beulah Summerall felt the leash jerk as her poor poodle tried to run away. She had her hand through the loop at the end of the leash, and there was no letting go now. She was tied to Max, and Beulah knew her fate and Max's would be one and the same.

The next few moments were sheer confusion and chaos.

Max released an earsplitting yelp, and the beast appeared to have the poodle in its mouth.

Without even thinking, Beulah rushed forward and began to swing wildly with her walking stick. She heard fierce growling, tremendous squeals from Max, and the pounding of her own heart in her ears.

She swung a few more times and felt the solid impact of wood on flesh.

Beulah couldn't be sure, but Max appeared to be fighting back. The light was too dim to be certain—but either Max was still in the beast's jaws or he had a fang of his own sunk into the animal's neck!

Beulah was out of breath now, her knees weak, her head spinning. She summoned the last of her strength, shouting, "*Get away!*" while swinging the walking stick as hard as she could from over her head.

The stick cracked and broke in two as it came down squarely on the animal's neck. There was a horrifying scream, almost human . . . and then it was over.

The animal bolted back into the woods.

Beulah dropped to her knees, using the remaining half of her walking stick to prop herself up.

Then she heard it. A bone-chilling sound that carried through the quiet night. It was almost like laughter. The animal was *laughing* at her.

Max immediately ran to her, whimpering but wagging his tail. Beulah reached down and carefully probed for injuries. His fur was damp, but he appeared to be okay.

Beulah took one last look toward the brush on the side of the road. "Let's go home, Max," she said. "I don't want to walk anymore."

Duke Waldrip had tried calling the game warden's home number several times that afternoon, but he hadn't gotten an answer. He'd even called the sheriff's office, but John Marlin wasn't there, either. It was obvious, though, that nobody was looking for Duke. He'd called Sally Ann earlier, and she had acted normal—meaning she'd been cold and unresponsive. Hell, half the time when he went to the trouble to go home, he expected to find his belongings dumped in the front yard. What kept him and Sally Ann together, he didn't have a clue. It sure wasn't the vast quantities of love they shared. It was probably just the convenience of it all, the fact that she lived two driveways down the road. Anyway, the good news was, she hadn't said anything about deputies looking for him. Still, though, Duke wanted to reach Marlin if he could. It was the best way to set his plan in motion. He grabbed his cell phone. As he dialed, he eyed Gus on the couch. His brother was reading a magazine, but he hadn't flipped a page in thirty minutes.

The phone rang, and this time, the game warden answered.

Duke used his friendliest voice, the one he usually reserved for rich customers. "Hey, John, this is Duke Waldrip."

"You talk to one of the deputies yet, Duke?"

Duke's heart thumped. "No, sir. About what?"

"Just need to ask you a few things."

"Shoot," Duke said, trying to sound nonchalant. He had three balls up in the air—the Searcy fiasco, the shooting of the sheriff, and the accident with Kyle—and it was damn near impossible to gauge what the cops knew about any of them. All Duke could go by was what the deputies, and Marlin, asked him.

"Any idea where Kyle Dawson is?"

Oh Christ! Had Cheri finally called it in? If she had, why weren't deputies pounding on Duke's door? But if she hadn't called, why the hell *were* Marlin and the deputies looking for Kyle? "No, sir, I haven't talked to him since—let's see—I guess it was yesterday."

There was a long silence.

"Tell me something: Did Kyle ever meet Oliver Searcy?" Marlin asked.

Jesus, what a perfect question! The entire purpose of Duke's call was to point Marlin in that direction—to make Kyle a suspect. Now Duke didn't have to plant that seed at all, because Marlin was already heading down that road. And that's why the cops were looking for Kyle.

"Funny," Duke said, straining to keep his voice even. "That's exactly what I wanted to talk to you about. You asked me to call if I remembered anything that might be useful. . . ."

"And?"

Duke knew he had to play this just right. Not too over-the-top. He started out slowly. "I kinda feel like a snitch, since Kyle is my friend and everything, but I started thinking about my conversations with Oliver Searcy. . . ." Duke intentionally took a long pause, just like the game warden sometimes did. See how he liked it.

"What'd you remember, Duke?"

"I think I might've mentioned Kyle's name to him, or at least the name of the ranch."

Duke let that lie there for a second, too.

Marlin said, "So you're thinking Searcy might've called Kyle direct and set up a hunt that way?"

Duke tried a laugh. "It wouldn't be the first time a hunter went around me to the ranch owner. Some of 'em decide they don't really need a guide and figure they can save a little money by cutting me out of the deal."

"But you don't know for sure?"

"No, I really couldn't tell you. I'd say it's a possibility. But it's probably nothing. Even if Searcy *did* hunt out there, there's no way Kyle killed him. He ain't got it in him to do something like that."

Duke could almost hear the game warden's gears spinning as he pondered this new information.

Marlin said, "Has he said anything lately about leaving town? Maybe taking a vacation?"

Leaving town? Could the cops have already discovered Kyle's car at the Houston airport? That would have been fast fucking work, especially for these yokels. But if they *were* that far along—Duke was really getting excited now—maybe they had even discovered the lock Duke had planted in the garage.

"Not that I remember," Duke said. "But if he was going anywhere, he woulda taken his Lotus. He only uses the truck around the ranch. Was the Lotus gone?"

Instead of answering, the game warden asked another question. "Does he allow anyone else to guide out on his ranch, as far as you know?"

"Kyle's friendly with a lot of guides and hunters all over the county, so there's no telling who's been out there. He hasn't mentioned anyone, though."

There was a long silence.

"Hello?" Duke said.

"I'm here," Marlin answered.

Damn it, those pauses made Duke jumpy. He wished the game warden would just ask his questions and get it over with.

"What kind of animals do y'all hunt out there?" Marlin asked.

Duke had been regaining his composure, but now he started to sweat again. "Whitetails mostly. Some turkey and hog. Why?"

"You ever hunt any type of exotics out there?"

He played it coy. "You mean axis, fallow, like that? Yeah, some-times." Those were the most common imported deer in Texas. All perfectly legal.

Again, the game warden didn't respond right away. It made Duke want to scream.

"If you talk to Kyle, have him call me."

"Sure, no problem."

As soon as Marlin hung up, the phone rang. It was Trey Sweeney, out of breath.

"John, I made a cast of its paws. They don't match."

"What paws?"

"The jackal's!"

"They don't match the tracks from Flat Creek?"

"Not even close."

Marlin knew what Sweeney was thinking: The tracks they'd found were made by some other exotic animal from Kyle Daw-son's stable. Marlin knew it was a possibility.

"How long before the lab can identify those samples?" Sweeney asked.

"Couple of weeks."

Trey laughed. "Well, I'd say we better keep our eyes open for something weird."

Marlin's call waiting beeped.

"Gotta go, Trey."

Darrell Bridges, the night dispatcher for the sheriff's depart-ment, was on the other line. "Sorry, John, I know you're trying to go ten-seven." Marlin had called Darrell before going to bed, ask-ing him to hold any calls that weren't urgent. "But we've got tres-passing calls coming in all over the county. Some of these landowners are pretty pissed off."

Just what Marlin had expected. Thrill-seekers were out look-ing for the chupacabra. Marlin got some addresses from Darrell and told him he'd respond.

He went to grab his gun belt, when the phone rang yet again.

"It's me," Darrell said. "Forget those trespassing calls for now. We just got a call from a lady on Flat Creek. Said she was attacked by some kind of strange animal."

21

THE SET THAT was used in most of Marty Hoffenhauser's films was really just an old airplane hangar on Marty's property. One half of the hangar housed a wide variety of furniture, clothing, and other props. Depending on the script, the small crew could slap together a bedroom one morning, then have a restaurant standing in the same spot that afternoon. Just outside the hangar was a travel trailer that the cast used as a dressing room between shots.

Marty asked Mike Hung to meet him at the hangar Saturday morning. Just the two of them, with no distractions. Shooting was on hold for the time being, while Marty tried to solve this delicate problem. This particular morning, the crew was prepared to return to the set on a moment's notice.

"So how's it going, Mike?" Marty asked, handing the star a glass of orange juice. He wanted to approach this topic just right.

Casual, not worried. Concerned, but not in a panic. They both took a seat.

"Aw, so-so," Mike replied. He appeared downright depressed. It broke Marty's heart to see this once-proud dwarf with such a hangdog expression.

"You been getting plenty of sleep?"

Hung nodded, but he stared into his glass.

"Yeah, well, that's good. Plenty of sleep can do you a world of good. I gotta have eight hours every night myself."

Mike was not exactly bubbling with conversation.

So Marty continued. "I've been thinking about something, Mike. Something that could be the answer to our small . . . issue." Marty shifted in his chair. "From what I understand—in your country—when a man isn't feeling quite as . . . masculine as he would like, there are certain items that can give him a . . . boost. Is that right?"

Mike made eye contact, but appeared confused. The language barrier was sometimes a problem.

"You know—aphrodisiacs?" Marty said.

Mike didn't appear to know that word. Marty didn't know how to say it in Chinese.

"For instance"—Marty had done some research on the Internet—"the penis from a horse? Bear gallbladder? Moth larvae?"

Mike began to grin. "Yes, yes, velly good stuff." He frowned. "But not available here."

"No, no, they're not," Marty replied. He leaned over and opened a brown grocery bag. "But there is something we have here that can do the trick."

Marty pulled the items out of the bag. Two matching antlers, four points on each. Junior Barstow had been kind enough to lop the antlers off what he had called a "basket rack eight."

Marty watched Hung's face, and was pleased to see that he appeared interested.

"You ever use these?" Marty asked.

Hung shook his head. "But I hear they much powaful." The little guy used a voice—a whisper, really—that one would normally reserve for talking about a saint.

Marty laughed. "Damn right they are! They'll make you more virile than you've ever been before!" Then Marty wondered if he was overdoing it. He sounded like a cheesy late-night infomercial for a Viagra knockoff. And besides—judging from Hung's expression—he didn't need to be sold. According to many different Web sites, deer antlers were one of the leading Chinese aphrodisiacs, their potency coming solely from the fact that they were considered phallic in design. The theory was, if you ingested something that had phallic qualities, your own phallus would be affected.

"I use it all the time," Marty lied. He knew that in reality the antlers worked the same way as a placebo. Mind over . . . well, in this case, penis. If Hung *thought* the antlers would make him a raging sex fiend, that's exactly what they would do.

A smile spread across Mike's face.

"And here . . ." Marty opened a large plastic Save Mart bag and withdrew a blender, still in its box. He'd purchased the most durable high-performance model available. Then he pulled a heavy-duty saber saw out of the bag. (Marty had received a strange stare when he had asked the salesgirl if the saw would cut through bone. "Yeah, I guess so," the young lady had replied, then quickly scurried down the aisle, leaving Marty standing there.)

Antlers were generally ground up into a powder, then sprinkled over food or into a drink. Marty decided the best way to grind them would be to cut them into small slivers and puree them in the blender. Probably not the way the Chinese did it, but Marty didn't think that really mattered.

Marty said, "Now, see, this blender has several different speeds. You just—"

But Hung wasn't listening. He was scooping the blender and saw into his arms, the antlers riding on top of the pile. "Thank you," he said, even going so far as to bow. "Thank you velly much."

Then he dashed to the travel trailer, the door slamming behind him.

* * *

Marlin pulled into the parking lot of the sheriff's department at five minutes before ten o'clock. After responding to Darrell's call last night, and then chasing trespassing calls all over the county, Marlin had managed to get to bed at five in the morning and get four solid hours of sleep. Then Bill Tatum had called at nine o'clock, wanting to set up a meeting. "I'd like to get everybody together," the deputy had said. "We've got some new developments, and I want to talk 'em through."

Inside the office, Marlin grabbed a cup of coffee and made his way to the small conference room. Already seated around the table were Bill Tatum, Rachel Cowan, and Ernie Turpin.

Marlin took a chair while Tatum finished up a conversation on the phone. When he hung up, the chief deputy rubbed his hands together and said, "Okay, things are moving damn fast and we need to get a handle on it all." He sat at the head of the table. "Let me bring you up to speed real quick, John. Kyle Dawson's house. The three of us finished the search about four this morning—and the short version is, we didn't find squat outside of that lock. No prints on it, by the way. We did find a pretty good stash of cocaine— about eleven grams. We *didn't* find any kind of travel documents— but Dawson had a computer, and we're sorting through it to see if he bought plane tickets on-line. If he *did* buy tickets"—Tatum slid a small item across the table to Marlin—"he's not going far."

Marlin glanced down and saw a passport. He thumbed through it and saw a photo of Kyle Dawson. "Maybe he forgot it," Marlin said.

Tatum shook his head. "Doubtful. We busted a few chops at the Houston airport, got them to hustle up some video from one of their cameras."

There was a laptop computer in the center of the table, and Tatum swung it around to face Marlin.

Rachel Cowan ran her fingertips along the computer's mouse pad. The young deputy was the unofficial high-tech guru for the department. She had set up a new computer system there the previous summer.

"They e-mailed this clip late last night, while we were at Dawson's place." She clicked on a file and a grainy black-and-white video began to play. It was a wide shot, showing a long row of vehicles in a parking lot lit by vapor lights. Behind the cars was a high chain-link fence and then a busy boulevard.

"Resolution's bad because each camera has to cover such a big area," Cowan explained.

Looking at the far end of the row of cars, Marlin saw a low-slung sports car—Kyle Dawson's car, presumably—pull into an empty spot at least forty yards from the camera. Bad luck. If the car had been closer, they would have gotten a much better look. When Dawson got out of the car, though, he would likely walk right past the camera on his way into the airport. After a few seconds, a figure climbed out of the car. The quality of the video made it impossible to make out any of the man's features. He was wearing a dark jacket . . . or maybe a long-sleeved shirt. Even details as simple as that couldn't be ascertained. It was all too blurry.

The man appeared to glance around, then leaned back into the car.

"We think he wiped away prints," Tatum said. "Houston didn't find any on the driver's side or the mirrors."

The man in the video reemerged from the car, carrying something bulky.

"What do you think, John?" Tatum asked. "Is that the deer mount from Searcy's house?"

It was impossible to tell. The man's body partially shielded the object, and if there were antlers protruding from it, the video was just too poor to make them out.

"Could be," Marlin said, but he knew he sounded uncertain.

Now the man proceeded to walk *away* from the camera.

Marlin started to state the obvious. "But—"

"Yes," Tatum said, "the airport is *behind* the camera."

Marlin watched dejectedly as the man walked out of the frame. Cowan paused the video. "The employees in the ticket booths never saw him. We think he climbed the fence."

"None of the other cameras picked him up?" Marlin asked.

Cowan shook her head.

"So Dawson didn't fly out?"

Tatum spoke again. "Hell, we can't even be sure that's him. We checked with all the airlines, and Kyle Dawson wasn't booked on any of them. At least not under his real name. He could've used a fake passport, but that doesn't seem likely."

Cowan said, "I'm checking with a few people to see if the video can be cleaned up a little, maybe give us a better look, but I'm not holding my breath." She leaned toward the computer. "Here's the next clip. . . ."

This segment of video showed a man from behind as he walked down the same row of cars. He stopped at the sports car, as if admiring it, then leaned over and peered into the window. He nonchalantly opened the door, climbed in, and drove away. It all transpired in about fifteen seconds.

"Terry Hobbs?" Marlin asked.

"Righto," Tatum said.

Cowan ran the clips again, but it wasn't much help. There simply was no way of determining whether it was or wasn't Kyle Dawson.

"What about the gun from the glove compartment?" Marlin asked.

"Registered to Dawson," Tatum said. "It wasn't the one Bobby got shot with. Wrong caliber."

As evidence, in its present state, the video wasn't worth much.

Now Tatum slid a large manila envelope across the table. "Early this morning, we got an overnight package from one of the nurses that worked for Oliver Searcy. She found this in Searcy's files, under the last name of 'Deer.' "

Marlin opened the envelope and pulled out an X ray. The item on the film was instantly recognizable. A deer mount, complete with antlers.

What Marlin noticed first were the bolts threaded upward into the base of each antler. Marlin had seen this type of work before, done by cheaters trying to win big-buck contests. The antlers were probably "sheds," meaning they had fallen naturally from a buck's skull, as they do every year. It was a fairly simple job to take a pair of sheds, attach them to a skullcap from another deer, and then cover it all with deer hide, making it more difficult to spot the fraud. Officials for some of the larger contests, however, had begun the practice of x-raying questionable entries. Marlin didn't need to explain any of this to the deputies. As natives of Texas, the state with the largest deer population in the country, they were more than familiar with this type of scam.

What Marlin noticed second was the long drop tine dipping down from the left antler. Drop tines were a fairly uncommon and therefore highly prized characteristic of a trophy buck.

"Is this actual size?" Marlin asked, holding the X ray.

The deputies glanced at one another. "I guess so. Aren't most X rays?" Ernie Turpin said.

"Because, damn, if this sucker wasn't a fake, it would score about one eighty."

"What's a buck like that go for nowadays?" Tatum asked.

"It varies, but five grand easy. Sometimes ten."

"Here's the theory we've been working with: Searcy hunted with Mr. X. He shoots a deer, and Mr. X passes off a fake later. Searcy figures it out, gets pissed off, and comes after him."

"Waldrip or Dawson?"

"Damned if I know. Could be either, or both. Or, hell, somebody else entirely. We do know that Searcy placed a call to Waldrip on Sunday, six days ago. He was officially missing as of Monday, and you found him Tuesday morning. Searcy made no calls to Dawson, and no recent calls to other guides. He did call those other two guides several weeks ago. . . ."

Marlin was trying to remember the conversation he and Garza had had with Duke Waldrip. He said, "What if Searcy hunted with somebody else—someone we haven't even talked to yet—and then he discovered the mount was a fake? Let's say he was embarrassed about getting ripped off and wasn't going to do anything about it . . . or maybe he was going to deal with it later. But with the deer season ending, he still wants to get a good deer . . . so he calls Waldrip again."

There was silence as the deputies mulled that scenario over. Cowan said, "But let's not forget about Bobby getting shot. I mean, we *know* it's gotta be the same guy, right? Whoever killed Searcy broke into the house to steal the deer mount. We agree on that?"

"I'd say so, at least for now," Tatum said.

"Then we're back to one of our original questions. Why steal the mount?"

Turpin said, "If the theory's right—meaning Searcy got ripped off and came to settle the score—then whoever killed him might be identified by that mount, right?"

"Some taxidermists put labels on the back," Marlin said.

"Excellent," Tatum said. "I imagine there'd be fingerprints on it, too. If not the guide's, then the taxidermist's."

Marlin gestured toward the X ray. "Here's something else, though. Normally, a guy like Searcy would get pretty pumped up about a deer like this and take photos after the kill."

Tatum clapped his hands together. "So we could find those photos and maybe identify which ranch he hunted on. Maybe there'd even be photos of the guide." He turned to Cowan. "Let's call the widow. See if there are any cameras lying around with undeveloped film."

"There's a problem with that, though," Marlin said. "If Searcy did see the deer after the kill, and if he took photos, when the mount got delivered to him—"

Turpin, an avid hunter, finished the sentence for him. "He'd recognize it as a different deer in a heartbeat. That crossed my mind earlier. Searcy—if he had any kind of memory at all—would *know* this wasn't the same deer he shot. He wouldn't need to x-ray it."

Everyone in the room was plainly stumped: Why did Searcy x-ray his trophy? They tossed a few more ideas around, but nothing cleared the confusion. Marlin could tell that Tatum was ready to end the meeting and start chasing down more information. "John, I appreciate your help," the chief deputy said, standing. "I know you've got your hands full. Speaking of which, what was that call out on Flat Creek last night?"

Marlin told them about the elderly lady who had described being attacked by a doglike animal she couldn't identify. "She chased it off with her walking stick."

"Coyote?" Turpin asked.

"Man, I hope so," Marlin said. He was starting to regret the interview with *Hard News Tonight*. He'd said that the animal troubles were over, but now he wasn't so sure.

"Well," Tatum said, "between chasing trespassers and wild animals, can you do one thing for us?"

"Talk to Waldrip again?"

"No. Actually, I want to hold off on that until we see where this goes. Apparently Dawson got married a couple weeks ago. . . ."

"Cheri? That woman is his wife?"

"Yep. Vegas quickie. Can you talk to her, see what she has to say about Dawson? Maybe she knows where he went. She might open up if she thinks it's about a hunting scam instead of a homicide."

22

"SSH! I THINK I hear something!"

"What is it, Red?"

"Just shut up for a second."

Red listened, but now all he could hear was the sound of Billy Don panting like a mule in labor. The trap was about fifty yards away, and both of them were already winded from the hike through the woods. The stock of the rifle was slick in Red's hands.

Red began to take slow, careful steps forward. Hell's bells, what if they'd already caught the chupacabra? Red figured this could be the turning point in his life. Granted, he was already what most people would consider an American success story. He owned his own Palm Harbor mobile home, complete with satellite TV. His 1977 Ford truck was nearly paid for. And just last month, he'd bought his own washer and dryer on revolving credit.

The rate was only eighteen percent, and they don't offer those kinds of terms to lowlifes.

But this thing here—the chupacabra—this could be his ticket to a whole new world.

He glanced back at Billy Don, who had stopped to take a leak. Of course, Red would need some new friends.

Billy Don zipped up and walked forward to meet him.

"Shit," Red whispered. "You had to go ahead and piss right here? We're trying to catch a wild animal, remember?"

Billy Don shrugged. "I hadda go."

"Well, keep it in your damn pants." Red turned and continued his slow approach to the trap. They were now thirty yards away, but the brush was too thick to see—

He heard something! A snort, or grunt, or some damn noise. Billy Don nodded his head, his eyes wide, meaning he had heard it, too.

Red double-checked the rifle to make sure a round was in the chamber. He'd brought along his .30-06 loaded with Nosler tips. If that wasn't enough to stop the chupacabra, they'd need a frigging bazooka.

Red picked his path carefully, stepping over sticks and around rocks. There was a clump of cedar trees ahead. Once they got around those, they'd have a clear view of the trap.

He heard another grunt.

Then a higher-pitched squeal.

Whatever it was, it was seriously pissed off.

Just a few more steps.

Now Red could see one corner of the trap. He saw movement!

Red took a quick look at Billy Don, who was several yards back, sort of shuffling sideways. Damn, the big pussy was ready to run back to the truck.

Red took another step forward—and he saw it!

It was . . .

It looked like . . .

Aw, damn. It was only a feral pig. Mr. Pierce had said he didn't have any wild pigs on his ranch, but he obviously didn't know what the hell he was talking about.

Red was dejected, but he decided to have a little fun with the situation.

He faced Billy Don. "You stay here. I've got the gun, so I'll go see what's what."

Billy Don nodded vigorously.

Red continued slowly around the cedar trees, out of Billy Don's sight. He placed the rifle carefully on the ground, sucked in a big breath, then ran back the way he'd come, screaming.

"Jesus! Billy Don! Get the hell out of here!"

Billy Don didn't need to be told twice. The huge redneck ran as fast as his size-fourteen work boots would carry him, plowing over cacti, uprooting stumps, leaving a trail of broken branches in his wake.

Red had stopped on the trail, and he was laughing so hard, he was crying. Billy Don was completely out of sight, probably back at the truck by now. Finally, when Red's laughter had subsided, he saw Billy Don peeking cautiously from behind a laurel tree. This brought on a new round of laughter, Red's ribs hurting so bad, he plopped to the ground.

Billy Don approached him, scowling. He walked past the cedars, and Red watched his expression change as he saw the pig. He glared back at Red. "Very funny."

"The man's a pig, you know that?" Cheri said. "A genuine pig."

Marlin could smell liquor on her breath. It was early Saturday afternoon and he was in her apartment on the north side of San Antonio, a forty-minute drive from Blanco County. Sprawled on the couch was a thin man with a long greasy mullet, wearing a muscle shirt and grimy blue jeans. Cheri had introduced him as "Goat." It seemed they had a regular barnyard theme going. A pig and a goat.

"You want something to drink?" Cheri asked. "Cold beer?" Her smile had some mischief in it. "I won't tell."

"Iced tea would be good."

"Be right back."

While Cheri went into the kitchen, Goat turned the TV

volume down and placed his bloodshot eyes on Marlin. "You a cop?"

"Game warden."

Goat nodded. "That ain't so bad." His eyes floated back to a wrestling match on the screen. "I ain't much of a hunter myself."

"Not everyone is," Marlin said.

"Hunted birds with my dad once," Goat said. "Back when I was a kid. Then he fucking passed out and I had to drive us both home."

Before Marlin could continue his scintillating conversation with Goat, Cheri returned with a beer for herself and a can of Coke for Marlin. Coke, not tea. Close enough.

Goat rose from the sofa and announced that he "had to blaze." He kissed Cheri on the cheek, nodded to Marlin, and was gone. Cheri sat where Goat had been sitting. Marlin remained standing.

Marlin went back to his original question. "Have you seen Kyle lately?"

Cheri wrinkled her face in disgust. "Two days ago, out at his place. This is Saturday, right?"

Before Marlin could answer, she said, "You know I got married to that asshole, right? Last month in Vegas. Yeah, we were just screwing around. I know that. But we *were* married, all legal and everything." She grabbed a pack of cigarettes off the coffee table and lit up. "Then when we got back, I kinda figured he'd say, 'Okay, that was fun, but it was just a joke.' But he didn't, so I thought I'd see where it went. I mean, I really cared for the guy and everything. If you can believe that."

Marlin thought, *Yeah, you're all broken up about it. With a guy like Goat hanging around.*

She exhaled a plume of smoke toward the ceiling, then took a swig of beer. "So then on Thursday, he finally says, 'You know it was all bullshit, right? We're not really gonna stay married.'" She shook her head. "I'm glad I hadn't canceled the lease on this apartment yet. What a prick. Why the hell did he waste my time like that?"

She glanced at Marlin as if he might actually know the answer to that question.

"Have you talked to him since then?" he asked.

"Hell no, and I don't plan to, neither."

"Did he say anything to you about going out of town?"

Again, she cut her eyes his way. "Is he wanted for something?" Marlin could tell that she hoped the answer was yes.

"I just need to talk to him about some of the hunting that was going on out there," he said.

She watched him for a long time. "What kind of hunting?"

Why would she ask that?

Cheri said, "Because they weren't just hunting deer out there, I can tell you that much."

Bingo.

Marlin played it casual. "Yeah, we stumbled over some of the cages he had out in the stable. Now we're just trying to figure out what kind of animals he was keeping. More of a formality than anything. It's a safety issue. We gotta keep track of the animals coming into the county."

"Were they illegal?"

She was quicker than Marlin gave her credit for.

"What, the animals? Like I said, that's what I'm trying to figure out. That's why I want to talk to Kyle."

"And you think he left town?"

"Possibly. We found his car at the Houston airport."

Cheri's smile was wide now, revealing straight, strong teeth. She wagged her cigarette at him. "I think you're leaving something out, Mr. Game Warden." She leaned forward. "You tracked his car down at the Houston airport, all because of some wildlife violation? Right. I don't think so."

Marlin was starting to lose his patience. He was asking questions but not getting many straight answers. "Cheri," he said slowly, "I need to find Kyle. And if you know where he is, you need to tell me. Otherwise, you'll be facing some charges of your own."

She winked. "Wow. You're even cuter when you're angry."

Marlin ignored her. "So I'm going to ask some more questions," he said, "and your job is to answer them. Are we clear on that?"

"Jeez, I'm trying to help, okay? God, from good cop to bad cop in ten seconds flat."

"Then just answer my questions. When was the last time you saw Kyle?"

"Two days ago, like I said. Thursday morning, he told me we were getting annulled, so I got the hell out of there."

"And you haven't talked to him since then?"

"Not a word. Haven't heard from his lawyer yet, but I'm sure it's just a matter of time."

"Do you know where he is?"

"Nope."

"Or how we can get in touch with him?"

"Try his cell phone. Damn thing's practically glued to his ear."

Marlin and the deputies had already tried that number. Many times. "Did you know he was leaving town?" he asked.

"News to me."

"Any idea where he might go on a spur-of-the-moment trip? Any favorite places?"

"Vegas, mostly. Sometimes Cancún. That's about it, as far as I know." She stubbed her cigarette out in an ashtray. "Listen, I really gotta go to work."

"Last question. Do you know what kind of animals they were hunting at Kyle's ranch?"

Cheri stared into space, thinking. "Damn, I heard them mention something just the other day. What was it? Some kinda foreign animal. Like from Africa."

Marlin gave her a moment to rack her memory, but she'd apparently had a little too much to drink. Finally, he said, "Jackal?"

She snapped her fingers. "Yeah, that's it . . . I think. Something like that."

"This is really important, Cheri. I need you to be sure. Was it a jackal or not?"

"Yeah, a jackal. That's what they said."

"Did you—"

Cheri stood up. "I gotta change clothes real quick. You mind?" She was already unzipping her jeans.

Marlin nodded, and she stepped into the apartment's lone bedroom, leaving the door open. "Did I what?" she called out.

"Did you ever see any of the animals?"

Her voice was muffled, as if she was pulling a shirt over her head. "No, just the deer."

"Did you ever meet any of the hunters?"

"Uh-uh."

"You never met a man named Oliver Searcy?"

"Nope."

Marlin could hear drawers opening and closing.

"Go ahead," she called. "I'm just putting on makeup."

"You ever meet any of the hunting guides?"

"Just Duke," she said.

"You ever meet his brother, Gus?"

"I heard his name a few times, but I never met him. They said something was wrong with him."

She came back into the room, looking like a different woman now. She was wearing black leather pants, a tight white crop top, and red pumps. Her hair was teased and her rouge was as thick as the dust on Marlin's hood. Lots of eyeliner and ruby red lipstick. The stuff of an adolescent boy's daydreams.

She turned to go back into the kitchen, and Marlin noticed a tag on the neck of her crop top. She came out of the kitchen with another beer.

"You're not driving, are you?" Marlin asked.

"Don't need to. The club's a block away."

He said, "Earlier, when we were talking about the animals, you said you heard 'them' mention something. Who did you mean? Kyle and who else?"

"Duke. If anyone knows where Kyle is, it's Duke. He was there when I was leaving on Thursday."

"When Kyle broke up with you?"

"Well, no, but he must've just showed up right afterwards. I saw him in the driveway."

That meshed with Waldrip's story. He said he'd seen Kyle on Thursday.

Cheri turned to grab a small red purse.

"By the way, your top is on inside out," Marlin said.

She looked down and giggled. "Oops. Thanks." She pulled the half shirt over her head, facing Marlin. She was braless, and her breasts were truly a marvel of modern-day surgery. Marlin knew she was doing it just to shake him up, make him feel embarrassed. He felt his cheeks flushing, but he didn't turn around. Underneath it all—the implants, the clothes, the overdone makeup— she actually was an attractive woman. She didn't need all the crap to catch a man's eye. Her body was lean and toned, and Marlin hated to think what it would look like after another decade or so of drinking and drug abuse.

She got her shirt back in place, the afterimage still strong in Marlin's brain. Marlin met her eyes, and a grin curled on her lips. She reached into her purse and handed him a matchbook from a strip club.

"I waitress the early shift, but I dance from eight till midnight. Come on by," she said, her tone making it a dare. "I'll buy you a drink."

23

MARLIN STOPPED AT a pay phone, called Bill Tatum's cell phone, and relayed everything he had learned from Cheri, which wasn't much. Marlin wanted to question Duke Waldrip about the imported animals, but Tatum told him he probably wouldn't have much luck.

"Why's that?" Marlin asked.

"Doubt he'll talk to you. We've been getting nowhere, so Cowan called him earlier. He was happy to talk, until she mentioned the airport. Then he shut down. Said he was tired of answering questions, he didn't know what happened to Searcy, he didn't know where Kyle was, and he wanted us to—quote—'quit pestering him.' She asked about his brother, Gus, and Duke said to leave him alone, too. Then he hung up."

"Houston getting anywhere on Bobby's shooting?"

"If they are, I haven't heard. I spoke to Bobby earlier, by the way, and he sounds pretty good. He's coming home tomorrow."

"Already?"

"Well, they're transferring him to Blanco County Hospital. I think he raised enough hell that they agreed to move him. I think he's going crazy—all this action and he's laid up."

"I imagine so."

"Hey, hadn't you better get on home? Your big show starts in an hour."

Duke knew only one good defense lawyer—a potbellied older guy named Danny "Boots" Baker, the man Kyle had hired to try to keep Duke out of the pen after the armed robbery. Duke had done his time, but he knew deep down it wasn't Baker's fault. Outside of turning black and hiring Johnny Cochran, Duke hadn't stood a chance in that case. Too much evidence.

During the course of the trial, Duke had learned a few things about Baker. Most important, Baker wasn't concerned much about justice. His chief goal was to ensure that his clients walked, or did as little time as possible. He was a showman, too, a guy who could embellish, exaggerate, distort, coerce, cajole, and mislead with the best of them. Facts? Fuck the damn facts. When this guy got on a roll, he could paint an entirely different picture. Plus, he looked damn spiffy in a pair of alligator boots. He always wore them in the courtroom—hence the nickname.

Duke hadn't talked to Baker in several years, but he still had the lawyer's home number, and he decided to give it a try.

"Well, goddamn!" Baker boomed over the phone. "Duke Waldrip. How the hell are ya?"

Duke was surprised Baker remembered him. "I'm holding up," Duke replied.

"Holding up what? Not any liquor stores, I hope!"

Duke held the phone away from his ear as Baker's vigorous laugh filled the air. "Hell no. I learned my lesson on that."

"I sure hope so. What can I do for ya, Duke?"

Duke wasn't sure where to start. "Listen," he said. "I need to talk to you about something. It's kind of . . . touchy."

"Hell, touchy's my specialty, you know that. Fact is, I oughta put that right on my damn bidness card. You been arrested?"

"No, not y—uh, no, I haven't."

"Well then, before you spill the beans, two things. First, let's talk in hypotheticals. You follow me?"

"Not really."

"You know, like *what ifs*. You say, 'Danny, what if this mighta happened or that mighta happened.' Like you're telling me a made-up story about some imaginary guy. It's called hypothetical, 'cause we're talking about what might hypothetically happen."

"Gotcha."

"And secondly, I do need to tell you that I have a five-hundred-dollar minimum fee."

Duke winced. "Damn, Boots, for a phone call?"

"Yeah, I know, it's steep. But there ain't nothing I can do. It's set by the bar association."

Duke was fairly certain that Baker was lying—but that was part of the reason the man was so desirable as a lawyer.

"You just drop the check in the mail on Monday and we'll be square, all right? Plus, see, it makes me your official attorney. That way, everything you say is confidential."

"Okay," Duke grumbled. "Monday. I'll mail it."

"All right, then. What's your story?"

Duke chose his words carefully. "I'm wondering what might happen . . . if a guy—an imaginary guy—was suspected in a murder."

Duke noticed that Baker had gone unusually quiet. "Murder, huh?"

"Yeah."

"Let me grab a notepad. Okay, start at the beginning."

"Well, let's say this guy knew another guy, and they had a business dealing together. Say the first guy supposedly guided the second guy on a dove hunt. Later, the second guy is found dead in the woods."

"Then the question is—speaking strictly hypothetically now—did the first guy do it? Now understand, in a real case, I would never ask that. But here, we're just shooting the shit, right?"

"Yeah, right."

"So then . . ."

Duke took a deep breath. "Yeah, he did it. But it was self-defense. The second guy had a gun."

"If it was self-defense, why the hell didn't the first guy call the cops?"

"Let's say he has a record, and he was afraid. . . ."

"Okay, good enough. The cops have already interviewed our guy about this situation?"

"Yeah."

"What did they ask him?"

Duke quickly recounted his conversations with the sheriff and the game warden. Then he mentioned that the imaginary guy's best friend had gone missing and was apparently also a suspect in the investigation. Duke could hear Baker scribbling.

"So this third guy owns the ranch where the first two guys allegedly hunted?"

"Yeah."

Baker continued with a long list of questions: How was the man killed? How was the body moved? How many times had the hypothetical suspect been questioned? What did the cops say when he told them to leave him alone? Baker grilled him for nearly fifteen minutes. Duke answered all of the questions honestly, except for one.

Had anyone ever seen the first two guys together?

Duke thought of Gus and said, "No."

"Well," Baker finally said, "I'd say this guy is in fairly decent shape. If I was this guy, I'd sit tight and see what happens. Now, even speaking hypothetically, and even if it *was* self-defense, I would never advise a man to destroy evidence. Say, for instance, that the guy still had the dead guy's gun. Never in a million years would I tell him to get rid of it. Or to throw away the clothes he was wearing at the time. Things like that."

"I understand."

"Also, if I was this guy, I wouldn't talk to nobody about it, and I mean nobody."

"What about the cops?"

"Now, see, it's different with the cops. If they're looking into this guy's best friend as a suspect, they can subpoena him as a witness for a grand jury. But at that point, our imaginary guy would be smart enough to call his lawyer, you know what I mean?"

"Yeah, I hear ya."

"Speaking of which, you got my cell phone number?"

"No."

Baker recited it and Duke wrote it on a scrap of paper. "I'll stick it in my wallet."

"Hell, son, considering your history, you might want to tattoo it on your arm."

Johnson City was bustling—Marlin could think of no other word for it. It was an odd sight to see. Johnson City might work itself into a mild buzz on occasion, but it rarely bustled. Driving north on 281, Marlin could see that every parking lot was overflowing, and the number of out-of-state plates had grown. Strangers were rearranging gear in trucks, carrying bags out of convenience stores, chatting in large groups as they threw tailgate parties. The population seemed to have tripled overnight. Marlin recognized a couple of the vehicles from trespassing calls the night before. Apparently, issuing citations wasn't enough to send some of these folks home.

He pulled into the parking lot of the Kountry Kitchen and managed to snag a spot as an SUV pulled out. He was bone-tired, too weary to cook. He'd grab an early dinner, then a nap at home, and be ready for a busy night.

Inside, it was standing room only, something Marlin had never seen at the small café. He changed his mind and was about to leave, when a local hunter gave up his chair at the counter. That was fine with Marlin, and he could still see the large TV mounted on the far wall.

Marlin ordered a chicken-fried steak, then thumbed through a copy of the *Blanco County Record* that had been left on the counter. On the front page was a photo of Kyle Dawson, along with an article stating that the Blanco County Sheriff's Department was seeking Dawson as a possible witness in a current investigation. It wouldn't take a genius to conclude that the crime in question was the Searcy homicide.

Just as the waitress placed Marlin's plate in front of him, a hush fell over the crowd.

"Turn it up!" someone yelled.

Hard News Tonight was beginning, the catchy jingle blaring from the TV, complete with flashy graphics and synthesized sound effects. Marlin turned to watch.

The two anchors—a well-groomed male and a perky blonde—were so damn excited they could barely contain themselves. It seemed that George Clooney—a shot of George grinning bashfully appeared on the screen—had been spotted with a certain female celebrity. Could it be true love this time for George, the confirmed bachelor? they wondered. Well, everyone would have to wait in breathless anticipation, because they'd have that story later in the program.

What's more, Brad Pitt had been seen purchasing a very expensive diamond necklace at Tiffany's. Was it an anniversary present for his wife, Jennifer Aniston? The good ol' *Hard News Tonight* team would have the scoop, coming right up.

Plus—wonder of wonders—there was a new garment that promised to "shape and accentuate the curves of the buttocks." The show would feature an exclusive interview with the designer, Giovanni Capestrano.

"But first," the blond woman said, "tonight's top story."

"As you know," the man said, "we've been following the strange story of the chupacabra down in Texas."

"It's quite a tale, too," the blonde added. "But this is one that's becoming more believable by the minute! One body's been found, and local residents are wondering if the chupacabra is to blame—but the police aren't saying."

Marlin wondered what *that* meant. If anything, the interview would let the air out of this whole fiasco.

"There's been another sighting, though," the male anchor said, his face deadly serious. "And this time, we're getting a report straight from the horse's mouth—a genuine Texas game warden."

"For an update, we take you to our correspondent Rudi Vee, on location in the Texas Hill Country. Rudi?"

Now there was a daytime shot of Rudi Villarreal in front of the courthouse. Marlin figured they must have shot it sometime today. "Thanks, Brad and Bonnie. The story of the chupacabra continues to unfold here in Blanco County. Late yesterday evening, an exotic animal of some sort was captured by Game Warden John Marlin."

People whistled and cheered, and a couple of men patted Marlin on the back.

"Is it the chupacabra? Has the elusive creature finally been caught? If so, it will rock the scientific community to its core. Until now, biologists have maintained that the chupacabra simply does not exist. I caught up with Game Warden Marlin late last night and got the full story."

Now there was a cut to the shot from yesterday evening— Rudi and Marlin on his front porch. Marlin had to grin, seeing his modest home on national television.

The interview began just as Marlin remembered it.

"What can you tell us about the animal you captured late this afternoon?" Rudi asked.

"Uh, I can say it wasn't a native species for the area," Marlin replied.

The screen now showed dramatic shots of the rolling Texas hills—twilight shots, meant to create a sense of mystery. Eerie banjo music faded in. *Banjo music?* Marlin had never seen an authentic banjo player in his life.

Then Marlin heard his own voice again—and that's when the trouble started.

"Well, I personally had never seen anything like it in Blanco County before," Marlin continued, "and we've had some odd animals get loose over the years. There's been somewhat of a frenzy around here. . . ."

Marlin frowned. What the hell was going on? The quotes were out of order.

Rudi's voice: "Okay, but you think this animal—whatever it is—was responsible for the so-called chupacabra sightings? Is this the animal that people have been seeing?"

"I imagine so. Sort of a cross between a flying monkey and a large reptile. Huge red eyes . . . long fangs."

Oh, Jesus, those sons of bitches! They had twisted everything around!

The audience in the café was babbling with excitement now, people tugging on Marlin's sleeves, wanting to ask questions. Marlin could feel his pulse pounding in his temples.

Charlie felt sorry for the chupacabra. That *had* to be what he had been seeing around his house. They were talking about it in the newspapers and on TV, saying it was some kind of animal that had never existed before.

Charlie had almost gotten a clear view last night, but the animal was too skittish. It would hang back in the trees just after sunset, staring at Charlie from a distance, nothing but a dark shape. It was probably hungry and scared.

And everybody wanted to kill it.

Some of the boys at school had said their fathers were trying to hunt it. They had set up traps, too, and none of it seemed fair to Charlie. If it *was* a rare animal—maybe the only one of its kind—why would everyone want to kill it? That just seemed stupid. Capturing it would be okay, because then the scientists could study it and turn it loose later. That's what needed to happen.

Charlie wanted to go to the police and tell them what he had seen. But first, he had to be sure. If it turned out to be a coyote or something, they'd probably be mad at him. So he had come up with a plan. He had started collecting leftovers from dinner, and he would use them to lure the animal closer. Charlie would hide way up in a tree and see what happened.

Maybe he could finally see it.

Maybe he could save the animal's life.

* * *

There were only two motels in Johnson City, and Marlin spotted the white van at the second one. He parked next to the van and slammed the door of his truck. Damn it, he'd make them air a complete correction on the very next broadcast.

Driving over, he'd already been in touch with Ernie Turpin via radio. He'd told him what had happened, and warned him to be ready for a wild night. The false interview would only fuel the fire. People were already wanting to believe in the chupacabra—and now that a game warden had apparently verified its existence, things were likely to get out of control. The highways all over Texas were probably already crowded with more thrill-seekers heading toward Blanco County.

Marlin didn't even need to go to the front office to find out which room Rudi was in. He could hear her shouting. He followed the noise to a door that was cracked open about two feet.

"No you didn't!" Rudi was yelling into the phone. "You damn sure did not!" Her eyes grew large when she saw Marlin through the opening. "You are such an asshole!" she screamed, and slammed the phone into its cradle.

She was wearing jeans and a light sweater, no makeup. As she approached the doorway, Marlin could see that her face was flushed with anger. She held both hands up, palms out. "Before you say anything—"

"Before I say what?" Marlin growled. "That I should bring a lawsuit against you and your damn program?"

Rudi winced. "I wouldn't blame you."

"I want an explanation. What was that bullshit just now?"

She sighed and swung the door wider. "You want to come in?"

"Hell no. I just want to know who was behind that little prank."

"You may not believe this, but that was the first I saw of it, too. I had no idea—"

"You're right. I don't believe you."

Her eyes flashed. "You know what? I don't really give a damn whether you believe me or not. But it's the truth, and I know it, and that's good enough for me."

Marlin noticed an open suitcase on her bed. He nodded toward it. "So why were you making a quick exit?"

"What, you think I was running away?" she sneered, her voice rising. "Well, just so you know, I thought the crew and I were leaving tonight. After what you said in the interview, I figured we were all done here. The lead-out I taped for that story said there was no chupacabra, just some unidentified imported animal. Did you happen to notice that they didn't give me a wrap-up for the segment? We always do a wrap-up, but not this time. They just cut back to Brad and Bonnie."

In the chaos at the café, Marlin hadn't caught the end of the story.

Rudi turned and sat on the edge of the bed. "If it's any consolation, I got screwed, too. I can already see where this thing is headed, and it's not exactly going to do wonders for my career."

She was telling the truth, Marlin could see that. If she'd been in on the scam, she would have no reason to be honest now. But there was something about her; he could just tell she wasn't lying.

"Who, then?" he asked.

She took a deep breath and said, "Chad. He went behind my back. That was him on the phone, because he won't open his door." She turned toward the wall and screamed, "You son of a bitch!"

Apparently, Chad's room was right next door.

In spite of the situation, Marlin could feel a small grin creeping onto his face. "I don't blame him," he said.

She didn't smile back. She was even angrier than he was.

Marlin walked outside to Chad's door and pounded firmly. He could hear the TV in the room, but nobody answered. He pounded again. A curtain moved slightly, as if Chad had been peeking out, but he didn't open the door.

"You're gonna have to talk to me eventually, Chad," Marlin said loudly. "You can count on that."

He stepped back to Rudi's doorway. Her face was no longer red. Now she simply appeared dazed and tired.

"Okay, I believe you," Marlin said.

Rudi nodded, staring at the floor. "Thanks."

He stood there awkwardly for a moment. Then he said, "You want to grab some dinner?"

"So it worked?" Drew Tillman asked.

"Worked, hell," Marty Hoffenhauser answered, the phone pressed to his ear. "It was a miracle. It's, like, the burning bush, the Red Sea, and these amazing antlers. I've never seen Mike go at it like that. The man was an animal."

Drew chuckled.

"In fact," Marty continued, "he was so good, I'm thinking of redoing a few of the scenes from last week. We'd have to bump the deadline just a tad. . . ."

Marty didn't hear any protest from Drew.

"But I think it would be worth it. Really, Drew, once word gets out about this, we're talking about a huge buzz. This could be the best-selling video of the year. Hell, of the decade."

"What, exactly, is so different?"

"Man, it's like he's on speed, but without being so sloppy and spaced-out. He just doesn't want to quit." Marty was getting excited just thinking about the possibilities. "I know this sounds crazy, but I'm thinking of trying a one-hour take."

Marty could picture Drew sitting up straighter in his chair. "You serious?"

"Drew, listen to me. He needs no extra time between each, uh, episode . . . you know what I mean? Can you imagine that? Like he's eighteen years old. Yeah, plenty of guys can keep going after one, but I'm talking two or three times straight, with no down-time. See, we'd use one camera. No fades, cuts, dissolves, or anything. One long take. Can you picture the publicity that would generate?"

"That's never been done before, Mart." Marty could tell Drew was getting caught up in it now, dollar signs dancing in his head.

"I'm talking about a landmark film. Adult video history, and not just in our subgenre, either. *Fortune Nookie*—right up there with *Bouncy Bonnie* and *Sluts from Hell*. Now's the time, Drew."

There was a pause, but a much shorter one than Marty had

anticipated. "Go for it," Drew said. "If it sets us back a few days, don't worry about it. If we're gonna do this, let's do it right."

"Oh, we will," Marty said, more confident than ever before. "I may need to bring in some extra female talent. . . ."

"Do it. We're already seeing some revenue from *Little China*. I'll cut you a check and send it on Monday."

Marty pumped his fist in the air.

"One thing, Marty . . . these antlers . . . you know it's all in his head, right?"

"Hey, as long as it works."

"Yeah, yeah, but what I'm saying is, if you're gonna expect him to tape the biggest money shot of his career, you're gonna need the biggest damn antlers you can get your hands on. That's my advice. Find the hugest deer in that whole damn county."

24

IT TURNED OUT that Rudi's story was a hell of a lot more interesting than the handful of tidbits Marlin had seen on *Hard News Tonight*. She had been born as Hortencia Villarreal ("Rudi" was a stage name) in Sasabe, Mexico, just south of the Arizona border. Her parents had come to the United States—without papers—when she was five years old. It was not a smooth trip.

Like many illegal immigrants, the Villarreals had hired a "coyote," a guide who specializes in smuggling people across the border. It was a small group—just Rudi, her parents, her two older brothers, and an uncle.

The coyote was a U.S. citizen, and he managed to slip them across the river without incident. But the trip didn't end there. The arrangement was that the Villarreals wouldn't pay until the coyote had delivered them to a safe house.

"What he didn't tell us," Rudi said, "was that we'd have to hike across forty miles of desert first."

Marlin had heard horror stories like that before. Every year, scores of hopeful immigrants died on ill-fated journeys into the United States. All they were looking for was a better life, and they were willing to risk everything to get it.

Marlin placed his hamburger on the truck seat beside him. Neither of them had wanted to deal with the hordes of excited chupacabra hunters, so they had chosen the drive-through at Dairy Queen. They were parked at an overlook beside the Pedernales River.

"Did you have enough water?"

"A gallon apiece."

Not nearly enough, Marlin knew.

He glanced over at her, unsure whether he should ask questions or let her tell it on her own. Dusk was beginning to cloak the hills, and he knew it was just a matter of time before the radio began squawking his name.

"The first day was cloudy," she said. "I remember that and a few other things. The rest my mother told me later. We made it about halfway across, our water was already running low, and then the coyote told my dad there was a misunderstanding about the price. He wanted three times the original amount. My dad knew it was a scam, of course. The guy had probably pulled that same trick a dozen times. They argued, and that turned into a fistfight. My dad was small, and not very strong, so my oldest brother, Miguel, jumped into it. He was only fifteen or sixteen then, but damn big for his age. Long story short, the coyote pulled a knife, and then Miguel took it away and beat the guy to death there in the desert."

Marlin could see the pain in Rudi's eyes. Or maybe it was fear.

"We all stood and watched. None of us had seen that kind of violence before, and we were all wondering if this was what we could expect of living in the States."

For a few moments, both of them listened to the river rushing over its shallow, rocky bed. The sun was just beginning to dip behind the hills to the southwest, painting flat-bottomed clouds a brilliant orange.

"Where did you end up?" Marlin asked softly.

"That night—and this was the luckiest thing that ever happened to any of us—it rained hard for a couple of hours. We used everything we had—hats, shirts, pants—to collect rainwater and fill our jugs. Then we took off walking again, all night long. When the storm broke, my dad used the stars to lead the way. We made it to a highway right at sunrise. A rancher stopped and gave us a ride." She smiled. "I remember that part—all of us piled into the back of his truck, looking like we'd just come from some kind of hellish camping trip."

"Your brother?"

She nodded. "My mother was worried that the police would be coming after him, so they decided he'd head further north and hook up with us later. We were working at the rancher's place. . . . We lived there for about a year. We got one call from Miguel when he was in Tucson, and then we never heard from him again."

Marlin couldn't even imagine the heartache that must have caused—the family wanting to believe that Miguel was okay, but never knowing for certain. Marlin had felt that way himself plenty of times, though to a lesser degree, when his father—a game warden before him—had stayed out all night chasing poachers. Even as a child, Marlin had understood the dangers that accompanied his dad's job. Occasionally, a poacher would resist arrest, maybe fire a shot or two, but his father would always downplay it. Marlin would get the truth from articles in the newspaper, and he came to realize that his dad was putting his life on the line every time he ventured into the woods. It made him proud, but it also made him fearful. Unfortunately, those fears were realized in 1976 when a poacher decided he'd rather shoot it out than face a stint in jail.

"I'm sorry," Rudi said, as if she'd somehow breeched the bittersweet memories playing through his head. "In case I didn't say it earlier, I'm sorry for the broadcast tonight. I didn't know that—"

Marlin shook his head. The incident seemed so unimportant now. "Not your fault."

"He's done it before, you know," she said. "Chad, I mean. He's phonied up stories like that, taken quotes out of context." She laughed, and Marlin was grateful for the change of mood. "One time, Anthony Hopkins had dinner with the queen of England. We'd interviewed him about it, and the reporter asked what it was like to be in the company of the queen. But Chad cut and pasted the answer from another question about some weird dessert they'd had. So the answer was, 'Somewhat smelly, actually. Quite unpleasant.'"

Marlin thought he remembered some kind of uproar about that a few years ago.

"You can imagine how pissed Hopkins was," Rudi said. "His attorney called and raised holy hell, and Chad had to air a complete retraction the next day. Blamed it on an editing error."

Marlin glared at her, trying to keep a straight face. "And this is the kind of thing you do for a living?"

She reached over and gave him a light swat with her fingertips. "Hey, I didn't do that one, either. And you gotta admit—it's pretty funny."

Marlin shrugged. "Well, maybe, in a lowbrow, very juvenile sort of way."

Rudi rolled her eyes. She tried a British accent: "'Somewhat smelly, actually. Quite unpleasant.'"

Now Marlin couldn't help but smile.

Rudi laughed with him. "Yeah, see, that's what I thought."

He decided she was even more beautiful without her Hollywood facade. He found her eyes, and held them a few seconds longer than he'd planned to.

"It's easy to fake something like that," she murmured.

Marlin reached for his burger, then stopped, thinking about what she had just said. She was right. She was absolutely right. Just about anything could be faked if the illusion was good enough.

Charlie pedaled faster than he had ever pedaled before. The convenience store on the outskirts of Johnson City was about three miles away, and he was already halfway there.

He had seen the chupacabra! His plan had worked, and he had seen it!

It sure was a funny-looking animal, unlike anything he'd ever spotted around Blanco County. It had come right up and eaten the leftovers, completely unaware of Charlie perched in a nearby oak tree.

Charlie's first thought was that he could tell the police now. Then he began to wonder, even now that he'd seen it, whether they'd believe him. He was just a kid, after all, and most kids had pretty wild imaginations. They might think he was making it all up, or that he was mistaken about what he had seen. That's when he decided he should try to get a picture of it. Then he'd have proof. The problem was, he didn't have a camera he could use. His stepdad owned some kind of fancy camera with a long lens, but Charlie wasn't about to mess with that. But he knew he could buy a disposable camera at the convenience store. He didn't know how much it would cost, but he had saved up about seventeen dollars from mowing neighbors' lawns. Surely that would be enough.

Charlie followed Flat Creek Road until he reached with Highway 290. His mom would tan his hide if he rode his bike on the highway, so he stashed it behind some trees, then walked the remaining half mile to the store.

"Evenin', Charlie," a voice called as he entered the store. "Ain't you out kinda late?" It was Bernice, the old lady who worked nights. She was propped on a stool behind the cash register.

Charlie shrugged. "I'm supposed to come up here and buy a camera," he said, stretching the truth a little.

"You mean one of these?" As Bernice reached back to pull a disposable camera off a rack, two men entered the store. One of the men was about the size of most regular men, maybe a little smaller. But the other man was huge, like a Dallas Cowboy lineman. Charlie didn't know if he had ever seen a man that big in person. They walked down the candy aisle without even glancing Charlie's way.

"This here's one of them Kodaks," Bernice said, lowering her reading glasses. "Let's see . . . twenty-four exposures. Water-proof, too."

She handed it to Charlie.

"Bernice, you all outta pork rinds?" the smaller man called out.

"Naw, Harry moved them to the next aisle. Next to the peanuts."

"How much is it?" Charlie asked.

"Nine ninety-five," Bernice said. "I got some of them Fujis, too, if you wanna look at those."

The directions on the camera looked pretty simple. All you had to do was point it and push the button. Then you turned the little knob to advance the film for the next shot.

"If you need the flash," Bernice said, pointing, "you just push that button there until that little light comes on. That means the flash is ready."

The two men approached the counter and plopped a large carton of beer down next to the cash register. They also had four bags of pork rinds, six different candy bars, and a box of dough-nuts. "Gimme a coupla packs of Red Man, too," the small one said.

Charlie saw that Bernice seemed to study them, like a school-teacher eyeing a tardy student. "What kind of trouble y'all got planned tonight?"

"Hell, Bernice, if I tole ya, ya wouldn't believe me," the small one said. The big man still hadn't said anything, and Charlie was beginning to wonder if he could even speak.

Bernice rolled her eyes, just like Charlie's mom sometimes did when she was being playful.

The man leaned in closer. "Don't tell anyone, but we're gonna catch the chupacabra," he whispered.

Charlie turned his head in surprise, and the small man frowned at him.

Bernice laid two packages of chewing tobacco on the counter. "Yeah, you and everybody else in the county."

"No, see, there's a difference. We actually know what the hell we're doing." Both of the men laughed, and Bernice shook her head, pushing buttons on the register.

"What you want to catch that thing for, anyway?" she said.

"For the good of the scientific community, what else?" Both men laughed again, but Charlie couldn't figure out what was so funny.

"Twenty-nine forty-four," Bernice said, bagging everything up.

The man handed her a couple of bills, told her to keep the change, and turned for the door. "Wish us luck," he said.

"You're gonna need it," she mumbled as the door closed.

"I'll take this one," Charlie said, shoving the camera forward.

Bernice rang the register again and said, "With tax, ten seventy-five."

Charlie handed her a ten and a one, got a quarter back, and darted out the door, saying, "Bye, Bernice" as he went.

The two men were sitting in an old Ford truck, both doors still open, the engine running. The big man had already torn into a package of pork rinds.

"Excuse me," Charlie said, standing by the passenger's side.

Both men glared in his direction. "Yeah?" the big man said. He *could* speak after all.

"You really gonna catch the chupacabra?" Charlie asked.

"What's it to you?" the smaller man said.

"Uh, it's just that, well . . . everybody has been talking about shooting it. You said you were gonna catch it instead."

"So?"

Charlie shuffled his feet nervously. These men weren't very nice. Maybe he was making a mistake. "I know where it is," he said quietly. "I can help. We could catch it together."

The driver reached out and turned the engine of his truck off. "Where you live, boy?"

Charlie gestured to the west. "Down Flat Creek Road."

The smaller man gave his friend a quick look, and Charlie wondered if they thought he was lying.

"I'm Red O'Brien," the smaller man said, finally smiling, being a little more friendly. "This here's Billy Don Craddock. Billy Don, give the kid one of your candy bars."

"Do what?"

"Give him a candy bar."

The big man—Billy Don—didn't move.

"Damn, don't be so stingy," Red said as he grabbed the sack.

"A deer decoy?" Bill Tatum said. "Really?"

"I'm checking on it," Marlin replied. "I left a message with Howell to call me back. But it's the only thing that makes sense. Searcy was an experienced hunter, so if he'd shot at a real live deer, chances are good he would've hit it—and that would've ruined the whole scam. But what about a decoy? I mean, Searcy's fake deer mount had to be attached to something, right?"

Game wardens across the country used roadside decoys to bait potential poachers. Marlin himself used one that featured a head, ears, and tail that could be moved by remote control. Poachers had shot at it from as close as thirty yards.

The phone line buzzed as Tatum considered the possibility. "So Searcy shoots at a decoy. Then what? When he walks up on it, he's gonna see it's a fake."

"Yeah, I'm still working on that part."

Tatum paused for a moment. Like many of the deputies, he was a hunter, though Marlin knew he was in it for the venison, not the trophies. Still, though, Tatum was aware of the wild antics that took place in the world of high-dollar whitetail hunting. "I guess it's worth checking into," Tatum said. "One problem, though. We've already searched Dawson's house, all the outbuildings. . . ."

"But you haven't searched the entire ranch."

"Not hardly."

"If I wanted to hide a decoy, I think I'd leave it out in plain sight."

"Just stick it out somewhere in the woods."

"That's what I'd do. Especially a decoy without any antlers on it. Nobody looks too hard at a doe."

"One other problem . . ."

"What's that?"

"Even if it *was* a decoy," Tatum said, "it doesn't bring us any closer to knowing who killed Searcy."

25

AS MARLIN HUNG up the pay phone, lightning danced in the sky to the west and the wind began to pick up. He ducked into his truck. "Sorry that took so long," he said. "And actually, there are a couple more calls I need to make, so maybe I better drop you off back at the motel."

"I can't believe you don't have a cell phone," Rudi said. "You want to use mine?"

"Thanks, but—"

"Or you could just use the phone in my room."

By now, despite his anger earlier, Marlin had decided he liked this woman. Plus, using her phone *would* be easier than going back to his house. "You don't mind?"

"Nope. Not like I have a lot on my schedule. I won't be taping any new segments anytime soon, that's for sure."

Marlin dropped it into DRIVE and pulled out. His first call—one he should have made right after the *Hard News Tonight* broadcast—would be to Gerald Klein, a producer with KHIL, a TV station that covered the Hill Country. Marlin wanted to get the word out that the broadcast had been faked, and Klein would be happy to have the scoop dropped in his lap.

Next, Marlin would call Jacob Daughdril, a helicopter pilot who was frequently hired by area ranchers to conduct deer censuses. Marlin wanted to look for the possible decoy, and if there *was* a way to scan Kyle Dawson's ranch quickly, it would be by air—assuming the weather cooperated. Marlin tuned his scanner to the National Weather Service. A front was moving their way, and temperatures were expected to drop by fifteen degrees. The front was dragging some thunderstorms with it.

"That should put a damper on things tonight, huh?" Rudi said. "Maybe keep some of the nuts indoors."

"If I'm lucky."

"See, I've always had an interest in mammals and reptoids and whatnot," Red said. The kid was sandwiched between Red and Billy Don. His bike was in the back of Red's truck. "And now, to think we might be the first to discover something that's sort of a half-breed between the two . . . well, that's just plumb exciting."

Almost as exciting as the speedboat I'm gonna buy when we catch him, Red thought.

"It's reptile," Charlie said.

"Do what?"

"The word is *reptile*."

"That's what I hear. Part reptile, part mammal. Could be damn dangerous, too, which is why you're gonna have to leave everything to us. You just show us where you seen him, and we'll take care of everything after that. When we catch him, you'll be the first to know."

Red knew the key was trust. If the kid was willing to trust him and Billy Don, they'd be home free. "Care for another candy bar?"

Billy Don glowered at Red over the kid's head.

"Yeah, sure," Charlie said.

Billy Don dug a Snickers out of the sack and grudgingly handed it over.

"Now . . ." Red said. "Where exactly on Flat Creek do ya live?"

Jimmy Earl Smithers popped a small pill into his mouth, gulped from a bottle of Mountain Dew, and shoved his truck into a lower gear as he approached the edge of Johnson City. He'd made damn good time on this trip—from New Orleans to El Paso in twenty hours flat—but there was some nasty weather biting him in the ass as he headed back to the east. His return trip was likely to be slower. Colder, too, according to the bursitis in his shoulder. Cold and wet—a trucker's nightmare. He'd have to ease off some, maybe get back to New Orleans by this time tomorrow night. Then he could sleep again. But right now, what he needed was some grub to keep the pill from eating a hole in his stomach.

He backed the big rig down and stopped at the traffic light in front of the Kountry Kitchen. The parking lot was jam-packed, so he left his truck idling across the highway, halfway off the wide shoulder. He wouldn't be inside for long. Shouldn't be a problem. Cops never did give him trouble for parking like that.

He shut the door to his rig, began to cross 290, then turned around. He had almost forgotten the deer mount in his truck. It wasn't any use to him, so he figured he might as well ask around in the café, see if anyone knew the man who owned it. Kyle Dawson—that was his name.

Inside, Jimmy Earl squeezed his way through the crowd—damn, he'd never seen the place this busy—and found a stool at the counter. He placed his order, then doctored his coffee just the way he liked it.

"That shore is a nice rack." It was the guy to Jimmy Earl's right. A younger guy, maybe mid-twenties, eyeballing the deer mount, which Jimmy Earl had placed on the countertop, drawing a frown from the waitress. There wasn't anyplace else to put it. "You shoot that round here?"

"Naw, it ain't mine. In fact, I'm looking for the guy who left it in my truck. Name's Kyle Dawson."

The young man shook his head. "Kyle's on the run, what I heard. Some kinda murder investigation."

"You're kidding me. Murder?"

"Damn right."

Jimmy Earl got the chills for a second. Had he had a killer right there in the cab of his truck?

Now the man to Jimmy Earl's left spoke up. "Naw, he's just a witness. Dale, don't be spreading a buncha bullshit around."

"That's not the way I heard it. Cops're after him."

"Well, yeah, they're after him, but as a witness. Don't you read the paper?"

The younger man shrugged.

"Either of y'all want this mount, then?" Jimmy Earl held it up. "Good-looking drop tine right here. It'd look damn nice hanging on your wall. I'll let it go for five hundred bucks."

"Shee-yit," said the man on the left.

"Don't think so," said the man on the right.

Now a third guy poked his head forward. Some kind of slick guy with round eyeglasses and a ponytail. He was sitting two stools down from Jimmy Earl, next to the young guy. "Excuse me, did you say you're selling those antlers?"

"Ain't no use to me."

"May I ask where you got a deer that large?"

"Damn, boy, ain't you been listening?" Jimmy Earl laughed, showing he was only being good-natured, and the men on either side of him joined in.

The waitress placed a plate in front of Jimmy Earl. Eggs, hash browns, and a side of Virginia ham. Just like home.

Jimmy Earl had the first forkful halfway to his mouth when the ponytailed guy said, "Will you take a check?"

"I'm seriously thinking about quitting," Rudi said. "You think I ought to quit?" She was lying on top of the bedspread in her motel room, leaning back against the headboard, her shoes kicked off on the floor.

Marlin was sitting in a chair next to a small table against the wall. He'd finished his calls thirty minutes ago, and they had been talking ever since. He had a handheld radio with him, but no calls had come his way. The only action on the airwaves was about a traffic accident in the southbound section of 281. Somebody had probably lost control in the rain. It had started coming down, and coming down hard, just after they'd made it back to the motel. As far as Marlin was concerned, he was officially off the clock unless a call came in.

"Rudi, I barely know you. I don't think I ought to be giving you life advice just yet," he said.

"Aw, what a cop-out," she said, slinging a pillow at him. "You've been listening to me babble all night, haven't you?"

He tossed the pillow back at her gently. "I haven't had much choice."

She smiled. "Smart-ass. Anyway, you do know me now. A couple hours is all it takes. I truly am that superficial."

He smiled back. "I don't think so."

She placed the pillow neatly in her lap. "Anyway, I've told you all about working on the show, about all the shit Chad has pulled . . . so basically you have all the facts. Damn it, I just need a fresh eye. If I told my friends back in L.A. what I was thinking, they'd say I was crazy. But they're all wrapped up in the Hollywood bullshit. I need someone on the outside looking in."

"What would you do if you quit?"

She stared into space, thinking. "There are a couple of ways I could go. I could keep trying to get on one of the major news shows, or maybe cable—something on CNN or MSNBC."

"But . . ."

"But what?"

"You tell me. You say you could try it, but you don't sound very enthused about it."

"Yeah, I don't know." She smoothed the pillowcase with her hand. "Maybe I'm getting kind of burned-out. I mean, I know the real network shows aren't anything like *Hard News Tonight*, but if there's even half the bullshit . . ."

"That would suck," Marlin offered.

"Yeah. It really would. I don't know if I'd be prepared for a disappointment like that. Up to now, I've only wanted to do the news."

She looked up, her eyes dancing. "You know, you somehow feel like you're doing something worthwhile when you're informing people . . . telling them what's going on around the world. People *need* information. On politics, world events, the economy. It makes me feel good to know I'm helping people form opinions on things. I don't mean the bullshit on HNT, but real news. I did the local news back in San Diego for a while, and that was great. But God, for the last four years . . ."

For a few moments, both of them listened to the rain drumming on the roof of the motel.

"What was the other thing?" Marlin asked. "You said there were a couple of things you could do."

She cast her eyes downward again. "Don't laugh, okay? I've never told this to anyone but my mom."

She glanced at Marlin and he nodded.

"I think I might be a pretty good journalist."

"You mean like newspapers?"

"Or magazines. *Time. Newsweek.* I don't know, maybe it's a stupid idea, but I majored in English in college. Yeah, I know I haven't ever even written a newspaper article, but I *can* write. At least I think so."

Marlin had an idea this woman could accomplish just about anything she set her mind to. "I think it's worth looking into," he said.

"Really?"

"Why not? You're sick of what you're doing now, right?"

"Absolutely."

"Well, how long do you stick with something like that? If you just sit around and wait for something better to come along, it probably won't. You need to find it yourself. My opinion anyway. You asked."

Rudi said, "I do have some money saved up. I could take some time off, kind of regroup."

"There you go."

"It's a big step."

"You're a big girl. You can handle it."

A quick giggle escaped from her mouth. "That's exactly what my mother always says."

"Wise lady. Listen to her."

A tremendous clap of thunder shook the small room.

"Wow," she said when the windowpanes finally stopped vibrating. "So let it be done," Rudi said. She glanced at the television set. "What time does the news come on? You want to watch, right?"

"About ten minutes."

"Well then, tell me more about being a game warden. How long've you been one?"

"Twenty-one years," he said. Marlin could practically see Rudi doing the math in her head, calculating his age from his answer. He figured she was in her mid-thirties, though she appeared even younger.

"That's a long time. Always here in Blanco County?"

"Born and raised." He went on to describe what it was like living in a small Texas town. Sure, the pace was slower, but that's what made it so special. Instead of strip malls and Yuppie bars, you had feed stores and beer joints. Most everybody knew everybody else . . . or one of their cousins. There was a sense of community you didn't find in places like Austin or San Antonio.

"What about work, though?" she asked. "I mean, doesn't it get kind of boring sometimes?"

"Yeah, I wish." He told her being a game warden meant more than writing tickets for hunting and fishing violations. In a county this sparsely populated, he was frequently involved in all sorts of interesting cases—from DUIs to drug busts all the way up to homicides.

"Like this Searcy thing?" she said.

"What, you don't think it was the chupacabra that got him?" Marlin said, laying on the sarcasm.

She snorted.

"Yeah, like Searcy," he said. "I'm helping with that a little. Not full-time or anything. I just help out when the sheriff needs me." He took a quick peek at the clock on the nightstand. "You mind flipping the news on?"

Rudi grabbed the remote and turned to KHIL. After a couple of national reports, the anchor said: "*In area news, the chupacabra chaos continues in the Hill Country. But now, perhaps the strangest twist yet. A segment this evening on the national television show* Hard News Tonight *included an interview with the Blanco County game warden, John Marlin. In the interview, Marlin appeared to be confirming reports of a lizardlike animal that has been allegedly sighted around the county. However, we spoke to Marlin earlier and he states that the report was edited in such a way as to be deliberately misleading. Marlin strongly denies that any evidence has been found to support the existence of the chupacabra. He would not comment on the possibility of any legal action against the program. But Marlin did say that anyone attempting to trap or shoot an exotic animal could possibly be charged with interfering in an investigation.*"

"Well done," Rudi said, her voice sounding much closer than before.

Marlin turned, and Rudi was standing next to him. She reached out and placed a warm hand gently on his cheek. "Thanks for the advice earlier."

Several years ago, Red had mail-ordered two camouflage hunting caps with small penlights attached to the bills—designed to allow a hunter to keep his hands free for field-dressing a deer after sundown. Red soon realized, however, that if the caps made it easy to gut a deer in the dark, hell, it'd be just as easy to shoot one. So he had tried it out. He'd hide in a tree near his deer feeder, wait till he saw shadowy shapes moving in the moonlight, then flick the light on and open fire. A big ol' double-aught surprise from his twelve-gauge. Worked like a charm.

Tonight, though, the hunting caps were serving another purpose. While the rain was coming down—in cold sheets now—the lights were helping Red and Billy Don make their way through the woods with the hog trap. Son of a bitch seemed even heavier this time around.

Billy Don wasn't happy about the whole situation. Every time lightning would flash, Red could see Billy Don across the top of the trap, madder than a ... well, madder than a wet three-hundred-pound redneck.

Billy Don dropped his end of the trap. "Damn, Red, let's take a breather."

It was raining so hard, Red could barely make out the words. Cold water was spilling off Red's cap in torrents, running down his neck, under his shirt, and into his Wranglers. A school of guppies could set up house in his Red Wings. His toes were going numb.

"Fifty more yards to the truck," Red hollered. "Don't puss out on me now." Red wasn't going to let Billy Don's grumpy mood get him down. No, not now. Things were looking too good for that. The boy had shown them exactly where he'd been seeing the chupacabra—just across the fence line, on a ranch behind his house. Red was familiar with the ranch, owned by some rich guy who drove a fancy imported car. The same guy who was wanted by the law, at least according to the rumors Red had been hearing. The guy's place didn't have a gate, just a cattle guard. That meant easy access. All Red and Billy Don had to do was set the trap.

26

MARLIN WOKE AT 3:47 A.M. with the heater running and a warm body in the bed next to him. Unfortunately, this warm body had a hairy face and bad breath. At some point, Geist had climbed up into the bed with him, probably skittish from the thunderstorms. The dog was snoozing soundly, her snout about two inches from Marlin's nose.

Wide awake now, watching bolts of white-hot lightning split the sky, Marlin had time to think.

Howell Rogers, the Burnet County game warden, had never called him back. Or if he had, the message had been lost. When Marlin had gotten home, the clock on his VCR was blinking, meaning the power had gone out. And the backup battery in Marlin's digital answering machine was dead. He'd have to try Howell again in the morning. Jacob Daughdril, too. If this weather kept up, the chopper would be grounded.

Then Marlin thought about Rudi. Intriguing lady. Smart and funny. After caressing his cheek, she'd given him a light kiss on the lips, then pronounced herself officially bushed. Marlin had taken the hint and cleared out.

"You leaving town?" he asked her at the door.

She pondered it for a few seconds. "No, not yet. Hey, I figure if I'm gonna quit, I might as well enjoy a vacation, right?"

She'd given him the number for her cell phone.

The solitary black boar weighed 360 pounds on the hoof and had a thick plate of scar tissue on each shoulder from years of fierce territorial battles. Its tusks were gnarled and chipped from repeated clashes with one particular opponent that was equally large. That hog, however, had not survived the winter, and now the black boar enjoyed dominance in its home range. It roamed the hills unhindered, hunting, scavenging, and breeding at will.

Tonight, as it trampled through the underbrush in the rain, it heard familiar grunts and squeals. Some primitive trigger in the boar's brain was released, and it knew two of the lesser boars—its own offspring, in fact—had located food.

It found the pair rooting in the dirt around a large stone. The alpha boar charged forward, and the smaller boars gave way and vanished into the night.

Curious, the boar nosed and rooted around the stone, which seemed to be sunk into a hole. An enticing scent wafted up around it. With one powerful flip of its tusks, the boar dislodged the stone and cast it aside. Underneath, a dark pit. The aroma grew stronger.

The hog proceeded snout-first into the hole, but its massive shoulders prevented it from entering. It tried to force its way inside with sheer strength, but the opening was too small.

So it did what was only natural.

It began to dig.

* * *

When Marlin woke again, it was 7:20. He started a pot of coffee, then dialed Howell's number. Marlin knew Howell and his wife well; they would have been up for several hours by now.

"You got my message, huh?" Howell said.

"No, actually, I had some trouble with my answering machine."

"Well, hell, you're a damn psychic. You should know exactly what I said."

"How's that?"

"Tell me something, smart boy. How in the hell did you know I'd lost a decoy in that burglary?"

Marlin mulled it all over as he drove.

Even if Marlin did find a decoy on Kyle Dawson's ranch, it wouldn't do much for the case, just as Tatum had pointed out earlier. It could've been Dawson who pulled the scam, or Duke Waldrip. In fact, *both* of them could have orchestrated it, with only one of them being involved in the murder. What mattered was finding out where Searcy had gone when he returned to Blanco County after discovering he'd been ripped off. Who had he come to see? That was the blank that needed to be filled in. But with Dawson missing and Waldrip stonewalling, that was a tall order to fill.

Marlin wouldn't even have been pondering the whole matter if he hadn't found himself with some unexpected time on his hands. The rain, combined with last night's news broadcast, appeared to have put a serious dent in the enthusiasm of the chupacabra crowd. Driving through town, Marlin noticed a marked decrease in the amount of traffic. Parking lots were no longer full. There were no crowds at the convenience stores. Darrell, the dispatcher, hadn't reported any trespassing calls. Maybe the buzz was dying down.

But something is still running loose.

He was worried that whatever had attacked Beulah Summerall's dog on Friday night might be something more dangerous than a jackal. On one hand, he kept wondering whether he should alert the public. On the other, he didn't want to cause panic unnecessarily. And he'd already seen how quickly the public's collective imagination could go wild. He'd decided it would be best to wait until the forensics came back. Then he'd know what he was dealing with, assuming the animal hadn't been captured or killed by then. Via the news broadcast, Marlin had warned the public to leave the animal alone—but that was chiefly a ploy to minimize trespassing calls and other mischief. If a rancher saw another jackal, for instance, and shot it dead, Marlin would have no problem with that. In fact, it might be the best thing that could happen.

Meanwhile, Jacob Daughdril had, as Marlin expected, declined to fly in the current weather. At the moment, there was a break in the rain, but more was on the way. Weather radar showed a second line of powerful thunderstorms trailing the first.

So Marlin had decided to give it a shot by truck. He'd drive the roads of Dawson's ranch and see what there was to see.

Mike Hung said something in Chinese that Marty Hoffenhauser couldn't understand. But judging from the way his eyes were bulging, he was quite pleased. Hung took the massive trophy in his small hands and gazed at it in awe.

"Yes. Velly good."

"I thought you'd like it," Marty said. "Listen, Mike, we've got a big day ahead of us. Wanda is gonna be here in a little while, and we've got a couple more treats in store for you, too. We've hired some additional talent. Other actresses."

Mike's face was like a kid's on Christmas morning.

"I want you to be ready to—"

But once again, Mike Hung was up and gone. Seconds later, Marty could hear the drone of the saber saw inside the small trailer.

Marty walked to the hangar, inspected the set, and sat down to enjoy a cup of coffee. Three industrial-size space heaters were humming away, slowly raising the temperature in the cavernous structure. He thumbed through a copy of the local newspaper, enjoying a rare moment of solitude.

A few minutes later, Tony, Marty's sound technician, wandered over and joined him. "What's going on, chief?"

Marty was about to tell him what was in store for today. Marty's mood was upbeat, his biggest star was ready, willing, and extremely able, and the whole damn crew was about to make adult-video history.

That's when he heard a horrific scream . . . followed by shouting. Then a longer scream.

"The hell was that?" Tony asked.

Marty stood just as Bill, the cameraman, came racing into the hangar. "Jesus, Marty, you better come have a look at this!"

"What's going on?"

"It's Mike, man. He's got some kind of saw blade sticking out of his eye!"

"Heads up, Bubba, we got company," Billy Don said.

Red peeked at his rearview mirror and saw the game warden, John Marlin, thirty yards off his rear bumper. Of all the shitty luck.

Red gave a small wave through the back window, but Marlin didn't wave back.

"What now?" Billy Don asked.

"Gimme a minute. For now, hold this." Red passed him the half-finished beer he'd just been drinking. Maybe it was God's way of telling them they shouldn't crack the first cold one before noon.

They were on Flat Creek Road, heading toward Kyle Dawson's place. The rain had slackened, and Red wanted to use the opportunity to check the trap. Last night, they'd simply ignored the sheriff's sign at the ranch entrance, which warned people to stay out. Couldn't do that again, not with Marlin on his ass.

After a few miles, when it became obvious that Marlin wasn't going to pull them over, Red's nerves settled. "We'll just mosey on down the road until he pulls over somewhere," Red said. "Then we'll give it a couple and head back."

Billy Don grunted an affirmation.

A minute later, Marlin *did* pull off the road—right into the

Macho Bueno Ranch. "Well, shit," Red said. "There goes *that* plan."

Bill Tatum hated to admit it, but it was probably time to call in the Texas Rangers. As the investigative branch of the Texas Department of Public Safety, the Rangers provided assistance to smaller police forces on an as-needed basis. Unfortunately, with the Searcy investigation at a standstill, the need was quickly becoming apparent.

Tatum had been a deputy in Blanco County for ten years, with eight years in Gillespie County before that. He had no aspirations to become sheriff, and he had supported Bobby Garza wholeheartedly for the two years Garza had been in office. Bobby seemed to handle the politics and tackle the administrative issues with ease, whereas Tatum wanted nothing to do with any of that. Something he did have in common with Garza, though: He wanted the Blanco County Sheriff's Department to be a capable and highly independent agency. Neither of them wanted to have to call for help when things got nasty. He and Garza agreed that the more forceful and competent the department became, the less crime they'd see.

There was evidence to support their theory, too. In the past decade, the Hill Country had seen a tremendous rise of meth labs in rural areas. Even Blanco County had had its problems. But under Garza's watch, the number of drug-related crimes had taken a nosedive. Simply put, most of the dealers had either been locked up or run out of the county, and new dealers were afraid to replace them. Why set up shop in Blanco County, where justice was swift, when it'd be easier to ply their trade somewhere else?

Some crimes, though, didn't respond to this type of approach— or any other. Homicide was one of them. There weren't many murders in Blanco County to begin with, but when they did occur, they were almost always spontaneous, products of anger, jealousy, or stupidity. The good news was, the lack of planning made these crimes easier to solve. Physical and circumstantial evidence were usually available by the boatload, and it was just a matter of figuring out who and why.

Not always, though. Sometimes you came across a tough nut like the Searcy case. They'd tried every possible tack they could think of—and nothing had panned out.

Tatum had called a meeting of the investigative team this morning, and now, with the room quiet, he bluntly stated his feelings. It might be time to call in reinforcements.

Kyle's ranch was crawling with deer; that much was certain. But after two hours, Marlin hadn't spotted any that failed to go on alert as his truck approached. None of them stood motionless in the brush—glassy-eyed and stiff-legged—waiting to be discovered. Granted, Marlin had to stick to the roads or risk getting bogged in the mud, so he couldn't survey the entire ranch. He'd get a more thorough look when he went up in the chopper. Now, though, as the rain began to fall again, Marlin called it quits and left the ranch.

He wheeled back onto Flat Creek Road and drove east, planning to stop for a late breakfast in Johnson City. As he passed the Waldrips' driveway, he glanced toward the house and saw a man sitting in the shadows on the covered front porch. He brought his cruiser to a halt. *Worth a shot*, Marlin thought. He reversed and pulled in. Approaching the house, he recognized Gus Waldrip swaying gently in a rocking chair. Marlin parked, stepped from his truck, and climbed the porch steps.

"Gus Waldrip, right?" Marlin asked, buttoning his down vest.

"How ya doing, Sheriff?" Gus said. The guy was all smiles, as if he'd just heard a good joke. Something odd about it, though. Like the guy'd inhaled too many paint fumes. The temperature was in the upper forties and the guy wasn't even wearing a jacket.

"I'm not the sheriff, Gus; I'm the game warden. John Marlin, remember? We've met a couple of times."

Gus nodded but didn't answer.

"You been out of town lately?"

"Here and there."

Marlin gestured toward a second rocking chair on the porch. "Mind if I sit down?"

Gus grinned from ear to ear. "Knock yourself out."

The voices on the porch woke Duke from his nap on the couch. He cracked the curtains a smidge and saw John Marlin sitting in one of the rockers, just as comfortable as you please. Son of a bitch had made himself right at home. His back wasn't more than two feet away from the window.

Duke's heart was picking up speed, so he took a deep breath to calm himself. He knew this moment was bound to happen eventually. They'd get to Gus, ask him all kinds of questions . . . and Duke would have to sit back and see if his brother could weather the storm. With any luck, Gus would tell the game warden to go fuck himself.

Duke listened in.

"You being gone, you missed a lot of excitement around here, you know that?" Marlin said.

"I'm not supposed to be talking to you," Gus said.

Good boy, thought Duke.

"Why's that?"

"Duke says somebody got killed and y'all are running in circles on it. Trying to pin it on him."

Gus was ad-libbing a little. Duke didn't have a problem with that, as long as Gus didn't get in over his head.

"I'm not here to talk about that," Marlin replied.

"Good. I don't have nothin' to say anyhow. I don't know nothin'. You want more than that, you can talk to my attorney."

Way to go, bro!

"That's fine, Gus. No problem."

There was a long pause, and Duke was tempted to peek out the curtain again. What the hell was happening out there? Had Marlin left? Then Duke heard him speak again.

"Let's talk about something completely different, then. You ever meet a guy named Oliver Searcy?"

Duke saw what Marlin was doing—trying to trick Gus into talking. Duke realized he was holding his breath, waiting for Gus to answer. *You're smarter than that, Gus. Don't let him fool you!*

"Yeah, I think so," Gus finally said.

Duke quietly slipped down the hallway to retrieve his shotgun.

27

RED AND BILLY Don waited a good ten minutes after the game warden left before they chanced it. Sneaking onto that ranch was probably some sort of felony, Red knew, especially with the sheriff's warning sign staring them in the face.

Red crossed the cattle guard and came to a stop. "Run back there and toss that sign in the weeds, will ya? I figure if they catch us out here, we can say we didn't know better."

Billy Don pulled his hunting jacket tight and clambered from the truck. He yanked the sign from the stone column and flipped it into the woods.

Five minutes later, Red had negotiated the slick roads of the ranch all the way to the south pasture. The trap was no more than two hundred yards from the kid's north fence line, but Red had decided it was better to take this more indirect route through the ranch. As far as Red could tell, the kid, Charlie, hadn't said anything to his parents about the chupacabra. No sense in getting them involved, because sure enough, they'd want a share of the loot. This way—with Kyle Dawson gone—Red could move the animal and claim he'd caught the chupacabra on his own land. How, exactly, would he move it? Well, Red hadn't gotten to that part yet. First things first.

Red reached behind the truck seat and came out with a couple of rain ponchos.

"Hell no. I'm staying in the truck this time," Billy Don said.

"The hell you are."

"I had enough of this bullshit last night. Go check the damn thing yourself."

Red held up one of the ponchos. "And here I went to the trouble of buying an extra-extra-large, just for your oversized ass."

Billy Don shook his head. "Leave the heater running."

"Fine." Red wrestled with the poncho and finally got it in place. Then he opened his gun case, removed his Colt Anaconda, and tucked it under the folds of his poncho. "Be right back. Don't play with yourself."

"Did you see him?"

"Dunno. What'd you say? Oliver Searcy?"

Duke was back at the window now, the shotgun leveled at the curtains. Double-aught buckshot. One blast was all it would take.

"Your brother met him, Gus. I'm just wondering if you ever did, that's all. Where did you meet him?"

"Duke said he met him?"

"Yeah, over at your office. No big deal, really."

"Now wait, isn't that the guy that was killed?"

No answer. Duke risked a look through the curtain. He could see over Marlin's shoulder, and the game warden was unfolding a piece of paper. A flyer with a photo of Oliver Searcy on it. Duke had seen them posted around town earlier in the week. But Marlin had folded this one so that the MISSING headline wasn't showing.

"You know him? I think your brother said something about hunting with him," Marlin said. "Said the guy wanted a big whitetail."

Duke was in full panic mode now, the shotgun trembling in his hands. *The son of a bitch isn't playing fair!* If Gus said he knew the guy—or, even worse, if he said Duke had hunted with Searcy—all hell was going to break loose.

But Gus didn't say anything.

"You met him, right?" Marlin asked. "Out at Kyle Dawson's place, or maybe over at your office?"

Still nothing from Gus.

"I'm even thinking y'all might have hunted with him, but you're both a little worried about telling the sheriff. There's no reason to be nervous at all. Take a good look, Gus."

Marlin held the flyer up for Gus to see.

"What kind of deer did he get?" the game warden asked. "Wasn't it a big ten-pointer with a drop tine?"

How the hell does he know that? Duke pressed his finger against the trigger, ready to give the oh-so-slight tug it would take to send the buckshot roaring out the barrel.

And then Gus said, "Beethoven."

Duke watched Marlin, who craned his head as if he was listening for music. Duke's knees nearly buckled in relief. *Jesus, he's listening for the goddamn music!*

"Squab," Gus said.

"Pardon?"

"Alabaster."

Red picked his way carefully through the trees, trying to follow the same path as the night before. He wanted to get a good look at the trap from a distance, so he wouldn't spook anything they might have caught. He couldn't believe Billy Don was such a big baby, complaining about a little rain. Now where was that trap, exactly? The clumps of trees were all starting to look the same. Should've marked the spot somehow last night, with some surveyor's tape or something. Red thought he'd gone too far, so he doubled back and came at it from a different direction. Then he saw a deep footprint in the mud. Had to be one of Billy Don's. Red's feet wouldn't have sunk that deep, and he didn't wear shoes the size of a pancake griddle. Now he was back on track. Had to be getting close. Okay, there—a huge oak he remembered from the night before. The trap was just on the other side of it. Red eased along, moving slowly, holding his revolver out in front of him. He wanted to be ready, just in case. He finally saw one corner of the steel cage, but he couldn't see the inside of it. Just a few more steps . . . and then he saw the trap was empty.

Damn.

"What's the gun for?"

Red nearly fainted. He swiveled his head, searching for the source of the voice. *There.* That damn kid, hiding in some bushes.

"Shit, Charlie. You trying to give me heart failure?"

"I saw you drive by, so I climbed the fence." The kid stepped from the brush and pointed at Red's gun. "What'd you bring that for? I thought you said you weren't gonna shoot it."

Red looked down at his weapon, which was now dripping with rain. "What, this? Well hell, boy, what was I gonna do if I ran into a big ol' hog? I'm getting a little too old to climb trees."

"You don't mind that I talked to him?" Marlin was in the interview room at the sheriff's department, sitting across the table from Bill Tatum. The other members of the team had gone back in the field after the meeting.

"Hell no," Tatum said. "He probably wouldn't have talked to any of the deputies anyway. Glad you took a shot."

Marlin had recounted his entire conversation with Gus Waldrip. Twice.

"'Squab'?" Tatum asked.

"I think that's what he said. Man, I've seen some strange stuff, but *that* was weird. One minute we're talking, the next he's completely zoned out."

"Faking maybe?"

"If he was, he belongs in Hollywood. I've only met him a couple of times, and he's always been pretty quiet, but I've never seen . . . that."

"But right at first—he *did* say he'd met Searcy?"

"Well, yeah, sorta. Then he said no." Marlin blew on the mug of coffee he had poured minutes ago.

Tatum was eyeballing him—looking, Marlin knew, for some sign that they'd learned something useful. Marlin hated to let him down. "Bill, I don't know. It's like talking to a six-year-old. Fantasyland, you know? I don't think we can trust any of it."

Tatum expelled a long breath and leaned back in his chair. After a pause, he said, "This thing's eating me up. I'm this close to calling the Rangers."

Marlin nodded. "Hey, man, if you gotta do it . . ."

There was a rap on the door and Ernie Turpin stuck his head in. He was smiling. "Y'all got a minute?"

"Come on in," Tatum said.

Turpin entered and closed the door behind him. "I just drove over to the hospital to see Bobby. . . ."

Marlin remembered that the sheriff had been transferred to Blanco County Hospital that morning.

"Anyway," Turpin continued, "I was parked near the emergency room entrance, and as I was walking in, I see this guy walking out—carrying a deer mount." Turpin smiled again. "I want y'all to meet someone."

He opened the door to reveal a civilian standing in the hall—a man around fifty, with round eyeglasses and a ponytail. He was carrying a green garbage bag. Turpin ushered him into the room. "This is Marty Hommenhoser."

"Hoffenhauser," the man said. "Hi."

"Mr. Hoffenhauser," Turpin said, "why don't you tell them what happened?"

The man plopped the garbage bag onto the table. "A friend of mine got injured. Pretty bad, too. Might lose an eye."

"What happened?" Tatum asked.

"An accident with a saw. The guy who sold me this thing didn't warn me about the bolt."

"Why don't you just start at the beginning?" Tatum said.

Hoffenhauser looked from Tatum to Marlin and back again. "I know this is kinda weird, but I bought a deer head from a guy. I was over at the Kountry Kitchen. . . ."

At that point, Marty Hoffenhauser paused, then pulled the trophy deer mount from the bag. He continued explaining, but Marlin, for one, wasn't hearing a word. He was leaning forward, then standing, anxious to see the amazing, familiar specimen on the table in front of him.

"Ernie, go grab that X ray," Tatum commanded, interrupting Hoffenhauser.

"Got it right here."

"You want to keep your job, don't you?" Chad Reeves asked. "I mean, if I remember right, your wife just had a baby a couple of weeks ago."

The man on the phone, Marvin something, didn't answer right away. "It was twins," he finally muttered. "And that was four months ago."

Whatever. All Chad remembered was that somebody had brought a cake and everybody'd made a big deal about it. Like babies weren't born every single goddamn day. The man was nothing but a video editor anyway—just one of dozens who had passed through the *Hard News Tonight* offices over the past few years. Chad couldn't imagine why they always left so quickly.

"You're asking me to lie for you," Marvin said, sounding like a whiny ten-year-old girl. *For God's sake, whatever happened to employee loyalty?* Chad wondered. Chad himself was as loyal as they came. When the conglomerate that owned *Hard News Tonight* was bought by a German media tycoon, had Chad's dedication to the job wavered? Hell no. He'd been willing to fall right into line, goose-stepping all the way to Berlin for the salary he was receiving. Sure, those German execs were a little more tight-assed than Chad was used to, but hey, those were the fortunes of the entertainment war. They had made one thing clear, though, right after the Anthony Hopkins debacle. They didn't want sleaze. They didn't want to be viewed as the on-air equivalent of the *National Enquirer.* They liked innuendo, they loved titillation, and, as far as they were concerned, rumor-mongering was just another tactic to boost ratings. "But for

Gott's sake," the chairman had chastised Chad, "no more lies. Ve vill haff no more lies." Chad was worried that if this game warden fiasco came to light, the Germans might not return the loyalty he himself had shown.

"No," Chad said to Marvin. "No, that's not it at all. All I'm asking you to do is to believe what I'm saying. And what I'm saying is that it was all Rudi's idea. I didn't even know what she was planning until the segment aired. End of story."

"But . . ." Marvin said. "But *you're* the one who called me. *You're* the one who told me what to do."

Chad snorted. "I don't think that's relevant at all."

"Of course it's relevant!" Marvin shouted. "How much more relevant can it get?"

Chad let the phone line hum for a few seconds. He wanted to let the man calm down and get his head around this whole idea. He'd come around. "Marvin, I'll be blunt with you. I think you have a promising career ahead of you. You've been a hell of a team player. Don't think I haven't noticed. You're the kind of guy people can count on. The kind of guy who advances lickety-split up the corporate ladder. Know what I mean? Raises, promotions . . . before you know it, you're the executive producer. You following me?"

Silence. But Chad knew he almost had him. He just needed to push him over the edge. Make him realize how this industry really worked. "Marvin," Chad said, "have I ever told you how I got my big break in this business?"

It was the same deer mount. Marlin had no doubt about that. They all knew it, even before they had taken an X ray for comparison. Which was why, four hours later—after fingerprinting it, verifying the results, and then typing up the proper documents— they were in front of Judge Hilton, asking for a warrant. They'd interrupted his dinner, but he'd been happy to carry a leg of fried chicken into his den with him. The judge's eyes roved from Tatum to Marlin, then to Turpin and Cowan. "Out in force tonight, ain't we?" he said as he studied the papers.

Tatum gave a nervous laugh. Nobody wanted to sit this one out. They were all vested in the case, and each of them knew it could hinge on the next few minutes. The silence was overwhelming as the judge methodically reviewed Tatum's affidavit. Turpin shuffled anxiously on Marlin's right. Tatum remained stock-still, military all the way.

Finally, the judge placed the papers on his desk and removed his glasses. "First Kyle Dawson and now Richard Waldrip, huh?" he said. He clasped his hands together. "Why?"

"Sir?" Tatum said, speaking for all of them.

"What's changed? Here, let's back up for a minute. When you came for that warrant on Dawson, you seemed to have your ducks pretty well lined up. Searcy was dead, Dawson was long gone, and you had hard evidence—that lock from his garage. Hell, it all looked good to me. Now you've got this new evidence—this deer mount—and you want a warrant for Waldrip's place. I'm not following the logic here."

"Sir, Duke Waldrip's fingerprints were all over the inside of that deer mount."

None of the fingerprints on the antlers themselves had matched Duke Waldrip's. The mount had obviously passed through too many hands by that point. But then they had removed the deer hide and exposed the prefab taxidermy form made of synthetic materials. There they'd found what they were looking for.

The judge nodded. "That may be, but that doesn't mean he's a murderer, does it?"

Nobody spoke. The judge wasn't expecting an answer.

"You haven't located the trucker yet?" Hilton asked.

"We're working on it," Tatum replied.

Marty Hoffenhauser had been able to give a fairly good description, including a cap with an arrowhead design the trucker had been wearing. If they could just find the trucker, perhaps he could shed some light on who was in possession of the mount before he was.

"Folks, what you've got so far is circumstantial evidence—and I'm not saying it isn't promising stuff. But from where I'm sitting, it doesn't add up to probable cause yet. I'm not even taking the deer mount into account at this point, because Searcy might very well have hunted with Waldrip, and Waldrip could've done the taxidermy for him. Waldrip might've even cheated the guy, but I'm afraid that just ain't enough. All it says is that Waldrip lied to y'all—something ex-cons are inclined to do on occasion."

"Sir, what about Gus Waldrip?" Tatum asked.

"What about him?"

"Well, when John talked to him, Gus indicated that he *had* met Oliver Searcy, which goes against what his brother told us."

The judge's gaze fell on Marlin. "That right?"

"Well, yes, sir . . . at first."

"'At first'?"

Marlin snuck a peek at Tatum, and the deputy's eyes were pleading: *Go on, stretch it a little.*

But Marlin couldn't do it. "He changed his mind later," he told the judge. "He's a pretty confused guy."

Hilton passed the papers back to Tatum, unsigned. "Sorry, folks. If you found anything, it'd get tossed later. You'll thank me for this. Believe me."

28

AT HOME, MARLIN took a quick shower and changed into jeans and a flannel shirt. He was sorting through leftovers in the fridge when the phone rang.

"How about dinner again?" Rudi asked. "My treat this time. I'm celebrating."

"Let me guess. You quit."

"Actually, no. I was fired, if you want to get technical."

She promised to tell him the full story when she picked him up. "I've got the keys to the rental car," she said with a wicked laugh, "and I'm not giving it back. Before I'm done, I just might make a cross-country tour."

She said she'd be there in thirty minutes, and they hung up. Marlin turned to feed Geist, who was hungrily watching his every move, when the phone rang again. It was Tatum.

"I talked to the trucking company, this outfit called Arrowhead Freight, out of Cary, North Carolina. Anyway, you hear about that ten-fifty on Two Ninety last night?"

Marlin groaned. This morning, he'd gotten the details about a wreck that had happened during the storm. A trucker had failed to make a curve, plowed through a guardrail, and plunged into a steep culvert. "Our guy?"

"Would you expect anything else? I swear, just when we think we're getting a break . . ."

"Jesus, you're saying he died?" The last Marlin had heard, the trucker had been taken to a hospital in San Antonio.

"No, but he's still unconscious, in critical condition." Tatum had left word with the nursing staff to call if there was any improvement. "Hey, listen," he said. "I've got this devious little plan running around in my mind. Tell me what you think. You haven't lifted prints from those metal bowls in Dawson's stable, right?"

"No, I figured it was kind of low on the list of priorities."

"Yeah, but here's what I'm thinking. Let me dust 'em, and if we find Duke's prints, we'll bust him for the illegal animals. Except I'll run him in instead of you. And I won't tell him what I'm arresting him for."

Marlin chuckled. "Damn, that *is* devious."

By the letter of the law, a suspect didn't have to be formally charged until arraignment. And normally, Marlin would be the one making an arrest for a game violation. If Tatum did it, Duke would definitely be confused.

"If he happens to think he's getting busted for the Searcy homicide . . . well, that's certainly not my fault," Tatum said. "That just might rattle his cage a little, get him talking again."

They both knew the fingerprints on the bowls probably weren't enough to convict him for hunting illegal animals, but in this instance, that wasn't the point. "You cool with that?" Tatum asked. "Might spoil your case."

"No problem." The homicide was much more important.

"I'll check for prints," Tatum said. "If we pick him up, I'll let you know."

* * * *

"How about that one?"

"Ease off the gas, Red, and let me see what the hell it is."

"I think it's a dead coon."

"Naw, it's just a—damn, stop for a second, will ya? Huh. It's a shirt."

"A shirt?"

"Yeah, someone's work shirt or something."

"You sure?"

"I know a shirt when I see one. Keep on moving."

"Any other day, you're driving along, there's dead shit all over the road. Now—when we need a coupla good animals—nothing."

"Man, this is just stupid. That squished armadilla should be plenty."

"Then why didn't anything show up last night?"

"Dunno. The rain?"

"Damn, what is it with you and the rain? Animals don't care about the rain. No, I'm thinking the chupacabra don't like armadilla. Can't be any easier than eating a damn lobster. Big ol' shell to crack and everything."

"Shit, when've you eaten a lobster? You can't even spell *lobster*."

"I've eaten my share of lobster."

"I'm gettin' hungry."

"See, what we'll do is load that trap up with a whole damn smorgasbord of roadkill. Coons, possums, cats, whatever."

"Smorgasbord of roadkill. Sounds like a Black Sabbath album. I like that."

"So will the chupacabra."

They picked Johnson City's one and only pizza joint, where they were the sole customers. Riding over in the light rain, Marlin had noticed that the town was back to its quiet Sunday-evening self. Very few cars on the road. Most of the restaurants were already closing for the night. Now, over slices topped with pepperoni and jalapeño, Rudi told Marlin what had happened.

"I've been pretty much ignoring Chad since last night. Barry already flew back. I took him to the airport in San Antonio this morning. He's as disgusted as I am, and he said he was going to start looking for another job. Anyway, my phone rang a few times this afternoon, but I didn't answer it. Finally, at about two o'clock, Chad knocks on my door, saying he won't leave until we talk. So I let him in. He's looking all nervous, which is completely out of character for Chad. He's usually Mr. In Control. I ask him what he wants and he says he wants to talk to me about, quote, 'responsible journalism.' Get this: He starts going off about how we have a sacred pact with our viewers and hypocritical bullshit like that. I ask him what the hell he's talking about, and he says, 'Based on last night's segment, I'm afraid I have no alternative but to let you go.' His exact words."

"You're kidding."

"I wish I was. That self-righteous prick."

"What'd you do?"

Rudi smiled. "I threw the phone at him. The whole damn thing."

"You get him?"

"Hell yeah, I got him. But there's more. It bounced right off his chest, and it made this weird noise, like it hit metal or something. So he fishes into his front pocket and comes out with one of those miniature tape recorders. *He was taping the conversation.*"

Marlin could see where this was headed. "You better watch yourself. He's trying to pin it on you."

She nodded. "Then he says, 'You're paying for this thing, you know.' Can you believe that asshole?"

"You got a lawyer?"

"You better believe I do. Called her right after. And let me tell you, she's one tough bitch."

Marlin gave her a deadpan look. "I have no doubt. Takes one to know one."

Rudi tried to glare at him, but she couldn't hold it. They laughed in unison.

"God, I feel so good, though!" she said. "Am I supposed to feel this good, without a job and everything? I mean, here I am, unemployed, two thousand miles from home, and I feel great!"

"Plus," Marlin said, nodding toward the front window, "you've got a luxury sedan with unlimited mileage."

"Damn straight I do. Grand Canyon, here I come. Then maybe Vegas, or up to see the redwoods in Oregon. Wanna tag along?"

Marlin knew she was kidding, but it was a tempting thought. Just to be able to pick up and take off, without a care in the world.

They finished the pizza and—just as she'd promised—she insisted on paying. Outside, the air was crisp, though not as cold as the night before.

She stopped for gas, and Marlin got out to pump it.

"Quite the gentleman," she said, coming around to stand beside him. "I'm going to run inside and get a Coke. Want anything?"

Marlin noticed the steam from her breath as she spoke, and how she had her hands tucked deep into her jacket pockets for warmth. Their eyes met, and for some reason Marlin couldn't determine, it was an oddly intimate moment. Like they were old lovers, stopping for gas, following the same routine for the thousandth time. "How about a six-pack of beer?" he said.

She took one step closer. "Are we going back to your place?" she asked softly.

"Yeah, I think so. I'd say it's time for a little celebration."

Her jacket came off first, followed by his. Their lips were pressed together, tongues dancing.

Rudi shrugged her blouse off her shoulders, and Marlin placed his hands on her rib cage. "Too cold?"

She shook her head and untucked his flannel shirt, running her hands up his torso, her fingers combing through his chest hair.

He caressed her breasts, tracing the lines of fine lace on her bra, slowly sliding his hands around to the back.

"It hooks in front," she whispered, her breath making Marlin's ear furiously hot. "Hurry."

29

"DAMN, I FIGURED you'd have called me by now," Jacob Daughdril, the chopper pilot, said. "Have you been outside? Clear skies, light wind. It's perfect."

It was 7:55 A.M., and Marlin was still in bed, wishing the weather hadn't changed quite so quickly. He cradled the phone to his ear and slid his free hand over the curve of Rudi's hip. "I'm ready when you are," he said, hoping Daughdril would be tied up until the afternoon.

"I'll be at your place at nine."

Marlin hung up and told Rudi his plans for the morning. "He's picking me up in an hour."

She stretched and yawned as she glanced at the clock on his nightstand. "I'd say that's plenty of time."

* * *

Daughdril's chopper was a Robinson R22 two-seater, and he touched it down expertly in a clearing on Marlin's seven acres. As they gently lifted back into the air, Marlin could see Rudi's rental car parked in front of his house. She'd promised to be there when he got back. "Where am I gonna go?" she asked. "I'm a woman of leisure now, remember?"

"We doing a deer count this morning?" Daughdril asked as he guided the chopper north. Marlin had told him the destination of their mission but not the objective. "Not exactly," he said. He told the pilot they would be attempting to spot a deer decoy on a thousand acres of wooded ranchland. Not an easy task.

Daughdril gave a low whistle, but he didn't ask any questions.

Marlin had ridden in helicopters plenty of times, but he could never get over the view. From one thousand feet, he could see thirty or forty miles in every direction. He'd been up at six thousand feet one moonless night and had spotted the glow of lights in Houston, two hundred miles away. Truly an awesome experience.

The flight to Kyle Dawson's ranch took about seven minutes, and Daughdril asked Marlin what kind of pattern he wanted to fly. "Is north-south okay," the pilot asked, "so we won't have to face the sun?"

"Fine by me," Marlin said. "I realize we can't check every nook and cranny on the place, so let's just see what we can see. Let's start on the western fence line."

"Ten-four."

On the first pass north, they spotted at least a dozen deer, plus a flock of wild turkeys congregated at a feeder. Most of the animals became skittish when the chopper flew over, ducking for cover or, in some cases, simply sprinting away from the thrumming of the rotors. A few deer stood in place, but Marlin could always see them crane their necks to stare at the strange object in the sky.

Coming back south, Daughdril pointed out a pack of coyotes sneaking along the bottom of a ravine. Gazing through his binoculars, Marlin figured it to be a female with five or six juveniles born the previous spring.

They continued cutting swaths up and down the ranch, with

each new pass pushing farther to the east. Fortunately, Kyle Dawson's father had removed most of the scrub cedars and other brush from the ranch years ago; otherwise, surveying the property by air would be, for the most part, a futile effort.

As the survey continued, Marlin asked Daughdril on several occasions to decelerate for a look at a particular deer. Each deer, though, bounded away, disappearing into a distant oak motte or field of tall native grasses.

"What the hell you think he's doing?" Billy Don asked, staring out the window on the passenger's side. He and Red were parked on the shoulder of Flat Creek Road, along the southern border of the Macho Bueno Ranch.

Red recognized the helicopter as one belonging to a man named Jacob Daughdril, who lived just south of Round Mountain. Every ten minutes or so, the chopper would approach from the north, reach the road, and turn around. It was obvious that Daughdril was scoping the ranch from one end to the other.

"What you wanna bet he's trying to rustle up the chupacabra?" Red said, not feeling too happy about the whole situation.

It was damn unfair, a man taking to the air like that. What chance did he and Billy Don have against a chopper? Daughdril could get a good look at the entire ranch that way, whereas Billy Don and Red were limited—legally anyway—to what they could see from the county road. Worse, they couldn't even check the trap until Daughdril left, because he was the kind of guy who'd raise a ruckus about a trespasser.

When their path took them over Dawson's house and the horse stable, Marlin asked Daughdril to fly in an expanding circle above the surrounding acreage. Maybe the decoy was stashed nearby, although Marlin was beginning to wonder if there *was* a decoy at all. Truth be told, he was beginning to lose his ambition for the project, knowing that even if he found the decoy, its evidentiary value would most likely be nil.

They had been in the air for more than an hour now, and their fuel supply was mandating no more than fifteen more minutes over the ranch.

"All right," Marlin shouted over the noise of the engine, "let's take a few more passes over the eastern pastures and call it a day."

Daughdril gave him a thumbs-up.

Duke heard the *whoop-whoop-whoop* of the chopper and stepped onto the back porch of the Waldrip homestead.

Jesus, what the hell are they up to now?

Duke had been following the news, and he didn't think the copter was looking for the chupacabra—not after John Marlin's warning on Saturday night. Most of those idiots had already left town. What a bunch of wackos, thinking an animal like that actually existed. All that uproar over a hyena. Stupid spick who reported it had done Duke a favor, keeping the cops busy with a bunch of bullshit.

So what, then, was that damn chopper doing flying over Kyle's ranch? According to the reports, the cops were calling Kyle a "person of interest" in the Searcy case—which meant to anyone with half a brain that he was a suspect.

He heard a car door out front. Gus coming back. Duke had finally made the decision: He was sending Gus away for a while. Not up to Alaska or anything that drastic, but maybe over to see a cousin in New Orleans. All in all, it was the smartest thing to do. Keep him tucked away somewhere until the heat was off.

Duke had sent Gus to the bank to get some cash, then began to pack a suitcase for him. Get him on a bus this very afternoon.

Then Duke heard another car door. And another.

What the hell?

He entered the house just as someone pounded firmly on the front door. "Sheriff's department!"

Duke peeked through the front curtains and saw three patrol cars in the driveway. He quickly turned and went out the back door.

"Hello, Duke."

Standing to the side of the porch was Bill Tatum, his hand resting on his revolver.

Just as they were making a final turn over the northeast pasture, Marlin saw it.

"Hey, Jacob, swing back to the left, will ya?"

Down below, something was catching the sunlight, twinkling like a jewel.

"See that thing shining?"

Daughdril veered toward the object, then began to hover overhead.

Marlin sighted through his binoculars.

Was that what he thought it was? He dialed up to maximum zoom. The object came into focus—and sure enough, it was a toaster. An everyday household toaster, lying in a remote field, half a mile from the nearest house. Weird.

"John, we gotta head out," Daughdril said, tapping the fuel gauge.

Marlin nodded, and Daughdril, eyeing his gauges, banked the craft back to the south.

As the chopper began to ascend, though, something else caught Marlin's eye. A shape, instantly recognizable by its contours, spilled across a rough caliche flat.

"Jake, stop! We're gonna have to land."

"But—"

"I'll have the deputies bring more fuel, but you gotta set her down!"

What Marlin had seen was a human body.

Bill Tatum calmly took a seat across from Duke Waldrip in the interview room. "Just give us a few minutes here, Duke. We want to set up a video camera." He gazed at Waldrip, and Waldrip stared back, unblinking.

To Tatum's surprise, Waldrip hadn't asked for a lawyer so far or said anything about not answering questions. Tatum had seen it before, though. Sometimes it was ego, or maybe it was stupidity, but guys like Waldrip often decided they could get through the proceedings just fine on their own. Waldrip, even with his criminal background, might not realize the smartest thing he could do was keep his mouth shut. The toughest offender was the type who forced the police to *prove* their case. More often, though, the break came when a suspect incriminated himself, or said something that inadvertently led to hard evidence against him.

Rachel Cowan entered with the camera, stood it on its tripod, and wordlessly ran a microphone to the table separating the two men. She pressed the RECORD button and said, "Anything else?"

"How about a decaf latte?" Waldrip asked.

Cowan didn't even look his way.

Tatum smiled. "No, that'll be it, Officer Cowan. Thanks."

She closed the door behind her, and Tatum let the silence settle in the room for a moment. Then he recited Waldrip's rights for the second time. "You understand your rights?"

"This is bullshit."

"Mr. Waldrip, do you understand your rights?"

"Yeah. Whatever."

"Thank you."

Tatum began to thumb through a pile of paperwork on the table in front of him, feigning interest. The truth was, the papers had nothing to do with Duke Waldrip. But Tatum wanted the man to think a great deal of evidence and documentation had been amassed against him. Likewise, the deputies had covered one wall of the room with materials meant to rattle the suspect: an enlarged photo from Waldrip's driver's license; a mug shot from his arrest for armed robbery; an aerial photograph of Maggie Mason's ranch, where Oliver Searcy had been found, and another of Kyle Dawson's Macho Bueno Ranch. Copies of interviews with Searcy's friends and family were thumbtacked to the wall, and meaningless notes had been scrawled all over them. The intent was intimidation—to make Waldrip think the full force of the Blanco County Sheriff's Department had been dedicated to bringing him to justice. It wasn't far from the truth. So far, Tatum had noticed Waldrip's eyes wandering to that wall on several occasions.

After a full ten minutes, Tatum finally placed the paperwork back on the table. "This is big stuff, Duke. Big stuff."

Duke shrugged. "I don't even know what the hell you're talking about. You still ain't told me what you arrested me for."

"You'll be arraigned tomorrow," Tatum said. "Meanwhile, I want to give you a chance to tell your side of it. Hell, Kyle's run off and left you holding the bag. You're the one we got, so you're the one that gets charged. But see, that's not so bad. You can tell us what happened, and Kyle's not around to say you're lying."

Tatum was walking a thin line here. Later, if the videotape was used in court, the questions had to be seen as applying to the illegal animal charge. If Waldrip misinterpreted them, though, and began giving information on the Searcy homicide, that was all fair game.

"The big question is," Tatum said, "was Kyle even involved? Right now, to be honest, Duke, everything's pointing at you. Maybe there are mitigating circumstances, though, or maybe the evidence isn't showing things the way they really were. All of us want to be fair here, and nobody wants to charge you with something you didn't do. That's why it's so important to tell us what happened."

Tatum did his best to present a cool demeanor, but inside, his heart was firing like a piston. The bluff came down to this moment. If Waldrip was going to give them any kind of toehold on this case, it would be now.

Waldrip looked up at the wall, his eyes roaming over every scrap of paper, and then back at Tatum. "You ain't got shit, do ya?"

Never in a million years, Tatum thought, *would an innocent person ask that question.* It renewed Tatum's feeling that the investigation was on the right track. In his experience, innocent men didn't taunt. But he kept a poker face and didn't answer. Clearly, this approach wasn't working as well as he had hoped. Waldrip didn't seemed cowed in the least.

The door opened again, and this time it was Ernie Turpin. Something showed on his face—urgency maybe—as he stepped into the room and handed Tatum a note.

Tatum unfolded it and read Turpin's scrawl: "*Marlin just found Kyle Dawson's body.*"

30

FOUR HOURS LATER, Tatum and Marlin stood back and watched the Bobcat operator tear at the soil. Marlin was impressed by how quickly Tatum's team had responded to his radio call. Within thirty minutes, Tatum and his deputies had arrived, along with the medical examiner, Lem Tucker, and the forensics technician, Henry Jameson.

A cluster of county vehicles was parked thirty yards from the site of the body, with a KHIL news van looming behind the yellow tape that had been stretched in a wide arc around the crime scene.

So far, the deputies had bagged the following evidence: the toaster, what appeared to be the remains of a swimsuit that had been torn from Dawson's body, and an extension cord found inside the hole that had obviously served as Dawson's tomb.

But Tatum wasn't content with merely peering into the hole or having a deputy crawl inside. He wanted every last scrap of evidence possible, so he was having the hole slowly excavated by the Bobcat, a small tractor equipped with a backhoe.

Meanwhile, Ernie Turpin was back at the office, typing affidavits for a search of Duke Waldrip's office, his home on Flat Creek Road, and his truck. "Yesterday," Tatum had said earlier, frustration in his voice, "Hilton didn't think we had probable cause on Waldrip. Now I'd say we do. I'd say he and Kyle teamed up on Searcy, and then their little partnership went south. Hell, we got Waldrip's fingerprints on the deer mount, calls from Searcy to Waldrip . . . and now somebody offed Kyle. Am I crazy, or is that probable cause?"

They were all hoping the judge would see it the same way. Just after three o'clock, they received the news they were waiting for. Ernie Turpin came over the radio to Tatum: "On that matter with Judge Hilton, we're a go. Repeat, we are a go."

"Ten-four," Tatum replied. "First things first, Ernie. Let's get his truck towed to the lab."

"I'm on it."

Tatum turned to Marlin. "I've got two locations to work, and I need every warm body I can get."

"Tell me where you want me," Marlin said.

Duke stretched out on the cot and waited.

Weak bullshit, that's all this was. A lame attempt to unnerve him. The county jail cell was easy time compared to Huntsville. If they were trying to scare Duke, they'd have to do a lot better than that.

And all those photos and documents on the wall of the interview room—what a goddamn joke. Then that deputy coming in, making a big production of handing Tatum some mysterious note. Fucking Barney Fife could come up with a better plan.

They were desperate, grasping at straws, because they didn't have a single piece of physical evidence, the kind that really mattered. Duke knew all about that stuff from his trip to the joint. He'd heard story after story about some poor slob getting tripped up by a carpet fiber or a single drop of blood. That's why he had taken care of everything.

Searcy's gun, the screwdriver, the bolt cutters—they were all at the bottom of Pedernales Reservoir. The plastic dropcloth and the clothes Duke had been wearing were now ashes in a barrel in his backyard. He'd tossed his boots in a trash bin at a roadside park on Highway 290. He'd even gone back and mopped the floor of his office three damn times with bleach, sponging away any last trace of Searcy's blood that might have remained.

Now all he had to do was keep quiet and he was home free.

Marlin had never seen a team of officers more dedicated to searching every square inch of a structure—and he was more than happy to take part.

They started with the Waldrip house on Flat Creek Road. Henry Jameson went in first, because the deputies didn't want to contaminate any trace evidence by walking through the home. His job was to scour the house for any possible forensic evidence and collect a broad sample of available hairs and fibers, on the chance they might be able to link it to Searcy later. If they could prove Searcy had been to the house, they'd be catching Duke Waldrip in a lie. When Henry was finished, he took three additional items with him for testing: screwdrivers he'd found in a desk drawer. He left the scene and moved on to Waldrip's office next to the feed store, where a reserve deputy was standing guard. Meanwhile, Marlin, Bill Tatum, Rachel Cowan, and Ernie Turpin began a methodical search of the contents of the house.

"Every last shred of paper, every photograph, under every stick of furniture," Tatum called out, "I want every last thing checked out. And if you find a pair of bolt cutters, I'll personally buy you a steak dinner."

It was slow, painstaking work, and they bagged any items of interest as they went. A list of phone numbers. Photos from hunting expeditions. Bank statements. They'd have to explore all of these more closely later. For now, if any item had any possible value in the case, they took it with them. They searched the small attic and the crawl space under the house, they checked for loose floorboards, and they even removed air-conditioning registers and peered into the ventilation ducts. Five hours later, however, they had found nothing that was blatantly incriminating. Marlin sensed the mood of the officers sinking. Tatum, especially, was looking more grim-faced by the minute.

They loaded the bagged items in the trunks of two cruisers, then proceeded over to Waldrip's office.

When they arrived, Henry was down on his knees in the back room. "Been waiting on you," he said.

"Find something?" Tatum asked.

"Just one thing, right here on this chair leg. A small streak of what looks like blood."

The deputies moved in for a closer look, and Marlin could feel their hopes rising. Jameson placed a numbered placard on the floor next to the chair leg, then swabbed the blood carefully as Rachel Cowan photographed the process.

Bill Tatum said what they were all thinking: "He's a hunting guide. Could be deer blood."

What Bill Tatum had been hoping for was direct evidence linking Duke Waldrip to the murder of Oliver Searcy, or even to the death of Kyle Dawson, which couldn't be ruled a homicide until Lem Tucker had done an autopsy. Wild pigs had worked the body over pretty well, and nobody knew yet whether Lem would be able to discern the cause of death.

When they were finished with the searches, at six o'clock in the morning, he was afraid they had come up short. They had bagged a wide variety of items from both locations, but Tatum's intuition told him they were chasing red herrings. The blood evidence might lead somewhere—but then again, it might not.

Tatum, the other deputies, and John Marlin gathered around their cruisers outside Waldrip's office. Cowan reached into her car for a thermos of coffee and some paper cups. "Anybody?"

Turpin took a cup, but Tatum shook his head. His hands were trembling from the amount of coffee he'd already consumed.

"We'll get right on this stuff," Ernie Turpin said, gesturing toward the trunks full of Waldrip's possessions.

Tatum nodded. "I really appreciate all of you working so hard. Y'all have busted your asses on this case, and we've made some good headway. But the truth is . . . we're hitting a dead end."

Tatum could tell each member of the group knew what he was saying. It was time to ask the Rangers for assistance. Turpin slouched against his cruiser. Cowan stared at the pavement.

"I know it ain't easy," Tatum said. "But we're all beat, we've been working nonstop, and we need a fresh set of eyes on this one. I've already talked to Bobby about it, and he thinks it's a good idea."

"We've got the blood," Turpin offered.

"I know it, Ernie, but let's face it—Waldrip probably has blood on his boots or pants every time he steps into this place. Besides, it's gonna take weeks to get the DNA results. I hate it as much as you do, but we can't afford the time."

"That's it, then?" Cowan asked.

Tatum glanced at his watch. "Listen, I'll make one more run at Waldrip, see if I can get anything new out of him. After that, I'm gonna have to make a call."

Duke was startled awake by the sound of his cell door opening, and for one brief moment, he was back in Huntsville, the dark early morning suffocating him like a woolen blanket. Panic began to grip his insides . . . until he remembered exactly where he was. His eyes adjusted and he saw a deputy watching him. Tatum, the short, beefy son of a bitch. Guy looked strong as a bull moose.

"Damn, what now?" Duke said. "Can't a guy sleep to a decent hour around here?"

Tatum stepped into the cell and stood silently for several moments. Fine. Duke was more than happy to play that game. He rolled over and faced the wall.

"It's not looking good for you, Duke," Tatum said behind him. "In case you haven't heard, we found Kyle."

Duke's eyes popped wide. He rolled over slowly and sat up, his back against the wall, one knee up. "What're you talking about? What happened to—" Duke snapped his mouth shut. The deputy hadn't said they'd found Kyle's *body;* he'd simply said they'd found *Kyle.* From the deputy's standpoint, as far as Duke knew, Kyle was still alive. He tried to cover his slipup. "What happened to him? Where'd that cocksucker run off to?"

The deputy leaned against the bars but didn't answer. Duke was fully awake now and already craving a smoke, but these jerks didn't allow it in the cells. He'd have to ask Boots about the legality of that bullshit.

"You got something to ask me?" Duke said. "Otherwise, I'd just as soon—"

"I'm wondering about the blood on the chair in your office. You care to tell me about it?"

Duke tried to study Tatum's face in the dim light, but the man was a stone. *Is he bluffing?* After all of Duke's cleaning, could they have found blood? "Something I might've left out the last time we talked. That time when Searcy came to see me, the man had a nosebleed."

The stout deputy smiled, and that threw Duke off balance a tad. Guy had no reason to smile. Tatum walked to Duke's cot, bent right over into his face, and said, "Bullshit."

"Hey, whatever. Believe what you want. You could use some Listerine, by the way."

"I'm not buying it, Duke. You're saying he just stood there and bled? No handkerchief or nothing?"

"That's what I'm saying. Bled real fast at first. I got the guy some towels from the bathroom, end of story. Blood on my floor, on the chair. I cleaned it up later."

"Why are you just now telling me this?"

Duke waved his hand, going for disgusted. "Y'all already made up your minds I done it. What, I'm supposed to say, 'Oh, by the way—that dead guy? You'll find his blood in my office.' Don't think so. How dumb do I look?"

The deputy crossed his arms. "Tell me about Kyle."

"What about him?"

"You wanna tell me what happened?"

"What happened where? Man, you're talking in goddamn riddles again. You ask me a question I understand and maybe I'll answer it."

Then Duke changed his mind. Talking to this guy—any cop, for that matter—was plain stupid. Just an idiot's way to get locked up. "On second thought, I'm all done. You got any more questions, ask my lawyer. I'm tired of trying to help you out."

Bill Tatum knew it wasn't enough, not even for an indictment. That smug asshole could sit in there and tell lie after lie, and there wasn't a damn way Tatum could prove otherwise. Not with what they had so far. Waldrip was either lucky as hell or smart enough to realize the implications of forensic evidence.

Nosebleed, my ass.

The problem was, Waldrip's story sounded just plausible enough to be true. A trial jury would think, well, hey, we've all gotten nosebleeds at some point. Could've happened here. With today's advancements in forensic technology, even grand juries expected each case to be a slam dunk. For God's sake, in the biggest fiasco of all, O.J.'s team of lawyers had shrugged off a mountain of DNA evidence to set him free. In comparison, what they had in this case was paltry.

Bill Tatum was just so damn tired. Maybe he and Garza should have called the Rangers right when this thing began.

Sitting in his cruiser outside the sheriff's office, Tatum made the call. "This is Bill Tatum with the Blanco County Sheriff's Department. Is Lieutenant Foster in yet?"

31

JOHN MARLIN DIDN'T usually eat chocolate-chip cookies for breakfast, but since these were left on his kitchen counter by a sexy, nationally adored TV personality, he figured he could make an exception. The only question was, where had she gotten the ingredients? She'd left a note:

> *John—*
>
> *Got bored and played around in your kitchen a little. Hope you don't mind. Did you know there are places known as "grocery stores," and you can give them money in exchange for food? (Ha!) I bought a few things, so now that six-pack from last night doesn't look so lonely. That white stuff in the jug is milk. It comes from cows. Enjoy.*
>
> *Rudi*

P.S. I'm back at the motel—or maybe out exploring the Hill Country by the time you get this. I've got my cell phone.

Marlin munched a handful, then brushed his teeth and climbed into the shower. When he got out, there was a message on his answering machine:

"John, it's Tatum. Listen, I already told Ernie and Rachel, but I wanted you to know . . . I called Lieutenant Foster in Waco and he's sending Brad Anderson down here tomorrow morning. I appreciate all your help. I'll keep you posted."

Tatum sounded none too happy, and Marlin couldn't blame him. Brad Anderson was a tough, smart Ranger out of Llano, but for Tatum, it would be tough giving up control of the case.

Marlin picked up the phone and dialed.

"Hello?"

"It's John. Where are you?"

"On my way to Enchanted Rock," Rudi said.

"Hey, good choice."

Enchanted Rock, forty minutes from town, was a massive dome of pink granite that loomed hundreds of feet in the air and covered more than six hundred acres. Visitors from around the world came to the state park to hike to the top of the monumental batholith. The view from the top was breathtaking.

"By the way, thanks for calling me yesterday. Are you just getting up?" Rudi asked.

"No, just getting home."

"You're kidding."

"Wish I was. Long night. Anyway, I wanted to thank you for the cookies. In person. Maybe tonight?"

"Are pigs dangerous?" Charlie asked.

Mr. Townsend, Charlie's English teacher, said, "Pigs? You mean like barnyard pigs?"

It was right after class, and most of the students had already filed out of the room. Mr. Townsend was wiping the blackboard.

"No, wild ones."

"Well, not really. Some of them might get pretty upset if you cornered 'em, or if they were wounded. And the mama pig doesn't like you messing with her piglets."

Charlie liked Mr. Townsend a lot, and the teacher was a hunter. Charlie figured Mr. Townsend knew what he was talking about.

"You've hunted them, right?" Charlie asked.

"Plenty of times. Are you going on a hunt, Charlie?"

"No, I don't think so. I just wondered what they were like."

"Just like any other pig, really, except feral. That means wild."

Charlie nodded. "Are they scary? I mean, are most men scared of them?"

Mr. Townsend chuckled. "Not anybody who's hunted them. Most pigs run the other way as soon as they see you. There's really not much to be scared of."

For six hours, Marlin slept like he was getting paid for it—the kind of deep, dreamless sleep that comes from being thoroughly whipped and mentally exhausted.

He didn't hear the ring of the cordless phone, which he'd left in the kitchen, and he never budged when Trey Sweeney left a message:

"Marlin, are you there? Pick up, will ya? Hel-lllooo? You're not gonna believe this. I just got some film back from my automatic camera. You remember—I set it up on Kyle Dawson's place, in the woods near the stable? Threw a deer carcass in front of it last night. Anyway, I checked it this morning, and the whole roll of film was shot up. I figured varmints at first, but . . . man, this is too weird . . . I've got it, John. I know what the chupacabra is. Call me as soon as you can. I don't want to just blurt it out on your answering machine. So call me."

The machine beeped and a small red light began to blink. Fifteen seconds later, the phone rang and the machine picked up again.

"*Aw, what the heck. It's a hyena, John. I know, it sounds crazy . . . but I've got twenty-four photos of a friggin' hyena. Swear to God. Call me as soon as you can.*"

Jimmy Earl Smithers, you do-si-do that girl like you mean it! His fifth-grade teacher, fat ol' Mrs. Griffith, always loved square dancing. Where was he? Who said something about morphine?

Had he paid his electric bill?

Babies really aren't that cute, when you stop to think about it.

Jimmy Earl couldn't open his eyes. His head hurt.

I bet kangaroos can kick really, really hard.

He had to get that load of something over to El Paso.

The black guy at the gun shop thinks I have a small penis.

Something wasn't quite right. Jimmy Earl was so tired.

Six days on the road and I'm gonna make it home tonight.

"Jimmy Earl, can you hear me? You're in the hospital."

He wanted to respond, but he couldn't move his mouth. Or his arms.

Gotta cage that rabid squirrel.

It was nearly one o'clock before Duke finally saw the judge, and he took that as a good sign. If it *was* a murder charge—which would have been damn big news in Blanco County—they'd have rousted him bright and early, paraded him around for everyone to see. The courthouse would've been buzzing with reporters, but when the deputy walked Duke over from the jail, just across the street, there wasn't a news van in sight.

Three minutes later, he was sitting in the courtroom of Judge Daniel Hilton. He was an older man, maybe in his sixties, and he didn't look like he had much of a sense of humor. Place was nearly empty, except for an assistant district attorney, a couple bailiffs milling around, and a few sorry-looking punks with their lawyers. Duke had to sit there and listen to their stupid, shitty cases.

One guy was a Mexican busted for driving drunk. Didn't know

a word of English, and there was a lot of confusion about whether he did or didn't want to plead guilty.

Next came a skinny white boy, maybe eighteen, charged with burglary. Apparently, he'd broken into a hunting cabin and stolen a bunch of rifles. Turned out the cabin was owned by one of the county commissioners. Kid was dead meat.

There were a couple more small-potatoes cases, and then Duke finally heard his name read aloud. Duke stood and faced the judge, a deputy still by his side.

"Richard Anthony Waldrip," the judge said, reading from some papers. He raised his eyes and glared at Duke. "I notice you don't have an attorney with you today."

"Judge, they never even told me what the hell they arrested me for."

"Mr. Waldrip, you will watch your mouth in my courtroom, do you understand?"

"Sorry, Judge. Just a little pissed . . . uh, upset about the whole thing. Seems wrong to lock a man up and not tell him why."

"You are receiving a prompt arraignment, sir, and that's all that's required. Now then, the charge against you is possession of a dangerous animal, a Class-A misdemeanor. How do you plead?"

A fucking misdemeanor? Duke had been right all along. It had been a bluff. That deputy had filed this crappy case, one he could never win, purely as a fishing expedition, just so he could pump Duke about Searcy.

"I'm gonna go with not guilty, Judge. In fact, I make a motion to dismiss based on lack of evidence." What the hell, it was worth a try.

Now the judge gave Duke a stern look, maybe ready to do some cussing himself.

"This isn't the place for motions. Besides, have you even *seen* the evidence in this case, son?"

"No, sir."

"Motion denied."

Five minutes later, Duke was released on his own recognizance and was free to go. Trial date in two months—but Duke knew it would never get that far.

It took Duke thirty minutes to walk home, and when he got there, the Explorer was still sitting in the driveway. A notice on the front door informed Duke that the sheriff's department had searched the place, which Duke already knew. They'd searched the office, too, from what the deputies had told him, and hauled his truck away.

Duke swung the front door open, expecting to find Gus on the couch watching TV. But the place was quiet. He walked down the hall and saw that the suitcase was missing from Gus's bed.

"Gus?"

"Well, you're right," Marlin said, scratching his head, still waking up. "No doubt about it. That's a hyena."

Trey had fanned out a selection of photos on Marlin's countertop. All of the photos had been taken at nighttime as the hyena feasted on the deer carcass, and the flash from the camera didn't appear to have scared the hungry animal at all.

Trey said, "I compared the tracks I lifted to some images I found on the Web, and it's a match. And the hair we collected from Kyle Dawson's place seems about right."

Marlin nodded. "Guess we're lucky it wasn't one of the big cats, or something even worse."

"The question is, what do we do now?"

"What do you mean?"

"How do we go about catching the dang thing? And do we alert the public or not?"

Marlin picked up one of the photos and studied it more closely. The hyena was a fairly fierce-looking creature, with a powerful muzzle and sloping muscular shoulders—but how on earth this animal could have been mistaken for the mythical chupacabra, he had no idea.

"I'm not sure we need to do anything at all, Trey," he said. "This thing is no more dangerous than a coyote, actually. Chances are, someone will shoot it or trap it. But it's not like it poses any immediate threat."

"No, I guess not." Trey dropped the photo to the counter.

Marlin eyed him. "Disappointed, huh?"

"What? No, not really."

"You were hoping for something a little more, I don't know . . . momentous. Hell, you can see one of those in a zoo." Frankly, Marlin was relieved. Now they knew exactly what they were dealing with, and it wasn't much to be concerned about. But if Trey wanted to mount a campaign to capture the hyena, more power to him.

Trey gathered up his photos. "You know, everybody thinks hyenas are just scavengers and cowards, but they're not."

Here was Trey, dejected, trying to gather one last ounce of excitement out of it.

"They're not?"

"Not at all. People think hyenas wait around for lions to finish their kills and then the hyenas creep in and scoop up the leftovers. But most of the time, it's the other way around. Hyenas are very capable predators."

Marlin didn't point out that Trey's own photos showed the hyena dining on a long-dead whitetail.

"I think I ought to at least let the newspaper know," Trey said. "Maybe give them a photo or two."

"Yeah, you're probably right," Marlin said. "Good idea."

For nearly three months—since the beginning of deer season back in November—Marlin hadn't had a spare moment. Now, suddenly, he found himself with time on his hands. Unless a call came in, his afternoon was free.

He threw a load of laundry into the washing machine, then sat at his computer and did paperwork for several hours. At four o'clock, he put a roast from a wild pig into the oven, nice and low at three hundred degrees. By seven or eight, it would be falling apart.

At five o'clock, with an hour of sunlight left, he and Geist stepped out the back door and took a stroll around his seven-acre homestead. The air was crisp, and the dog was full of pent-up energy from being left alone so much in the past few days. She bounded after white-wing doves and even flushed a small covey of quail, but Marlin could tell it was nothing but play. She wasn't a born hunter and wouldn't know what to do with one of the birds if she caught it.

Back at the house, Marlin straightened things up, ran the vacuum, and even lit a few candles to freshen the air a bit.

At seven, he returned to his computer, Googled the words *spotted hyena*, and got a hit from the San Antonio Zoo Web site. The site informed him that the spotted hyena can grow as large as 190 pounds, with females generally larger than males. Bigger than he thought. They can gallop at speeds approaching forty miles per hour and can easily top thirty for several miles while pursuing prey. Trey was correct, too, in that the hyena does more hunting than scavenging. Most of the hyena's power is in its forequarters and its powerful jaws, which can crush bone. And, of course, there is the hyena trademark: the laughing sound it makes when being attacked or chased.

Maybe Trey was right about trying to trap it. So far, all of the reports had come in from the Flat Creek area, but the Web site didn't mention the size of a hyena's home range. Would it remain in the area, or roam into another county? As Marlin searched for more information, the doorbell rang.

He opened the door, and there was Rudi, looking great in the glow of the porch light.

Gus leaned back and listened to the bus engine roar.

This was a lot of fun, really, not knowing where he was going. When he had come back from the bank, Duke was gone, but Gus's suitcase was sitting right there on the bed. So he'd grabbed it, thumbed a ride to Austin, gotten a cab to the bus terminal, and bought a ticket. But he'd had an episode at the counter, and then, the next thing he knew, he was in a seat. Couldn't remember what he'd told the ticket agent. Then again, did it really matter? This was an adventure.

Only problem, he'd forgotten his Altoids. He turned to the man next to him, a chubby guy in a business suit.

"You got a mint?"

"No, sorry," the man said.

"Gum?"

"No."

He'd have to buy some at the next stop.

"Where're we going, anyway?" Gus asked.

"I wanted you to know I'm leaving tomorrow. This is outstanding, by the way."

Marlin finished a bite of his dinner, then said, "Back to L.A.?"

Rudi frowned. "What, are you kidding? Not yet. No, I'm thinking Florida. I've always wanted to go to Key West, and I figure now's as good a time as any. I can stop in New Orleans along the way, maybe poke around in Mississippi and Alabama. A nice slow tour along the Gulf. Get my head back together, *then* I can go back to L.A."

Marlin took a drink of wine, giving himself time to think. What would she say if he said, *Mind if I come along?* He'd made that same drive himself a couple of times, but it had been many years ago. *I wonder if Sloppy Joe's Bar is as much fun as it used to be.* People sometimes danced on the bar, and how could you not like a place like that?

But he couldn't just up and leave, could he? He had things to take care of around here. On the other hand, he *did* have a lot of vacation time piled up. He was starting to feel a nice connection with Rudi, and he hated to see it end so quickly.

"When I do go back home, I'll be coming right through Texas again," Rudi said.

Marlin nodded. "Interstate Ten."

"Which goes right through San Antonio . . . and I was wondering . . . you ever been to the Riverwalk?"

He woke sometime in the middle of the night and didn't bother to look at the clock. From his side of the bed, looking through the east window, Marlin could see the moon just climbing over the trees.

Rudi stirred beside him, and he placed his hand on her flat belly. She covered his hand with hers and, as she woke, began to rub his calf with one of her feet.

He rolled onto his side and slipped his hand down her hip, along her outer thigh. Her breathing had become deep and slow.

After a moment, she placed a hand on his shoulder and gently rolled him onto his back, nuzzling his neck as she climbed on top.

32

MARLIN WOULD BE asked, several days later, to recount the details of the next morning in painstaking detail. Some of it was fuzzy, but he remembered exactly how it had started.

At about eight-thirty, while Rudi was in the shower and Marlin was making pancakes, he heard a loud knock on his door. Geist barked and ran to look out the window. Marlin opened the door and saw a boy standing on the porch, a bike lying in the yard behind him.

The kid was maybe eleven or twelve, wearing a thin jacket and blue jeans, breathing hard. "Are you the game warden?" he asked.

Marlin said he was.

"The chupacabra," the boy announced. "It's in a trap behind my house."

* * *

Most of the out-of-town morons had given up on the chupacabra, but Red still had faith. After all, you couldn't always believe what a government employee told you. Just because the game warden had talked to some news reporter, swearing up and down that the chupacabra didn't exist, that didn't mean he was telling the truth. Red could almost smell a conspiracy. It would be just like the government to try to cover this thing up, but Red was smart enough to see through it.

He emerged from his bedroom, to find Billy Don on the sofa, watching some dumb game show. Apparently, a housewife from Arkansas was trying to win a new washer-dryer combo. Yippee. Maybe she could quit washing her clothes in the creek, or turn around and sell the damn things so she could afford some dental work. She looked like she needed it.

Red eased himself down into the La-Z-Boy. "You 'bout ready to go check the trap?"

Billy Don gave him a look. "Think it's safe?"

Sheesh. Red hated the way Billy Don always worried about shit, afraid to take a chance every now and then. "Guess we'll just have to go and see for ourselves, won't we?"

Yesterday, right after they'd seen the helicopter, a whole convoy of patrol cars, ambulances, and the like had come streaming down Flat Creek Road and pulled into the Macho Bueno Ranch. Later on, Red found out why. The ranch's owner had been found dead, right there on his ranch, which was awful damn inconvenient. Red and Billy Don hadn't been able to check the trap all day. Now, though, Red figured all the official hubbub would be done with and they could sneak back onto the place.

Red stood. "C'mon now. Get your boots on."

"Gimme a minute, will ya? She's about to win a Maytag."

Duke wasn't what he'd call worried. More like puzzled. Had Gus really gone for good? And where exactly would that simpleton have gone anyway?

Duke had spent the night at the old homestead, as he had for the last week or so. He'd expected Gus to come home sometime in the night, or to at least call. But nothing. It made Duke a little uneasy not to be keeping tabs on Gus, but maybe it was better this way, Duke not having to watch after his brother all the time. It could be a real pain in the ass. Let somebody else worry about him for a while, maybe a mental institution, which was where he was likely to end up.

Duke swung out of bed and went straight to the refrigerator, hoping for some cold pizza or a leftover breakfast taco. All he found was beer, a jar of hot sauce, and an unidentifiable ball of moldy fuzz in a Tupperware container.

Sally Ann's place was a quarter of a mile down the road, and she always had something good in the fridge. What the hell, he'd hoof it down there and check it out. Sally Ann would be at work, so he wouldn't have to deal with her. But maybe—if he was feeling charitable—he'd leave a nice lovey-dovey note, see if he could get back on her good side. Now that everything had blown over, Duke was ready to make nice and start getting laid again.

Deputy Ernie Turpin was at his desk when Bill Tatum buzzed him.

"What are you doing right this minute?" Tatum asked.

"Not a whole hell of a lot. Putting paperwork in order so the Rangers can—"

"I need you to go down to San Antonio. Our boy is waking up."

"The trucker?"

"Yep, and I want you and Cowan down there."

"Leave now?"

"Right now."

"Slow down a minute, son," Marlin said, stepping out onto the porch. The kid was wide-eyed and excited, shifting from one leg to the other, like he had to take a pee. "Just take it easy and tell me what you saw."

The boy nodded. "There's a hog trap on the ranch behind my house, and, uh, I went out to check it this morning before school and I saw this animal in it. I've seen it before. It has a huge head and lots of teeth, and I figured it had to be the chupacabra, because I've never seen nothing like it."

"Where do you live?"

"Over on Flat Creek Road."

Well, of course you do, Marlin thought. Everything had happened on Flat Creek Road so far. Why should this be any different? "Which ranch are you talking about?" he asked.

"It's got a green gate, and I think a man named Kyle owns it." Once more, all roads led to Kyle Dawson's place. The boy was getting excited again. "But we have to hurry, because I think they're gonna shoot it."

"Who's gonna shoot it?"

"The men who set the trap."

Marlin wanted to ask more questions, but the youngster was obviously agitated and ready to lead him to the trap. Marlin figured the boy would calm down on the drive over to Flat Creek. "Wait right here."

Marlin stepped inside, donned his uniform, and told Rudi, who was dripping wet and had a towel wrapped around her hair, that he'd be back in an hour or two. She said she'd wait.

Mary, Queen of Scotch, we've done it! Red thought.

There was something in the trap! Not a damn hog this time, or a coyote or badger or any damn thing like that. This was something wild and nasty, with a God-awful muzzle and a head the size of . . . well, something pretty damn big.

Billy Don was breathing heavily, eyes wide, unable to even speak at this point. They were seventy yards from the trap, downwind, hunkered low in the brush, and the animal hadn't spotted them yet.

"Gimme the binoculars!" Red hissed.

Billy Don passed them over.

Red glassed the animal, and he was . . . confused. This beast didn't look anything like he'd expected. It wasn't a freaking lizard or flying monkey at all. He and Billy Don had even gone to the Johnson City Library, which turned out to be a nice place, and located some drawings of the chupacabra. Those people had it all wrong. This animal didn't have big alien eyes or wings or spikes along the ridge of its back. But it was just as scary, looking huge and pissed off as he peered at it through the binoculars.

"What ya think?" Red asked, passing the binoculars to Billy Don.

The big man took a look and gave a shudder. "Thing's a damn monster!"

"Yeah, yeah, it is."

"So what the hell do we do now?"

"What do you mean?"

"What I mean is, are *you* gonna walk right up to that thing? I know *I'm* not."

"Well, we sure as shit don't want to shoot it, not unless we have to. Worth more alive than dead."

"What, then?"

"Just give me a damn minute, Billy Don. Lemme think." Red put his powerful mind to work, sorted through the possibilities—and then he had it! "What we need," he said triumphantly, "is a tranquillity gun."

"Tranquilizer gun?"

"Exactly!"

But the only person they could think of who would have one was John Marlin. Red wasn't about to fool around with him. Then he remembered someone else.

Duke's key still worked, and he took that as a good sign. If Sally Ann had written him off, she would've changed the locks. As he expected, nobody was home.

He found some fried chicken in the fridge, and he ate it cold, chasing it down with a couple of beers. He threw the bones in the trash and grabbed another beer. It was nice to sit and drink a cold one in peace and quiet, no worries hanging over him. Gus was gone, Kyle was dead, and nobody on earth could pin him to the murder of Oliver Searcy.

He stretched out on the couch, feeling a nap coming on.

All it took was one phone call—Red acting all excited, giving a fake address on the west side of Blanco, saying he had a genuine king cobra in his swimming pool—"Hurry! It's flaring its damn neck at me!"—and Trey Sweeney said he'd be right there.

When they got to Sweeney's place, sure enough, the biologist was gone. He'd even left his front door unlocked. Billy Don went inside (Red had to explain to him the importance of a lookout man, of course) and in less than five minutes he returned with a hard-sided gun case. Inside was a tranquilizer gun and equipment.

Moments later, they were back at the ranch. The first time through the gate that morning, they had discovered that the sheriff's department was no longer content with a sign warning people to keep out. Now there were wooden police barriers, which Billy Don had dragged to the side earlier.

"Want me to close 'em behind us?" Billy Don asked.

"Naw, we'll be outta here in no time. Get your rain gear on. Tops and bottoms."

"It ain't raining."

"No, for the camo, dumbass. I don't want that creature seeing us and flipping out. Grab those camo hats, too."

Red pulled off the road into a grove of cedar trees, hiding his truck as well as he could, just in case a deputy came by.

"You bringing your gun, too?" Billy Don asked.

"Damn right."

They dressed themselves in camo, then test-fired the tranquilizer gun at a stump. Easy as pie. Ol' Trey Sweeney had even left an instruction manual in the gun case. Red slipped his Colt Anaconda into a holster on his hip, and then they began a slow stalk through the woods.

Now, knowing what was waiting for them in the trap, every

stick they stepped on and every stone they stumbled over seemed to make a noise that was ten times louder than it should have been.

They moved at an excruciatingly slow pace, circling around to the south to keep the wind in their faces. Finally, nearly fifteen minutes later, the trap came into view.

Red hoisted the binoculars. "I think it's sleeping," he whispered.

Billy Don nodded. "What now?"

It was an agonizing moment for Red. What he *wanted* to do was hand the tranquilizer gun to Billy Don and tell him to go get the job done. But Red knew Billy Don was about as stealthy as a gut-shot cow. He couldn't sneak up on the chupacabra even if it was deaf and blind. No, the sad truth was, Red would have to do it.

"You wait here," he said, but Billy Don was already finding a hiding spot in some brush.

Red crouched low and began to approach the trap, one hand clutching the tranquilizer gun, the other pinning the binoculars to his chest, keeping them from swinging.

At fifty yards, he could clearly see that the animal was lying down on the floor of the trap.

At forty yards, he could make out its backside. Perfect. The animal was facing away from him. Even if its eyes were open, it wouldn't see him coming.

At thirty yards, Red realized his hands were trembling and sweat was running down the sides of his face. *Gotta get my shit together,* he thought. *This is a million-dollar shot.*

Then, at twenty yards, he heard a wonderful sound. The chupacabra was snoring. Deep, rhythmic snorts with each incoming breath.

Red froze for a moment. Should he try to get closer? Or take a shot from here? Considering his shaky condition, he decided he wanted as short a shot as possible.

He took another step, and then another. His own breathing sounded like a windstorm. He could feel and *hear* his heart thudding in his chest. His mouth was as dry as a flattened frog baking on a road in the August sun.

One last step. He'd shoot from here, fifteen yards away. He felt a little dizzy, light-headed.

He didn't waste any time. He lifted the rifle, took a deep breath, squeezed the trigger . . . and the sound of the dart whooshing out of the barrel nearly made Red soil his camo.

"You ever seen a wild hog?" Marlin asked.

"Yes, sir."

"Did this animal look anything like that?"

The boy, whose name was Riggs, looked small and nervous over in the passenger seat. He kept glancing through the rear window to make sure his bike was okay in the back. "No, sir, this was something different."

"You've seen a coyote?"

"Yeah, a lot of times. It's not a coyote."

"You sure?"

"Yes, sir."

"How about a bobcat?"

"I've seen pictures, but this ain't one of those."

"Tell me exactly what it looks like," Marlin said.

"Like some kind of weird dog. It's got spots all over it."

That could be a hyena, Marlin thought. *It could also be a Dalmatian.* He hoped this boy wasn't wasting his time.

"What color was it?"

"Mostly brown. Except for the spots. Those are black."

Back at the house, Marlin had been tempted to show Charlie a photo of a hyena, but he was afraid Charlie would automatically say, yeah, that's it. Now that Charlie had described it, though, Marlin removed the photo from his shirt pocket. "Does it look like this?"

Charlie sat up straight. "Yeah, that's it! Definitely."

Okay, now we're getting somewhere, thought Marlin. Maybe they could officially close the chupacabra case. He said, "That's a hyena, Charlie. They come from Africa."

The boy appeared confused. "It's not the chupacabra?"

"I'm afraid not. See, the thing is, the chupacabra doesn't really exist. It's kind of like Bigfoot or the Loch Ness Monster. You've heard of those?"

"Yeah."

"What happens is, sometimes people let their imaginations run away a little, mostly because it's fun. It's exciting to think something that weird is for real. But it's really a myth. There is no such thing."

Charlie seemed okay with that explanation. "How did the hyena get over here from Africa?"

"It might've gotten loose from a zoo, or sometimes people get permits to import them."

"Do they hunt them?"

"Some people do, but they're not supposed to."

Charlie looked down at the photo again, then handed it back to Marlin. They drove in silence for a moment.

Marlin said, "You been on Kyle's ranch much, Charlie?"

A funny look came over the boy's face. "Not really. Just a couple of times."

Marlin knew what it was: Charlie was afraid Marlin would lecture him about trespassing. "I used to roam the woods when I was a boy, too," Marlin said. "But you gotta be careful out there, especially during hunting season. It's probably best if you don't cross any more fences, okay?"

Marlin gave him a smile and the boy nodded back, finally grinning.

"If we drive through the ranch gate, can you lead me to the trap?" Marlin asked.

"Uh, I don't think so. I just know the part behind my house."

"Okay, then, we'll park at your house and climb the fence."

"But you just said I shouldn't do that."

Quick kid. "Well, this time it's okay, because you're with me."

"Cool."

Marlin turned onto Flat Creek Road. "Charlie, who were the men who set the trap?"

He shrugged. "Just some men I met at the store."

"You remember their names?"

"Red and Billy Don."

Should've known.

"Are they in trouble?" Charlie asked.

If Marlin was going to file charges on anyone, it would be those two goofballs. "Well, maybe a little."

"Good," Charlie said.

33

"MR. SMITHERS, CAN you hear me all right?"

Cowan could see Smithers's recessed eyes blinking, and his voice came out as a raspy croak. "I hear ya."

It sounded like his windpipe had been mangled in the wreck. *That's gotta hurt*, Rachel Cowan thought as she surveyed the poor man. She could see nothing of him except his eyes and mouth. Even with all those bandages, she could tell that his face and head were tremendously swollen, much larger than they should be. In addition to the head trauma, both ankles were broken and one lung had been punctured by several splintered ribs.

Ernie Turpin was on the other side of the hospital bed, ready to take notes. Both of them were as excited as they had ever been in their careers. Depending on what Jimmy Earl Smithers told them, the deputies were very possibly on the brink of discovering who had shot Bobby Garza, and that same person had likely killed Oliver Searcy or knew who had. They knew Smithers himself wasn't involved, because travel records indicated he was nowhere near Houston when Garza was shot. Besides, Smithers had absolutely no connection to Oliver Searcy. So the question was, where had Smithers gotten the deer mount?

Cowan leaned in low and spoke softly. "This will only take a few minutes. We're here about a deer mount that you sold to a man in Blanco County. You remember that?"

Smithers gave a nearly imperceptible nod.

Good. His memory wasn't totally shot.

"What we really need to know is, where did you get it?"

Smithers acted as if he wanted to sit up, but he groaned and eased back onto the mattress. Then he muttered something Cowan couldn't understand.

"I'm sorry? I didn't catch that."

Smithers said it again.

"Hitchhiker," Turpin said softly.

Cowan said, "Was that it, a hitchhiker?"

Another small nod.

Cowan did her best to remain calm, but her palms were getting sweaty. They were hot on the trail now. "Where did you pick him up?"

"Houston," Smithers said, forcing the word out.

Cowan wanted to ask for details: Where in Houston? When? Had he been alone at the time? But all of that would have to wait.

"Good. Very good. Can you tell me where you dropped him off?"

For a few seconds, Smithers closed his eyes. Then he opened them and said, "Johnson City."

Cowan wanted it all: Where did you drop him? What time? Was anybody waiting for him? But again, it was more important, at the moment, to get the basic facts—while Smithers was still conscious.

Now the most important question of all. "What was his name?"

It was a long shot. Injury aside, it was easy to forget the name of a passing stranger. Would he even remember?

Then Smithers spit it out in a voice thick with grit. "Kyle . . . Dawson."

For one stunned moment, Cowan didn't know what question to ask next. *Kyle Dawson?* Everybody on the investigative team had been certain the answer would be Duke Waldrip. So far, everything pointed toward Waldrip, and they had become convinced that Dawson wasn't involved. Still, though, with Dawson found murdered (which was an assumption, since they were still waiting on autopsy results), there was the possibility he'd had some part in Searcy's homicide and was killed to silence him.

"Kyle Dawson?" Cowan said, almost to herself.

At this point, Turpin opened the manila envelope and removed a photograph. He held it in front of Smithers, saying, "Is this him?"

Smithers said, "No."

Turpin showed the photo to Cowan. It was Kyle Dawson. Cowan smiled.

Turpin removed another photo and held it for Smithers to see. "Is this the man?"

Cowan was literally crossing her fingers.

Smithers said, "Not him, either."

Charlie pointed out his driveway and Marlin followed it to a small weather-beaten house with a sagging roof. Paint was flaking, the yard was nothing but weeds, and Marlin, when he stepped out of the truck, could smell the unmistakable odor of a septic system that wasn't quite doing its job. Hell of a way for a kid to live.

Marlin unloaded Charlie's bike from the back of the truck; when they were done here, Marlin would drop him off at school and he could ride the bus home.

Charlie came around the truck and Marlin knelt on one knee. "Listen, Charlie, I know you think it's a neat animal, and neither of us wants it harmed. But I need to take a rifle along, just to be safe, you understand?"

"Yes, sir."

"Tell me something: When you go to check the trap, how far away are you when you first see it?"

"I dunno. Maybe the length of a football field."

"Okay, good. Then here's what we'll do. You stay behind me the entire time, okay?"

"Okay."

"You'll point the trap out to me, but we want to stay as far away from it as possible. Don't go anywhere near it, okay?"

"Yes, sir."

Marlin grinned at him. "You're a smart kid. You did the right thing by coming to me."

Charlie looked at his shoes, but he was beaming.

"Okay, just let me gather a few things," Marlin said, standing. Inside his truck, an overhead gun rack held a .270 and a 30/30. Marlin removed the 30/30, then opened a box of cartridges and slipped a handful into his pants pocket. He grabbed a pair of binoculars from behind the seat.

"Okay, where're we headed, Charlie?"

"Behind the house there's a deer path leading onto the ranch. That's the way I go."

They set out, and as they reached the corner of the house, Marlin noticed that Charlie wasn't wearing the jacket he'd had on earlier.

"Where's your coat?"

"In your truck."

"Why don't you run and get it?"

"I'm not cold."

"It'll keep the barbed wire from snagging you."

Charlie turned and trotted back to the truck.

Charlie opened the truck door and quickly grabbed his jacket, which was lying in the middle of the bench seat.

But then something stopped him. Something he hadn't noticed before, because his jacket had been covering it up.

The game warden's truck was kind of sloppy, with empty soft-drink cans on the floorboard, maps on the dashboard, and right there, among some other loose papers on the seat, was a sheet of paper that said MISSING! Underneath was a photo of a man.

Charlie recognized him.

The writing underneath the photo said the man's name was Oliver Searcy.

For a second, Charlie thought about leaving the paper where it was. The game warden, even though he was a really nice man, would probably think Charlie was lying. After all, Charlie had already claimed he'd seen the chupacabra, when it was really a hyena. Just a regular animal.

But then . . . if this man was missing, Charlie figured he'd better say something.

He lifted the paper and climbed back out of the truck. The game warden was still waiting at the corner of the house.

The animal made a surprised yelp and sprung to its paws, whirling in a circle and looking for whatever had just bitten it.

Red had nailed it perfectly, and he could see the dart dangling from the chupacabra's haunch. The animal was so busy looking inside the trap for an unseen attacker, it didn't even notice Red standing fifteen yards away.

Red eased backward, slowly, step by step . . . and then the chupacabra spotted him. It locked eyes with Red and let loose with a series of grunting growls and snarls, baring its yellow teeth.

Red had had enough. He turned and began a clumsy gallop back the way he had come, glancing over his shoulder nervously, certain the animal would burst from its cage and run him down.

Up ahead, Billy Don was out of the bushes now, prancing in place, and Red ran to him, gulping for oxygen.

"Did you get him? Did you get him?" Billy Don asked.

Red nodded, his hands on his knees now, the tranquilizer gun on the ground at his feet. "Yeah, I got him." He removed the binoculars and handed them to Billy Don, who lifted them to his face.

"He's just standing there."

At least the damn noises had stopped. Those sounds gave Red the chills.

He was still wheezing, but he took the binoculars back from

Billy Don. "Looks like . . . he's starting to sag some. Oops, now he's sitting. Kind of lost his balance."

"You all right, Red? You're lookin' kinda puny."

As a matter of fact, Red's head was feeling kind of woozy at the moment. But he'd done it! He'd faced down the monster, and now he was about to become an international celebrity! He'd be rich and famous and important people would want to interview him, but damn, he was feeling awful strange and his vision was getting dark, and why was the ground coming up at him so quickly?

John Marlin had been in the woods of central Texas all his life, and he'd never heard animal vocalizations quite like those he had just heard. They were faint, a couple hundred yards away. An animal in distress. Eerie as hell. Then he heard dogs yapping, the barks coming from behind the house.

Charlie, over by the truck, didn't appear to have heard the animal wailing. Marlin was second-guessing himself now, thinking he probably shouldn't take the boy onto the ranch. Charlie could give him a general description of where the trap was located, and Marlin would find it himself. He was even thinking it might be best if he called someone else to go with him, maybe Trey Sweeney. His mind was pondering all of these issues, wondering how to proceed, when, in the next few seconds, everything changed and none of those concerns mattered anymore.

The boy was standing by the truck, holding his jacket in one hand and a sheet of paper in the other. Charlie held the sheet up and said, "I've seen this man."

What is he talking about? Marlin wondered. He couldn't see the paper clearly. *What is he holding?*

Charlie said, "He hunted with my stepdad."

Who did? Marlin took a few steps forward. . . . Charlie started coming his way, holding the sheet of paper out. And then Marlin's palms began to tingle as he recognized it. The flyer about Oliver Searcy. That's what Charlie was holding. The dogs were still barking.

"Who's your stepdad, Charlie?" Marlin was vaguely aware of a sound behind him, but he was too focused on the boy, waiting for his answer. Everything depended on the answer.

And Charlie said, "Duke Waldrip."

Then Marlin saw, just for an instant, a look of sheer terror in Charlie's eyes. But the boy was looking past Marlin, at something behind him. Charlie began to open his mouth to yell something.

Marlin had just enough time to turn and see Duke Waldrip—and to realize that the man's large, hard fist was sailing directly toward his face.

34

ERNIE TURPIN GAVE Rachel Cowan a coy smile and showed her the photo. She was pissed at Ernie for having a little fun with her, but she was relieved to see that the man in the photo was Gus Waldrip, not Duke as she had assumed.

Now Turpin extracted a third photo from the envelope, this time letting Cowan see that it was indeed Duke. He held it in front of Smithers, who immediately coughed out the most beautiful words Cowan had heard in a long time: "That's him."

"This is the hitchhiker who said his name was Kyle Dawson?" Turpin asked.

"Yeah." Smithers's eyelids were halfway closed.

"You got the deer mount from him?"

"Yeah."

Cowan was elated, ready to sprint into the hallway and call Bill Tatum, but they needed to ask a few more questions. Smithers's voice was growing weaker and it was obvious he was becoming too tired to talk.

"Anything else you can tell us about this man?" Cowan asked. "Did he mention any of his friends, any of his hunting buddies?"

A long pause.

"Girlfriend," Smithers said.

"A girlfriend?" This was something new. Cowan didn't remember anything about Duke having a girlfriend. "What was her name?"

"Sally Ann."

Cowan and Turpin exchanged glances, and she knew they were thinking the same thing: *Who the hell is Sally Ann?*

Minutes earlier, before Duke had been forced to make yet another quick decision that would likely turn his world into a fucked-up mess, he had been sleeping quietly on the couch.

Then something had woken him up. Voices right outside. He'd glanced out the window and seen Charlie—why the hell wasn't he in school?—standing in the yard with the game warden.

Jesus, what now? What is that snot-nosed kid doing with the game warden?

John Marlin was kneeling in front of Charlie, saying something, but Duke couldn't make it out. Whatever the reason for this visit, Duke didn't want to be in the house when they came inside. Up to now, the cops hadn't asked him about Sally Ann or her boy. As far as Duke knew, Marlin and Tatum and all their punks *still* hadn't figured out that he had been living here for the last six months, that Sally Ann was—as she'd been saying, anyway—his common-law wife, and that Charlie was his stepson, whether Duke claimed him or not.

So Duke leapt off the couch and scrambled out the back door. Damn it! Charlie's mangy dogs started to bark. Duke made his way to the front corner of the house and hid in a small space between the house and an oleander bush, where he could keep an eye on Marlin and Charlie. He peeked around the corner, concealed by the bush.

Crap. He knew he'd made a huge mistake. The game warden was now holding a rifle, and he and Charlie were walking this way. Duke pulled his head back and tried to think. What would happen if they noticed him? How would he explain himself? Why was he hiding in the bushes? A few seconds passed, but Marlin and the boy still hadn't rounded the corner.

Then Duke heard Charlie say, "I've seen this man." The boy's voice sounded much farther away than Duke expected. Wherever they were going, had they turned and gone the other way? The oleander leaves caressed Duke's back as he flattened against the side of the house and risked one more peek around the corner.

Fuck!

The game warden was standing right there, about six feet away. But he hadn't heard or seen Duke yet. Neither had Charlie, who was back at the game warden's truck, holding up a sheet of paper. What *is* that? What in God's name is the kid talking about?

"He hunted with my stepdad," Charlie said.

And in one horrifying second, Duke realized exactly what was happening. Charlie was talking about Oliver Searcy. He was holding a flyer, like the ones Duke had seen around town. The kid was slipping a noose around Duke's neck.

"Who's your stepdad, Charlie?"

"Duke Waldrip," Charlie said, and Duke would have gutted him alive if he'd had the chance.

He saw no options. Once again, as with Oliver Searcy, he was forced to react, without having time to think things through. He slipped from the bushes, stepped toward John Marlin, and put every ounce of strength into a crushing right hand.

"Yoo-hoo, wake up."

Red's eyes fluttered, then opened just in time to see the stream of beer coming down from the can in Billy Don's hand. It caught him squarely in the face, most of it running right up his nose. He coughed and sputtered and said, "Christ, you tryin' to drown me?"

Billy Don extended a hand and helped him up. "Well, I damn

sure wasn't gonna give you mouth-to-mouth. I don't believe I've ever seen a growed man faint before."

Normally, Red would have been embarrassed. But at the moment, he didn't give a damn. It was his lucky day—like he'd just won the lottery or managed a sneak peek down some hot babe's blouse—and nothing was going to ruin it.

He wiped his face and peered through the binoculars at the trap. The chupacabra appeared to be down for good. But what next? The problem was, the area between the trap and the truck was too heavily wooded to drive through, and with the added weight of the animal in the trap, Red was certain they couldn't carry it. They'd have to remove the chupacabra from the trap; there was no way around it. Red was wishing he'd planned in advance and brought some sort of muzzle, and maybe some rope to tie its legs together.

"Okay, I did the hard part," Red said. "Now it's your turn."

Billy Don eyed him suspiciously.

"What I want you to do," Red said casually, "is go get it out of the trap and—"

"You're out of your friggin' mind."

"But Billy Don, we've got to—"

"No damn way. Uh-uh. End of story."

Red really couldn't blame him. Who knew how long the drugs would last? If that thing woke up halfway to the truck, it could be a real nightmare. But Red wasn't ready to give up.

"How about we both go get it?" he offered.

Now Billy Don looked a little more agreeable. "I'm listening."

"I'll even carry the front part," Red said, wondering where he had gotten this newfound courage. He figured the promise of a big payday had something to do with it. "And if it starts to wake up, we'll just drop it and run like hell."

"Okay, but I get to carry the pistol."

Red had to mull that over for a good long time. "Deal," he said finally.

Red passed the holstered pistol over to Billy Don, who strapped it on. Then they both stared toward the trap.

"Good a time as any," Red said.

"Yep."

Neither of them moved.

"Might as well get after it," Red said.

"I imagine so."

Red took a step forward and, to his surprise, Billy Don followed.

They started slowly, then picked up steam as they realized it would be best to get it over with quickly. They began taking large strides, covering ground swiftly, before they lost their nerve. Soon, they found themselves standing next to the trap, the chupacabra completely unconscious inside.

"Ugly sumbitch," Billy Don said.

Red nodded.

Delicately, as if he might wake the sleeping animal, Red opened the spring-loaded door to the trap. He poked the chupacabra in the hindquarters with his fingers.

"AARRRGGGHHH!" Billy Don said, goosing Red in the ribs. The door slammed shut, and Red stumbled backward, falling onto his butt.

Billy Don was laughing so hard, most portions of him were jiggling. "Gets you back for the other day," he said, hardly able to contain himself.

"Quit screwing around!" Red said. "We got important business here."

Billy Don stifled a laugh and allowed himself only a mild giggle. The chupacabra hadn't budged.

Red, trying to redeem himself for being so spooked, opened the door again, grabbed the animal by its front legs, and dragged it out of the trap.

Billy Don wasn't laughing anymore.

"Okay," Red said, keeping a close eye on the animal's teeth, "grab your end and let's get this thing to the truck, pronto."

Texas Ranger Brad Anderson arrived from his hometown of Llano by nine o'clock, and Bill Tatum, despite his regrets about the Searcy case, was happy to see him. The men had gotten to know each other over the years, and Anderson was, in Tatum's opinion, one of the best cops in the state. Damn nice guy, too.

Tatum carried all the files related to the Searcy case into the small conference room; then for a solid hour, he brought Anderson up to speed. Tatum was distracted, though, waiting for a call from Cowan. He knew the trucker could be the key to all of this, the one thing that could bring Duke Waldrip down. But Tatum still hadn't heard from the deputies.

Finally, just as he was finishing with Anderson, his cell phone rang. "Excuse me a minute, Brad."

Rachel Cowan was on the line. "It was Waldrip," she said, breathless. "Smithers had no doubt at all."

Tatum pumped his fist in the air. The team's determination had finally paid off. He listened as Rachel mentioned another item of information Smithers had provided. Duke Waldrip had a girlfriend named Sally Ann—a fact that somehow had never come up in the investigation. "I'll check the voting records and tax rolls," Tatum said, "and see who we can come up with. You and Ernie get back here ASAP," Tatum said. "Great work, Rachel."

He cut the connection and told Anderson what had just transpired. "I think we've got a handle on this one now. I might've brought you all the way down here for nothing. Unless you want to help me bring the guy in."

"Hell yeah," Anderson said. "Be my pleasure."

Marlin honestly didn't know whether he ever lost consciousness, but he did know he had never been struck that hard in his life. The blow knocked him to the ground, blood gushing from his nose, which was surely broken. When he opened his eyes, the ground rose and fell repeatedly, making him nauseous. Worse, swelling around both eyes was already beginning to limit his field of vision.

He couldn't remember feeling hands on him, but there was Duke Waldrip, holding Marlin's .357 revolver, as well as his rifle.

"Charlie, get over here!" Waldrip yelled.

Marlin could see the boy cowering over by the truck, still clutching the flyer and his jacket. He walked over to his stepdad.

Duke pointed the handgun at Marlin. "Roll over on your belly."

Marlin did as he was told. He could feel Duke removing the pepper spray and handcuffs from his belt.

"Okay, sit up."

Marlin complied.

Duke handed the cuffs to Charlie, who was visibly trembling. "Go cuff yourself to him, Charlie."

Marlin knew he couldn't let that happen. With the boy cuffed to him, he would have no chance of making a move on Duke. And there was always the possibility that Charlie might get a chance to run free. If nothing else, Marlin wanted to give the boy a shot at getting away.

Charlie leaned down with the cuffs, tears now running down his cheeks.

"I'll do it, Charlie," Marlin said softly, taking the cuffs from his hands.

Before Duke could protest, Marlin flipped the cuffs over his head and onto the roof of the house.

"Shit!" Duke yelped. He took a step toward Marlin, shoving the gun into his face. "Real fucking smart, asshole."

"Give it up, Duke."

"Shut up!"

"You've got no chance." It came across as corny and clichéd . . . and a little hopeless, Marlin thought. His own voice sounded odd, and he realized it was because of the blood and phlegm flowing down the back of his throat. He felt weary and defeated.

"I said shut up! Now get to your feet."

Waldrip was glancing nervously toward the county road. The line of trees at the front of the property provided privacy, but there was always the chance a passing driver might notice the commotion. Marlin didn't know what Duke was planning to do next, but he knew it would be a good idea to stall.

"I have double vision. I don't think I can walk."

"Get the fuck up! Now!"

Marlin got to his knees, then made a production of getting to his feet, lurching like a sick horse. It didn't take much acting. His head was pounding and the world around him was swaying. He knew he very likely had a concussion, if not something worse.

Duke cranked the lever on Marlin's rifle until it was empty, then tossed it to the ground. "Around the house!" Duke barked.

So that's it. Onto Kyle Dawson's ranch. Nothing good had happened there so far, and Marlin didn't think this would turn out any differently.

Carrying the chupacabra wasn't so tough, but Billy Don kept making growling sounds and it was starting to piss Red off. The animal was like a bag of wet laundry, its big head lolling to one side as they carried it. Now Red had to figure out where they were going to go with it once they'd put it into the truck.

There was a small exotic zoo a few miles north of Johnson City, but most of the animals there were imported deer, antelopes, zebras, even a camel. Nothing too dangerous. Red thought he remembered a bear, though. Maybe they'd have a big cage he could use. That would be a much shorter ride than a trip to the zoo in San Antonio. *Somebody* had to keep this animal for him. The alternative was to trek back and get the reinforced trap, but Red didn't know if he'd have that much strength left. His legs were already wobbly as it was.

Duke was nearing a state of frenzy, breathing hard, having a difficult time figuring things out. *Where am I going with them? What am I gonna do next?*

He could have handcuffed them together over a tree limb, but that was no longer an option, thanks to the damn game warden. He'd have to come up with something soon, because he needed to hit the road as soon as possible. *Mexico?* He had no idea where he was going to go. But there would be a manhunt, and he wanted to put some serious mileage behind him. *What about a vehicle?* He couldn't risk taking Marlin's truck; in fact, he'd have to hurry back and hide it somewhere. He'd have to figure all that out later.

He ordered Marlin and Charlie to cross the fence onto the Macho Bueno Ranch, and then told them both to lie facedown on the ground. That would keep them from running while he climbed the fence himself. He wasn't taking any chances.

There were only two registered voters with the first name of Sally Ann in Blanco County, and one of them was seventy-eight years old. The other—Sally Ann Riggs—was thirty-three and lived on the same road as Duke Waldrip. Bill Tatum figured it had to be her. If Duke wasn't home, they'd check her place next.

He and Brad Anderson had strapped on Kevlar vests and were now in Tatum's cruiser, heading toward Waldrip's house. They had decided it would be best to wait until Cowan and Turpin could join them—which shouldn't be more than thirty minutes more—but Tatum wanted to watch Waldrip's house until then.

"This guy gonna be armed?" Anderson asked.

"Shouldn't be. We took all his guns during the search. But you never know."

Marlin kept an arm around Charlie, who seemed to be holding up well. He tried to engage Duke in conversation, hoping it might slow things down.

"Tell me about Searcy," Marlin said over his shoulder. Duke was ten feet behind him. If Marlin saw a chance to jump him, giving Charlie a chance to escape, he'd take it.

"Shut up!" Duke spat. "I don't want to talk about him."

"You killed him, though, right?"

They walked in silence, crossing a dry creek bottom.

Then Duke spoke up. "It was self-defense."

Good. Even if Duke was lying, maybe Marlin could use this information to his own advantage.

"Then the thing to do is—"

Duke cut him off. "Nobody would ever believe me. I'm an ex-con. Shit, I wouldn't believe it myself."

"But Duke, if it was self-defense, you don't want to—"

"Keep your damn mouth closed!"

Duke sounded even farther behind now. Marlin whispered, "Run when I tell you."

Charlie looked up at him, eyes hard and determined, and Marlin could see in that instant that the boy was a survivor. Regardless of what kind of life the kid had had and whatever abuse or neglect had been heaped on top of him, he was going to come out all right. Charlie nodded that he understood.

"Quit talking," Duke said sternly. "No more talking."

35

RED STOPPED ABRUPTLY. "You hear that?"

"What?"

"Voices. Someone yelling."

They stood in silence, the chupacabra hanging between them.

"Don't hear nothin'."

Red waited, but all was quiet. They started walking—and Red heard it again. He looked at Billy Don.

"Yeah, I heard it that time."

Someone was nearby, on the ranch.

Red looked in the direction the voices had come from. And then he saw the unmistakable khaki-clad figure of John Marlin, two hundred yards away, walking out from a grove of oak trees.

"Shit, hit the ground!" Red hissed.

It took Billy Don a good five seconds to manage that feat, but by the time they were both prone, settled in the tall grasses, the game warden still hadn't looked their way.

"He's got a boy with him," Billy Don said. "And some other guy."

Red suddenly realized that his face was about ten inches from the chupacabra's jaws. But that wasn't his biggest concern right now. His biggest worry was getting caught red-handed on Kyle Dawson's ranch with the chupacabra. Marlin would take it away in the blink of an eye.

Red lifted the binoculars and studied the group. Something wasn't quite right. John Marlin appeared to be staggering along . . . and the other guy, behind Marlin . . . Christ, he was carrying a gun!

"Christ, he's carrying a gun!" Billy Don said.

"I can see that."

They watched as the trio continued tromping through the woods and disappeared into another grove of trees.

"What we gonna do?" Billy Don asked.

Red glanced at the chupacabra, which was still slack-jawed, its tongue hanging out. But how long would it be out cold? If they left it here, would it be gone when they got back? Hell, would he and Billy Don even *make* it back? "We could go call the cops," Red ventured.

"There ain't time for that."

Red paused, and Billy Don struggled to his feet. "Do what you want," the big man said, "but I'm going after 'em."

Red didn't say anything. *Damn, why does everything always have to get so screwed up?*

Billy Don started walking.

"Okay, damn it," Red said. "Wait for me. And gimme my gun back."

Tatum slowed when he saw a mailbox with Sally Ann Riggs' house number on it, trying to sneak a peek through the cedar trees that choked the front property line.

"That's the woman's place?" Anderson asked.

"Yep, and I figure we should—"

Hold on a second, Tatum thought as he took another look.

He stopped the car and put it into reverse. Peering through a small gap in the tree line, he had seen a vehicle that looked like John Marlin's Dodge truck.

"What's up?" The Ranger was following Tatum's line of vision.

The white Texas Parks & Wildlife emblem was easy to spot on the driver's door.

"I'm just wondering what Marlin's doing here. Let's duck in here real quick."

Tatum backed up farther, then dropped into forward gear and swung the cruiser into the driveway. He parked behind the truck, noticing that the door on the passenger's side was standing open. Marlin was nowhere to be seen.

Both men got out, and as they approached the truck, Brad Anderson was the first to spot it: Marlin's rifle lying in the dirt, surrounded by six fresh cartridges.

The men exchanged glances and didn't need to say a word. They drew their weapons, went to the front door of the house, and flanked it on both sides. Tatum rapped hard with his knuckles. Immediately, dogs began barking behind the house, but there was no sound from inside.

Anderson motioned that he was going around the back, and Tatum nodded. He gave it a minute, then knocked again. Then he tried the doorknob and found it locked. All was quiet.

Anderson appeared at the corner of the house and motioned for Tatum to join him. The Ranger was bent at the knees, and Tatum soon saw why. On the ground, a few feet from an oleander bush, was a pool of blood.

"I'm calling for backup," Tatum said.

"At least tell me how you scammed Searcy," Marlin said. "I still haven't figured that one out. Must've been pretty clever."

Marlin glanced back and saw that Duke was smiling.

"He shot at a decoy," Duke bragged.

"The one you stole from Howell Rogers?"

"Yep." Duke didn't sound contrite at all. "See, I'd take a hunter out to Kyle's place, let him sit for an hour or so, stare at a few average bucks and get all worked up. Gus'd be about three hundred yards away, hiding over a hill. He had this string tied to a branch, and when he'd pull it, the branch'd move and you could see the decoy."

"And the hunter would shoot?"

"Not right away," Duke said, disgusted. "Some of those guys couldn't spot an elephant in a parking lot. Most the time, I'd have to point it out to them. Finally, they'd take the damn shot. Gus'd pull a second string and the decoy would fall over. We'd wait a few minutes and then go searching for it. But by then, Gus and the decoy would be long gone. We kept blood in a bottle to leave a trail."

Marlin was appalled that Duke appeared so pleased with himself. "Then what?"

"We'd look around for an hour or two then I'd say it must've been a flesh wound. Call the search off."

Marlin saw where this was going. "Until you called 'em up a few days later."

Duke whistled. "You catch on quick. I'd tell 'em I found their deer and ask did they want the trophy or not?"

"And of course they did."

"Damn right they did. Every time."

"Where'd you get the sheds?" Marlin asked.

"Breeders."

Many area ranch owners held scientific breeder permits for whitetail deer. In essence, the deer became livestock, and some massive bucks were grown through selective breeding. Most breeders were willing to sell the antlers that were shed by their prize bucks every spring. As Marlin had seen, it had been a simple matter for Duke to bolt a set of monstrous antlers onto the skull-cap from another deer, then cover the whole thing up as the taxidermy job was completed. Marlin had heard of all kinds of scams, cheats, and swindles in the hunting world, but this was one of the most despicable. It was also pretty damn shrewd.

"What about Kyle?" he asked.

"What about him?" Duke replied.

Marlin slowed his pace, hoping Duke would come closer and Marlin could risk rushing him.

"What happened to him? Why'd you kill him?"

"Keep moving," Duke said.

They were cresting a hill, and Marlin was getting winded from the uphill climb. His legs felt like jelly. Charlie was still doing fine, and Marlin was as proud of him as he had ever been of anybody.

"If you wanna know about Kyle," Duke said, "you're gonna have to ask Cheri. She did it."

Marlin couldn't keep the disbelief out of his voice. "Cheri killed Kyle?"

"That's what I'm telling you. It was Cheri's fault."

Moments after making the radio call, Tatum and Anderson discovered another disturbing item. They were circling the house, looking for more evidence, when they spotted a sheet of paper a stone's throw from the rear porch.

They walked to it, and Tatum flipped it over with the barrel of his gun. It was a flyer announcing the disappearance of Oliver Searcy.

Tatum looked to the north, toward the Macho Bueno Ranch. There was no wind today; the sheet of paper hadn't been blown to this location. Someone had dropped it here, on their way into the ranch. It could have been mere moments ago, and Tatum felt the need to act immediately.

Tatum contacted the dispatcher on his handheld radio. "Be advised that Anderson and I are entering the Macho Bueno Ranch. The responding deputies should enter with caution."

"We gotta do something, Red!"

The men were shadowing the gunman and his hostages, moving as quietly as they could, ducking from tree to tree. Occasionally, Red would lift the binoculars and take a closer look. There was now no doubt whatsoever that Marlin and the boy were in danger. The man with the gun was keeping his distance, marching them farther into the woods.

"How far you think they are?" Red asked. "Hundred and twenty yards?"

"More like one fifty."

Billy Don had always been a better judge of distance than Red, something they had learned on their late-night poaching excursions.

"We gotta get closer." Red had equipped his pistol with a scope for hunting, but a shot that long was out of the question. Even a hundred yards would be pushing it. Fifty would be best, or even less, if they could manage it.

Billy Don gulped and nodded. "Let's do it."

"Okay, this'll do," Duke said.

They had descended the hill and were now in a low basin beneath some towering pecan trees. The canopy was thick and dense, screening out the sunlight. A couple of bodies could lie here undetected for a damn long time if nobody knew where to look.

Marlin's arms were twitching, sounds seemed to be muffled, and he didn't know if it was from his injury or the massive amounts of adrenaline pumping into his system. This was the end of the line. He had to buy some time.

Marlin said, "You're telling me Cheri—all hundred and twenty pounds of her—dragged Kyle into that cave?"

Duke's eyes were darting back and forth, as if he was searching for a solution to his problems in the trees or the grasses.

"I don't believe it, Duke."

"What do I care? Both of you, get down on your knees."

Once the gunman disappeared over the hill, Red and Billy Don began closing the distance quickly. They could move without fear of being seen, but they had to be careful to keep the noise to a minimum.

Billy Don was panting hard, his face a vivid red, doing his best, Red knew, to keep up.

"If something happens to me," Red said between breaths, "you can have my Elvis CDs."

Marlin refused. He wouldn't go down on his knees. He knew what would happen then.

"Let Charlie go," Marlin said. "Please, Duke, let him go."

"I told you . . . get down!"

Marlin took a casual step to his left, away from Charlie, hoping Duke would keep the gun trained on him rather than on the boy. He did.

Red didn't know where weird thoughts came from, and it didn't really matter, but as he rushed up the slope, possibly about to face death square in the face, he wondered, *Is this what Teddy Roosevelt's boys felt like, busting their humps up San Juan Hill?*

He hoped not. Because he felt like he was going to vomit.

"We can take my truck, Duke. We'll drive wherever you want, and nobody will stop us."

Marlin made another small step to the left.

"Won't work." Duke was holding the handgun on Marlin, ignoring Charlie. The man's face was contorted with anguish.

"Sure it will. We'll be able to hear everything on the radio. We'll keep to the back roads. I know 'em all. I can get us out of the county."

"I'm telling you . . . I want you down on your knees."

"Don't get down, Charlie."

"Down on your damn knees!"

Red and Billy Don dropped to their knees and scurried to the crest of the hill. *Just like Injuns would do*, Red figured. Another weird thought, coming from nowhere. Red had to force himself to focus.

They scooted slowly, and then they could see down the other side into a tree-filled hollow.

Red saw the three of them, Marlin with his hands in front of him, the other man pointing the gun right at him.

"How far?" Red said.

"Sixty . . . maybe seventy."

Red longed for his .270. With his rifle, a shot like that would be a no-brainer. But his revolver, even with a scope, well . . .

"If he shoots, I want you to run, Charlie."

"Shut up!"

"Run as fast as you can and don't stop."

"I will."

"Shut up!"

They were yelling like crazy down there, and Red knew the time was now.

"Do it, Red. You gotta do it."

Red pulled the hammer back on the big .45 and sighted through the scope.

He couldn't hold it steady. The crosshairs were jumping everywhere.

Marlin took one more small step to his left. Charlie was now at least fifteen feet to his right. Duke couldn't shoot and then swing the gun on the boy, not with any kind of accuracy. With luck, Charlie could scamper through the trees and get away. Especially if Marlin was doing everything he could to slow Duke down.

It was time to charge.

"Take a deep breath," Billy Don said.

"I know, I know." Red sucked it in and held it. Yeah, that was better. Not perfect—things were still jiggly—but at least he could see the guy in the scope now. Red thought Marlin and the boy were spaced far enough apart that he could shoot without hitting them.

Probably.

He began to pull back on the trigger.

He felt the resistance, but he moved it, a millimeter at a time.

It was about to give, to set the hammer free and send the bullet home. . . .

"*Freeze!*"

Red jumped. *What the hell?*

The yell had come from behind him, down the hill.

All three of them heard someone yell, and Duke took a quick look behind him. He couldn't see anybody.

"They're coming, Duke. It's no use."

Red turned and saw two cops on the flat below the hill, aiming rifles up at him. *Son of a bitch, I don't have time for this!* Red thought. *Those guys don't understand the situation.*

He looked back at the gunman. The guy's arm was stiff now, straight out, bracing for a recoil, and Red knew he was about to shoot.

Red found the guy in the scope again.

"*Freeze!*"

Red ignored the men behind him.

"Shoot, Red."

Red squeezed the trigger, all the way this time.

Marlin flinched at the sound of the shot, but it hadn't come from the gun in Duke's hand. He wasn't sure where it had come from. Marlin was heartbroken to see that Charlie hadn't run. There had been a shot, but he hadn't run.

Even when there was a sharp report of a second shot, this one farther away, Charlie didn't move. He was frozen in place by fear.

For a moment, Marlin and Duke stood there, staring at each other. Marlin saw a large red stain spreading across Duke's left shoulder, growing rapidly, but the gun was still dangling in his right hand. He raised it again, but this time he pointed it at Charlie. Later, in hindsight, Marlin would wonder why Duke had done that. Maybe because, in Duke's twisted mind, the boy was the witness against him. The one who had caused his downfall.

The gun was up, but Charlie wasn't budging.

Marlin bent low and rushed toward Duke.

The bullet the cops fired slammed into the dirt next to Red, and he immediately dropped the gun. He and Billy Don both rolled over onto their backs and put their arms in the air.

"You did it," Billy Don said.

"Man, I hope so."

As Marlin hit Duke and drove him to the ground, the gun roared in his ear, and Marlin could feel the heat from the muzzle on his cheek. But he was on top of Duke now, straddling him, trying to pin his arms.

Marlin managed to grasp Duke's right forearm, then his left, but Duke twisted the revolver upward with his right wrist and let another round fly. Marlin collapsed onto Duke, trying to stay low, out of the line of fire.

Despite his injury, Duke was astoundingly strong, and Marlin knew he couldn't hold him down for long.

Marlin decided to relinquish his hold on Duke's left arm and try to use both hands to wrest the gun away. As soon as he released, though, Duke slammed his left fist into the side of Marlin's face. His right eye was now totally swollen shut.

Tatum and Anderson cringed when they heard the shots, thinking the two men on the hill were returning fire. But neither had moved. Who was doing the shooting?

The chief deputy and the Ranger pumped their legs and hustled up the incline as fast as they could move.

Marlin was lying on top of Duke now, their heads side by side, their arms out to the left and right. He could see Duke bending his wrist again, struggling to bring the barrel horizontal.

Can't give him a target, Marlin told himself.

The big gun roared again, and Marlin felt a sting along his left bicep and shoulder. He knew he'd been hit, but he didn't know how badly. The next shot could be the last.

Marlin was sapped of strength, almost powerless now, and he decided to try something desperate. Once again, he released Duke's left arm, and Duke began to rain powerful blows on the side of Marlin's head.

But this time, Marlin quickly moved his right arm across Duke's body and slipped it underneath Duke's right forearm. He had Duke's arm in a fulcrum now, and Marlin began to press downward with his left hand.

Duke let out a horrible scream as the bones in his arm snapped. He was bucking and kicking now, and then Marlin's right ear exploded under the force of one last powerful strike from Duke's left fist.

The sheer power of the blow launched Marlin to the left, and he was unsure where the gun was now. He was on his back, unable to lift his head, struggling to see through a left eye that was a mere slit.

He heard Duke rising to his feet, moaning like a wild beast, and Marlin could picture the gun in his hand. *Any second the shot will come.*

But instead, he heard Duke shout, "Don't do it, goddamn it!" Then the sound of heavy footfalls.

A shot rang out, loud and close. Marlin managed to roll to his side. . . . And he saw Charlie, who was wielding the gun with both hands as he tried to shoot his fleeing stepfather.

36

"HOW DOES THAT feel?"

"Okay."

"Doesn't sting?"

"Yeah, a little."

The nurse, a woman in her fifties, said, "I thought so."

It was quiet in Blanco County Hospital, except for the incessant ringing in his ears.

"What time is it?"

She checked her watch. "Eleven-thirty. Why, you got a hot lunch date?"

Marlin gave her a small smile, all he was up to at the moment. He was certain he looked like some kind of gargoyle, eyes swollen and starting to go black, nose broken and puffy, cheek cut, ear red and inflamed. He'd broken a finger, too, something he hadn't even felt at the time. Then there was the wound along his arm and back, where the bullet had dug a furrow half an inch deep and eight inches long. "Not too bad," the doctor had said, "but you're gonna have a nasty scar."

He could live with that. What he couldn't live with was the thought of Duke Waldrip getting away. Tatum had promised to call and give him an update, but so far, Marlin had heard nothing. He hadn't wanted to leave the scene, but Tatum had insisted. Marlin hadn't had the will to argue.

"How's the boy?" Marlin asked.

"He's over in Social Services," the nurse said, "but from what I hear, he's fine. Must be a tough kid."

"Yeah," Marlin said. "Yeah, he is."

Tatum phoned Marlin's hospital room thirty minutes later. He sounded grim. "Nothing yet."

Marlin was sitting up in bed, with no intention of staying the night, despite the doctor's recommendation. He let out a low sigh of exasperation.

"Relax," Tatum said. "We've got thirty men on the ground, ten of them on horses, and Jacob Daughdril's got his chopper in the air. We've got dogs coming, too. He's weak, he's wounded. Believe me, John, he ain't going nowhere."

That wasn't much comfort. Nothing would feel right until Duke was in a cell. If only Tatum and Anderson had gotten down the hill a little sooner. Marlin still wasn't clear on what had happened at the top of the hill, about what had stopped Tatum and Anderson from chasing Duke immediately. Everything had been too chaotic at the scene. Now Tatum filled him in.

"I've only got a minute, and then I need to get back to it. . . . But do you remember seeing Red O'Brien and Billy Don Craddock?"

Marlin did, but at the time, he had thought he was hallucinating.

"Well," Tatum said, "it was Red who put that bullet in Waldrip."

Marlin was too mortified to speak. Red O'Brien was one of the most incorrigible poachers in the county, and here he had very likely saved both Marlin's life and Charlie's. What could Marlin possibly say about that?

Tatum let that sink in, then said, "They were all camoed up, so we didn't know who the hell they were. When we figured it out, they said they were out there about the chupacabra. Said they pulled it from a trap, were hauling it to Red's truck, and then they saw the three of you go marching by." Tatum paused. "Chupacabra. Is that a crock or what?"

Red was royally, supremely, and totally pissed off. He couldn't remember ever being this angry. They hadn't even let him look. Just one quick look, that's all he had wanted. Just a quick scamper through the woods to see if the chupacabra was still there. But as Ernie Turpin had driven them off the ranch, all he'd said was, "Sorry, guys. Can't do it."

Red leaned back on his sofa and pouted. "Save a couple of lives and that's the thanks we get? Well, that's bullshit."

Billy Don, sitting in the La-Z-Boy, shrugged. Red didn't like it.

"A little support here, Billy Don, that's all I'm asking."

"I know it, Red, but hell, what do you want? They called you a damn hero."

That was news to Red. Somebody had called him a hero? Really? "Who?"

"'Member near the end, when all the deputies showed up? Tatum had you off to one side, asking questions, and the Ranger was talking to me?"

"Yeah?"

"That Ranger asked me who fired the shot, and I said you did."

"And?"

"And then he said, 'That boy's a damn hero.'"

Red wasn't all that sure Billy Don was telling the truth. "If you're telling me stories, Billy Don, I swear I'll—"

"Honest to God," Billy Don said, sounding sincere.

Imagine that. Weren't many millionaires in the world, but there weren't that many genuine heroes, either. Hell, it felt pretty good, in a way.

"What say, hero, you want a beer?" Billy Don pushed his bulk out of the recliner.

"Yeah, okay. Sure."

A few seconds later, Red could hear Billy Don opening the refrigerator.

"I'm a damn hero," he said softly to himself.

"What?" Billy Don called out.

"Nothing."

By four o'clock, Marlin was feeling pretty good and he decided it was time to leave. He slipped the hospital gown off his shoulders, then found his clothes in a cabinet by the door. He managed to get down the hall and into a stairway without being noticed. Then he remembered he didn't have his truck. He retraced his steps back to his room and picked up the phone.

Rudi answered on the first ring.

"It's me again," Marlin said. He'd already called once and told her the complete story, or least everything he could remember.

Amazingly, she hadn't flipped out. Marlin guessed she had seen all kinds of chaos and destruction when she'd done the local news. She had, however, sounded very concerned, as she did now. During the earlier call, he'd had to insist that she stay at the house instead of coming up to the hospital. "What's going on?" she asked now. "How're you doing?"

"I'm fine, Rudi, really. Beat to hell, but fine. I'm ready to get out of here."

There was a pause. "What did the doctor say about that?"

"Not much. I didn't ask him."

"But if you have a concussion—"

"I don't. He said I didn't." It was the truth. "I'm ugly as hell, though, so you'd better prepare yourself."

"Oh?"

"Yeah. I was wondering if you could come get me."

"Where's the hospital?"

Marlin told her.

"I'll be there in ten minutes."

"I'll be waiting out front."

The four German shepherds and their handlers crossed the shallow, narrow creek, but the dogs couldn't pick up the scent on the other side. The oldest trick in the book. Waldrip had entered the creek and walked upstream or downstream to throw them off.

"Split 'em up," Tatum called out.

He glanced at his wristwatch, even though he'd promised himself ten minutes ago he'd quit doing that. Nearly five o'clock, and the sun would set in an hour. If the dogs couldn't come up with something, Tatum would have to call it off for the night, start fresh in the morning.

Every so often, when the wind was right, Duke could hear the far-off barking of a dog. Or maybe it was all in his head. He knew he'd lost a lot of blood, and his head swam with every forward step. He was so tired. So damn tired.

But he'd made it off the Macho Bueno Ranch, and he figured it would be hours before they'd expand their search beyond its borders. He'd gone north, intentionally stopping at Kyle's house—going in the front door and out the back—to confuse the dogs and waste the deputies' time as they searched it.

Now the sun was setting, and if he was lucky, he could find a place to stop and rest. Just a few minutes was all he wanted. Some time to regain his strength and come up with a plan. Maybe if he could make it to town, find a phone, he could call Gus and—no, he couldn't do that. Gus was gone. Gone, like Duke should've been a long time ago.

Duke was walking into a small, steep ravine when his knees buckled. He collapsed to his butt and slid the rest of the way down. Here. Here would be a good place to stop and clear his head.

The wound was bleeding again. He knew the deputies and the dogs were at least a mile away, maybe more, but he couldn't shake this feeling that he was being watched, that something was stalking him.

Just after seven o'clock, Marlin called Tatum's cell phone. The reception was poor, fading in and out.

". . . at Kyle's house," Tatum was saying. "But he wasn't in there."

"Have you widened the search area?" Marlin asked.

Tatum replied, but it was garbled, the deputy saying something about the dogs.

Then the connection was broken. Exactly the reason Marlin hated those damn things.

"Maybe I should go out there," he said.

Rudi, who was bringing another ice bag for his face, said, "Yeah, and do what?"

The dogs never could pick the scent up again, and Tatum sent them home. Let them rest, and maybe they'd do better in the morning.

Ernie Turpin's voice came over the radio: "Dark as hell out here, Bill. What you wanna do?"

There was only one thing to do: call it off until first light.

Duke faded in and out of consciousness for several hours. Later, judging by the half-moon climbing into the sky, he knew it was late, maybe three o'clock.

The night was cold and damp, but Duke was burning up. He could barely lift his good arm to wipe the sweat from his forehead.

He heard a noise nearby, a stick cracking under a foot. Or a paw.

He found a small rock and tried to throw it into the brush. It went ten feet.

His head fell back to the ground. His breathing was rapid and harsh.

Something was speaking to him now. An animal out there,

mocking him, telling him it was only a matter of time . . . *laughing* at him.

His eyes never closed, but they stopped seeing.

He was long gone before the teeth sank into his flesh.

37

IT WAS A beautiful day for the ceremony—sunny, cloudless, temperature in the sixties. Marlin's face bore little reminder of the events from eleven days earlier. There was still some minor discoloration around his eyes, but his nose was feeling much better and the wound on his back was healing quickly.

"You ready for this?" Bobby Garza asked. He was sitting across from Marlin in the coffee room at the Blanco County Sheriff's Department. Garza had been at work for eight days and had been making his way around on crutches. It was good to have him back.

They could hear a marching band torturing some unrecognizable melody on the lawn of the courthouse across the street. After that, the mayor would speak, and then John Marlin would climb to the stage. He'd volunteered to be the one to bestow the honors on Red O'Brien and Billy Don Craddock. The city council had conjured up something called the Superior Citizen Award, and the two poachers would be the first ever to receive it. Marlin could barely stand the irony.

But this wouldn't close the books on it all. None of them— Marlin, Garza, Tatum and the other deputies, even Charlie and his mother—would feel a sense of closure until they knew what had happened to Duke Waldrip, who had never been found. After several days of combing the woods, the search party assumed they would stumble upon a body eventually, but they never did. Had Duke escaped? They might never know.

They knew what had happened to Kyle Dawson, though. He'd been electrocuted, most likely by the toaster that had been found with his body. The hot tub behind his house seemed the most likely scene of the crime, considering that he'd been wearing a swimsuit—and Duke Waldrip was the chief suspect. All his bullshit about Cheri just didn't add up, and she had volunteered to take a lie-detector test. Actually, she'd taken two, and she had passed them both. There was one odd fact, though, that couldn't be explained. Henry Jameson had lifted a number of partial fingerprints off the extension cord that presumably was used to plug the toaster in. Some matched Duke's. Some matched Kyle's. None matched Cheri's. But right at the end of the cord, on the plug, Jameson found the largest print of all. And it matched Gus Waldrip's. *Gus Waldrip.* Of course, he was nowhere to be found. Maybe he'd reappear someday and they could question him. For some reason, Marlin didn't think that would ever happen.

They had no doubt it was Duke who had shot Garza, but there was never any physical evidence to support it. It was merely the most logical conclusion, and there were no other suspects. The Houston Police Department had filed that case as "open but inactive."

Likewise, they were certain it was Duke—not Kyle—who killed Oliver Searcy. Charlie had been given a few days to recover from the trauma, and then a social services worker had gently questioned him. He'd skipped school one day—which he swore he rarely did—and that was when he'd seen Oliver Searcy with Duke Waldrip. Charlie had been in the house alone, watching television, when he'd heard a truck pull up outside. Then another.

He ran to his room and peeked out the window. Duke was out there with another man in camo. Charlie had gotten a good long look, and Marlin felt the boy's identification of Oliver Searcy was indisputable. Duke, who had come home to retrieve a rifle, never knew Charlie had been home that day. He never knew there was a witness who could verify that he *had* hunted with Searcy. He never found out, apparently, until that morning eleven days ago.

"Quit dwelling on it," Garza said, and Marlin looked up at him. "Won't do any good anyway."

"Well now, those are some words of wisdom," Marlin replied.

"Don't get all ornery on me. All I'm saying is, we'll find him or his body. You *know* we will."

The band fell silent and Marlin could hear the mayor's voice over a loudspeaker.

"Better get out there," Garza said, "It's redneck-appreciation time."

Marlin slowly stood.

Garza put his weight on one leg as he hoisted himself out of the chair and onto his crutches. "I got an idea. Tonight, let's load up some sandwiches and go hunt for the chupacabra. There's bound to be some kind of reward, don't you think?" He pronounced it *ree-ward*.

"And right after that," said Marlin, playing along, "we can throw a net over the Sasquatch. Maybe track down a unicorn."

"That's the spirit."

They got to the front door of the building, and Marlin opened it to let Garza through. As the men walked down the sidewalk and began to cross the street, the crowd rose and began to applaud.

 **Epilogue**

THE DAY AFTER the ceremony on the courthouse lawn, a dog returned to its home north of Macho Bueno Ranch with a bloodstained rag in its mouth. Closer examination revealed that the rag was a portion of a shirt much like the one Duke Waldrip had been wearing twelve days earlier. John Marlin, Bill Tatum, and a small group of deputies searched a wooded area behind the dog's home the next afternoon. In a ravine half a mile away, the search party found more shredded clothing, and then a badly decomposed partial corpse. DNA testing revealed that the body was, in fact, that of Richard Anthony Waldrip. The medical examiner, Lem Tucker, noted several fang marks on the remaining bones.

Four days later, a fourteen-year-old named Tiffany Sloan, driving without a license, hit an animal with her mother's car on Flat Creek Road. John Marlin and Trey Sweeney quickly identified it as a spotted hyena. After much debate, the animal was sent to the forensics laboratory at the Texas Department of Public Safety in Austin. The contents of the stomach were extracted, but testing for human remains proved inconclusive.

Immediately after the ceremony, Red O'Brien and Billy Don Craddock approached John Marlin and professed that their poaching days were over. "This doing the right thing is kinda cool," O'Brien said. Billy Don nodded vigorously in agreement. One month later, John Marlin arrested them for shooting three whitetail deer out of season.

Sheriff Bobby Garza discarded the crutches after nine weeks, three weeks short of the twelve the doctor had recommended. Two months later, he began a rigorous regimen of rehabilitation therapy. Today, his limp is nearly unnoticeable.

After inheriting Kyle Dawson's estate, Cheri quit her job at the strip club and went into a pricey rehabilitation facility. She *has* slept with most of the male counselors, but she was stone-cold sober each time. She plans to attend college and earn a teaching degree.

In November of that year, Mike Hung won Actor of the Year at the Adult Entertainment Awards. As he gave his acceptance speech, right after he thanked "all the little people," his glass eye popped out of its socket, rolled down the stage toward the audience, and caused pandemonium as scantily clad porn starlets screamed and fled in horror. Hung and Marty Hoffenhauser went on to produce three more films together, grossing a total of more than twenty million dollars.

In February, Rudi Villarreal met John Marlin in San Antonio, just as planned. But she hadn't been simply enjoying a long vacation; she'd struck a deal with the *Blanco County Record,* and they'd agreed to run a lengthy article, written by Rudi, about deception and dishonesty within the media. When she asked Marlin if he would be willing to be interviewed regarding the false broadcast on *Hard News Tonight,* he readily agreed. Her reputation opened many doors for her, and she was able to go on record with many high-profile politicians and celebrities who had been libeled or slandered by disreputable and legitimate media outlets alike. Her article garnered national attention and became a frontrunner for the Pulitzer Prize. Shortly afterward, she took a position with the *New York Times*. She and Marlin talk often on the phone, and Marlin is planning to visit her soon in her new apartment in Manhattan.

In the spring of that year, Kate Fulmer, a college student and part-time volunteer for an organization called People 4 People, worked ten hours a week at a soup kitchen in Lincoln, Nebraska. On her second day, she noticed a quiet man sitting by himself in one corner of the room. Kate approached him and made small talk, which became a daily routine, and the two quickly became friends. He was an odd individual, who, on occasion, would stare into space and blurt out a bizarre amalgam of words. All in all, despite his peculiarities, he seemed to be a content person, a gentle and peaceful man who smiled often. That's why Kate was so surprised when, on his ninth day at the kitchen, he casually mentioned that he had intentionally electrocuted a man. Further, he said, he had arranged it so his brother would take the blame. Initially, Kate assumed he was either delusional or joking. He flatly said he wasn't. Kate, starting to believe him, asked why he had done it. He said that both men had made fun of him. Also, he said, they were mean to animals, which was why he had let some of their animals loose. And then he giggled and said something confusing about sousaphones. *Maybe he is joking*, Kate thought. You could never tell with these people. The man continued to laugh as Kate rose and made her way back behind the counter. She wondered if she should call the police and report what the man had said. But it wouldn't have been any use anyway. He left a few minutes later and she never saw him again.

KEEP READING FOR AN EXCERPT FROM
BEN REHDER'S NEXT BLANCO COUNTY MYSTERY

GUILT TRIP

AVAILABLE IN HARDCOVER
FROM ST. MARTIN'S MINOTAUR

ON FRIDAY, MAY 7, a beautiful spring morning fairly bursting with promises of hope and renewal, Texas state senator Dylan Herzog received a phone call that grabbed him by an extremely sensitive part of his anatomy and yanked him to a place he definitely didn't want to go.

Before the unwelcome interruption, Herzog had been minding his own business, thumbing through a copy of *Esquire*, contemplating the possibility of cheek implants. A senior aide named Rusk was in Herzog's office with him, both of them moving slowly, sort of easing into the morning. They were seriously hung over, having spent the previous afternoon on a cabin cruiser with a couple of hard-drinking lobbyists and their bikini-clad dates. These were young ladies with scruples; their tops hadn't come off until the third round of margaritas.

"You seen this yet?" Rusk asked, hefting a document three inches thick.

But Herzog was too distracted by the article, a somewhat facetious piece on cosmetic surgery. For a price, you too could look like a Hollywood hunk! There were before-and-after shots: Some loser who'd spent a cool twenty grand for a complete makeover. Hair plugs to give him a thick mop like Hugh Grant's. Liposuction for the trim waist of Russell Crowe. And cheek implants for the Brad Pitt look. But now, in Herzog's opinion, the patient simply looked like a hairier, skinnier, cheekier loser.

Rusk repeated his question, and Herzog glanced up. "Seen what?"

"The prelim report on the red-necked sapsucker."

Herzog tossed the magazine aside. Cheek implants? The very idea. He was a devastatingly handsome man as is, even if he was approaching fifty. "The red-necked . . . ?"

"Sapsucker."

"What about it?"

"They want to move it from endangered to threatened, but they need more funds to continue the study."

Screw the sapsucker, Herzog was about to say, but right then Susan buzzed in on the intercom.

"Senator Herzog, there's a call for you on line one," his executive assistant said, sounding somewhat less chipper than normal. Herzog frowned at the phone. He had asked her to hold all calls unless it was important. And for God's sake, he'd told her, don't put the wife through.

"Who is it?" he snapped, running a hand through his hundred-dollar haircut.

"Well . . . he didn't say."

"Didn't I tell you—"

"You need to take this one, Dyl."

Herzog shot a quick look at Rusk, thinking: *Jesus, how many times have I told her not to call me that in the office?* He lifted the phone from its cradle.

She whispered: "Sorry about that, but it's some guy . . . he didn't give his name. He says he has photos—"

"Aw, Christ," Herzog said, wondering why she would interrupt with a call from a person he didn't even know. And why was she whispering? "Just take a message, Susan, and tell him—"

"Of us!" she hissed. "He says he has photos of us."

And just like that, everything changed.

Herzog sat up straight. His forehead suddenly felt like a furnace. A million invisible pins pricked at his scalp. The hair on his neck would have stood on end if it hadn't been meticulously trimmed with a GroomMaster Deluxe. He tried to smile at Rusk, who was looking more curious by the minute. *Everything okay?* the aide mouthed. Herzog nodded.

"I wasn't going to put him through," Susan said gingerly, "but when he said that, well . . ."

Herzog stared down at the red blinking light on the phone's base. The caller was waiting patiently. "What were his exact words?"

"He said he'd been watching us . . . and he has photos. He sounds pretty creepy, Dyl."

"Okaaay," he said, drawing the word out, giving himself time to think. But it most definitely was not okay. He covered the mouthpiece. "Can you give me a few minutes, Ken?" Rusk gave him a questioning look, but nodded and left the office.

Herzog took a deep breath, then pushed the red button and mustered up as much bravado as possible. "Who the hell is this?"

There was a moment of silence, then a harsh backwoods twang: "Mind you damn manners, Herzog, or every newspaper in the state's gonna know you cain't keep your pecker in your pants."

Play it tough—that's what his instincts told him. Herzog had dealt with his share of blowhard rednecks before, and they usually backed down when he got firm with them. Besides, the caller might be bluffing. "I don't know if this is a sick joke or what," he said, "but if you think—"

"Have you checked your mail this morning?"

"No, I haven't, but I have no intention—"

"Just shut the hell up and check with your secretary. She seems to take care of all kinds of little things for you, know what I mean?" There was a taunting quality to the caller's voice.

With one hand, Herzog began to rummage through his overflowing inbox. "You leave her out of this," he demanded. "My relationship with Miss Hammond is purely professional." He meant to issue the words in a bark of indignity, but they came out in a frantic squeak.

"'Purely professional,'" the caller mocked. "I wish I had me a setup like that. Now you just find them photos and we'll all see how professional it really is. I sent you a little care package on Wednesday. Would've been in yesterday's mail, today's at the latest."

And it was. Herzog found it buried in the middle of the pile: a plain manila envelope, Herzog's name and address in block letters, with the word PERSONAL below that. The return address said *Kimberly Clark*. Why did that name sound familiar? "I've . . . I've got it right here," Herzog said.

"Well, hell, boy, don't be bashful. Take a look."

Herzog swallowed hard, tore the envelope open, then braced himself and pulled the contents out.

Oh my God.

He felt an iron fist grasp his balls and squeeze. Sweat was beginning to trickle from every perfectly exfoliated pore.

The photos were grainy and of poor quality, but they did the job. They had been taken through the rear windows into the living room. His stomach went queasy. Someone had been spying on them from Susan's backyard!

The first shot wasn't too troublesome—just him and Susan kissing, fully clothed. He even remembered the night, Friday of last week, when his wife was out of town.

Herzog flipped to the second shot and a wave of nausea churned in his abdomen. Much more incriminating. Now they were undressing—Herzog unbuckling his belt, Susan with her blouse off, her skirt at her feet. The important question was, how long had the photographer hung around? Was the last shot worse than the first two? After all, Herzog had certain, well, "predilections" that the average constituent simply would not fully understand. He might be able to survive a run-of-the-mill infidelity scandal, but if these photos ventured into—

His thoughts were interrupted.

"That gal's sure got some nice titties," the caller said. "Them store-bought or what?"

Herzog couldn't answer. He was beginning to hyperventilate. Everything depended on the third shot, and he couldn't bring himself to look. His hands were trembling and his eyes had watered up. Why was this happening? He played golf with all the right people, greased all the right palms, followed the code of the modern-day politico. For God's sake, he was supposed to be governor some day! "Who are you?" he managed to mumble. "Why are you doing this?"

"We'll get to that. But first, have you seen 'em all yet? That last one's a beaut."

Herzog summoned up his courage, what little was left, and flipped to the final photograph. He almost passed out at his desk. A bolt of pain stabbed from temple to temple.

The shot was from later in the evening, after they'd both had plenty to drink. Susan was wearing her black leather outfit—corset, thigh-high boots, and a G-string. A riding crop completed the fetching ensemble. But that wasn't the worst part. Not by any stretch of the imagination. What Herzog was wearing made the photo an unmitigated disaster.

Dylan Albert Herzog—the distinguished representative of Senate District 32, chairman of the Natural Resources Committee—was now on foreign soil. Rather than being the one in power, the one who commanded others to jump through hoops, he was at the mercy of a stranger at the end of a phone line. It was his worst nightmare. "What . . . what do you want?" he chirped.

"Oh, I see I've got your attention now. Okay, listen up." The caller's tone had gone from chiding to militant. He spat each word out like curdled milk. "I'm sick of laws that favor the rich folks and screw small landowners like me. I'm sick of the government meddling where it don't belong. I'm sick of letting a bunch of dirtbags screw me out of a dollar every chance they get. And it makes me sick when I know the chief dirtbag"—here there was a diabolical cackle—"is a guy who likes to wear a friggin' diaper."

Herzog pulled his trashcan from under his desk and neatly launched his breakfast. *Kimberly Clark.* Now he got the joke.

"What do you want?" the senator croaked, with much more sincerity this time.

Late Sunday afternoon. Annie and Horace Norris, retirees who proudly hailed from Madison, Wisconsin, had just left the Snake Farm & Indian Artifact Showplace (an attraction they had found rather odd, to be honest), when they spotted the drunk driver.

"No doubt about it, the guy's smashed," Horace growled, stooped over the wheel of his Winnebago, heading north on Highway 281 toward Johnson City, Texas. "A regular menace, that's what he is."

"Oh, dear," replied Annie, his wife of forty-six years.

Horace didn't like it. No sir, he didn't like it one bit. It was hard enough to maneuver his RV in a safe and prudent manner under ordinary circumstances, but when you had to share the road with a drunk driver, well, that was entirely unacceptable. He hadn't survived four decades in the dog-eat-dog world of actuarial analysis to be killed by some hotshot in a flashy red Corvette. Looked brand-new, judging by the temporary dealer plate in the rear window.

"This fruitcake is all over the road," Horace grumbled. And the sports car was, too—floating from lane to lane, forty yards ahead of the Winnebago's massive front grille. He glanced down at his speedometer, which was sitting on *30*. A measly thirty miles per hour. Horace couldn't believe it. Not only was this joker weaving, he was doing it at roughly the same velocity at which Horace could break wind.

Horace had seen enough.

"Climb back there and grab the video camera," he said. "I wanna get some tape of this guy."

Annie was perplexed. "Why . . . what for?"

"To show to the cops!" Horace barked. "I'll flag one down if I have to. Show him what kind of lunatics are using the roads nowadays. Evidence, that's what for!"

Annie unbuckled (she never sat in the front seat without buckling up), and as she made her way toward the rear of the vehicle, Horace continued to rant. "In all my sixty-six years," Horace proclaimed, "I've never seen a guy drive like this. But come to Texas and what do we get? A friggin' demolition derby. Well, we may not be Texas taxpayers, but we pay our federal taxes, for Chrissakes. And since this is a U.S. highway, we got our rights! We have a right to be safe on our freeway system!"

"Oh, dear," Annie murmured again, opening a storage compartment above the Formica-topped dinette.

Horace was good and angry, boiling really, now a mere twenty yards behind the Corvette, breaking his own strict tailgating rule. He wanted the driver to notice him back here and know that his appalling behavior wasn't going unobserved. "What we'll do— you find that camera yet?—what we'll do is stop at a pay phone and report this nutcase. Show him what's what, this guy. And when the cops pull him over, we'll—"

Horace's train of thought was interrupted by movement in the Corvette. Until then, Horace had seen only one occupant in the car. But now a woman's head popped up—*from the driver's lap*— and she returned to her place on the passenger's side. She appeared to dab her lips with a tissue and then buckle her seatbelt.

Horace couldn't believe his eyes. The man driving the Corvette wasn't drunk at all. No, sir. Horace knew exactly what was going on. Hanky panky! On the open highway! Right in front of Annie, for God's sake!

Horace was shocked. He was outraged. He was envious.

The driver, finally glancing in the rearview, gave a small wave to Horace out the window, then goosed the vehicle up to highway speed, leaving the Winnebago behind.

Horace could only watch it disappear on the horizon.

"Here's the camera," Annie said, returning to her seat and buckling in. She glanced out the windshield. "Wha—where did he go?" She looked over at her husband. "Horace?"

"Never mind," Horace mumbled.

BUCK FEVER

A Blanco County, Texas, Mystery

BEN REHDER

Blanco County, Texas. It's one week before the start of deer hunting season, and everyone in town has come down with a case of buck fever. The fury begins with Red O'Brien and Billy Don Craddock, two drunken poachers who fire a shot in the direction of Blanco County's most important resident: a wide-eyed, white-tailed deer named Buck who lives on the Circle S ranch. Now Buck is on the loose, and no one knows where to find him. Navigating all this turmoil is Blanco County Game Warden John Marlin, with a little help from his best friend, Phil, and a beautiful nurse named Becky. But when a dead body turns up, the real mystery in madcap Blanco County soon boils down to a single question: Just who is hunting whom?

"A complete success…There's sure to be a long career for this happy, wacky series."　　　　　　　　　　*—Publishers Weekly*

"Briskly paced, amusing, spiced with deftly drawn good-old-boy portraits: an altogether promising debut."　　　　*—Kirkus Review*

Visit www.benrehder.com

AVAILABLE FROM ST. MARTIN'S / MINOTAUR PAPERBACKS

ISBN 0-312-99220-3

BF 05/05

BONE DRY

A Blanco County, Texas, Mystery

BEN REHDER

Edgar Award Finalist

The opening of deer season always brings a Texas-sized wave of excitement to sleepy Blanco County, but this year game warden John Marlin is finding mysteries as thick as ticks on a whitetail's rump. First, there are reports of a blonde bombshell who's been raising Cain with hunters, scaring away wildlife and trashing vehicles. Then, there's the tragic discovery of a local man shot to death and left in his deer blind. And when a feisty old rancher disappears, he leaves behind a trail of blood and enough questions to keep both John Marlin and the local sheriff chasing their tails for some time to come.

"Imagine Carl Hiaasen with a Texas accent."
—*Denver Post*

"You don't need an invite to the Bush ranch to have fun in Texas. Ben Rehder, whose *Buck Fever* earned him an Edgar nomination for Best First Mystery last year, is back."
—*Chicago Tribune*

Visit www.benrehder.com

AVAILABLE FROM ST. MARTIN'S / MINOTAUR PAPERBACKS
ISBN 0-312-99460-5